# Sylvia's Solace

## By Cinda Brea

I dedicate this novel to my loving Mother, Bennie Louise
Solomon (Jacobs) Smith
June 21, 1923 to May 14, 2008

## Acknowledgments

As always, first I give thanks to God from whom all blessings flow. A special thank you to my Aunts: Ruthie Solomon Porter, Lessie Solomon Wingo, and Gertrude Solomon Hall; to my exceptional sisters: Freddie Jacobs, Lessie Smith Solomon, Martha Smith Robinson; my wonderful lady cousins, my daughters, my nieces and all my lady friends. You ladies have provided the flavor and seasoning to what might have otherwise been a boring life. Each of you has brought so much knowledge, excitement, and laughter into my world. Thank you for allowing me to live through you and sharing your lives with me. You are the reason I love.
I also want to send out a special thank you to my cousin Brenda Smith for reviewing this novel and providing her invaluable input. Brenda Joyce, I love you and thank you for taking the time to do this for me!

Cover art by Shally Brady. Thank you, Shally!

Table of Contents

Chapter 1: Sugar's Legacy

Sylvia Solomon stood in the men's room of her family-owned restaurant scowling at the crud forming in the corners of the otherwise immaculately clean facility. "God, I wish I didn't need to go behind these tired people and inspect so often. I have told them time and time again to clean these corners when they clean the floors."

Sugar's Place was closed Sunday evenings so that afforded Sylvia the time to take a good look at the place and find discrepancies and she usually did, fortunately, not always in the lack of cleaning. As usual she wrote a reminder to discuss the cleaning with Rudy, her front of the house manager, the following day. She'd had this discussion with Rudy before and he was always receptive and the cleaning would be flawless for a few weeks until the next time Sylvia honed in on some area the cleaners had neglected.

As owner of 27% and manager of the San Antonio eatery, Sylvia was responsible for 100% of the business's daily operations. The remaining 73% of the restaurant belonged to her late husband Sugar's children and nieces. Sugar's nieces, Jessie and Retha each owned 12.5% and his four children, Cheryl, Terence, Nathaniel, and Gerald each owned 12%.

All had questioned Sugar's reason for leaving the ownership of his restaurant broken down so strangely. Not long after his death, the wisdom of Sugar's bequeath became apparent when Sylvia's stepchildren, none of whom had ever worked the restaurant, tried to push her out. They had proposed sending her a check from the profits once a year, if there were any profits. By that time, Sylvia had been working as assistant manager or manager of Sugar's Place for well over two years which seemed more like ten. She had been distraught about her stepchildren's proposal. She had grown to love the business which had proven to be the most lucrative job of her life. She feared how she and her three children would manage financially. Sylvia would have found another job but that would have taken time and of course she had dreaded starting over. Sylvia had felt so vulnerable the day she heard about her stepchildren's desire to fire her, but Sugar's nieces, Jessie and Retha, had stood with Sylvia and shut down any effort to move her out as the manager of the profitable business.

More than two years had passed and Sylvia still felt threatened whenever Terence, Sugar's oldest son, contacted her. She was in quite a tiff today because Terence had called a meeting of the owners to discuss some matter of great urgency. One niece, Retha, lived out of state but called Sylvia earlier to say she wanted to attend via Skype. Jessie, the other niece and family matriarch, would be present for the meeting.

Thankfully, Jessie was the first to arrive for the meeting with Sugar's youngest two sons, Nathaniel and Gerald, right behind her. The two older children, Cheryl and Terence, lived in Houston, so they were normally the last to arrive.

At Sylvia's direction, the front of the house staff had set up a sideboard of refreshments for the meeting attendees. Jessie helped herself to a cup of coffee and made small talk but her young cousins responded only grudgingly. Once Terence and Cheryl arrived, he was ready to dive right into the meeting. Sylvia stopped Terrance, explaining that she needed to Skype Retha in before they began. He did not hide his annoyance at the delay.

Upon starting the meeting, Terence pulled no punches and got straight to the point with the announcement that he and his siblings wanted to sell the restaurant and already had an interested buyer; Sylvia was floored.

Jessie sat up straight in her chair and looked from Terence to Nathaniel to Sylvia before commenting, "Sugar's is operating in the black and we're all making money. Why would you want to sell?"

"We've been offered $200,000 for Sugar's. I know we can get significantly more because there is more than one group interested in purchasing the business." Terence answered excitedly.

"Sugar's is clearing between five and six and a half thousand a month. That's good money," Sylvia protested.

"Not when it's divided seven ways and you get the largest percentage by yourself. The rest of us don't get half of your share. I need to get my hands on enough capital to invest and put in to my own business," Terence complained in a heated voice.

"I've got a guy coming out to give us an appraisal on what the business is worth, not counting the income," The youngest son, Gerald, informed the others. In the three years since Sugar's death, Gerald had not once voiced an opinion or made a suggestion about the management of Sugar's Place or the partnership. Jessie, Retha, and Sylvia would have found it astounding for Gerald to recommend a hire for wait staff duties and were certain he was over his head hiring a company to place a valuation on their business.

Retha voiced her skepticism. "How much will that cost you Gerald or is this person doing the appraisal for free?"

Hesitating for a moment before a glare from his older brother Terrance spurred him to respond, Gerald informed the partners, "No, we'll have to pay the appraiser."

Retha objected. "Gerald, we have to discuss and agree on things that will cost us all money. You can't just go and hire an appraisal company without discussing it with the rest of us."

"Damn, Retha, I didn't know you were hurting for money!" Terence interjected.

"That is not the point." Retha started but Jessie took over. "No, that's not the point. I think we first need to agree to sell the place or at least be in agreement that we will consider selling Sugar's Place before we start paying for appraisals. This is the first I've heard about selling Sugar's. I need to tell you all right now, I am not interested in selling." Jessie took a sip from her coffee and looked around, waiting for someone to say something in response to her declaration before she continued. "My uncle loved this place and it makes damn good money. Gerald, Terence, you guys might think that lump sum of thirty or forty thousand is a lot of money but once it's spent you will regret your decision."

"I want to sell also and so does Nate. I want to buy a new house and I need the money as a down payment," Cheryl chimed in.

"Well, I'm not willing to sell." Sylvia drew her line in the sand.

"Even if we don't sell, we are getting new management," Terence countered belligerently.

"Why is that?" Retha yelled over her poor connection and the now heated mumblings circling the room she could only partially see.

Finally Nathaniel added his discontent to the conversation. "I don't see why Sylvia should be in here calling all the shots."

"Stop it, Nathaniel!" Jessie gave her young cousin a look no one in the room would dare challenge.

Sylvia watched the stepson she had been closest to during her marriage to Sugar and longed for the physical strength and size to pop him in the mouth and get away with it but feared he would hit her back and lay her out flat on the floor. She felt angry, tired, and frustrated until Jessie said, "Me and Retha will buy you out."

"What?" Retha exclaimed.

"If they want out, we'll buy them out. Okay?" Jessie said.

"Lord have mercy, people just spending my money left and right," Retha fussed.

The siblings looked at each other with eyes wide open. Only a moment passed before they heard Retha's "okay," in agreement.

"Is everyone in agreement that we will get an appraisal completed?" Jessie asked, taking over the meeting at this point.

Terence was not happy. "Wait a minute, Jessie! Why are you buying us out?"

"So we can keep Sugar's in the family," Jessie answered coolly.

The room was now dead silent as the siblings looked at one another with questions on their faces. All four of Sugar's offspring were unhappy with the prospect of their late father's business belonging to his nieces and young widow. Each would have preferred strangers take the business rather than see it grow under Sylvia and their cousins' control.

"I think me and my sister and brothers need to talk amongst ourselves before we make a decision. I kind of promised it to this guy." For the first time during the meeting Terence seemed unsure of himself.

"Well 'this guy' ain't getting my uncle's place. I am amazed that you believed you could promise someone a business that you only own twelve percent of," Jessie declared in a huff.

Sylvia was relieved to see her stepchildren up and leave her tiny office. No sooner than they exited and Retha got off the line, Jessie started talking. "Sylvia, what you need to understand is that Nathaniel and Gerald will follow Terence's lead like mosquitoes after blood. They idolize their older brother. Terence is the reason those younger boys wouldn't help Uncle Sugar in the restaurant. He started all that dissension."

"I always wondered why they were so stubborn about helping Sugar, no matter how short-handed we were," Sylvia commented thoughtfully.

Jessie explained further. "Terence used to have Sugar all to himself when he visited during the summers or for long weekends. Cheryl usually stayed up in Houston with Bonnie, their mother.

Nathaniel and Gerald's mother was much younger than Sugar and not ready to settle down and raise those boys, so Sugar brought them from LA to live with him. Sugar didn't treat Terence much different but Terence got jealous and resentful about Sugar having those younger boys with him all the time. Terence spent a lot of time with Nate and Gerald whenever he'd visit but he and Sugar grew distant after the younger boys came. I could see it. He took his anger out on Sugar not his brothers and I guess that was preferable. He rebelled against anything Sugar wanted. After a while he started saying Sugar didn't care about his children, that all he cared about was the restaurant. Sugar got so tired of Terence's resentful ways he stopped encouraging him to come to San Antonio. I believe that only made Terence more resentful."

"What about Cheryl?" Sylvia asked.

"Cheryl loves Terence too. She's just going along with him. Terence pulls all their strings. Uncle Sugar knew what he was doing when he left Retha, you, and me with the majority ownership. He was protecting you. I'll talk to Nate and Gerald but they probably won't listen. I'm afraid they're gonna walk off into a swamp following behind Terence."

Jessie stopped bad-mouthing her younger cousins and looked around the restaurant, eyeballing everything. "It looks better in here every time I come. I like that new commercial. Business still picking up?"

"You know the only complaints we're getting is that we need to open longer hours. People want you to work yourself to the grave to feed them," Sylvia shared.

"People appreciate good food. We need to have a serious talk about expansion." Jessie said.

Chapter 2: Until the Party's Over

Randall Craig hated the hesitancy, the lack of assurance that remained with his decision to move back to San Antonio. He had not spent more than five days in the city in the past five years. His Aunt Izola had visited him in DC. When was that -- three or more years ago? She had been worried about him. Said she could not sleep at night until she put her eyes on him and saw for herself that he was doing alright, that he was still her baby. His cousin Jerome had also visited several times. Those were short turn-a-round or passing through visits that did Randall a lot of good. Both their visits had lifted his spirits while they lasted and made him lonely and hollow when concluded.

Aunt Izola and Jerome were two of Randall's closest relatives. For a long time, more than ten years, he had tried to distance himself from them. As much as he loved his relatives he had wanted to not need them. He did not like the emotions and the memories seeing his family dredged from his insides. Oh he had many good memories associated with his aunt and the rest of the family in San Antonio, even the city itself, but Randall had told himself she was a transitioning place in his life. She was the place that had held him during his adolescence and through the turmoil of being a teenager and coming into the years of his manhood.

Leaving the Alamo City for college had been one of the happiest days of Randall's life. No more Aunt Zoe hovering over him and fretting after him, escape from the endless barrage of words of wisdom. He had known he would miss his aunt's babying. He even missed all her fussing because no one could fuss like his Aunt Zoe except maybe his Aunt Vi.

Randall could still see the hurt on Aunt Zoe's face when he announced he would not be returning to San Antonio to live after college. He remembered that conversation like it happened a few days ago. "You know Randall, everybody told me to keep it secret, but we giving you a big welcome home graduation party." Aunt Zoe was glowing like the brightest porch light in a neighborhood with no streetlights. She had not been able to stop her tears -- "her baby" had just graduated college, just like his mother, Izola's baby sister Evelyn.

Not only had Randall graduated but he graduated with honors. Aunt Izola, Aunt Viola, and Randall's cousins Jerome, Martha, and Mark were joined by his old girlfriend, Debra and her parents at the graduation. It was a wonderful and scary day. Randall had reservations about Debra and her parents attending the graduation. He had been certain they were hoping for a husband and son-in-law, but Randall had made up his mind that he was not going backwards, not to his old town or an old love. He had just graduated college and wanted everything new in his life, but he needed to stop putting off the inevitable and tell his aunt he would not be returning to San Antonio. He knew his aunts would be hurt over his decision but he could put the conversation off no longer.

The entire group had stood and mingled in one general area of the campus grounds. Before that day, Randall had never noticed how beautifully green and well kept the grounds were. The Texas air even smelled sweeter than usual. It seemed as if every member of every family had a camera or video camera up recording this special day in Randall's life. He had posed for so many shots his jawbone ached from grinning.

*Let me take this bull by the horn.* Randall thought about his dilemma not his aunt. "I need to talk to you in private, Aunt Zoe." Randall had a smile on his lips but distress in his eyes.

"What's the matta, baby?" Izola asked with great concern after looking directly in his face as she had done every day that he was in her presence since his parents' death.

*Hell, she's already worried.* "Nothing's wrong. Everything is good. I just need to discuss some things with you when we can get time alone." Randall did his best to hide his discomfort.

"Well then we need to get some time now." That was Aunt Zoe. She never believed in putting anything off. "We need to talk long?" she asked with eyes darting back and forth across his face taking in every muscle twitch as she tried to discern what was going on before Randall told her.

"No, Aunt Zoe, well, maybe. I don't want to talk now, maybe later."

"No, child, unh unh, I want to hear what you got to tell me right now." Izola turned around and looked at her entourage who were all watching her and Randall and told them, "Listen, I'm going to ride with Randall. We'll meet y'all at the restaurant in," she turned and looked at Randall, as did all the others. "What you think, Randall – half an hour, forty five minutes?"

Randall felt conspicuous by that time because everyone's curiosity was up and they were not hiding the fact.

"Hey Randall, I'm gonna ride with you," Jerome had yelled.

"Me too," young Mark pleaded running toward Randall.

"No man, you ride with your mama! I get tired of you following behind me." Jerome had rebuffed his young cousin.

"Hush! Neither one of y'all are riding with us," Randall's Aunt Zoe had rebuked the boys.

Randall finally answered the question his aunt directed at him earlier. "We can meet them in an hour." He did not dare look at his Aunt Viola or any of the others, avoiding the scorn that would greet him in their stares.

Aunt Viola had been mad about being left out. She had always been jealous of Randall and her sister Izola's relationship. She knew they loved each other more than either loved her. Randall loved his Aunt Viola almost as much as Izola but Izola raised him; she was his mother now. Randall had imagined his Aunt Vi complaining, "That damn Zoe is always bossing people and trying to control things," as he had heard her protest so many times before. Izola was aware of Vi's jealousy and complaining but by that time no longer cared. Back then, Izola often said that Viola lived to complain. She never had a solution, just complaints and problems. Izola had long since stopped trying to please her younger sister Viola.

Randall's Aunt had taken his hand and held it lightly in hers as they walked to the car his family helped him purchase. Seeing that 1990 Camry made him dread sharing his decision even more. His family had sacrificed to help get that car. Sure he worked and paid the insurance and monthly payments but they had come up with the down payment and Aunt Zoe had co-signed for him. He had been ecstatic at how easy his family made it for him to have that car after his first year of college -- that substitute family of his.

"You sure do take good care of this car, Randall. You remind me of your daddy. He was real good with cars. You know Mark is figuring you'll give it to him when he graduates." Aunt Zoe snickered. Randall smiled back as he opened the car door and held it for his aunt.

Izola looked around in the car and thought about what a perfectionist her nephew was. He had sure rubbed off good on her Jerome and Viola's son, Mark. They both looked up to Randall and wanted to be like him. No chance of that. They were beautiful children, just like all children but Randall loved deeper than those younger boys ever would. His love was great for his family and when he lost both his parents in an automobile accident, Izola feared he'd be lost also because he adored his mother and father. She had feared he might become hard and callous but, thankfully, he did not. Then Izola worried Randall would be too gentle, loving and easy. People take advantage of kind folks, but her nephew had proven himself to be no one's fool either. He seemed perfect. That scared her too. She felt like she was walking down a wet slippery staircase with a pair of brand new five inch heels on when it came to Randall. She was always waiting for the fall. She hated feeling that way. She prayed not to expect bad things for "her baby" but he was just too perfect.

Izola and Randall had ridden along quietly until Randall turned on the radio, pulling Izola's attention back to the situation at hand. "So, nephew, what you need to talk about?"

"It's not anything bad, Aunt Zoe."

"I know that's what you say."

Randall pulled the car over to a nice little park and got out and walked around to open the door for Izola. She took his offered hand and stepped from the car thinking, *this must be serious. Please don't let anybody be pregnant and don't let him be gay. I'll love the baby and I love him. I don't know about that girlfriend or boyfriend but if I have to, I'll accept them. Lord but just please don't let it be that.*

Randall found them a nicely situated spot on a bench under a large oak tree. He then jumped in with both feet. "Aunt Zoe, I've got a job offer."

"A job, already, that's good news!"

"Yeah, I told you I had good news. I'll be able to work and do my graduate work at the same time. They have a great tuition assistance program. The job is with a pharmaceutical company in their accounting department. It'll be good experience for me, a career builder and the pay is more than I ever imagined I'd make starting out.

"Why such a secret Randall?"

"Aunt Zoe, the job is in Maryland. I'll have to move to Maryland."

"You're not coming back to San Antonio?"

"Try and understand, Aunt Zoe. This is a good job. I may not get another opportunity like this."

Randall could see the color drain from Zoe's face as her dark skin began to gray. Although she was somber she was as always reasonable. "Jerome will be so hurt by this, Randall, but you got to do what's best for you. I knew you'd do well after school. I'm so proud of you and I want what's best for you. I know how hard you worked in that school and I know it was not easy. Believe me it was not easy for me to let you come here. I figured once you left you'd never come back to my house. That's the way it's supposed to be, you know. When a child goes off to college, he's not supposed to come back home. That means everything is falling into place as it should. Nothing is wrong if a child comes back home. It just means things are happening a little bit out of place. I guess it never occurred to me that you'd be so far from us." Randall's aunt had shaken her head and looked at him as if a light had just come on before asking, "do you have to go so far?"

It still stung when Randall thought about the hurt on his aunt's face that day. She had tried to help him feel better and laughed and told him she was glad he didn't have anybody pregnant and didn't have a boyfriend. She had managed to get a laugh out of him with that.

As stunned as Izola was about the news that Randall had taken a job 2000 miles away, the real drama started when Aunt Vi heard the news. Aunt Zoe had made the command decision that no one other than Randall and she needed to know his news until after the party the following evening. At first Randall had thought Izola wanted to keep his new job a secret from the others out of consideration for their feelings, but Zoe wanted to protect herself as well as Randall. She had spent a "pretty penny" organizing a party for him and she did not want her money and effort to go for naught because the family was going through histrionics over Randall's good fortune. Zoe knew that between her sister Viola, niece Martha, and son Jerome they could easily ruin the remainder of the fine graduation day enjoyed by all and the next day's planned celebration.

"Jerome might still let me whip his ass if he acts the fool, but that Vi has put on so much weight, she might be a little hard for me to get down," Aunt Zoe had chuckled and told him on their ride to the restaurant to meet the others.

So Randall's Aunt Vi did not learn about his leaving until two days later. It was as if a hurricane was blowing shit. When Randall told his Aunt Viola his "good news" she broke down and cried right there at his Aunt Zoe's kitchen table. Randall's cousin Martha looked at him like he was a sadist and called him an "ungrateful bastard." This resulted in Aunt Vi slapping Martha in the mouth, causing Martha to cry. Jerome marched into his bedroom and slammed the door behind him, not allowing entry for hours. Little Mark kicked and yelled at Jerome's door, begging to be let in.

The cherry on top was the reaction by Debra and her mother who had stopped by unannounced during the rampage. Martha was happy to enlighten the newcomers with the news that Randall was leaving San Antonio for good. Initially, Debra took on the grief-stricken demeanor of a pregnant bride abandoned at the altar. When that tactic failed, she got so angry she tried to jump Randall but her mother and Martha held her back. Denied any possibility of getting her way, she bolted out the door. Now this was a woman Randall had not had sex with in three years. Just three months earlier, Debra had ended a relationship with a longtime boyfriend, so she had contacted Randall and once again started acting as if they were a couple. The "jilted" woman's mother fussed Randall out for not telling her daughter how things stood between them earlier.

Randall had been stupefied at the mayhem his news caused and turned questioning eyes to his Aunt Zoe, who calmly said, "I told you it was best not to tell these Negros until the party was over."

Chapter 3: The Homecoming

Randall was not sure if he was back in San Antonio for good, but he was certain he would be home for a while. He had missed his family and given thought to coming home for some time. It felt good to be back in Texas. If he had returned earlier, when he had first started longing for home, he would have been running from changes in his life. He recognized that he needed to stay in DC, get his life back on track as a single man, and get comfortable being alone.

When he learned that his Aunt Izola was battling diabetes and high blood pressure, he was certain it was time to return. Randall had immediately started putting things in place for a move back to Texas. He contacted a realtor to line up properties for him to consider and got all necessary information for his CPA certification to practice in the state. Then his Aunt Viola had a minor stroke and he felt the urgency to make the move happen as quickly as possible. He hoped his family welcomed him home with one tenth the fervor they showed on his departure.

Randall spotted his cousin Jerome standing near the baggage carousel. This was quite a welcome. In the past Jerome picked him up in front of the terminal. "Hey, man," Jerome greeted him with a warm embrace and big smile. "I'm sure glad to see you. I need some help with these women of ours. My mother and aunt are working me, man. Let me shut up. I don't want to run you off again. They're waiting on you. I'm surprised they didn't ask me to find a fatted calf to slaughter." Jerome pushed Randall in the shoulder with his fist and grinned so hard his cousin had to laugh.

"Why you grinning so hard, man?" Randall asked.

"I can't believe you are voluntarily coming back into this din of controlling women. You couldn't find anywhere else to live but San Antonio? I need someplace to visit," Jerome joked.

"I need to be here close to family. You have been here all along so you may not recognize how good it is to be near people that really got your back like Aunt Zoe and Aunt Vi and for me that includes you. I wanted to get back here so I could keep track of your mother and that aunt of ours. How are they doing?"

"Moms is good as long as no one mentions her illness. She seems to be doing everything the doc ordered but don't want to talk about it. She just about crucified me for telling you she was sick. But when you told her you were moving back to San Antonio she was grinning like she'd just hit the Powerball. I don't think I've seen her that happy since Martha and Trace had Tristin. Her and Aunt Vi acted like Martha had just given birth to a princess when she had that girl. I guess after five knuckle head boys straight in the family, they were happy to finally get a girl."

"So, Vi's doing okay, too?" Randall asked.

"Aunt Vi is coming along great. I can't see any changes in her since she had the stroke. She still goes to therapy and has started a good walking routine. Her and Moms are both walking regularly. Vi's taking less blood pressure medicine and her pressure is still good."

Randall was pleased to hear that his aunts were working hard at improving their health. He had never known Izola or Viola to put their minds to a task and fail.

The men made their way out of the airport with Randall's luggage and found Jerome's car in the short term lot. Randall was not surprised to see Jerome was driving a brand new BMW 550i. His cousin also owned an old Chevy Silverado pickup for dirty work, but Jerome never kept a car more than three years. Cars were his only frivolity, cars and women that is. Jerome managed his finances well in every other aspect but he had to have that new car, always wanted his ride shiny and smelling new.

"You know Aunt Zoe kept telling me not to come back here. She was serious too until I explained that I was coming home for my own benefit as much as hers and Vi's. That mother of yours has never been one for wanting people to go out of their way or make sacrifices for her."

Jerome nodded his head in complete agreement as they climbed into his car.

"So what y'all got to eat at the crib; I'm starving. That food at the airport did nothing to curb a brother's appetite."

"I'm not sure what they're cooking but whatever it is, you can bet it will be good and plenty." Jerome pacified his hungry cousin.

Five years was a long time and it had been that long since Randall stepped foot on Texas soil and fifteen since he lived in the state but here he was moving back. What did he know about San Antonio now? Well it was certain the concrete fixation was alive and well. He hardly recognized Loop 410 with its new overpasses and hotels. From what he'd heard the real growth was outside Loop 1604. Randall could remember when the only structure on that loop was the Alzafar Shrine Temple for miles.

Randall was disappointed to see only two vehicles in front of Izola's well kept but way too busy yard when they arrive. Flowers and plants covered the landscape. Bougainvilleas, azaleas, roses, mums and anything Izola thought might grow populated the outside of her home. He shook his head in awe. ***It is good to be home.***

"Where is everybody? I thought y'all were glad I was coming." Randall said, commenting on the number of cars in front of his aunt's home.

"Moms didn't want no whole slew of people when you got here. Aunt Vi doesn't even know I'm picking you up; Moms is surprising her."

"Is that Vi's car?" Randall pointed to a slightly dated Toyota Avalon.

"Yep, that's her."

"So she's here but doesn't know I'm coming today?" Randall asked, holding out hope that his Aunt Vi was not inside with his Aunt Zoe, because if she was, he expected a great deal of drama.

Jerome gave only a raised brow in response.

"Sometimes I think your mother likes to get shit started. She knows Aunt Vi hates to be kept in the dark. If I had known Aunt Zoe was not going to tell her I would have told Vi myself. I hate to come home and cause her to have a conniption. Hell, she was having one when I left. My return is supposed to be a happy occasion."

"Don't worry brah; it will be a happy occasion for Moms. I don't think she has been able to upset Aunt Vi since her stroke. This should do it." Jerome nodded his head toward Izola's house as he grabbed up Randall's luggage. "Welcome home."

Izola's cramped East Side home was more crowded than her yard was busy. Randall could hear his aunts in the kitchen toward the back of the home cackling in laughter. They obviously did not hear Randall and Jerome enter because there was no break in their conversation.

"Girl, I thank she bought that dress ten years and two sizes ago. I don't know why Eugene lets her come out in those too-little clothes," Viola said to her older sister.

"I thank he likes to see her in those tight short dresses. Then she always wants to be up in front of the church showing every roll and every bulge. She is hard on the eyes but not to some of those old men at the church, especially Brother Jemison, that old dog," Izola gave her opinion on some of her fellow churchgoers.

Randall walked quietly through the living room, entered the kitchen, and leaned on the door frame before asking, "What's that you ladies are cooking that smells so good?"

Izola looked up at her nephew with a pleasant smile as if he had just come in from a day's work. Viola looked at Randall as if she was not quite sure who or what she was looking at. Was it an apparition or her imagination? She then looked at Izola for confirmation that her eyes were not playing tricks on her. When Izola's grin doubled in size, Viola jumped from her stool straight into her nephew's arms yelling, crying, and laughing all at once. "I can't believe y'all kept this secret from me. Boy you look good." Randall's aunt held him away from her at arm's length and looked him up and down assessing him. "Look at this, Zoe," Viola said excitedly.

Izola came around the counter and gave her nephew a hug and a kiss on the cheek. Randall had one of his beautiful teary-eyed ladies on each side of him and he had never been happier. "I was expecting a welcome home party. I'm a little disappointed," he said with a smiling face.

Viola pulled away and punched him gently in the side. "You can see all those other people tomorrow. You belong to me and Zoe tonight."

Jerome looked on wondering if he would ever be first in his mother and his aunt's eyes. He could never match up to Randall, not with them. He had long ago gotten past being jealous. Besides, the sisters had more than enough love to give to everyone in their orbit and Jerome was happy Randall was home to help sop up some of that love. Yet, he felt the need to remind them of his presence. "Don't forget about me."

Jerome's Aunt Viola couldn't pass up an opportunity to tell him about himself. "You know you gonna get out of here to a club or something first chance you get."

"If I go anywhere, I'm taking Randall with me," Jerome declared.

The sisters looked at Jerome as if he was absolutely out of his mind. No way were they releasing Randall from their presence tonight. That realization now dawned on Jerome who had thought he might get Randall out to one of his haunts. Not that he was hanging out much anymore, but the thought of going to some of his old places with Randall had been exciting. Randall would definitely attract some different women. Women like fresh meat as much as men. Boy, he envied Randall, coming to what must feel like a new place and starting life anew.

There was nothing odd about Jerome envying Randall. He had envied his older cousin his entire life. Randall always had this air about him that Jerome once tried to emulate. Randall looked like he didn't give a damn and that attitude of his attracted women like raindrops to the earth. Jerome remembered how the older girls tried to kiss up to him to get to his older cousin. The girls from Grace First Baptist Church were the worst. Jerome always thought it was such a waste that Randall did not get with more girls before he went away to college. Of course, once he got tied up with Debra there was no chance of Randall getting involved with another woman; Debra was full time.

Jerome had long ago given up on emulating his cousin. In his mind, Randall was the man. Once Jerome grew older, he realized that although Randall appeared disinterested, he actually cared deeply about others and took on the hurt and pain of those around him. Randall, Jerome learned, was loyal to a fault. He had never known his cousin to date two different women at the same time. If Randall was dating one woman there was not room in his romantic or sexual life for another. He might notice another woman's good points or faults and when he was younger he'd discuss those traits with his buddies but that was as far as he would go. He was not a player, but that aura of his made women flock to him, begging to get their hearts broken, when the most they would receive from Randall was an examining gaze, a flirty grin, and possibly some polite conversation so superficial it would not include the day's weather.

Jerome, on the other hand, would give as many women as possible the time of day, weather, local, national, and international news reports if that was what made them happy for a day or maybe longer. Jerome would be their friend and sleep with them, take them on a nice date, cook them dinner, babysit their children, meet the parents, whatever it took. He just wouldn't love them, at least not one of them exclusively. He did love them all, every one of them. Jerome had just never been in that type of love that made a man want a woman to the point that she lingered on his mind and he longed to spend time with her, but then neither had Randall.

Chapter 4: Reacquainted

Friday's lunch crowd was larger than any of Sugar's staff had anticipated. The restaurant closed its doors for the day at two thirty Sunday through Wednesday. Guest flow was usually slow by one thirty or two o'clock at the latest on weekdays but today's lunch rush had extended into the two o'clock hour.

On Thursday and Friday afternoons, Sugar's closed from two thirty to five thirty to give staff a chance to eat, run errands, prep for the dinner meal and change shifts. Sylvia was amazed at the number of tasks she could squeeze into that three hour break: dental and doctor appointments for her and the children, grocery shopping for the house, a nap, paying bills, housework, laundry, even parent teacher conferences. Most importantly, Sylvia or Jim, her long-time head cook and assistant manager, held a management meeting on Thursdays and a full staff meeting on Fridays. Those meetings were usually short and efficient because each person in attendance wanted to move on to another task as quickly as possible.

With no personal business on her schedule for the day's break, Sylvia planned to help the kitchen staff prep for dinner while Jim ran out to the dentist. On this particular Friday, Sugar's was short of staff, a circumstance not apparent to those dining on some of the best cuisine to be had in the city, if not the state. Comfort food – that was what the patrons of Sugar's expected and the staff worked hard to ensure no customer left unhappy.

Sylvia and her crew were on their final sprint to that much awaited three hour break. With ten minutes to go, two guests walked in. "Shit," Sylvia whispered under her breath. She had hoped they could get the place closed without guests in the house. The policy at Sugar's was to allow customers to sit and enjoy their meal even if they ordered right before the closing of the doors.

"Syl, hey, Syl!"

Sylvia recognized the voice as a long-time regular and good friend Jerome Keys. Jerome required lots of attention and Sylvia didn't usually mind. *He will need to entertain himself for a while today. Oh good he brought a friend.* "Hi, Jerome," Sylvia returned Jerome's wave and yelled, "I'll be right out." She knew at a minimum she must stop by Jerome's table and talk for a minute. She and Jerome had been friends since their school days. He was a big flirt and the wait staff loved him because he treated them like good friends and was a big tipper.

Just moments before the wait staff closed the doors for the afternoon an elderly couple came in wanting soup. Sylvia sighed and was grateful none of the late arrivals needed anything cooked. She recognized the elderly couple as Elder and Sister Ware, the pastor and wife from her church. She stopped chopping, washed her hands, and went out to visit and chat with the cherished souls for a few minutes before attending to her most demanding guest.

"She looks familiar." Randall watched Sylvia with a squint on his face.

"That's Debra's cousin, Sylvia. You remember Sylvia. She was at Roosevelt when you were there."

Randall thought maybe he remembered the woman but was uncertain. Jerome refreshed his memory. "I used to have a crush on her and you and Debra teased me and told me I didn't stand a chance."

"Yeah, man, yeah." Randall laughed now, remembering what a hard time he had given his cousin about the busty beauty. "I don't think I've seen her since I left for college. We had some fun with you about her. So she manages this place now or what?"

"She's part owner. You know Old Sugar died?"

"Nah man, when? Sugar wasn't that old." Randall said excitedly.

"Shhh," Jerome nodded slightly in Sylvia's direction as she approached their table. He then stood up and hugged her long and hard. "Wow! That was just what I needed." Looking at his cousin he reintroduced Randall and Sylvia. "Syl, you remember my cousin Randall don't you?"

"Sylvia turned her head toward Randall and smiled as she sized him up. "Sure I remember Randall. When did you get in town? You visiting with your aunts?"

Randall began to see the girl he remembered inside the woman standing before him. There was a slight family resemblance to his old lady love Debra. "I've been in town a couple of weeks now. Actually, I'm not visiting. I've moved back to San Antonio."

"No! Really! Well good. I know your aunts are happy." Sylvia laughed as she turned to look at Jerome. "Maybe you can get this guy to settle down. You're going to have some competition now, aren't you fella?" she teased her friend.

Jerome shrugged and blushed slightly. Just then the cousins' food arrived and Sylvia felt free to return to her duties in the kitchen. "Welcome home Randall. Tell both your aunts and your cousin Martha hello for me." Then thinking he may not remember her name she said, "Sylvia."

Randall watched Sylvia until he was sure she was out of earshot. "Why'd you shush me when she was coming up?"

"That was her husband." Jerome chomped down on a baby back and then wiped his mouth as he shook his head in appreciation. "Hey baby, can I get some of that hot barbeque sauce? We only got the mild one here."

"Sure, Jerome," the young waitress responded as she filled condiment containers on the tables.

"Who was her husband?" Randall asked, at a loss as to what his cousin was talking about.

"Sugar." Jerome was totally absorbed in his lunch now. "Man, eat your food."

"Are you saying Sugar and Sylvia were married?"

"Unh huh."

"You bullshittin' me?"

Jerome raised his eyes to Randall's face but barely raised his head as he continued chomping on his lunch.

"How long were they married?"

"I don't know; two, three years maybe."

"Man Sugar's your mama's age. What did she want with that old man?"

"You askin' the wrong person, dude. I tell you one thang, he didn't last too long after they said I do."

"She didn't kill him did she?"

"Cancer," Jerome informed his cousin matter-of-factly.

Randall wasn't sure why this revelation about people he barely knew surprised him. He remembered Sugar well; the man was an institution. Randall and his friends would pool their funds and head to Sugar's for ribs or barbecued chicken. The restaurant was much nicer and cleaner these days. It was little more than a juke joint with a pool table back then. He and his friends liked to listen to Sugar talk smack. Sugar might tell anyone off, sometimes he'd curse his employees or even a customer if one got out of line. Randall and his friends felt truly lucky when they caught Sugar and his pals telling stories about the Army or street life. The boys had learned a lot from Sugar and his buddies.

Randall had seen Sugar on his last visit to San Antonio. The restaurant was going through renovations during that time. That was just a little over five years ago. Sugar hadn't remembered him; at least he hadn't acknowledged him. He remembered Sugar looking tired and old. He was certain he did not see Sylvia around. He would have remembered her. Wow! He wondered what made her marry that old dude.

--

"Hello," Aunt Zoe answered the phone with so much glee in her voice, the person on the other end had to feel uplifted. "Hey, baby! How long has it been since I talked to you?" Izola was quiet for a moment before she cracked up with laughter. "Well, I knew I'd see you soon," Izola added with a loaded glance at Randall who was sitting at her kitchen table drinking coffee. "How's the rest of the family?" Izola listened and laughed again before telling the caller goodbye and handing the phone to Randall.

"Hey handsome, I heard you were back in town."

Randall chuckled lightly before commenting, "I'm afraid you've got one up on me. I'm not sure who I'm talking to."

"You don't even recognize my voice anymore; shame on you."

"Debra? Hey, what's going on, girl? I hear you're stacking that swag left and right. Who told you I was back in town?"

"You know nothing stays quiet around here. I saw Romey at Ma Harper's eating lunch today. He wasn't volunteering any information until I asked when you were getting here so he had to give you up."

"Okay, okay. How you been?" Randall felt as if he had been caught in a lie. Debra was one person from his past he had no intentions of seeing.

"I'm good. Divorced and glad about it. My boy Trevon is nine years old now. Can you believe it?"

"Sorry to hear about the divorce; seems to be an epidemic," Randall said.

"Yeah, I put a lot of good years into my marriage but I was glad to get out of that mess. Life is much better now, especially with you back home. So when are you coming by to see me? I've missed you, baby."

Randall ignored the intimacy of her declaration and tried to lighten the conversation. "Jerome tells me your office is up on 281 outside 1604 somewhere in that area. I hear you've got some pretty nice digs."

"It's okay, but that's where I work. I live out in Cibolo. It's country as hell out there but quiet and I don't have to be bothered with people unless I want to. I'm sure you understand. You moved all the way back east to get away from your family."

Randall had been on guard for the knife Debra yielded with her words. She had only pricked him with that comment. It was best he end the call before she went for the juggler or worse performed a verbal castration. He was well aware of his old girlfriend's ability to cut anyone down with her words. "Listen, Debra."

"Oh, I know. When you start off with 'listen' you are ready to move on. I'm having a birthday party for my baby on Sunday. I already told Romey to bring you. It's at three o'clock. The kid's party will end at six when my ex picks up Trey. Then the adults can enjoy each other. Some of the old gang will be there. Don't worry – no one you're too special to be around. Come on out."

"I don't know, Dee. I'm just getting back in town and trying to."

Debra cut him off. She did not take no for an answer, at least not without a fight. "If you don't show up, I'm coming to get you."

"How old did you say your boy is?"

"He is turning nine and smart just like his mama." Debra paused for a moment. Her voice was low and sensual when she continued. "I'm glad you're finally back, Randall."

"It's good to be home."

--

Randall had been in San Antonio less than three weeks and had picked up three potentially lucrative clients without trying. His realtor, an old school friend from Roosevelt High School was so appreciative of Randall's business he had immediately introduced him to a contractor in need of an accountant. After checking Randall's credentials and references, the contractor was anxious for Randall to conduct an audit as quickly as possible.

Randall's most lucrative and demanding new clients were also attained by way of an old high school buddy. Ray Rutledge had fallen in love with Randall years ago when Randall and Ray's son, JT, played football together. Randall could do no wrong in Ray's eyes. He had more faith in Randall than he had in his own son, mainly because Randall had been a tougher and all around better player on the football field. No sooner than Ray had heard that Randall was returning to South Central Texas, he had picked up the phone and called, demanding that Randall become his personal accountant.

Randall had always needed to draw a line with Ray because the man could be all consuming. Two weeks after arriving in town, Randall had accompanied Ray to a charitable function where Ray introduced him to yet another client, Maris Kleinholz. Randall had noticed the woman from clear across the huge JW Marriot Ballroom where the function was held. She was hard to miss. She had a mane of golden blond hair and stood well over six feet in her Kate Spade pumps. Stunning was the only word that suited her. Randall had tried not to stare. He had not wanted to catch her eye but was certain she had her eyes on him. He was, after all, one of only a few blacks in attendance. He had been approached by three women and one man with questionable intentions before Maris worked her way around to where he and Ray were standing. "Rayford, you old dog, how the hell are you? I hoped I'd see you here tonight." Then looking at Randall, she added, "Please introduce me to your friend."

Ray was happy to oblige the lady's request after giving her a firm kiss on the mouth. "Maris Kleinholz this is my old friend Randall Craig, Randall, Maris. Randall and JT went to school and played high school ball together. He has only just moved back here from DC. Now he's working for me."

"Really, and what does he do for you?" Maris asked, never taking her eyes from Randall's.

"He's an accountant and a damn good one. If you know of anybody that needs someone smart and honest to handle thangs, Randall here is your man. Y'all excuse me just a moment. I'll be right back." Ray rushed off to greet friends across the room and Randall knew he was in for an interesting night.

Maris had eyed him with the look of a large cat that had cornered its prey. "An accountant; isn't that somethin'. My cousin Donny is an accountant working at state."

"And what does your cousin Donny do at state?" Randall asked.

"Honey, I truly do not know. I guess I should listen when he tries to tell me." Maris grinned, showed a mouth full of beautifully whitened teeth and continued eyeing Randall as she contemplated how long she needed to wait to make a serious move on the man.

Randall's friend, JT, had teased and laughed at him upon learning that his father had roped Randall into attending the event. As it was the third invitation Ray had extended Randall since his return to San Antonio, the younger man felt obliged to accept. Once he laid eyes on Maris Kleinholz, he was pleased he had made the sacrifice. "Well, now you know what I do. Tell me about yourself." Randall could not resist the impulse to flirt with the fabulous woman.

"I own an oil well excavation company. My father started the company decades ago and as he had no sons, I am the lucky heiress." She threw her head to the side and laughed lightly in a deep rich voice. As she did so, she kept her eyes on Randall to make sure he did not miss her well practiced subtleties. She ran her fingers through the front of that dense mass of hair and shook her head slightly. Randall wondered how many men she had captured with her hair alone.

Maris wasted no time in declaring her need of Randall's services for her personal accounts, explaining that her company used a large reputable accounting firm for the business accounts. Randall considered turning Maris away as a client, sensing she had an agenda that did not include accounting. Later Ray told him Maris was just a "big old flirt" who would make a good client. So Maris Kleinholz became client number three.

Before picking up these new clients, Randall tried to free himself of as many of his old clients back in the DC area as possible. A large number of his DC clients showed no interest in staying with Randall's old company and were determined to keep him on as their accountant, at least in the near term. Randall had to insist that his most demanding and profitable accounts make other arrangements because he simply could not put in the time to provide adequate service during his move.

Time off to get settled in to his new condo was slipping away. Aunt Zoe had begged Randall to stay at her place for a while longer but he knew he would not be comfortable until he was settled in a home of his own. The new luxury condo market in San Antonio was growing fast. Now was a good time to buy in. Later, when he was ready for a house, if ever, he could rent the condo out or sell for a profit. Randall had thought about using Debra as his realtor but had wanted to avoid her as long as possible. He was surprised she hadn't mentioned helping him find a place. She obviously did not know he had bought a home or she would have confronted him.

His new home was larger than he had planned but since he planned to work from home until his clientele list grew large enough to take on partners or employees, he would use the third bedroom as an office. Randall would definitely not work for another firm; he was his own boss from here on out.

Chapter 5: A Business Proposition

Getting Rudy to close up the restaurant and leaving early, Sylvia looked forward to an interesting evening at her cousin Debra's house, celebrating Debra's son's ninth birthday. Knowing Debra, there would be many adults at the party. Adult company was something Sylvia often craved when she had free time. She had planned to go home and hop in the shower, wait for Jessie to stop by and drop off her six-year-old grandson, Jevon, so he could go to the party with Sylvia and her youngest child, seven-year-old Bertani. The leaving the restaurant early part and getting showered and dressed worked out just fine. Sylvia was ahead of the game and would have arrived at the party at a respectable time if Jessie had not showed up at her house ready to talk business "for just a minute." Sylvia found herself in the midst of a business meeting with Jessie and Retha via Skype. Thankfully, she had purchased a gift for the birthday boy the week before so she did have time to spare, although she still needed to swing by her ex husband's home to pickup Bertani.

After some small talk and catching up, Jessie got to the point of the meeting. "I think we need to find another accountant for the business. Gerald was out with Chris on Friday night and after a few beers he forgot Chris and Nicola are brother and sister and that Nicola is my daughter-in-law, so he started talking. It seems Mr. Frisk is having a lot of contact with Terence about Sugar's Place. Gerald told Chris that Frisk found the buyers for Sugar's and that he has others lined up to buy the place. Didn't you hire Frisk, Sylvia?"

"Yes I did, right after Sugar died." Sylvia wished she had some plausible deniability but she had indeed done the deed.

"Well, Chris says our cousins are supposed to pay Frisk a finder's fee if one of the buyers he brings to the table actually purchases the place," Jessie said.

"How does that work?" Retha asked.

"Under the table. The buyer will pay a good percentage more than the amount we agree to on paper. Frisk and the kids will divide the extra money and tell us nothing about it," Jessie explained.

"Why was that fool Gerald talking to Nicola's brother about this? Every time I start to believe that boy is gaining a modicum of sense, he proves me wrong. Damn if you gonna cheat us could you please keep it to yourself," Retha complained.

"He got loaded and forgot who he was talking to -- just stupid." Jessie answered quietly, feeling a little sympathy for her young cousin.

Sylvia's insides were churning. An accountant had been her idea, actually she had insisted so that her co-owners would have access to a full accounting of the business. She had found Frisk and been given free rein to do so. "God, I can't believe this. I haven't trusted this man for awhile now and should have gotten rid of him when he started stonewalling me on information and documents I requested. I have to go over his reports so carefully and bug him to get documents and information I need to sign for taxes to me on time. You know we pay some pretty stiff penalties when we miss filing and payment deadlines."

"Well we need an audit of all the finances," Jessie advised.

"Not by Frisk I hope," Retha exclaimed.

"No. We'll need someone else. You think you have time to find a new accountant, Sylvia?"

"I feel bad about this. Maybe one of you should look for another agency. I hired Frisk."

"I could find someone but you're the one that will have to work with the person. You shouldn't feel bad about this. Frisk got greedy, not you," Jessie said.

"Well, Terence, Cheryl, Nate, and Gerald aren't going to like this," Sylvia responded.

"Humph," Jessie grunted. "Remember, we did an agreement that states you pick the people you do business with. You are running Sugar's, not us. If we have a problem with your decision we can vote on it but that would be a waste of time since the three of us are in agreement. Those cousins of ours will have a hard time objecting to a change they supposedly know nothing about."

"I'll start looking right away," Sylvia said.

"Go ahead and find someone but I think we should give it a few weeks before we actually make the change," Retha recommended.

"Why wait?" Jessie asked. "That snake Frisk might do more damage."

"First, I don't like the idea of Gerald guessing why we're letting Frisk go. We need to protect him from himself. He might run and tell

Nate or Terence that he told Chris about their scheme. If he tells Nate first, Nate will stop him from telling Terence. If he tells Terence, I feel very leery about Terence's reaction. He has always scared me a little," Retha explained.

"That's true. Gerald just talks without thinking. I hope he'd have sense enough not to tell Terence but you never know," Jessie agreed.

Retha continued with her reasoning. "Also I'd like to get an idea of what if anything they'll do from here. We've shut down the sell scheme for now. Thirdly, I'm afraid our entire partnership may become to adversarial if they know we are aware of their little kickback scheme."

Sylvia's mind was working as she listened to her nieces and she shared thoughts that had grown stronger over the past year. "I think the partnership as it currently exists is flawed. I think we should buy the kids out if you guys are serious about that offer."

"Sylvia!" Jessie grinned now because her uncle's young widow was ready to make a power play.

"That's what I'm talkin' bout. Buy them fools out and expand. We need a place in Austin, Houston, and another location in SA for starters, okay!" Retha was hyped. "That's the only way to really make money in the restaurant business; otherwise you're just working to pay bills. I'm tired of spending up Jaren's money."

"Well let's see if they accept our proposal. When is the appraisal supposed to happen?"

"Oh hell, I forgot! Frisk hired the company to do the business valuation. They are scheduled to come in next week," Sylvia groaned in frustration.

"Cancel it. Tell Frisk Jaren's lawyer has recommended a company we want to use instead," Retha says.

"Okay, but." Sylvia hesitated.

"You got to make it seem like there is no problem, Sylvia. Treat and talk to Frisk like always. I know me and Retha get on your nerves with our hands-on approach and I know Frisk is aware of that. Just give him the impression this is another one of our pushy demands. You know how you do," Jessie advised.

Sylvia chuckled at this. "Y'all don't get on my nerves too bad."

"Listen to her." Retha said and then asked, "So niece of mine, do you have the capital to buy out Sugar's brood. I'm not convinced

Nathaniel wants out at all. Gerald is too much the follower to know what he wants, but I am getting off track. It is important for you to hold on to your savings. Are you planning to take out a loan or what?"

"I was going to use money I got from Sugar's life insurance. I invested a good portion of that money but can get to it whenever I need to. It's growing well and I've made some money I can use."

Retha thought for a moment before she went on. "Well let's talk about that when we get to it. My uncle wanted you and his children and the business protected and that is what we need to do. He left a legacy and I'd like for at least one of his children to carry that legacy on."

"I plan to talk to both Nate and Gerald. Hopefully they'll have sense enough to hold on to their shares of the business," Jessie added.

--

"Wow, there are a lot of people here," Sylvia observed as she pulled up to her cousin Debra's large two-story Cibolo home. "Okay kids, we're here. Now I want you both to have fun and behave. Okay, Bertani, Jevon." She gave her daughter and Jessie's grandson "what'd I say" looks.

"Yes ma'am." Seven-year-old Bertani responded very sweetly and politely so she could fly from the car as quickly as possible and find her cousin the birthday boy, Trevon. Jevon did not bother to answer such a ridiculous request. This was a birthday party and whatever happened they would have to live with.

"Wait a minute. WAIT A MINUTE, Tani!" Sylvia yelled as the two children started a frenzied race toward Debra's front door. "Come back and get these presents."

"Come on Jevon; you too," Bertani bossed her younger friend.

The children grabbed up the gifts and once again took off at a fast clip to beat each other into the house. Sylvia maneuvered them from the front door to the side gate and into the backyard where they found the party in full swing with a water slide bounce, lots of balloons and several piñatas hanging from oak trees, and people everywhere.

Sylvia pulled up a chair with a group of ladies she recognized and took a much welcomed seat. No sooner than she got settled in, her cousin Janice approached. "Hey Sylvia, I'm glad you could get away from work. I never see you anymore. Are the kids with you?" Janice asked as she looked around for her young cousins.

"Just Tani. As always, Sean has some plans with the boys." Sylvia stood up and gave her cousin a warm hug, genuinely glad to see her.

Janice returned the hug and added a kiss on the cheek before she drew back and bestowed her usual sympathetic gaze upon her cousin before asking, "You doin' okay, baby?"

Sylvia hated the gaze and the whine that came along with it. "Fine, Janice; how about you?"

"Girl you know I'm always good." Janice smiled and sat down to visit a moment before moving on.

Sylvia realized years ago that Janice meant no harm with her patronizing ways. Janice just had no idea how to discuss Sylvia's life trials so the most she was able to offer her young cousin was hugs, kisses, back pats and rubs, that sympathetic gaze, and pitiable whine. As much as Sylvia hated the gaze and whine, she liked the rest and loved her cousin who was one of the few family members who treated her well after her marriage to Sugar Solomon.

"Mommy, can me and Jevon go on the slide?" Tani ran up to her mother with Jevon close behind. Sylvia helped the two children out of their top clothing and secured everything in the bag she had brought for that purpose before walking them over to the slide. She was quickly dismissed by Janice's teenagers who Debra had designated to supervise the youngsters on the slide. Sylvia reluctantly returned to her table of women, positioning herself so she had a full frontal view of the water slide.

"Girl, you better get you a plate. With all these people Debra got here that food is not going to last long," one of her table mates advised.

"I'm not hungry. I ate before I left Sugar's," Sylvia told the woman.

Sylvia watched the children for a while and after becoming comfortable that her cousins had a good handle on the kids climbing up and sliding down the slide, began paying attention to the conversation at her table.

"He's good looking and he doesn't have that player mentality like that brother of his. I used to think he was the one with all the girlfriends but he just looks the part." The ladies were clearly talking about Randall and Jerome.

"They're not brothers; they're cousins. Why did he move back here anyway? I thought he was married. Did his wife move here with him?" another lady shared her knowledge and asked for more.

"Debra didn't mention no wife, not that it would make her any difference." The ladies laughed and one of them glanced over at Sylvia who pretended not to hear the remark. Remembering that Sylvia and Debra were cousins, the ladies continued their conversation with a little less feline quality. "I hear he made good money back in the DC area but wanted to get back to San Antonio. He's a CPA and worked for some big firm out of DC. I heard him say he has already picked up several clients here without looking for them and still has a number of clients in DC."

*A CPA, exactly what we need. This is too good to be true. I'll have to ask Romey or Debra about Randall's qualifications*. Not one to put things off, Sylvia wanted to go and find her cousin or her friend right away but did not feel comfortable giving up her view of the water slide. Just then, she looked up and saw Jerome headed in her direction with a grin on his handsome face. She noticed a couple of the ladies at her table sit a little straighter as he approached. Jerome had a reputation as a player and a flirt but women loved his attention and he gave it freely.

"Hey ladies, I asked Debra where all the good looking women were and she told me y'all were right over here." Jerome worked his way around the table and gave kisses to the women he knew and nods to those he did not.

"You so full of shit," one of the ladies told Jerome but they all happily received his attentions with school-girl like giggles. He grabbed a seat on the grass next to Sylvia's feet and bestowed his marvelous smile on the ladies at the table.

"Where all these kids come from? Did I see Tani over there, Syl? Are the boys here too?" Jerome asked.

"Justin and Billy are with their dad. I brought Tani and Jessie's grandbaby, Jevon, to the party. Why didn't you bring your cousin's kids?"

"Martha's kids wear me out. I can only watch them in twos. The two oldest are not so bad but the two times I kept those younger kids, I had to sleep for twenty four hours straight after they left."

Jerome's attention was quickly diverted by an attractive woman across the yard getting ready to climb into the hot tub. He lowered his voice and asked Sylvia the identity of the stranger. Sylvia had never seen the woman before, so Jerome prepared to make his move. Sylvia stopped him to ask about Randall and his business.

"He's here; we rode together. When he can get away from Debra, ask him if he's taking on any more clients. He's already complaining about the workload but don't worry about that. If you decide you want to use him, he won't turn you down; I got you." Jerome pinched her on her outer calf as he bit down on the area just below his lower lip.

"Is he any good at what he does?" Sylvia asked.

Jerome gave Sylvia a skeptical look. "What do you expect me to say? I know he knows his stuff. He makes damn good money but the little me and Moms need he does for free. I do most of my own business accounting but he set me up and showed me how to save him time and me money. I'm pretty good now but if I have any questions he checks it out, explains things to me like I'm a four-year-old and boom – problem solved. Talk to him, but you better move fast. He doesn't want much more business while he's getting settled in. Let me know if I need to twist his arm. I got sway and you know I'll do anything for you girl." Jerome pinched Sylvia again before moving on to the next woman he wanted to charm as he made his way to the lovely stranger.

Sylvia finally got a small plate of food and sat there listening to and laughing with the others at her table, only contributing to the conversation when she was addressed. She spotted Randall and wanted to speak to him but noticed he and Debra were stuck to each other like glue. After the cake was cut and during the opening of the gifts, Sylvia saw Randall standing alone near the edge of the crowd and approached him. "Hi, you got a minute to talk shop?"

Randall returned her greeting and looked at her for a moment as he tried to place her before he responded, "Sylvia?"

Knowing she looked much better than she had on the few occasions Randall had seen her working hard at her place of business, Sylvia could not hide her embarrassment when he did not recognize her. "Yep, this is me when I'm not slaving at Sugar's." She smiled and looked around, hoping no other adult overheard their exchange.

Randall was ashamed of his reaction. It was obvious he embarrassed her. She was a good looking woman with a hairnet, worn apron, and sweaty face but he had no idea she would clean up so beautifully. "Sure, what can I do for you?" He smiled before averting his eyes to keep from staring and embarrassing her further.

"Romey says I need to ask you if you're taking on new clients. I need an accountant for the place. I'd like to discuss your availability when you have some time."

"Time for what?" Debra asked, catching the end of Sylvia's query. Debra was not smiling and looked at Sylvia with a challenge on her face.

"Hey, girl." Sylvia placed an arm around Debra's shoulder and drew her near. "I want Randall to consider looking over our books and maybe even taking on Sugar's as a client." She released her cousin but did not take her eyes from Debra's face and never turned her eyes toward Randall. He watched the cousins as Sylvia looked at Debra with a raised brow as if she was asking, "What do you think?" When Sylvia finally turned her eyes toward Randall there was no emotion directed toward him. It was as if he was not standing there. Randall recognized her behavior as an act for Debra and was surprised to see that Sylvia, who seemed demure but straightforward, had just handled Debra, who always needed to be alpha.

"He'd better make time for you and your business if he wants to stay in my good graces." Debra looked at Randall as if she held every ace in a deck.

Randall could only smile and act as if Debra had twisted his arm. "I'll call you next week Sylvia and we can set an appointment."

"Thanks Randall. I'll be looking to hear from you." Sylvia gave him a tiny smile with next to no eye contact before turning to Debra and giving her a full on hug. "Well baby, I guess it's the witching hour for those of us who came with children. Thanks for the party. I'm going to find the birthday boy and give him a big old wet kiss and gather up Tani and Jevon."

"Girl, you don't have to leave yet," Debra lied, not wanting to appear callous in Randall's eyes. If he hadn't been listening Debra would have thanked Sylvia for coming and nearly kicked her out of the yard. She planned for the few remaining adults to have a real party once the children were gone. Sylvia, even without children, would not fit in with Debra and her friends when it came to partying.

--

"Why did she say she wanted to cancel the appraisal?" an angry Terence asked Charles Frisk, who was beginning to hate his entanglement with the demanding man.

"She said Mrs. Daniels wants to use a business associate of her husband's to complete the valuation."

"Did you tell her that could be a conflict of interest and if the appraisal is too low we might not accept it?"

"I did, but you realize that the chances of the appraisal coming in lower than three hundred thousand is nonexistent. Sylvia says they will deal with any possible conflict later, if need be."

"You think Sylvia suspects something?" Terrance asked the accountant.

"No. She was the same as always – just spewing out information."

"I need to get control of that business with everything intact. I know we can open in Houston and Atlanta in no time and then expand all over the south and make a killing. It's a good business model. It's hard to make a profit in the restaurant business but my father and cousin found the formula. I've got investors who are willing to back me financially in the purchase of Sugar's Place. I've got a dummy corporation in place to hide the fact that I'm the one behind the purchase. I'd like to keep that under wraps for a while. But I need to get the business at a price that doesn't have me paying these people for the next fifty years."

"Terence, once they get the business valuation completed, you will have to make a good offer. From what you've told me, it sounds like the ladies won't sell. You should consider working with them to expand. They have the finances." Frisk tried to persuade Terence.

"Nah, Just about every dime that bitch Sylvia has should have been mine. She married my father and two years later he was dead. She gets a fat social security check. She got over two hundred thousand in life insurance, his home, and the largest share of Sugar's Place. She even gets a fat paycheck from managing the place. My dad was my father for thirty five years and her husband for two but she gets more than four times what I get just because she's got a split between her legs. I don't think so."

There was no reasoning with Terence so Frisk tried no further. He cursed the day he picked up the phone and agreed to have lunch with the man. Terence had been so friendly back then and the possibility of making twenty thousand dollars or more so easily had been irresistible. Frisk now feared that Terence was willing to go further than deception and fraud to get his revenge on his young stepmother. Frisk wished for a way out.

Terence snapped the accountant out of his wishful thinking. "I'm going to give this some thought and I'll tell you what I need from you."

"Maybe we should just wait until they get their business valuation completed and go from there," Frisk advised.

"Are you telling me you want out of our deal?"

"I see no way for me to make money out of the sale of Sugar's Place at this point," Frisk admitted.

"What about with the books? Anyway to make it appear that Sugar's brings in less than it does?"

"Not with Mrs. Solomon watching everything the way she does. She goes over every report diligently. She knows her business and becomes more astute each time I meet with her."

The last thing Terence wanted to hear was praise for his deceased father's widow. Frisk's assessment of Sylvia's wisdom and ability to learn angered Terence to near eruption. "Like I said, I'll tell you what I need." He ended the call without a goodbye. The time for pleasantries toward Frisk was over.

Chapter 6: Lots of Strong Women

"I'm calling to see what time you want me to pick you up for dinner tomorrow?" Randall spoke to his Aunt Zoe with assurance. He had been trying to take his Aunt Izola and Aunt Viola out for dinner since he moved back to San Antonio. One or the other always had a reason for not being available and each refused to go without the other.

"Randall you know I have church tomorrow. You supposed to go with me."

"Come on Aunt, Zoe. We'll go after morning worship. It'll be a nice change of pace for you and Vi."

"I don't know why you like spending up your money at these expensive places. You and Jerome act like money just grows on trees. I can cook right here and we'll eat better than we would at any fancy restaurant."

"How about Sugar's? When was the last time you were there?"

"Ooh it's been a long time since I ate at Sugar's, a very long time. I know it was before he married that young wife of his, Sylvia. You remember Sylvia, Debra's cousin."

"You know Sugar is dead, Aunt Zoe?"

"I know that. I hear it's almost impossible to get a table on Sundays. That place has really changed, so I'm told.

"I'll pick you and Aunt Vi up at one thirty sharp. We'll get a table but we've got to be there before two, okay?"

"Okay." Izola gave in because Sugar's was the one place she wanted to have dinner. Their Sunday brunch was purportedly other worldly. Being a connoisseur of delicious food she wanted to compare Sugar's cuisine to her own. Also, she often heard friends brag about eating at Sugar's as if it was some great experience. Izola wanted to see for herself what all the fuss was about.

Randall had not expected such an easy fight and was pleased he did not need to push his aunt any harder. He was tired after a full busy week getting settled in. He had more work than he had anticipated from his old clients back in DC. One client called in a crises and Randall could hardly tell him no, even though this was a client who had supposedly found another accountant. Randall knew the man's business better than he did. It took some serious man hours but Randall had put everything back in order. That had always been his specialty – finding errors, usually other peoples, and fixing them. The client was so grateful that Randall had already received payment for his services plus a hefty bonus. The downside was that the client wanted to remain with Randall for a while longer while he looked for another accounting agency. This was one of the businesses Randall thought he was free of.

Debra had been bugging him all week. Every time she contacted him, it felt as if a bit of his energy seeped away. She required so much from those in her life. Getting away from her after the party last weekend had been harder than he'd expected. He wished he had not attended the party but had not wanted to appear unfriendly or disinterested in his old friends, but Debra was one old friend he had no interest in reengaging. She was a strong beautiful woman who wanted all the people in her life to revolve around her. She clearly wanted a romantic relationship with Randall but he had no desire to be her lover or make love to her.

Randall had dragged Jerome to the party with him. Fortunately, Jerome had a six o'clock flight to Atlanta the following morning so he insisted on leaving Debra's by seven so he could pack and rest before heading to the airport. Debra had volunteered to take Randall home after her guests left but he had declined her offer stating that he had some work to finish for his clients. Debra was fuming when the cousins left her home. "So when are we going to get together?" she had asked Randall with as much innuendo as possible.

"Maybe we can do dinner or lunch next week," Randall had responded, appearing dense.

"I'm not talking about eating, Randall."

Randall could not remember a woman being so assertive since his ex wife, Jillian. She and Debra were cut from the same cloth. Debra had chosen him way back in high school and she was attempting to reclaim him. Randall had come a long way since his high school days. He no longer felt the desperation Debra had used to lure him and keep him. He sure understood that sexual arousal was not the same as love or passion. He never loved Debra or felt a passion for her but he had wanted sex, desperately. Debra used his desire for sex like a weapon. Only his ex wife, Jillian, was more adept at sexual weaponry than Debra had been when they were in high school.

How was it that his first love and his last were both such self serving controlling women? What was it about him that the two longest "romantic" relationships of his life had proven unbearable for him? He had never liked either woman. They were both smart, gorgeous, good in bed, ambitious, selfish and cold.

Jillian had claimed Randall just as Debra had in high school. Randall had been on a new job all of three months when he found himself locked down with the beautiful corporate attorney. He had dated one other woman who worked with him but Jillian, not Randall, had run her off. He had been flattered that two women on the job wanted him. He actually preferred the other woman but she had been the weaker of the two and not willing to fight for Randall. What it came down to was that there was no love involved nor was there any passion except Jillian's passion to win. There was money, power, and sex – lots of sex.

Life was exciting to Randall back then. He and Jillian with her six figures and his near six figures, spending money like they had two seven figure salaries. It did not take Randall long to wake up and realize they could not afford the life they were living; expensive home, cars, clothing and vacations. They were living a Louis Vuitton life on a Coach income. At first Jillian had ignored Randall's pleas for moderation and budgeting but when they started having trouble paying all their debts and attending every function of interest to Jillian, she agreed to a budget. Her acquiescence lasted just under sixty days. After that Jillian was like an addict who had fallen off the wagon. She consumed as much of her spending drug as possible.

When Randall refused to partake of the spending frenzy, Jillian spent time with friends and family who would. Soon all their finances were separated and she wanted nothing to do with him. They remained in the same home and slept in the same bed. They were civil but shelter became their only common factor. Randall tried to be heartbroken over the state of his marriage but felt nothing but relief that the end was near. He remained ashamed of that fact. Their decision to separate had been mutual. Randall and Jillian did not hate each other because they had never loved in any form. Both felt the other was an inconvenience and wanted to move forward without the encumbrance of a partner with diverging values.

Randall signed over his interest in their home to Jillian who did not wait long to let the house go into foreclosure. After a couple of years, she worked out an agreement with the bank in her favor. She told Randall about the new mortgage terms and seemed to think that change in circumstance would entice him back to the marriage or at least to her bed. He had considered both a number of times.

A woman in his bed every night was the one thing Randall missed about his marriage. He hated the dating game and could never see himself paying for sex. He soon concluded that it was better to pay for sex, masturbate, or occasionally date, wine, and dine for sex than deal with the stress of living with Jillian.

Randall continued living in his cramped one bedroom apartment, worked hard, saved, and invested most of his income. Time had gone by quickly. Major changes started taking place at his agency causing Randall to long for a change in his own career. He had developed a need to be his own boss. He worked too hard for other people, saving them tons of cash, knowing he was worth far more than he was paid. As soon as his company sold out to a larger corporation with a reputation for squeezing the life out of its staff, Randall handed in his resignation and started his own small accounting firm.

When he became aware of Izola's medical condition, he knew it was time for him to return to San Antonio and help the people who had raised him and given him a loving home. His partners had bought him out with the agreement that he would not solicit his clients to move their business with him but the firm would not hold Randall liable for clients who chose to continue his services.

--

When Randall walked into Sugar's with his two lady loves he felt special. His aunts were beaming and blushing like brides on their wedding day and they looked just as beautiful. The hostess greeted them and immediately walked them past numerous customers and right to a table Sylvia had reserved with Izola and Viola's names on the table top. "Oh they reserved a table for us," Viola whispered as she glanced back at the guests standing and waiting for tables near the entrance. "I heard they don't reserve tables on Sundays."

"I called Sylvia and asked her to hold a table for me but she told me that was not their normal practice. When I told her I was bringing my aunts to brunch, she said, and I quote, 'anything for Romey's mother and aunt.' I was a little put off that she wouldn't hold a table for me based on my good looks and charm. Thank God for Jerome."

"Stop lying, Randall." Aunt Zoe stopped looking around long enough to chastise her nephew with a chuckle as they settled in at their table.

"Miss Zoe and Miss Vi, it is so good to see y'all. I haven't seen you two in ages." The daughter of an old friend of the two sisters approached the table and gave the ladies hugs in turn.

"Hi, baby." Viola smiled and returned the hug.

"Hi, Patricia, how is your mother? It's good to see you too." Zoe beamed at the young woman.

"Mama is good. She is going to be so excited when I tell her I ran into the two of you."

"Be sure and tell her we said hello, you hear."

"And give her our love," Vi added.

"I will do that. She'll be so happy to hear from you both." Patricia showed her best smile and then hesitated for a moment.

Viola caught on quickly and responded to the young woman's unspoken request. "Tricia did you ever meet my nephew Randall. He has just moved back here from DC. Randall this is Patricia. She's Miss Laverne's daughter. You remember Laverne that used to do the taxes for me and Zoe?"

Randall stood and accepted the beautiful young woman's hand. She flashed that best smile again and said, "Nice to meet you Randall. I do remember you from our school days. I was a few grades behind you though."

"You went to Roosevelt?" Randall didn't remember Patricia but most likely they had not hung in the same circles.

"I did. So, you're back in San Antonio from DC. What made you do that?"

"Oh, personal reasons, the main one being a need to be close to my aunts." Randall made a point of only glancing at Patricia who had thrown him so many smoldering looks he was beginning to feel uncomfortable.

"I hope to see you again sometime. Are you staying with your aunt?"

"No, I'm not. It was nice meeting you Patricia. I'm sure we'll run into each other again." Randall gave her a cool friendly smile and looked away. A little of the glow vanished from Patricia's face and she said her goodbyes and left the table.

"Nephew, do you always have to cut women off like that? She might as well have asked you out on a date. These young women are so forward these days." Viola looked indignant.

"Randall is not only good looking, he presents and carries himself well. Patricia is just trying to get him before someone else snatches him up. I don't blame her," Izola said.

"My aunts." Randall blushed handsomely and shook his head.

All three ordered the buffet and settled in to enjoy their meal and each other. "This place is sure nice. I wish Sugar could see it. That young wife of his didn't let it go down like folks said she would. I'm proud of her. I knew that girl had it in her." Viola looked around with so much pride you'd think she had a first-hand part in the upkeep of Sugar's Place.

"And the food is still good. It might be a little better. There is so much to choose from. I am enjoying myself." Aunt Zoe chewed into her potato flan.

Randall spotted Sylvia headed toward them with a warm smile on her glowing face. "I tried to get out here earlier to greet you ladies but we are swamped. Seems we get busier every week. I hope you're enjoying your dinner. Where is that son of yours, Miss Izola? Why didn't he come?" Sylvia stood over Viola and rubbed her back as she smiled at the ladies.

"He's out of town on business," Zoe answered.

Sylvia looked at Randall with a question on her face which he interpreted and answered. "Jerome flew out first thing this morning. He's trying to get some fitness certification on one end and he's giving continuing education and certification classes on the other. I think this trip will be his last for a while. Join us for a bit." Randall wished Sylvia would sit with them for a few moments and not dash off as he had seen her do every time he patronized her place of business.

"Don't I wish I could. You've got to get these ladies in here on a slow day so I'll have time to visit." Sylvia continued to smile at her guests without really looking at Randall. "Please, if you all need anything special let one of the wait staff know. Miss Viola, it has been so long since you were in here but I recall you loving Sugar's banana pudding. Would you like me to have them box one up for you, on the house? It will hold for two days, so you don't have to eat it today. And Miss Izola what would you like to take with you?"

"Oh goodness, everything is so good. I couldn't eat another thing today but I will take a piece of that apple cake if you can spare it."

"You got it," Sylvia said.

Sylvia started to walk away from the table but Randall stopped her. "Hey boss lady, what about me?"

"Yes sir," Sylvia answered, caught a bit off guard by the question.

"I want something sweet too." The look Randall gave Sylvia made her and his aunts question what he meant by "something sweet."

Sylvia smiled at him, causing a stirring in his chest. "Well I guess it wouldn't be fair not to include you. What can I get you, Cousin Randall?"

"Can I get one of those banana puddings for later?"

"You got it, Cousin."

Randall watched Sylvia walk off and thought to himself, *She's fun.*

"That girl sure is happy isn't she? What a change," Izola said.

"She deserves some happiness in her life," Viola added.

"What did she have to be so unhappy about, losing her husband?" Randall asked.

"Yes, but she was unhappy before she married Sugar and folks talked about her and gave her such a time about marrying him. That girl was just trying to survive. That first husband of hers treated her pretty bad," Izola said.

"How long were they married?" he asked, not able to contain his curiosity about Sylvia.

"Not sure. You know, Vi?"

"Unh unh but they stayed married until he got tired of her and found somebody else. She moved on and has made a life for her and those kids."

"How many kids does she have?" Randall asked.

Izola thought for a moment. "Three or four I think. I don't think she gets much help from her people with them either but I heard the ex was doing a lot better and spending time with the kids these days."

"I think Sugar's people help out too, the nieces not the kids. Them boys were real mad when Sugar married Sylvia," Viola told him.

"What about her mother? I remember her, a real pretty woman."

Viola took Izola's turn and answered Randall's question. "Dianne. She and Sylvia's daddy were never married. That Dianne stayed busy looking for a man. When she got one she had even less time for Sylvia. Then she had two more children with Sylvia's stepdad, so they lost just about all interest in Sylvia after that. Sylvia was Raelene's baby, her father's mother. When Raelene died that girl might as well have been by herself. That's why she jumped up and married that boy so fast. I think she was going to one of the colleges but once she got pregnant, that was that."

"What about Debra's mother. Didn't Sylvia spend a lot of time with them?"

"Before she got married she did but once she married that boy and started having babies, I don't think they had much time for her," Viola said.

Randall's Aunt Izola tried to explain Sylvia's family. "Those folks got so wrapped up in their own business. Denise and Dianne always wanted to be high class. I'm not saying they didn't love the girl but once she got married they were glad to be rid of her. Debra is worst than her mother and aunt together. That oldest girl, Janice, is a little better but she's got five kids of her own. She could hardly take on Sylvia and help her with her children. I think they were all upset when Sylvia married Sugar but I believe marrying that old man was the best thing that ever happened to that girl. We just never know how the lord will provide."

"Ain't that the truth? Ain't that the truth," Viola agreed.

Randall had noticed a man with a familiar face watching him and recognized the man as an old friend from high school and college. He asked his aunts to excuse him and approached his friend's table. "What you keep looking at man?" Randall asked belligerently. The woman at the table did not see Randall approaching and was caught completely off guard. Her eyes widen as her face took on the scowl of one deeply insulted. Randall knew he had gone too far. "Excuse me ma'am; I was just kidding around. I've known this knuckle head for years."

The lady smiled and watched as Luis De La Cruz stood and grabbed Randall in a suffocating embrace. "Hey, bro! When did you get back in town? Man, it's good to see you. I see Romey in here eating once in a while. I was beginning to wonder if you were still alive. I wouldn't ask him something like that though. Wouldn't want him to break down and start crying." The men laughed, remembering how much Jerome used to worship Randall.

Randall gave his friend a quick recent history. Luis did the same after introducing Randall to his fiancé. The friends shared contact information and Randall rejoined his ladies. He counted this as one of his best day since his return to San Antonio.

Chapter 7: Circumstances Such As These

Randall found the demands of his one-man business more trying each day. The tedium did not stem from work per se but from the peculiar necessity to spend an inordinate amount of time on the phone and meeting with one of his new clients.

On this particularly lovely fall day, he found himself sitting across the table from Maris Kleinholz, in all her glory. This was Randall's third luncheon with the lady and he was not quite sure why, though he did have strong suspicions.

"Randall, sweetie, you're not eating your lunch. No appetite for food," Maris questioned with that ever present hint of a hidden meaning.

"No Maris, I've been a little under the weather."

"Oh, come and go home with me. My girl will fix you a nice soup that will have you right in no time."

Randall was tired of the cat and mouse. The woman had called him three to five times each week since he met her. Upon first laying eyes on Maris, he thought her the most beautiful woman he had ever seen. It took one evening in her presence to realize Maris was best admired from afar. She was Debra and Jillian all rolled up in one. But as easily as he could resist her charm on a personal level, he had a harder time turning down her offer of a lucrative accounting gig.

Admittedly, Randall had been flattered when the lady first started calling him but now found her attentions boring. He was not unaccustomed to women pursuing him but had far too many things happening in his life at present to play along with Maris. So there he sat, ignoring her not so subtle innuendos and considering dumping her as a client. "Maris, I think I may have made a mistake in taking you on as a client," Randall said.

His client watched him with a sly smile and both her beautifully manicured hands clasped together under her chin.

"Am I wrong in thinking that you are flirting with me or is this how you talk to all men?"

"No, of course not, only men I like," Maris answered, leaning in closer and looking directly into Randall's eyes.

"I don't want to appear dense but are you saying you are interested in me for something other than my professional services?" Randall asked.

Maris smiled even more suggestively. "You know you do sound naive. You knew when I hired you that I wanted more than my numbers crunched."

"Well I guess I gave you the wrong impression. I'm not interested in anything more than crunching numbers just yet."

She gave him a toothy grin and leaned back into her seat. "Are you kidding me?"

Randall smiled back at her, slowly shaking his head.

"So, I don't get to take you home with me?"

"Fraid not," he said, not the least bit apologetic.

"You're not quitting on me are you? I do need a good accountant."

"No, but I need us to keep things professional."

"Okay, if that's the way you want it. I sure hope you don't regret this decision. I don't usually give second chances, if you know what I mean."

"As long as we can work well together, I'll be fine," Randall assured her.

Maris got up to leave the table. "Yeah, but will I. I was going to treat you to lunch but I figure you owe me something. Think you can handle the check?"

"My treat. No problem."

Maris slung that marvelous head of hair and pulled it back with her fingers before telling Randall, "I'll be in touch," and walking out.

--

Sylvia had finished her work and was looking over the day's receipts when she heard a rapping on the front entrance door. It was late but the only time Randall had available for the next seven days. Sylvia wanted to either hire Randall or eliminate him as a possible candidate to handle the restaurant's accounting needs. She wished she had not volunteered to feed him but otherwise he would have stopped to eat dinner. That made no sense when Sylvia had food left from the day's menu.

A whiff of Randall's scent mixed with a light hint of his after shave greeted her as he stepped through the opened doorway, not at

all unpleasant. *He sure is a well groomed man, just like Romey.*
Suddenly Sylvia was embarrassed about her own appearance. Her
chef's coat was dirty, her pants also. She had her hair pulled back
and her face was greasy as usual. She smiled at Randall and did her
best not to appear self-conscious.

"You here all alone?" Randall asked as he looked around.

"That's not unusual," Sylvia responded.

"Is that wise?"

"It's my day to close up," she answered without further
explanation. Normally she would have left with the last of the
kitchen staff and be gone by this time. She led Randall to the back
area where there was a small office and employee break room. "I
saved you some of our Korean style short ribs, some brown rice, and
a salad. I hope it's okay."

"Sounds good to me. I haven't had anything from your menu
that wasn't delicious. This has got to be the best food in town."
Randall made himself comfortable at a table while Sylvia gathered
his food.

"So explain to me how I can help you while I eat, if that's okay.
It'll save us some time and you can get out of here," he said as she
placed his food on the table in front of him.

Sylvia had not given much thought on how much detail she
wanted to share with Randall and decided to play it by ear. "I have
reason to not trust my current accountant so I am looking to make a
change. I need someone to audit my books and make sure everything
is on the up and up."

"You have reason to believe your accountant has been stealing
from you? Does he or she have access to your funds?" Randall had
stopped eating and was watching Sylvia very closely at this point.

"No, he doesn't," Sylvia answered hesitantly.

"You only need to tell me what you think I need to know to do
the work you want me to do, Sylvia, but if you think the law is being
broken you need to report him to the authorities."

"I don't think he has broken any laws, at least not yet, but I
believe ethically he has stepped across the line." Sylvia went on to
explain about the family partnership and her stepchildren's desire to
sell Sugar's. She told him that she and the nieces wanted to keep the
restaurant in the family and possibly open a new location or two and
about their offer to buy out the stepchildren. Sylvia explained their

belief that her current accountant had planned to take a kickback from the sale of the restaurant. "At first Terence, the oldest son, said $200,000 but that he was sure we could get more because he had a couple of other buyers interested. Now that we've offered to buy them out, they say they want to think about it."

"Just glancing around and observing your business volume, I can tell you this place is worth much more than 200k. How much debt are you carrying?"

"None."

"None?" Randall was stunned.

"What kind of lease?"

"We own the property."

"Damn, girl! You guys are sitting on a gold mine. You know it's going to cost a lot to buy Sugar's children out."

Sylvia smiled when she thought about Jessie and Retha. Jessie and her husband, Robert, were well off financial and Retha and her husband, Jaren, were wealthy. "I know. My understanding is that money is not an issue. But I don't think Sugar's kids will agree to sell to us."

"Why would they prefer to sell to strangers? It's their father's legacy."

"They don't like me. Me and the youngest two boys, Nathaniel and Gerald, were beginning to get along but after my husband died they pulled away. The daughter, Cheryl, never came around. I only met her one time before Sugar's funeral. That oldest son, Terence, is the worst. When I first started working here, he visited. He asked me out almost every day the entire time he was in town. I ignored him just like I do every customer that makes a play."

Randall grinned, causing Sylvia to take offense. "Believe it or not, customers hit on me even when I look like this."

"I have no trouble believing that. I was smiling because you are so honest but you are not bragging. I take it that you don't consider it a compliment when men hit on you?"

"Please! That's what men do – they hit on women." Sylvia laughed and Randall found himself laughing along with her. He wondered if she realized that's what women do also.

"So I guess he was pretty embarrassed when you married his father. You think he holds that against you?"

"I doubt that's the issue. Terence was married then and had been for years. He may have just been flirting. He is ambitious and I know he plans to be a rich man. Sugar provided well for me and my children when he died. He left me his home, the largest share of the restaurant, life insurance and a social security pension. All of that, except the pension, would have gone to his children. That's what I think he resents."

"It happens hundreds, if not thousands of times a day. Sugar had a right to leave his assets however he chose. He left them to those he valued and wanted to protect the most. Did he leave his children anything other than part ownership in the restaurant?"

"He left them insurance money, quite a bit I'm told."

"But not enough. For some people, there is never enough," Randall said.

"I guess not." Sylvia appeared saddened by Randall's revelation. "Would you like some coffee?"

"That would be nice. Thanks."

Sylvia and Randall sat and discussed the restaurant for another hour with him picking her brain about every aspect of Sugar's. He had started taking notes when he finished his dinner. Finally he asked, "So when would you like me to start?"

"Well I guess I need to get some idea what we are looking at when it comes to your fees."

"What were you paying Mr. Frisk? That's my fee and I guarantee you I'll find ways to save you money."

"You don't know what I was paying him."

"I will after I go over your books." Randall said as he packed up his tablet and followed her to the kitchen.

"Can you start as soon as possible? Do you have an office yet?"

"No. I'll be working from home for some time to come. I'm not ready for the office overhead. We won't need to actually meet that often but when we do, I can come here if you like."

"Well I don't like staying here so late, so maybe you can come to my place. I usually come in late one or two days a week, so if you can do early mornings we're set. I prefer not to come in here during my off hours in the morning. I stay late a lot."

Randall looked at Sylvia and thought she might have been making a subtle play but quickly realized that was far from the case. He felt a twinge of disappointment as he watched her put away the dishes she just washed and wondered if she noticed that he was a single available man. "Whatever works for you," he said.

"I'll get all my records together for you to go over but Frisk has most of the paperwork." Sylvia did not look happy at the prospect of confronting Frisk.

"I'll draft a letter for you to sign and mail out registered mail to your old firm. The letter will ask them to forward all records concerning your accounts to me no later than a date specified by you. In that letter you will also ask for a final bill. It is always a good idea to thank the agency for their service but do not give praise just in case you become aware of a problem you need to address through litigation later."

"He's going to want to know why we are dropping him."

"You have no obligation to explain and it is best you don't. You don't want him taking your words and using them against you at a later date. I'm not insinuating that your Mr. Frisk did something criminal. I'm telling you the common practice under circumstances such as these."

Chapter 8: Sylvia's Savior

As inviting as Sylvia's bed was, it did not fulfill its promise of a restful night's sleep. Sylvia's children stayed with her ex husband, Sean, on Wednesdays so the house was peaceful though a little cold, lacking the warm it held when the children were at home. Her mind was busy – full of all the changes taking place in her life involving the business and others of a personal nature. Sylvia usually went in early on Thursdays so she could take off and spend time with the children the evening after their weeknight with their father and stepmother. This was Sean's weekend so the kids would be with him from Friday after school until Sunday evening. Planning around the visitation had been challenging for both parents and children but so far they were making it work. It hadn't been as hard at first because Sean was in such bad shape he stayed away from the children. Now that he had learned to control the abuse of his addictions, he worked hard at parenting.

Lately Sean was asking Sylvia for more time with their two boys, but she was unwilling to agree to any change in visitation, no matter how informal. The children had adjusted to their schedule and were doing well in school. Between Sean, his wife Camille, and Sylvia, the children were a priority and all their needs were met. Six years ago Sylvia had felt sorry for her children, for the circumstances they were born into -- a weak orphan of a mother and a bullying addictive father. Decent employment, Sugar and his nieces for Sylvia and rehab, counseling, and Camille for Sean had made a world of difference in their lives.

These days Sylvia hardly recognized the person who peered at her from the mirror each morning so motivated and full of confidence. She was the woman her Nana Raelene had worked so hard to form. Sylvia prayed everyday that her grandmother knew her life was good.

The circumstances of Sylvia's early life had often been precarious. She was born to young unmarried parents who were neither wise or in love. Fortunately, both her parents' families were strong. Dianne, Sylvia's mother, came from a family strong in number and pride. Sylvia's father, James, who died in a training accident while serving in Germany, had only Sylvia and his mother,

Raelene, a woman who had enough strength for a family of ten or more.

Since Sylvia's mother had little time for raising a child, by the time Sylvia was five years old her home was no longer with Dianne but with Miss Raelene. By every account, Sylvia's paternal grandmother was an intelligent and good-hearted woman who loved Sylvia greatly but suffered through mistreatment from Dianne on a regular basis. It was not uncommon for Dianne to show up unannounced and take Sylvia away, never telling Raelene when she would return the child. Sylvia's grandmother fretted whenever Sylvia was with Dianne's family but Sylvia always longed to spend time with her mother's people. She had cousins her age at her Aunt Denise's house and there was always a family cookout or a party taking place. Often on these visits her mother would give her bags of clothing, always the best brands and of the best quality.

As Sylvia grew older she became aware of her grandmother's concerns but did not quite understand the cause. Looking back, she believed her grandmother feared the values she might learn from Dianne and her people. They had always been very self-centered people who bad- mouthed everyone. No one was quite good enough. No one was pretty enough, had enough money, bought nice enough things, or lived in a nice enough house. The Samuels considered themselves elite and above everyone. They were a family but they believed in exclusion and had excluded Sylvia most of her life.

But Sylvia was a new person now. All those seeds her grandmother toiled so hard to plant were coming to harvest, not all at once but week after week, year after year. She felt strong now. She had needed strength to deal with the ups and downs of her life. There had been those times when she was down and thought she would never see the sun breaking through those dark clouds. God sends angels.

Sean was a new person also. He had been meaner after their separation than he was while they were together. He had stopped hitting Sylvia but he threatened her so often that she was afraid to leave her apartment for months.

One day out of cold desperation she steeled her nerves, went out in search of employment, and got hired on at Sugar's. It was her good fortune that Retha had just started working her magic on the place and Sylvia got to watch the transformation from one day to the next, day after day. Sugar had been resentful of the change but he wanted the money Retha was investing in the place. He also loved having his nieces come and work with him, something his own children refused to do. Jessie and Retha were closer to their uncle than his two oldest children were, much closer. He would have let those nieces of his do just about anything they wanted to Sugar's Place. Yes, he had raised hell while the changes were made. Sugar did not like losing control the way he had, but he knew the changes were for the best.

The turmoil in Sylvia's life had nearly caused her to lose the job at Sugar's. Sugar had threatened to fire her several times for being late or not coming in at all. On the morning of the day she failed to go into work she had seen Sean's car parked up the street from her home. Job or no job, she stayed locked up in her apartment. She had been terrified. Retha stood in the gap on those occasions and helped Sylvia keep her job. Sugar was not happy but let her stay on anyway. Looking back, Sylvia believed that Sugar and Retha had their suspicions about her situation. She was a lousy employee, could hardly concentrate on the simplest task but they kept her on.

Sugar had stopped the terror that was Sean. Sugar had walked up on Sean assaulting Sylvia one night outside of the restaurant when she was taking out the garbage. Sean had her by the hair and was sneering as he told her he could do whatever he wanted to her and no one could stop him. Sylvia's heart raced as she tried to get away but his grip was so tight she knew she would have to leave a handful of her hair in his clutches. She thought about her children and wondered if she would ever see them again or if he would leave her alive but in no condition to care for her babies. A million thoughts had raced through her mind.

Sugar didn't say a word as he approached and Sylvia had no idea he was nearby. She was holding onto Sean's wrist with both hands, trying to loosen his grip on her hair, as she watched him with fear, hate, and pleading in her wet eyes. She watched as his head suddenly fell to the side.

"Nigga, I'll kill you!" Sugar yelled as Sean released Sylvia's hair, causing her to fall to the ground. "Get, up Sylvia! This the son of a bitch been beatin' on you?"

Sylvia said nothing in response. She was too relieved and grateful.

Sean was leaning against the dumpster holding his hands to the side of his head where Sugar had hit him with the largest handgun Sylvia had ever seen. The blood was gushing and when Sean saw the thick red flow he must have thought he was dying. "Oh God, oh God, call me a ambulance," he moaned.

"I'm gonna call the fuckin' police, that's what I'm gonna do. You ever heard of pistol whipped boy. Well that's what you just got the front end of and you gonna get the middle and the back end if I hear tell of you around Sylvia again. You hear me?"

All Sean could do was whimper.

"You hear me, boy?" Sugar demanded a response.

"Yeah," Sean moaned as he bent over and held his bleeding head.

"Get yo black ass outta here!" Sugar yelled.

"I need a doctor. I don't think I can drive," Sean groaned

"You gonna need the fuckin' mortician if I ever see you again. If you can't drive, walk yo ass off my property but I'm gonna have that damn car towed to the impound lot."

Sylvia had been so fearful of Sean's reaction that her eyes barely blinked for several nights following his bludgeoning. She was constantly on the lookout for Sean even while she feared his death. She had heard, like most of us, that a wounded animal is the most dangerous of all. Sugar took her home every night and started spending every free moment with her. It wasn't long before Sylvia grew to love Sugar, not that heated, excited young love, but the comfortable, cozy, mature kind. Soon he started staying in her home and after only a few months they married.

Sylvia did not hear a word from Sean for more than two months after his run in with Sugar and that big gun. Her boys had been heartbroken and distraught with the absence of their father. Sylvia had feared he was dead, lying in a ditch somewhere rotting. When he finally called, there was a change in him. "I'd like to see my kids, Sylvia." No hello, no small talk, just a request.

"Okay," was her only response.

"I'm going to have a police escort when I pick them up. Can I get them on Friday?"

"That's fine, Sean. They've been asking for you every day."

Later Sylvia learned that Sean had been in rehab for his alcohol and cocaine use. He continued his counseling to this day. It took him a year to apologize to Sylvia and a month or so later he walked into the restaurant and sat down with Sugar and thanked him for not killing him that night, for knocking some sense into his head, and for taking care of Sylvia and the children.

"That's alright." Sugar told him. "You ain't the first nigga I had to beat some sense into. You the first one ever thanked me for it though." Sugar and Sean had both laughed at that.

Sugar and Sylvia grew strong together, fortifying each other. Sugar had so many ailments that their physical love was limited but Sugar lead people to believe he kept Sylvia on her back. Sylvia didn't mind the nonexistent sex life or Sugar's misrepresentations. She was safe and content for the first time since her Nana died.

Shangri-La had not lasted long. Sugar's health problems turned out to be fatal. He and Sylvia had been married just under two years when he died.

Sugar had been more of a father than a lover to Sylvia and she mourned him deep in her soul. He was the only father figure she had ever known and she expected her struggles to resume after his death but Jessie and Retha stayed in constant contact. Jessie made sure she saw Sylvia no less than four or five times a week for the first few months after Sugar's death. Retha, who was recently married and pregnant with her first child, had moved away but called so frequently that Sylvia sometimes avoided speaking with her.

Those sisters stayed in Sylvia's business until she handled it. There was much to be done and when Sylvia wasn't working she had wanted to lie in bed and cover her head but Jessie kept her moving forward. One morning Sylvia opened her eyes and all of Sugar's affairs were settled; she cried. It had been a trying task. Sugar's children had been angry and difficult but not impossible. They would not have dared cross Jessie back then. They were more emboldened now. They were more mature, had plenty of their own money, independence, and good jobs.

Sylvia rented out the little home Sugar left her on San Antonio's East Side and bought Retha's home near Jessie in Northeast San Antonio. Retha sold her the home well below market price and now Sylvia and the children had plenty of room in a beautiful home with a big back yard. Things had worked out for Sylvia and her children. She had lost one protector and gained two. Her children, Jessie and Retha, and their families were her closest relations now. She longed to become even closer to her nieces but was still a little afraid of pushing too much and turning them away. Sylvia had lived with so much rejection throughout her life that she couldn't help but watch for it, even from those closest to her. She accepted that she needed Retha and Jessie but did not believe they needed her also.

She laid awake thinking about her newest dilemma. *Just think how much easier life would be if Sean had the boys with him most of the time. Dealing with Tani is so much easier than Justin and Billy. They've got football and I spend so much energy getting them to do homework and eat right -- and those games, all the time those games. They are forever begging to be with Sean anyway.*

As Sylvia thought about all the reasons why she should let her boys spend more time with their father, one glaring reason against the change stayed in the forefront, football. Sean lived and breathed the sport. He had kept both boys involved in football since they were old enough to walk. Sean placed football ahead of school, illness, broken limbs, even death. Yes, he had been known to miss one or two family funerals because of a football game, not because he played the sport but because he breathed it.

Sylvia had no problem with her sons playing football. Justin had an amazing aptitude for all sports but liked football best. Her younger son, Billy, preferred basketball and track, but Sean insisted both boys play football first. Sylvia managed to maintain a balance in the boys' lives. She knew if they spent more time with Sean their choices would be limited with football as the only option. Camille would be of no help. She was as much a football junkie as her husband.

--

Nathaniel Solomon was not pleased about spending his Saturday afternoon at Houligan's Sports Bar. He liked the bar but had other plans for his day. His older brother, Terence, had started calling and leaving messages at five o'clock the day before. When Nate finally spoke with his brother, Terence wanted to set up a meeting. He said it was urgent.

Looking around the bar, Nathaniel spotted his younger brother, Gerald, approaching just as his phone beeped with a text from Terence. He and Cheryl were ten minutes away. Nate wondered what could be so important and had Terence so angry. *Must be that*

***damn restaurant and Sylvia.*** Like Frisk, Nathaniel had started to question his decision to participate in the scheme to make a little extra off the sale of Sugar's Place.

Nathaniel and Gerald had always accepted guidance from Terence better than their father. Sugar's children often felt neglected and acted out based on their anger toward him. The younger brothers knew their father disliked the way they followed Terence's lead so they made a point of becoming more dedicated to Terence, anything to upset Sugar. Looking back, Nathaniel could no longer recall why he had so often been angry with his father. Sugar could have left them with their mother out in LA but he had chosen to give them a better life with him. No, it was not always easy and there had been a number of different women passing through their lives, but Sugar kept them close and safe.

The sale of the restaurant was becoming a weight about Nate's neck. He liked getting those quarterly checks from Sugar's. This was the money his father had occasionally shelled out to his children on an as needed basis but more substantial. If you begged Sugar out of a few hundred dollars one month, you had better not try the next. At most, you might be able to get twenty or fifty after two months. Now the money from the restaurant just arrived in his account the last week of the month following the quarter's end. That money made Nathaniel feel wealthy, so he saved all of it. Although his lady brought in nearly twice as much as him, she was impressed when he told her about the income from Sugar's Place. There was something special about owning a piece of a business that paid out on a regular basis.

The two brothers greeted each other, grabbed a table, and ordered drinks. "I just got a text from Terence. They'll be here in a few," Nate told Gerald, getting only a nod in response.

"Sylvia fired Frisk," were the first words out of Terence's mouth when he sat down with his siblings.

Nate and Gerald looked from Terence to Cheryl who appeared more upset than Terence. "I had to make him pull over outside of Katy and take the wheel. He was driving like a crazy person. No damn money or restaurant means that much," Cheryl complained.

Gerald chuckled but quickly checked himself after an angry look from Terence.

"Why'd she fire him?" Nathaniel asked.

"Who the hell knows? I just know I'm tired of her shit. Hey, you think I can get some service over here, baby." Terence yelled at the waitress who ignored him.

Gerald wanted answers. "Wait a minute man. She didn't give him a reason or anything. Don't she need to give him a notice or something?"

"Frisk called me late yesterday and told me he received a registered letter from Sylvia stating that effective immediately his accounting services are no longer needed. He is supposed to send her a bill so he can get paid. She wants all the records turned over to the new company," Terence explained.

"What does this have to do with us? I cancelled a very hard to come by hair appointment for this meeting?" Cheryl was getting angrier by the minute.

Terence looked at his sister as if she was dumber than a toadstool. "Frisk has the connections to the buyers we want. The buyer pays significantly more than the price on paper but much less than the true value. Sylvia, Jessie, and Retha take their share from the bogus sale price on paper. We split the remainder after Frisk takes his cut. That's why it was important to use the business valuation from Frisk's man. The last tool we had available to keep the value of Sugar's on the low side was the projected receipts. I could have talked Frisk into fudging those numbers. He even has the real estate attorney in his pocket to make everything real nice and legal for the closing."

"Well if they don't want to sell, it doesn't matter about Frisk. And if you want to sell so bad why don't you sell your interest in the place to Retha or Jessie?" Nathaniel asked, more certain than ever that Terence was either hiding something or incompetent. Why all this agitation over selling the restaurant at a reduced price and cheating their partners?

"I wouldn't sell them the time of day. They already got too much of my shit and I want it back!" Terence hit the table angrily as he looked at his sister and brothers. "I need to know what put them on to Frisk. First they didn't want to use the appraisal company he set up. Now Frisk is out all together. Something is not right here." Terence stared at Nate as if he expected him to admit to the betrayal of their secret. Nate held his brother's gaze without flinching. He too had his suspicions about all the coincidences surrounding Mr. Frisk.

"Why don't we just ask Sylvia why she fired him? What's the big deal?" Gerald asked as he munched on a nacho chip.

"Because we don't know she fired him. She hasn't told us and we don't want her to know we know," Nate explained to his unconcerned younger brother.

"Ain't she supposed to tell us about stuff like this? I mean, firing your accountant is a big deal. It's our business too," Gerald said.

"Sylvia is owner manager. Remember, we didn't want to get involved with running the place. The short answer is no. She has the power to hire and fire, buy and sell, change, make minor renovations, whatever the hell she pleases; we gave her that power and she has done a damn good job. Maybe we need to leave things as they are and forget all about this sneaky bullshit. We are all getting money out of Sugar's Place. Sylvia's the only one working her butt off to make us money." Nathaniel hoped these words sank into the psyche of his companions.

"She gets paid a decent salary for her labor, damn good from what I understand," Cheryl smirked.

"No she doesn't, not for the hours she puts in. Sylvia is working our hours. In the restaurant business, the owner always puts in the extra hours. We don't do that. Sylvia does it for us, all of us," Nathaniel explained, getting more disheartened by the minute. He wanted all the scheming to end. He was certain Gerald was the leak and fearful of Terence's reaction when he found out.

"So, you backing out on me now too, little brother?" Terence's question to Nathaniel held a menacing tenor.

"If we can sell the restaurant with all the cards on the table, I will support that. I'm tired of all this subversive bullshit. It makes no sense to me. Why should we sell for $400K, pretend like we are selling for less when we might be able to get 800K? We'd be cheating ourselves to hurt Sylvia."

Cheryl and Gerald both looked at Terence for an answer they knew he had to have off the top of his head. Terence appeared cool and calm on the outside but was smoldering underneath his beautiful caramel skin. His plan was falling apart and he needed another tactic. His siblings were clearly not the sheep he had always thought them. He decided to play a little naive at this point. "What makes you think the business is worth so much more?" he asked Nate.

"We never talked about the building. It has got to be worth a lot – likely more than the business," Nathaniel explained.

"Isn't there a mortgage on the building?" Cheryl asked.

"I don't think so. The financial reports just show the property taxes, inventory taxes, insurance, utilities and other maintenance stuff but no mortgage, rent, or lease payment. Dad owned that building free and clear."

Cheryl looked at Terence as if a veil was lifted from her eyes. "Did you know the building was paid off? I thought it belonged to the bank."

"It's ours," Nathaniel said, without looking at Terence.

"Wow. That really puts a different light on things. I don't know why Frisk kept that from me. Maybe that's why Sylvia let him go. He ain't trustworthy." Terence was certain Cheryl and Nathaniel were on to him. He wouldn't push further but would seek another way to accomplish his goals. He glanced at his watch in a pretense at having somewhere else to be. "Listen, Sis can you ride home with Nate or Gerald and I'll pick you up in an hour or so? I've got another meeting."

"Another meeting!" Cheryl raged. "I could have driven my own damn car if I had known you were going to bring me down here and dump me. Drop me off at a shopping center. Nate and Gerald don't want to be bothered with me. And you better not leave me hanging too long."

Nathaniel and Gerald were both relieved they were off the hook and wouldn't need to entertain their older sister who could be difficult to please on a good day.

Chapter 9: Screw Her

"Hey, what you got going on today?" Jerome had Randall in the car with him on a gorgeous fall day. He should have been at home working on a training program for his special needs clients but wanted to hang out with his big cousin for a while.

"Jerome?" Sylvia questioned the caller, not able to recall the last time her friend called her at home. "I'm here with the kids. Sean is picking them up later to take them to Fear Fest."

"He taking the baby too?"

"She can't wait to go. Tani's not a scaredy cat like her mother. She went last year. What are you calling me about anyway? It must be snowing in your part of town." Sylvia laughed.

"I got my cousin in the car with me. Moms and Aunt Vi went to Wimberley with Martha. We're out your way so I thought we might stop by. You got any beer?"

Randall wondered who he was about to visit. One never knew with Jerome. Randall had been finishing a report for one of his new clients when Jerome knocked at his door a few hours earlier. Needing a break, Randall was glad to see his unpredictable cousin. He had nearly completed the report and would finish easily when he returned home later in the evening.

He had accompanied Jerome to a nearby furniture store and then the cousins had gone to Sugar's for lunch. No sooner than they had arrived at the luscious eatery, Jerome started his "Hey Syl" routine. Both men were deflated to learn that the ever present Sylvia was off for the day. Randall was surprised at how little he enjoyed Sugar's Place when there was no Sylvia in sight. The food was as good as ever but there was definitely something lacking in the ambiance with no visit to his table by his new employer.

"I'm going to run in here and grab a twelve pack; you want anything?" Jerome asked as he whipped his car into a parking space near the front of a Valero station.

"Nah man," Randall replied.

When Jerome returned to the car he heard Randall exclaim, "Good God!"

"What's up, man?" Jerome asked.

"Nothing, it's nothing." Randall placed his cell phone back in the carrier on his belt.

"Must be a woman. You ain't been in town a good fifteen minutes and you already got somebody hunting you down." Jerome grinned at his cousin as he pulled his car onto the roadway.

"It's Debra. She wants me to come way out there to the country and, check this out, install a new light fixture over her garage door. Who was doing these things for her before I came to town? She's got neighbors, two brothers, cousins, a father, and let's not forget hired repairmen or women. She's bugging the hell out of me, man."

Jerome glanced over at his cousin and grinned but said nothing.

"What?" Randall wanted to know what Jerome was thinking.

"Just screw her and get it over with. You know that's what she wants. Has she been to your place yet? She know where you live?"

"Nope, haven't told her. I think she believes I'm still at your mom's house. You'd think she would take a hint. If I wanted to be bothered, I would have showed up at her place a long time ago. Man I don't want to make an enemy out of that woman."

"Screw her. Maybe you'll run her off that way," Jerome teased.

"You know Debra as well as me. If I sleep with her she'll claim me as hers until she's tired of me. I'm not willing to go through a relationship with her to get her to leave me the hell alone."

"Is she calling you every day?"

"If she's not calling, she's texting. She texts like a fifteen-year-old. She tries to hold entire conversations via text. If I gave a damn about her, romantically I mean, I'd want to hear her voice not read some silly text message. Randall looked around when Jerome stopped the car in front of an unfamiliar home. "You think you could tell me who we're about visit?"

"Sylvia. You looked so sad when she wasn't at Sugar's, I thought you might want to see her." Jerome tilted his head and looked at his cousin with a smile and a raised brow. Randall could only smile back as he reached for the beers in the back seat.

A call from her "see ya when I see ya" friend, Jerome, caught Sylvia by surprise. She seldom had visitors because she worked such unpredictable hours. Also she became a bit of a pariah after her marriage to Sugar. Many of Sylvia's friends and acquaintances and much of her family felt sorry for her and thought she was disgustingly pitiful, far too pitiful to bother with. Others thought she was a conning woman taking advantage of an old man, which made her disgraceful. Most people were more accepting these days and she no longer got all those "poor thing" looks and seldom received out right snubs, but Sylvia had no desire to renew bonds with used to be friends who distanced themselves from her after she became involved with Sugar.

Jerome and his aunts had not changed, ever. Jerome's cousin Martha remained as self-absorbed, opinionated, and foul-mouthed as before. "Girl, tell them motherfuckers to kiss yo ass. If you like that old dick, it ain't no money out their pockets." Martha had made Sylvia laugh that day. She was serious when she made the statement but got tickled also when Sylvia laughed so hard.

So two of her business partners, Jerome and his family, and her ex husband and his wife Camille were Sylvia's closes associates. She was excited that Jerome and Randall were paying her a visit. *Wow, two good looking men coming to visit me. I'd better check myself out.* She hurried from the backyard, where she had been playing with the kids, into her room. Sylvia washed and moisturized her face, applied a little blush and mascara, and put on a bra with a fresh top. She re-twists her hair onto the top of her head and breathed deeply as she looked in the mirror. "I guess this will have to do."

She was glad her housework was done and that she didn't need to run around picking up the place. Two of her neighbors had a cleaning service and they came in on Sylvia's Saturdays off to clean so she was free to focus on her children on the Saturday afternoons they spent with her. They had just finished lunch and her neighbors had cleaned the kitchen and were gone by the time Jerome called.

"What time is Dad coming?" her middle child, Billy asked. "I'm ready to go."

"Is your bag all packed? Don't forget anything. Your dad will be here in thirty minutes," she told Billy.

The children loved and hated these Saturdays because even though the ladies came to clean, Sylvia made them help. They had to strip their beds and make sure all their dirty things were downstairs in the laundry room. They had to get out of bed by nine o'clock and were not allowed to watch television or play any form of video game. Once they had eaten and finished their house work they did their homework or read until lunchtime. After lunch, Sylvia would take her children out shopping, to the movies, a park or on an adventure. Sylvia's Saturdays off were full of family time which her children loved but also full of structure which the children despised.

Sylvia noticed Justin, her oldest, looking at her as if he had a question which Bertani gave voice to. "Mommy, you look pretty. Why you look so nice?"

"Romey is coming by."

"Cool." Justin headed toward the living room so he would be near the front door when the bell rang.

"Oh boy, Uncle Romey is coming over!" Tani yelled and left the room. Sylvia guessed her daughter was going to make sure she looked her best. Jerome had that effect on females, even seven-year-olds.

"You think Uncle Jerome will throw with us until Dad gets here?" Justin asked his mother.

"Don't bother him about throwing that ball. He's just stopping by for a minute. Did you pack up those games your dad asked you to return?"

"I forgot. I'll go get them now. That's why you put on makeup," Justin said sarcastically, "because he's just stopping by?"

Sylvia thumped her son on the head as he passed by her. No sooner than Justin walked off to his room and Sylvia went to check the mirror one more time, the doorbell rang. Both Billy and Bertani shot out of nowhere as if they were hiding in wait for the bell to ring and made frenzied dashes to the door yelling "I got it." "No, I got it." "Mommy, tell Billy, I got it." Then they stood at the door with both their hands on the knob yelling at each other.

"Get away from that door," Sylvia yelled as Justin cleared his brother and sister away from the door.

"Get off me boy," Billy yelled at his older brother who then pushed him into Bertani who started to cry as if one of her brothers had hit her hard in the mouth. Sylvia gave her oldest son the look and he immediately yelled, "She's not hurt. She's such a faker."

Sylvia cleared her children from the door and opened it to find Jerome bent over in laughter and Randall standing there with dumbfounded disbelief on his face. "I guess you can tell we don't get much company," Sylvia said with an embarrassing smile.

The children flocked to Jerome like he was the ice cream truck. He picked up Bertani and patted her back like she was a toddler and managed to shake the two boys on their heads.

"Where should I put this," Randall asked Sylvia, who seemed lost.

"Oh, I'm sorry, Randall. I'll put some in the fridge to cool." Sylvia answered as she reached for the case of beer.

Randall pulled the case out of her reach. "Just lead the way," he said.

Sylvia tried not to grin too hard but her mouth and cheeks seem to have a mind of their own. She and Randall left Jerome with the children and headed into the kitchen. "You have a beautiful home. How long have you been collecting art?" Randall asked.

"Since high school. There was a girl in band with me and Jerome who was an artist. You might remember her, Lessie Solms. I have several of her pieces. She lives out of state now."

"Is she still showing her work?"

"She sure is. She had a store on eBay for awhile. I don't think she has that any longer but she does have an online store. She does most of her work in acrylic but sometimes uses watercolors; she's prolific."

"I'll have to check her out. I need some help getting my place together, you know, making it homey and comfortable but with style." Randall leaned back against the counter and watched as Sylvia placed beers in the refrigerator.

"Where are y'all going?" Sylvia asked when she saw Jerome and the children walk through the kitchen and start out the back door, totally engrossed.

Jerome stopped in his tracks and looked at her just as Justin or Billy might, pointed to the door and said, "Oh, I was just gonna toss a few balls for the boys."

"Me too, me too!" Tani pleaded.

"You too, baby." Jerome assured the child.

"No no 'me too', no nobody," Sylvia admonished. "I told you guys not to bother Jerome about tossing that ball. Your dad will be here any minute."

"He asked us!" Justin shouted at Sylvia.

Jerome jumped in. "Boy, you don't yell at your mother or any woman like that."

Justin looked shamefaced and apologized to Sylvia.

"I did ask them, Sylvia. They never mentioned tossing the ball. How about it?"

"Okay, but first you guys go upstairs and bring your bags down. You know your dad hates to wait."

The kids took off running.

"Stop running on those stairs," Sylvia yelled after them.

Jerome looked at Sylvia with respect in his eyes. "I don't know how you do it, Syl."

"Do what?"

"Take such good care of these kids, your home, work an outside job and a half, and still stay so beautiful both inside and out. The gods must be smiling on you."

"You're so full of it, Jerome." Sylvia blushed appealingly.

"I'm not kidding. Those three would wear me out in fifteen minutes. Most people that do all you do, look all tired and run down. You just get prettier and more vibrant every time I see you. You must have a new man in your life." Jerome cut his eyes at Randall.

Sylvia scoffed at Jerome who smiled back at her. "Ain't she beautiful, man?" He deferred to his cousin who was looking at Sylvia and enjoying her discomfort.

"She's my boss. I can't comment." Randall said with a smile.

The children returned and got Jerome and Randall in the back yard throwing footballs while Sylvia sat on the patio searching her tablet and watching. She looked up when she saw Sean enter the back yard through the side gate. He did not try to hide his surprise when he saw men playing with his children. Sean smiled slightly when he saw Sylvia sitting on the patio but still did not look pleased. He and Jerome shook hands like two warring adversaries during peace time and Jerome introduced Randall to Sean.

Sean and Sylvia soon walked into the house following the children who had run inside to gather up their bags. Jerome and Randall remained out back throwing the football to each other. Once the kids were outside, headed toward their father's car and out of earshot, Sean commented to Sylvia about her guests. "It's strange to see you with visitors other than Jessie or her sister."

Sylvia just shrugged, not knowing how to respond.

"You dating now?" Sean looked directly into her eyes in a way he hadn't since they were young and in lust, before he became a monster.

Sylvia wished she had someone to date. "They're just friends." She tried not to show how sad her answer made her but Sean was happier when he walked away.

Sylvia entered the house and yelled at her guests, "You guys want a beer?"

"Thought you'd never ask," Randall replied.

Jerome didn't bother to respond. He had a question for Sylvia when she brought their beers out to the patio. "Did you get in trouble for having men at your house?" he asked with a straight face.

Sylvia took a seat at the patio table where the cousins were relaxing. "Why would you ask me something like that?" She was as uncomfortable with Jerome's question as she had been with Sean's a few moments earlier.

"I know how possessive your ex gets sometimes."

"You seem to have forgotten that Sean and I have been divorced for years and that I have remarried since I was married to him."

"Yeah but he might not like the idea of you getting involved with someone you might really want."

"Man, what are you talking about?" Randall asked, totally caught off guard by Jerome's words and turning to Sylvia for her reaction. She looked angry enough to fight Jerome on the spot, said nothing, but got up to leave the patio.

"Wait a minute, Syl! I didn't mean," Jerome began, knowing he had misspoken.

Sylvia cut him off "Excuse me." She marched off the patio as Jerome called after her. "Sylvia, come here."

From the patio they heard Sylvia's bedroom door close.

"Why would you say some shit like that to her?" Randall said, not hiding his anger.

"Man, I didn't mean it. I was just talking. Damn!" Jerome said in his defense as he rose to follow Sylvia. He knocked at her bedroom door but she didn't answer. Sylvia was closed up in her bathroom trying to stop the tears. The second time Jerome knocked and called out her name she let him in.

Once more Jerome tried to apologize. "Sylvia, baby, I didn't mean."

"Yes you did." Sylvia sat on the side of her bed and glared at her friend defiantly. "Yes you did. I guess everyone either felt sorry for me or Sugar. I hate that sympathy bullshit. Sugar was the best thing that ever happened to me. He saved me and gave me and my children a decent life. He made us safe and secure and I loved him." Sylvia was crying again.

Jerome sat down next to her and wrapped her in his arms. What she said next surprised him. "And I miss him so much." Sylvia sobbed and Jerome wanted to run away. He couldn't believe he had made such a mean verbal blunder and dredged up so much pain for the friend he loved so dearly.

"Sylvia, I'm sorry."

"Stop apologizing. The hurtful part is that I wanted a young healthy husband. I wanted to feel that romantic love and never felt it for Sugar but I loved him."

Jerome felt terrible. He had not wanted to make Sylvia cry and he sure had not wanted her to start spilling out all her thoughts and emotions on him. He did his best to avoid situations involving high levels of emotional drama. He was speechless at this point. Sylvia was full of pent up feelings and she was spewing all over him.

"I feel so guilty for living so well. I've got a nice home, a good income, a partnership in a prosperous business. I've even got some family now, all because of Sugar. Is it any wonder people say I married him for what he could do for me financially? Do you know they've said I had someone do something to him to make him sick? I'm so tired of it."

"That's stupid talk. Don't pay attention to what people say, especially not me," Jerome said.

Sylvia smiled upon hearing this, helping Jerome breathe freely again. The friends sat in silence for a few moments. Finally, Sylvia took a deep breath and rose from her bed. She reached for Jerome and pulled him toward the bedroom door. "Come on. We left Randall out there alone. He's our guest and he's not going to think very highly of either of us."

"Sylvia." Jerome stopped her just inside the door. "Do you forgive me? You know I love you, don't you?"

"Yes I do and I want to thank you and your aunts and Martha for being so good to me when just about everyone else was so mean or disinterested." Sylvia started tearing up again.

"No, no, no, no, no more crying today," Jerome urged as he pushed her toward the door.

When they got back outside Jerome noticed Randall tapping his foot. That was a sure sign his cousin was pissed. Randall looked at Sylvia and asked, "You okay?"

"I'm fine. I'm so sorry. That was really rude of me," Sylvia said.

"I understand. Who could blame you? Maybe we should go." Randall looked at Jerome who knew he had fallen into disfavor.

"Please don't go, you guys. We haven't visited yet. I get so little company and now the kids are gone with Sean. Can you stay a little longer?" Sylvia pleaded.

Randall gave her a close hard look, trying to determine if she really wanted them to stay longer. "You drink a beer with us and we'll stay," he told her with a lightened mood.

"That's a bet." Sylvia got herself a beer and put two more in a bucket of ice for her friends. She turned on some mellow jazz and before long they were enjoying stories from long past school and church days.

They were in the middle of a good laugh behind one of Randall's stories when Sylvia jumped up and ran into her kitchen to answer the house phone. She walked back out to the patio with her mouth half open and a question on her face as she turned her eyes on Jerome. Her expression changed into a gotcha smile as she turned to look a Randall. Her demeanor signaled trouble for the cousins and they passed questioning looks between them.

"Just a minute." Sylvia placed the phone on hold. "It's Debra and she wants your number, Jerome."

Randall clapped his hands hard one time and started to laugh but Sylvia turned to him and said, "because she's been calling and texting you all day and you're not answering the damn phone -- her words not mine -- or responding to her messages. So you must be with Jerome." Now it was Jerome's turn to laugh.

Sylvia held the phone out between the cousins. "Who wants to talk to her?"

"Just give her my number," Jerome said.

"That would be deceitful. I don't want to be in the middle of this," Sylvia protested.

Randall started shaking his head with frustration and took the phone. "Hello."

Debra's shock was palpable over the phone. "Jerome?" she asked.

"This is Randall."

*What the hell is he doing at Sylvia's?* Debra hardly knew what to say at this point. She wanted to scream at him; she was at a loss for words, a first for her. Finally her brain started filtering and processing again and she asked "Is Jerome there with you?"

"Yeah, you want to talk to him." Jerome was across the table shaking his head fast enough to cause whiplash as he waved his hands across his face in a universal sign for "NO!"

"I was looking for you. I thought you were going to call me about coming out today."

Randall walked out into the yard so the others couldn't hear his end of the conversation. "I told you I might call you this weekend. The weekend just started. What's going on?"

"I thought I might come out your way and meet you somewhere, have a couple of drinks or something. How long before you guys leave Sylvia's?"

Randall did not like the way the conversation was going. "Yeah, sounds tempting but I've got plans for the evening and I'll be tied up tomorrow. Why don't we meet at Sugar's for dinner on Wednesday?"

Debra did not want to be put off one more day. She had plans for Randall and did not want to wait. She knew he had changed and she could no longer control him like she had in the past. "Between me and you, I don't care for Sugar's. How about you come over here and I'll cook you some really good food and give you dessert afterwards – as much as you want."

Fighting the urge to laugh out loud, Randall thought, *Why is she so determined to be with me? She has not changed a drop. Always wants what she can't have.* "Listen Debra, I'm so wrapped up with new clients and getting settled in, I don't have time for much socializing. I'm willing to make time for you because you're one of my oldest friends. Why don't you meet me half way and pick a restaurant that's halfway between us. I'm not familiar with the area once you get past Walzem headed north, so I'll let you choose the place."

"You sound like you don't want to see me," Debra complained.

"I'm just so busy right now," Randall replied dishonestly.

"Then why is your ass sitting up at Sylvia's today?"

Randall had known that was coming but refused to answer. "Look, I've got to go. I'm being rude. Let me know by Monday if you want to meet for dinner on Wednesday. We'll talk later." Randall hung up the phone and rejoined Jerome and Sylvia on the patio.

"I hope you guys haven't gotten me in trouble with my cousin," Sylvia said with a serious expression on her face.

"I'm afraid the only way you could have avoided Debra's wrath today was to lie to her and you didn't want to be deceptive as I recall or was it deceitful. Oh yeah, that was it – deceitful." Randall toyed with Sylvia.

"I'm tryin' to tell you." Jerome got profound and then continued. "I've got tickets to the Spurs versus Grizzlies tomorrow night, seven o'clock tipoff. How about it Sylvia?"

"You're inviting me?" Sylvia sounded like she had just won the lottery.

"Yeah, I'm inviting you. I know you're a fan."

"I've never been to a Spurs game."

Randall felt his heart actually ache at that moment. What adult who had lived in San Antonio their entire life had never been to a Spurs game – maybe two, and before him sat one.

"Well, come go with us tomorrow," Jerome implored.

"I'll have to get a babysitter." Sylvia's excitement was almost tangible.

"We'll pick you up at six. Be ready."

As the cousins left Sylvia's home and approached the car, Jerome who liked to pick at those he loved, offered, "You know, I've actually got four tickets to the game tomorrow night. You want to invite Debra?"

"Hell no!" was Randall's hostile response.

Chapter 10: A Confession

Robert Polanco stood inside his opened garage doorway watching an unfamiliar truck park in front of his home. The questioning look on his face turned into a huge grin as he saw Nathaniel Solomon exit the truck and approach. Robert didn't hesitate to meet his wife's young cousin with a handshake and bear hug. "Cabezon, I thought you and your brother had forgotten we are still in town. What's going on, bro? I been missing you. Where is Gerald?"

Nate was touched by his cousin's welcome. Over the years he had been closer to Robert than Jessie and had missed him also. "Gerald is around. He's still working out at USAA, doing pretty good there. I'm still on at Toyota."

The men entered the house and found Jessie in the family room watching television. "Look who the wind blew in," Robert declared.

Jessie was as happy to see Nate as Robert was. "Nate, hey baby! What's going on to get you to stop by here?" she asked.

"I thought you might have something sweet. I miss your cakes." Nate grinned and tried to lighten things up. Jessie looked in his eyes and sensed he was troubled. "I need to talk to you, Jessie. It's about the restaurant. I'm worried about Sylvia." Nate looked at Robert and added, "Robert I'd appreciate it if you'd listen in. I need some advice."

"Let me get you something to drink. You want that cake now or later?" Jessie asked.

Nathaniel had to smile. "Later. What kind you got?"

"Coca Cola cake. I made it yesterday for Catrina's birthday."

"Where is she, anyway?" Nathaniel asked, looking around for Jessie's daughter.

"She went on an outing with Linda. I think they're going to the park. You just missed 'em."

Nathaniel accepted the glass of water Jessie offered him and took on a serious tone. "You're going to be disgusted with me and Gerald, Jessie," then glancing at Robert, he added, "you too, Robert." The young man paused for a moment to collect his thoughts before going on. "Me, Terence, Cheryl, and Gerald tried to cheat you guys on the restaurant deal." With his head hung low and not looking up at either of his cousins, he continued. "We were involved with Frisk." Nathaniel chanced glancing up for moment before dropping his eyes again. "The plan was for us to try and get a few extra thousand a piece – maybe as much as a hundred thousand or more total divided between the four of us after Frisk took his cut."

"Why would you guys do that? Are you hurting for money?" Jessie asked, not at all surprised by the revelation.

"I don't know how I let me and Gerald get caught up in this." The young man dropped his head and said nothing more.

Jessie looked at her husband and back at her cousin. "Do you need money, Nate?"

"Nah. It's just me and my lady. We both got good jobs. I haven't touched the money my dad left me. I'm set."

"It was Terence wasn't it?" Jessie said quietly not wanting Nathaniel to feel the need to defend his older brother.

He didn't answer for a moment but squirmed almost imperceptibly in his seat. "Jessie, I can make my own choices. I messed up. I'm not blaming Terence but he wants Sylvia out of the restaurant. He believes she married Dad just to get what she could get out of him. Terence says everything Sylvia has should be ours. I don't feel that way. I like Sylvia. She was really good to Dad." Nathaniel rose from the table and walked away holding his head with both hands. "I love my brother but I don't want him screwing over Sylvia. She doesn't deserve that. I can't disrespect my father's wishes any longer. He loved Sylvia and the kids and wanted to make sure they would be okay after he left. I'm proud of Dad for that. He planned and saved and did the best he could by us all."

"Are you afraid Terence might still go after Sylvia in some way?" Jessie asked.

"I don't know what my brother will do. He's like a different person. I don't think I ever really knew Terence. My father always told me he was trouble. On his dying bed he told me not to let Terence lead me. I just thought he was being hard on Terence like always. I was angry at him for talking so bad about Terence, wondered if he talked about me the same way. Now I understand. I remember Dad trying to talk to Terence about things like not trying to play women, gambling, drugs. Terence would never listen. Dad knew about life. He had lived a lot and knew a lot about the streets but Terence acted like Dad was a chump. He hated him; still does. He wants to get Sylvia because it's his way of hurting Dad."

"Well, if you're worried for Sylvia's well being maybe you should tell her," Robert advised.

"I don't want to scare her," Nathaniel said.

"It's not about scaring her. Your gut is telling you Sylvia is in danger. You have to tell her what you told us," Robert urged.

Nathaniel had hoped after telling Jessie about his misdeed he could wash his hands to this situation. After all, he had come clean. Now Jessie and Robert wanted him to take full responsibility. He stood in their kitchen, leaning back against the counter with his arms folded across his chest, legs crossed at the ankles, and head hanging down. Leave it to his cousins to ask him to do all that was required of him. He realized that he would not be free of this mistake until all was out in the open, if ever. He tried to convince himself that Terence would not harm Sylvia physically. "I don't see what Terence would have to gain by hurting Sylvia. It's not like he would get her money or her share of Sugar's. Her children are her heirs. He has to know he would lose money because Sylvia manages that place down to the penny. There is no waste and she is making us all a nice little bit of money."

"I think Terence is an angry man looking for someone to blame because his life is not what he hoped it would be. He's focusing on Sylvia when he should be looking at himself. What is Gerald saying about all this?" Jessie asked.

Nathaniel gave a sarcastic little chuckle and shook his head without looking up. "Nothing, nothing at all. I'm scared for him too. He'd follow Terence off a cliff without hesitation."

"Have you told him how you feel about this situation?" Robert asked.

"No, not yet."

"You should and like Robert said, you've got to tell Sylvia. I hate this for her. That girl has been through a lot of mess in her life. She was terrorized by that first husband of hers. I hate for her to return to that place of fear. We are her family and we have to protect her, so she needs to know about your concerns," Jessie explained.

--

Sylvia had just experienced one of the best weekends of her life. After Jerome and Randall left her home on Saturday, she treated herself to a full body massage and facial, got her nails shellacked and her hair washed, trimmed and twisted. She picked up a new novel by Nia Forrester and dinner before returning home to a clean quiet house. Jim was surprised to see her at Sugar's so early the next morning, looking and acting like a new person. As usual, she humped from the moment she stepped in the place until she locked the door on her way out that afternoon. After leaving the restaurant, she stopped by Sean and Camille's home to visit with the kids for a bit. This was actually Sylvia's weekend with the children but since Sean wanted to take them to Fear Fest, the kids would stay with their father until after dinner on Sunday. Sylvia's regular sitter agreed to adjust her hours and watch the children in the evening instead of during the day so Sylvia could show some spontaneity and go to the Spurs game.

Camille and Sean seldom had a problem with watching the children when Sylvia needed extra help and Sylvia did the same for them. The children loved Camille to the point of causing Sylvia little twinges of jealous at times when they spoke of her so fondly. Sean was the only one who was cool during Sylvia's short visit to his home. He was so aloof that it surprised her when he walked her out. She assumed he wanted to discuss the children. She was more surprised when his conversation was about her. "So you got a date tonight?" Sean asked.

"Just going to the game with some friends." Sylvia answered feeling uncomfortable with the question.

"Jerome and that cousin of his, Randall?"

"Why you say it like that, 'that cousin of his, Randall?'" Sylvia copied Sean's manner of speech.

"I remember him from school. He was what we called a 'ladies' man' back then."

"Randall?" Sylvia appeared skeptical and scornful all at the same time.

"So you telling me he's changed?" Sean asked.

Sylvia smiled now. "I never knew Randall was considered a ladies' man. He had Debra wrapped around him whenever I saw him. Now Jerome, there was your ladies' man."

"Jerome was a player. The girls had little crushes on Jerome but no one took him seriously because he flirted with everyone. The girls were in love with Randall. Sure, Debra put him out of reach because no one wanted to deal with her bitchiness. Anyway, you didn't answer my question. Who are you going to the game with?"

Sylvia did not like the jealous lover vibe coming from her ex husband. "Why are you asking?"

Sean was surprised at her resistance to answering his question. "Is it a secret?" he asked.

"I'm going with the fellas," she told him as she turned to enter her vehicle. "And thanks for keeping the kids longer this evening."

"Not a problem. Have a good time." Sean yelled over his shoulder as he walked off like a dejected lover.

Sylvia wanted to spit and wondered if Jerome had been onto something when he said Sean didn't want her with anyone.

Sylvia's weekend ended with her at the Spurs game with two handsome eligible bachelors who both had great personalities and wanted to show her a good time. The best part of that dynamic was that she was not dating either; she was with friends and she was safe and secure. The Spurs won in a close enough shootout to keep the game interesting and the fans screaming their throats raw.

The friends stopped for a late snack and drinks at Barriba Cantina on the Riverwalk where they sat and talked until the eatery closed its doors. When Sylvia got home she thanked both Jerome and Randall profusely for a good time and told them she would not hangout with them again for a long time because they had taken all her energy for the upcoming week.

--

A late morning call from Randall the next day caught Sylvia by surprise. He had not mentioned the restaurant when they were together over the weekend but sounded like he needed to see her on important business. They scheduled an appointment for three in the afternoon. When they sat down, Randall went over some basic information about the business accounts before having Sylvia sign a couple of documents. He presented her with a bill for services rendered and told her he had received what appeared to be all the accounting documents and reports from Frisk and Associates. By the end of the meeting Sylvia still did not understand why Randall wanted to meet so urgently. Not that she objected to seeing the man but she got an inkling that the business meeting was a mere pretense.

"I guess that's all I've got," Randall announced after nearly twenty minutes of paper shuffling, hemming, and hawing."

Sylvia felt sympathy for the brother but was not sure why he was out of his comfort zone. "You want another cup of coffee or how about something sweet?"

Randall looked at her hard, hoping for some hint of a flirt but nothing.

Sylvia continued before he answered. "I've got some of that banana pudding you like. There is one slice of Italian cream cake and a few pieces of our cream cheese coffee cake; it's not too sweet." She gave him an encouraging smile.

"I'll try the coffee cake. You gonna keep me company while I indulge?" Randall patted his abs and Sylvia tried not to admire his physic. He was such a good looking man and so friendly, it was hard to keep her feelings in check. She reminded herself that Randall was Debra's playground, not hers.

"You know Sylvia, when I first came in here with Romey I was impressed with the 180 degree change in Sugar's. I'm curious how you managed that but kept so much of the feel of the place. It's great in here." Randall said as she placed his cake down and took a seat.

"I wish I could take credit for the change but it was Sugar and his nieces. Sugar wanted the place to continue to have his vibe and Retha wanted everything clean, attractive, well-organized – you know, inviting to the women of our community. Those two fought nonstop with Jessie refereeing. It took a lot but they did a good job."

"Well you can sure take credit for keeping it going. I hear nothing but praise for Sugar's Place. Every time I come to eat I run into old friends or new business associates. I ran into one of my best friends from high school, Luis de La Cruz. We played football together at Roosevelt and hung out up at A&M. He invited me to his wedding in two weeks and wants to hire me on as his accountant for his construction business."

"You know Luis? Me and his fiancée, Olga, were in band together. They invited me to that wedding too," Sylvia said with a big smile on her face.

Randall grinned back at her as he chomped on his coffee cake. "He told me to be sure and bring a date. Why don't we go together?"

Sylvia pursed her lips, folded her arms across her chest, and looked at Randall with attitude. "Wouldn't that be cheating? Besides, what makes you so sure I don't have a date?"

"What makes it cheating? Just because you and I are friends doesn't mean you can't be my official date. But excuse me, do you have a date?" Randall watched her quizzically.

"Don't I wish," Sylvia said. "I'd be happy to ride with you or I can drive and meet you there. The wedding and reception are in Seguin at some event center out there, so I'm closer."

"I'll pick you up but you'll need to help with the navigation," Randall negotiated.

"Gladly. I'm happy I don't have to go alone," Sylvia said.

"Me too, beautiful, me too."

Sylvia couldn't help but blush. She got up from the table to get more coffee when a rap came on the front door. Recognizing Nathaniel, she went directly to the door and opened it. No sooner than Nate walked in he caught Sylvia up in a warm hug, something she had not experienced since shortly after Sugar's death. Sylvia was now on high alert. All she said was, "Hi."

"How you doin' Sylvia? Is Jessie here? I told her I'd meet her here at three thirty."

"No. I haven't seen Jessie. I didn't know you guys were coming by."

Nate started to respond until he saw Randall watching him closely.

Sylvia could tell the two men were sizing each other up. "Come and meet Randall." She introduced them and told Nate that Randall was Jerome's cousin.

Nathaniel warmed at the mention of Jerome's name. "Hey, I remember you coming in here with Romey a long time ago. You live in DC, right?" Nate asked as he and Randall shook hands.

"Nah man, I'm back here now. I did live in DC up until a couple of months ago. So you're Sugar's oldest son?"

"My brother Terence is the oldest. He lives up in Houston. It's good seeing you, man. Tell Romey Nate said hey."

"Bet."

Nathaniel turned to Sylvia. "I need to talk to you, Syl but I can come back or come by your house. Jessie is supposed to be here too."

Sylvia glanced at Randall who was drinking coffee and eating his coffee cake, showing no intention of leaving any time soon. "We can go in the office." She turned to Randall. "Randall if my niece comes to the door, will you let her in?"

"Sure."

No sooner than Sylvia and Nathaniel entered the office, Jessie began knocking on the restaurant door. As requested, Randall opened the door for her. Jessie halted in the doorway and peeped around Randall with a question on her face. "I'm Randall. You must be Jessie. Sylvia's in the back. She asked me to let you in."

Jessie extended her hand. "Nice to meet you. Are you the new accountant?" Jessie couldn't hide her appreciative smile. Sylvia had failed to mention Randall was such an attractive man.

Randall stared at her for a moment and smiled but not in a flirtatious way and Jessie would know. She may be middle aged but she received her share of attention from men of all ages. "How'd you guess?" he asked.

"You've just got that bookish look about you," Jessie said with a smile. "No, I'm kidding. Sylvia told me your name." Jessie's eyes travelled to the table where Randall was sitting and saw his half eaten dessert. "I see you're hard at work," Jessie continued her banter.

"Somebody has to do it." Randall played along. "Sylvia is in the office with Nate."

"Thanks, Randall. I'm sure we'll talk some more later."

Randall watched Jessie march toward Sylvia's office. *Now that is one confident woman!*

--

As Sylvia sat in her office listening to Nathaniel, she became more forlorn with each passing moment. No one spoke a greeting when Jessie entered the office and sat down. Nate continued to speak, barely pausing to breathe. Sylvia remembered Sugar's words to her as Nate talked. "You watch out for that Terence. He's my son but he is dangerous. I've warned my boys about him but they won't listen and besides, he cares about them, a little. He don't give a damn about me and he don't like you. Oh that boy can be a charmer when he's tryin' to get somethin' from you, but he'll resort to anything to get what he wants. Don't you trust him or depend on him for anything and keep away from him. Jessie, Retha and Robert, if you need anything, that's who you depend on." Sylvia had promised to deal with Terence carefully but had paid little heed to Sugar's warning. Weeks later when Sugar learned she had asked Terence's advice concerning Sugar's business affairs, he had yelled at her. Other than the night he had hit Sean with that big gun, that had been the only time she could remember him raising his voice at her. Sylvia had forgotten the nature of Sugar's warning until this very moment.

Terence had only visited with his father twice after his diagnosis of cancer. She remembered Sugar asking that she, Retha, Jessie or Robert always be present in his room when Terence paid him a visit at the hospital or in hospice. Like Sylvia, Terence likely had no idea of the sizeable estate Sugar would bequeath. Had he known, he would have been kinder to his father over the years. During his first visit with Sugar after the diagnosis, the oldest son had attempted to gain information about his father's affairs but it had been impossible for him to dig deep because Retha had been in the room the entire time. Terence had called regularly to check on Sugar but showed no genuine concern about his father's well-being.

Jessie was the executor of Sugar's estate and he had left her with very strict and detailed guidance about his affairs. He had made her and Retha sit with him several times to clarify all the details. One issue he was adamant about was that his children not know anything about the insurance monies he left for Sylvia and her children. Sugar had left his children proceeds from insurance policies also but he was certain they would feel slighted that he had provided for Sylvia. "That cain't be helped. I know where the money is needed most and who should have it. I'm being as fair as I know how. Terence is a snake and a deadly one. That's all I'mo say on that. I already warned Sylvia about him and I told Nathaniel and Gerald time and time again about Terence. They have to get burned for they selves. I need y'all to protect Sylvia and look after her. You the only real family she's got now. Please don't let me down."

Sugar's repeated warnings about Terence and pleadings for Sylvia's protection now filled both Jessie and Sylvia's heads as Nathaniel repeated his confession. By the time he stopped talking, Sylvia's cherry wood colored skin was ash gray. Nate's arms dropped to his side and he wished he had not shared his concerns with her.

Jessie left the room to get Sylvia something to drink and found Randall just outside the office door preparing to knock. She stepped aside, allowing Randall access to the office. Once Randall saw Sylvia, he looked at Nate with both anger and accusation in his eyes. He looked at Jessie for an answer but she said nothing and left to get water for Sylvia. "What's going on, Sylvia?" Randall asked.

Sylvia shook her head swiftly without looking at him. "Just restaurant business."

Randall walked closer to her. "You look terrible. What is it?"

Jessie returned with a glass of water for Sylvia who looked at her and asked. "Jessie, what am I suppose to do with this information?"

"Together we have to decide what's best. We just thought you needed to know," Jessie told her.

"I'm sorry, Randall. You have to excuse me." Sylvia took the water and sipped.

Randall's concern was heightened and he wanted to help in any way possible. "Listen, I'm your accountant. If there is something going on with the restaurant, I should know; tell me."

"I think we should tell Randall, Sylvia," Jessie declared.

"Nate," Sylvia directed, glancing at her stepson who was all but distraught at this point about his role in such a seedy plan. He saw himself in a worst light each time he told the sordid details as vague as they were. He and his siblings would never have been able to pull such a haphazard scheme on their partners. The women were far wiser than the schemers had credited. Now he needed to describe his actions to a man who did not know him and who clearly had a strong affinity toward Sylvia. Relaying the scheme to Jessie and Robert had been hard. They had looked at him like disappointed parents. Telling the story to Sylvia had been torture. She hadn't looked at him at all during the retelling. These people cared about him. Now he had to relay the story to a stranger who cared nothing for him. Randall had already looked at him with malice in his eyes. Nathaniel had avoided Robert and Jessie's eyes when he told them the plan but he was determined to hold Randall's threatening gaze. He could not let this stranger see his guilt, his betrayal, his shame, his weakness.

Nathaniel regretted his decision to listen to his older brother more with each passing moment.

At some point, Randall stopped staring at Nate and turned his gaze to Sylvia. He realized that Nathaniel's story of lies, deception, and fraud came down to one real problem, hate. The irrational hate Terence felt for Sylvia. That was the unspoken truth behind the plot. "So why are you telling your stepmother this now?" he asked.

Nathaniel looked at Sylvia who returned his gaze. "Because I'm afraid for her. I don't trust my brother. Sylvia, I'm sorry. If I had any idea it would come to this, I would have."

Jessie stopped Nathaniel. "You've apologized enough, Nate. Now what do we do? I think we should at least talk to the police."

"No." Sylvia said calmly, looking at Jessie and then Nate. "You say you are afraid of what Terence might do to me, Nate. Are you afraid of what he might do to you if he learns you told us about this stupid scheme of yours?"

"I'm not afraid of Terence. I don't want him mad at me but that's not important," Nate said.

"So you think he's a danger to Sylvia but not to you?" Randall asked.

"I have come to believe my brother is a dangerous man, but I'm not afraid of him. If he weren't my brother I believe I would steer clear of him."

"I think we should meet and put everything on the table. Terence needs to know we know about his plan and he needs to know I know he dislikes me as much as he does." Sylvia said.

"That sounds dangerous to me Sylvia," Jessie said.

"Are you afraid of him too, Jessie?" Sylvia wanted to know.

"I don't know Terence. I know about him. I know he has never been warm or cared about family and I know he has had a bad influence on his brothers all their lives." Jessie looked at Nathaniel, daring him to comment, before she went on. "My uncle didn't like him around them but felt he owed Terence his time and attention also. I've never had a hug or a kiss from Terence. I've given them, but never received one in return. I'm not afraid of Terence but I am afraid of what extremes he may attempt to achieve a goal, however misguided that goal."

"Can we talk to Robert and Retha about this before we decide on a course of action? I'll call Retha. I owe her that much." Nate looked from Sylvia to Jessie.

"Does that work for you, Sylvia?" Randall asked.

"I think that is a good idea, Nate." Sylvia's color had returned to her face and the light was back in her eyes. "And Nate."

"Yeah."

"Thanks for telling me and Jessie this. I forgive you."

Nathaniel moved over to Sylvia and gave her a hug as he whispered in her ear. "I'll do my best to make this right, Syl. I promise."

Jessie and Nathaniel took their leave but Randall remained behind to talk to Sylvia. "How worried are you about his guy, Sylvia?" he asked.

"When Nate first started telling me how he thought Terence resented me and I realized what he thought but didn't want to say, I got scared shitless."

Randall had to laugh at her. Sylvia was smiling now. "But when you made him put words to it, I began to feel better. Thanks for being so direct. Jessie is usually like that but she was afraid to say what needed to be said out loud, so was I and Nate just couldn't."

Sylvia felt safe enough to share her history with Randall. She was certain he must know a lot of it already. "When Sean used to beat me and threaten me, I never said a word to anyone. It was as if I thought as long as I didn't say what was happening to me, it wasn't real, at least not during the quiet times. My mother knew. Lots of people knew but no one ever put words to the violence that was my life." She stopped speaking, took a breath, and smiled at Randall. "Okay, that's enough, at least for now," she said.

Chapter 11: You Do Your Thang

The groan that escaped the manager of Sugar's Place late
Wednesday afternoon was irrepressible. Looking out into the dining
area and seeing her cousin Debra who had stopped in for a late lunch
was a sign of bad things to come. Sylvia could guess the
conversation awaiting her when she joined Debra. Sylvia waved at
her cousin and headed back into the kitchen to help get the last of the
orders out before closing. Once the dining room started to empty out,
Sylvia accepted her fate and approached Debra's table with a bowl
of potato corn chowder in hand.

"Girl this place is really jumpin'. It's nice in here too. I'll have
to eat here more often when I'm down this way. These are the best
fish taco's I've had anywhere." Debra turned on her charming smile.

"Thank you! What brings you down this way?" Sylvia asked.

"I have to show a property at four thirty and I've got a dinner
date with Randall later." Debra watched for a reaction from Sylvia
but saw nothing.

"Where you guys eating?" Sylvia questioned her cousin. She
tried not to appear too interested or acknowledge the twinge of pain
she felt but her feelings were hurt.

"A little Italian place in the Quarry called Piatti. It's nice and the
food is good. What kind of soup is that?"

"It's the potato corn chowder. Want a taste?"

Debra took the spoon and helped herself. "Ooh, how often do
you have that?"

"A couple of times a month during cool and cold weather. We
put our soups on the website and Facebook each day so you can
always check."

"I might take a bowl of that with me for dinner tomorrow."
Debra gave Sylvia a sneaky little grin and asked, "What's going on
with you and Jerome? Have y'all finally decided to spend some
serious time together?"

"What made you think that? Me and Jerome are like brother and
sister, have been for years."

"Well he was at your place the other day. Jerome's gonna make
a good catch for some lucky lady one day." Debra gave her cousin
the "I'm making a point" look.

"Yeah but she's gonna need a strong rope and will have to be quick on her feet to catch Romey. He doesn't stay still long enough for anyone to hold his attention."

"I guess he hasn't changed that much," Debra agreed and was quiet for a moment before broaching the subject foremost in her thoughts. "What do you think about Randall?"

"Oh Randall is different. He takes life more seriously that Jerome."

"Yeah, but he's kind of standoffish. I wonder if he left someone back in DC or if he's met someone here."

"I think Randall would tell you if he was involved. Are you trying to start back up with him?" Sylvia could not hide her disapproval.

"What's wrong with me dating Randall?" Debra asked indignantly.

"Nothing I guess, but I thought you had already rode that wave and washed out." Now Sylvia had made her point and watched her cousin in wait for the breaking storm.

Debra was speechless. Sylvia had never criticized her in any way. In their relationship Debra did the criticizing, the critiquing, she gave the feedback. What could Sylvia have been thinking? "Since when do I need you to tell me who I should date, Sylvia?" she said with dead calm in her voice.

"Don't get pissed off. I just hate to see you getting so wrapped up over Randall."

"And why is that? You say he doesn't have anyone so what's the damn problem?" Debra glared at Sylvia, seeking answers she was certain her cousin held.

"Lower you voice!" Sylvia admonished as she caught sight of a couple of wait staff looking over at their table. "I don't know why I try to tell you anything. You've got all the sense. What can poor little pitiful Sylvia tell you. You do your thang, Debra. Forget I opened my mouth." Sylvia started stacking the dishes on the table. "You need anything else?"

Debra felt she had to be in an alternate universe. "No. I don't need another thing out of this shit hole." She grabbed her things, threw a twenty on the table, and told Sylvia to "keep the damn change" before stomping out like the world's most dramatic diva. Sylvia sat and watched her cousin leave and questioned her judgment in discussing Randall with Debra. She and Debra had not been close since their school years. She hated that Debra was so determined to be with Randall when he was clearly not interested.

Sylvia went into her office, sat and considered her actions. Was she trying to protect Debra or was she jealous of her cousin? Sylvia liked Randall and her feelings for him were different than those she held for Jerome. She tried not to think about Randall as more than a friend or someone who provided a service to the business. She made a point of dealing with him in a straight forward way but there were feelings inside her that she could not deny. Her stomach, head, and heart all felt different when she saw or spoke with Randall. Until now she had ignored the emotional mayhem he caused. She told herself that Randall was Debra's, whether he knew it or not. He was hallowed ground.

Over the years Debra had never stopped talking about Randall as if he would someday return to her. On her wedding day, as she stood before the mirror admiring her image in her bridal gown, she declared, "I wish Randall could see me in this dress; he wouldn't stand a chance." Sylvia remembered answering the phone years later to an excited Debra, joyously announcing that Randall and his wife were getting a divorce.

"Forget about Randall and forget about Debra too." Sylvia stomped from the office and got back to closing down for the day.

--

The following day Jessie Polanco and Retha Daniels enjoyed their almost daily hour-long conversation which was a recap of much of what they had discussed the past week and hopefully some new tantalizing and even informative pieces of news. Much earlier in the year, Retha and her husband, Jaren, had invited Jessie and Robert and their family to spend the Thanksgiving holiday in Tampa. Jessie and Robert's youngest child, Catrina was deaf-blind and mentally retarded and although she did okay on flights, the person flying with her was usually bruised and exhausted by the time the plane landed, so the invite included a chartered flight from San Antonio to Tampa and back. The private charter would alleviate some of the stress caused by flying with Catrina on a commercial flight, which would be cramped and confined.

"How is Sylvia doing with all this crazy talk? I cannot believe Terence is as obsessed as Nathaniel made him out to be. I used to think it was so unfair for Sugar to mistrust Terence the way he did," Retha told Jessie over the phone.

"Terence is just like his mother. Bonnie is conniving and just plain evil and Terence learned from her. Sugar could see that. I don't think she ever spoke a kind word about anyone to Cheryl or Terence. She fed them poison nonstop. I'm surprised they turned out as well as they did. Sylvia will be fine. Nathaniel will not allow Terence to mess with her." Jessie hoped she was speaking the truth.

"Poor Nate. His bubble has burst when it comes to his older brother. I'm glad he is taking on some responsibility for Sylvia. She needs someone other than us looking after her," Retha said.

"Looks like Sylvia's back is well covered. What has she told you about our new accountant?" Jessie asked.

"She said he's an old friend and Jerome's cousin. She did say he had just moved back to town from DC and he'll do a good job for us. Why?"

"Did she tell you he is fine?" Jessie dragged out the word "fine" for emphasis.

"You know Syl doesn't talk about stuff like that. Is he good looking?"

"Good looking is an understatement and you'd think he doesn't know it. He's friendly, courteous, well dressed and really into Sylvia," Jessie told her sister.

"Not married?" Retha got to the real deal.

"Nope," Jessie responded to her sister's grilling.

"How old is he?"

"I'd guess in his thirties. Retha, I could hardly stop grinning when I saw the man. You remember how our cousin Minnie Faye used to grin whenever she was around a good looking man? That was me. I had to make myself not flirt with my old behind."

"What about Sylvia. Is she interested in him?" Retha asked hopefully.

"Who knows with Sylvia. Sometimes I don't even know if Sylvia likes me," Jessie said.

"That's not true, Jessie. You know Syl loves you." Retha gave her older sister some unnecessary reassurance. "When are we going to meet our new accountant? I plan on coming to San Antonio after

Thanksgiving and staying until just before New Year's. We promised Jaren's parents we would spend the New Year with them in Tampa this year."

"I remember. You don't need to remind me. Are you flying back from Tampa with us?"

"No, a few days later. I might send Sugar Babe back with you if Lizzie will watch her for me. That way I can have a couple of days alone with my husband." Elizabeth, aka Lizzie, was Jessie and Robert's oldest daughter. The couple had three children: Mykol the oldest who was the father of Jevon and husband of Nicola, Elizabeth their dependable middle child, and their youngest who Retha referred to as "old bad ass Catrina."

"You want me to ask Elizabeth about watching the Babe? If she can't, I can handle the Babe; she's a good girl," Jessie offered.

"I'll ask Lizzie. She won't give me any lip like she would you. I think you should know your young niece has declared that her name is Morning and she no longer wants to be called Sugar Babe or Babe," Retha informed Jessie.

"No, she didn't tell you that. She can't even talk that well," Jessie said with a laugh.

"She has made that clear to me and Jaren. She said 'My name is Morning, not Sugar Babe, no Babe needer.'"

"Thanks for the heads up. I will pass the word along that the little princess wants to be called by her given name. That girl is too grown," Jessie said with a chuckle.

"I know," Retha responded and quickly changed the subject. "I asked Nate to join us with his girlfriend for Thanksgiving. He told me his girl will probably want to be with her family."

Jessie shook her head as she thought about Nathaniel. "I think him and this girl are pretty involved. She might be the one."

Retha agreed, "I think so too but I told him he better get her accustomed to spending time with his people too. I'm not going to charter a plane every year to bring my family to Tampa. The only reason I'm doing it this year is because it's easier on you, Robert, and old bad ass Catrina. If she wasn't so difficult, I wouldn't go through the expense.

"Everybody's so excited about you guys coming to Tampa this year. Susan and Charles are planning for your visit harder than we are and you know Rachelle can hardly wait for Lizzie to get here. I asked Rachelle what she's got planned but she refused to divulge the details," Retha said.

Susan and Charles Daniels were Retha's mother and father-in-law and Rachelle was her sister-in-law. Rachelle and Jessie's oldest daughter, Elizabeth, were close in age and became good friends after Retha and Jaren started dating.

"Everybody is excited about coming out there. Mykol and Robert are walking around with their chests sticking out because we will have our own chartered flight. Thank you and thank my brother-in-law. You guys are too good to us. Did you invite Gerald and Sylvia?"

"Gerald is not taking my calls. Nate told him though. He told Nate he couldn't make it. I told Sylvia too, but she says she can't leave Sugar's at Thanksgiving. It's one of the busiest seasons. I think we need to talk about increasing her holiday bonus. Her kids will be with Sean. I hate to think of her spending the holiday alone but hopefully she has some plans. I know she usually spends it with you. You think she'll be with the CPA?"

"I really don't think she and Randall are dating but I sure hope she gives him a chance so I'll get more opportunities to grin at him," Jessie said.

"You silly," Retha chuckled.

--

Between earning a living, spending time with his aunts and family, and the demands of old friends; Randall was finding little time for relaxation and beginning to wonder if life wasn't simpler back in DC. The aunts were pretty easy to please and not very demanding but his friend Ray Rutledge was constantly seeking a spot on Randall's calendar. Overbearing was an understatement when it came to Ray. The man meant no harm, but he liked to have his way. There had been times in the past, after Randall's Uncle Jake died, when he needed the advice of an older wiser man. Rayford Rutledge always made time for Randall. Ray always tried to do more for Randall than the young man needed. He had no hidden agenda; he just wanted to be of assistance to his friend. Randall had grown to love the man and would never want to deny him the pleasure of his company.

He accepted an invitation to a good old fashioned barbeque at Ray's home one Sunday when he should have been at home working. Ray promised not to keep Randall long and lured him by telling him that JT would be in town. Randall always looked forward to seeing his old high school pal, so he threw in the towel and drove the thirty five miles out to Ray's Thorny Horn Ranch.

In addition to JT who had driven in from Arlington along with his wife, Rhonda, and their two children; Ray's fiancé, Karen; and Maris were also present for dinner. Randall wondered if Ray called himself matchmaking but didn't question his friend.

Maris had been cool and professional with Randall since he clarified his expectations of their business relationship weeks earlier but she greeted him in the best of spirits, acted as if they were long time friends, and seemed to harbor no bad feelings toward him. When they eventually sat down and talked, Maris started off with some refreshing small talk which had been none existent in their recent conversations.

It ended up being an altogether pleasant evening for everyone and Randall was pleased he took the time from work to visit with Ray, his family, and friend. He thought he would get away without a conflict but when saying his goodbyes, Maris extended an invitation. "I know this is very late notice but it has taken me a while to work up the nerve to ask," she said almost shyly. "Would you consider being my guest for my company's Thanksgiving dinner this coming Saturday? I understand if you have other plans, but it will be a really good time and I promise to behave. Haven't I been a good girl tonight?" she asked with only a hint of the old Maris showing.

The pleasant invitation brought a smile to Randall's handsome mouth. He had one of those smiles that made women want to know him better. Although he smiled, the invitation was a dilemma. Unless a man thought a woman was completely vile and disliked her greatly, he would find the act of turning down an invitation for a simple date highly distasteful. Though more enticing, Randall found sexual advances much easier to decline than an offer of dinner and a movie. Maris's cool treatment of him over the past weeks made her seem more vulnerable than the femme fatale he first met. If he had not made plans for the Saturday in question, he might have seriously considered Maris's invitation. "I appreciate the thought but I do have plans for Saturday," he explained with a smile and a twinkle in his warm brown eyes.

"So there is a special lady. Is that why you have been so distant with me? You work fast or does she?" Maris asked with no evidence of malice in her question.

Randall chuckled as he thought about Sylvia. "She's just an old friend."

"Sounds like you're hoping for something more. I understand why you are not at all tempted by my offer but the invitation stands. Bring your lady friend; I'd like to meet her. It's going to be a fun romantic evening. We've got two live bands and Mariachi's, a beautiful venue. You can book a room on the resort, so you and your lady friend will enjoy yourselves."

"How about if I buy a ticket and you can donate it to one of your employees? Better yet, let me buy two so some nice couple can attend," Randall said by way of appeasement.

"Oh there is no cost to my employees. We do two events for them each year. If you change your mind just let me know and I'll leave tickets at the entrance for you and your lucky lady."

"Thanks, Maris. It was good of you to think of me."

"I do all the time. Keep that in mind."

Maris left him with food for thought and Randall did dwell on their conversation.

Chapter 12: That Man Is Not For You

Telling herself to forget Randall did not prevent Sylvia from looking for him each day at Sugar's place. Her disappointment was substantial when he did not make an appearance. He did call her to discuss business but the sound of his voice did little to alleviate her desire to look upon his person. The calls were quick and to the point. Jerome had been in for lunch three times since Sylvia last saw Randall. Each time Jerome came in Sylvia hoped Randall was not far behind but he never showed.

She was reserved and distant when she answered her phone the Friday leading up to Thanksgiving and heard Randall's voice on the other end. Sylvia was certain he had gotten her cell number from Jerome and wanted to tell one, the other, or both off for sharing her number without her permission. She did not bother to verbalize her complaint because she realized that her angst was actually due to Randall's absence from her life for the past eleven days. She had thought about that dinner date between Debra and Randall more than once, actually daily, well actually many times each day. She wondered if they were back together. Did they spend the night together? Were they having sex? Regularly? Was marriage written in the stars? Would they invite her to the wedding? Would Debra let Randall keep her accounts? Would they even come to the restaurant? She had told herself to stop worrying about things that were out of her control. *I just hate for Debra to make a mistake. Stop lying to yourself, Sylvia. You're not worried about Debra. You can hardly stand her most of the time. That man is not for you. Debra put her brand on him long ago, so don't pretend like this is about her.*

"I was calling to see what time you want to head out tomorrow," Randall said with no preliminary small talk.

"Oh, the wedding. I had forgotten. You're still going?" Sylvia asked, somewhat relieved.

"I responded that I would attend. Did you?" Randall asked, sounding worried.

"Yes, I did? It's a five o'clock ceremony so we should be on our way by four. It'll take us about thirty five minutes to get there."

"Okay, so I'll see you tomorrow about four; be ready."

"I'll see you then." Sylvia wanted to ask something childish like "Do you have Debra's permission to go?" or "I thought you might be taking Debra." She decided against silliness and in favor of relishing the joy she could feel welling up inside. She was excited when she hung up the phone. The thought of Randall and her alone together riding to Luis and Olga's wedding was invigorating.

--

When Randall pulled up in front of Sylvia's home the following evening, she had been sitting in her living room looking out the window in wait. She exited her front door before Randall got of his car. Bertani stood in the open doorway along with Andrea, the babysitter who was holding a one-year-old baby. They watched as Sylvia walked out to the car. Bertani waved with excitement and shouted, "Hi Uncle Romey's Cousin," when Randall stepped from his car.

Sylvia stopped and turned around to wave at her daughter who she found running toward her. "Tani get back in that house," she yelled and pointed toward the front door, all the while looking at Andrea for assistance with her determined child.

"I forgot to give you a kiss Mommy. You look so pretty." Bertani wrapped her arms around her mother's hips.

"Thank you, baby. I love you, too. You be good for Andrea, okay."

"I will, Mommy."

"Now go." Sylvia watched Bertani run back to the house before turning toward the car and finding Randall only inches behind her.

"You really don't want me to mistake this for a date do you? I was coming to the door for you," he said with an unmistakable gleam in his eyes.

"That's not necessary." Sylvia stepped back, took in Randall's custom suit with open shirt collar, smiled seductively, and released a long low whistle before telling him, "You look good."

"Thanks. You look beautiful." Randall was not smiling as he took her hand in his and walked her to the car." Sylvia was thrown completely out of kilter by this gesture. *We are only riding to the wedding together. This is not a date.* When he closed her door, she rubbed the palm of her hand on her dress to wipe the feel of his hand away. *God, I hope this is not a mistake.*

"I thought your kids would be with their father this weekend?" Randall said once he was in the car and they were on their way.

"Yeah, this is his weekend but he called and asked if we could switch because he had some special event he wanted to take Camille to; that's his wife. He'll have the kids from Thanksgiving through the following Sunday, so I understand them wanting a break this weekend."

"Whose baby?" Randall asked.

Sylvia smiled, slightly embarrassed, and looked down at her hands. "She's Sean and Camille's baby. Camille's mother is the usual babysitter but she's not feeling well so my sitter didn't mind keeping the baby."

"You are one understanding woman, Miss Sylvia."

"We have to work together with the kids," Sylvia answered defensively. Over the past hour Sylvia had begun to feel like a fool in regards to Sean. He had known for days that she planned to attend the wedding. First he had called begging to switch weekends with Sylvia because Camille was in such a rut and he had an opportunity to take her to the symphony for free. Sylvia reminded him that she had plans but he offered to pay for the babysitter if she kept the children at her home overnight. Sylvia, recognizing that Camille would appreciate the night out and not having to come home to the children, agreed. Then Sean called her at the restaurant in a panic, asking if the baby could come also. Sylvia had wanted to say no but felt she did not have a good reason other than she did not want to babysit the child when she returned home. Now Sylvia would need to be out of bed first thing in the morning because the baby did not sleep in.

After the call from Sean, Sylvia remembered telling him she was riding to the wedding with Randall and became skeptical of the whole "Camille needs a break" story. Now, sitting in the car with Randall, she was certain Sean was trying to sabotage her evening. He had not left her house immediately when he brought the children home. When Sylvia excused herself to finish getting ready he commented, "Oh that's right. This is the big night." She wondered if Sean was trying to play foil to her nonexistent love life.

--

The wedding ceremony was short and traditional. Luis was nervous and Olga was beautifully radiant throughout the service. Sylvia and Randall were among the first to arrive at the event hall where the reception was taking place. They sat at a table for ten all alone. Randall got them a couple of drinks from the bar. As the place began to fill up, Sylvia spotted some old band members and Randall saw some former classmates and team members. It was not long before the hall was lively with conversation, laughter, and Tejano, Conjuncto, and Country music played by a DJ. Soon the Mariachis started their stroll and serenade. Finally the wedding party arrived and the speeches began followed by the special dances. The cake was cut and the party took off at warp speed. Randall and Sylvia were observing all the festivities and not doing much talking because it was far too noisy to hear each other.

Their table mates were quite friendly but did not speak English. Sylvia and Randall did a lot of smiling and nodding but not much conversing. Randall left the table for a restroom break and was stopped by an old school mate on his return. After talking with his friend for a few minutes, he went to the bar and got a couple of more drinks and headed back to the table, feeling he had left Sylvia alone long enough.

Randall was happy to hear some familiar music as he returned to their table but Sylvia was nowhere in sight. He looked around and thought she might have gone to the restroom also. He sat at the table and smiled at one of the ladies who grinned real big and said something to him in Spanish. Randall shrugged and answered with, "Sorry." The lady then pointed to the dance floor where Randall spotted Sylvia dancing with one of her old band members as if they were on a date together and had been dating for a while. Randall stared for a moment. He never would have guessed Sylvia was such a good dancer. No longer smiling, he looked at the lady who pointed Sylvia out to him with disbelief written on his face. The lady elbowed her friend and started to laugh as they watched Randall. She pointed to the dance floor, said something to her friend and laughed some more. Randall shook his head at how he had been left alone. Then his table mate got up from her seat, walked over to him, and pulled him onto the floor. It happened so quickly that Randall found himself on the floor right next to Sylvia and her provocative dancing partner before he knew it. His new friend started to move to the music so Randall joined in the dance. The woman really didn't need him or music for that matter. She was in a world unto herself, having a good time. When the song finally ended, Randall met Sylvia back at their table and took her hand before she sat down. The DJ was playing a nice slow two-step and Randall wanted to hold Sylvia close to him.

"I'm not good with these slow dances," she said as she looked down at their feet.

"Just follow me but you'll need to stay real close." Randall smiled and pulled her closer.

***Oh God, he is flirting with me***! Sylvia gave in and relaxed in his arms as he started a nice smooth two step around the floor with her. Before she was aware of what was happening, Randall spun her and pulled her back to him. She stayed in step and grinned real hard at such an achievement.

"You're a natural, Sylvia." He glided her around a few moments longer then whispered in her ear. "I love that dress on you. I meant it when I said you are beautiful." Sylvia missed a step and tripped over Randall's toe but he held her a little tighter and his entire face lit up with the biggest most beautiful smile Sylvia had ever seen.

"Would you please shut up and just dance." Sylvia growled, wanting him to stop flirting so she could concentrate. It felt good moving with Randall on the dance floor. He held her with confidence and moved like butter, smooth; light; and just plain good. Randall pulled her still closer and she did not resist.

The friends spent the remainder of the night partying with their fellow table occupants who were serious old school partiers. Randall stopped drinking after his third round but not Sylvia. She was having the time of her life. By night's end Sylvia was using her limited Spanish and their "friends" at the table were showing off their English. The newlyweds stayed until the reception ended. No point in missing the end of the best party of their lives to pretend there was an urgency to do something they had enjoyed for years together. Sylvia nearly captured the bridal bouquet but had it snatched from her grasp by a woman twice her size. The groom told Randall loud enough for all to hear, "Man, you dodged a bullet on that one."

Randall laughed hardily.

As they walked to the car, Randall held onto Sylvia tightly. She wasn't slurring her words but she was definitely intoxicated. "You want to stop and get coffee before I get you home. You seem pretty toasted," he said.

"No, I'll be fine."

"What about the kids? You've got the baby, remember. Will the babysitter stay over?"

"Oh hell! I forgot about the kids. I forgot about the baby. Oh shit! What kind of mother am I?"

"A drunk one." Randall made fun of his friend. "Maybe you should call your, I mean Sean and tell him to pick up the baby."

"I can't call Sean. He didn't even want me to go out with you." Sylvia sat in the car with her head back on the headrest. "Coffee might help. What time is it? I told Andrea I'd be home by twelve. Coffee and water, that should help."

Randall took Sylvia to a Mickey D's not far from her home and ordered two large coffees and two medium fries. He was certain if she ate a little more she would sober up. They sat and laughed and talk about the great time they had at the wedding, drank coffee, and ate their fries. After her second large coffee, a bottle of water, and one and a half order of fries, Sylvia felt a little less drunk.

Randall got Sylvia home and went inside with her. Andrea had everyone settled in for the night and was all packed up and ready to leave. She started giving her report, but Sylvia ignored her and headed off to see the children. "The baby is in the portable crib in Sylvia's room," Andrea said to Randall. "Tani had a fit because I wouldn't let the baby sleep in the room with her and wouldn't let her sleep in the room with the baby."

Randall smiled. "How much is it?" he asked as he pulling bills from his pocket.

Andrea looked toward Sylvia's room door, not sure she should answer this stranger. "Well, ah, seventy five."

"Thanks. I'll get the seventy five back from her." He handed Andrea five twenties. She looked pleasantly shocked and said "Are you sure?"

"I'm sure. Thanks again."

"I'm leaving Sylvia." Andrea called out quietly.

Sylvia exited her bedroom. "Okay, baby, let me get my purse."

"Not necessary. Your friend took care of it." Andrea waved the cash at Sylvia and took her leave. She stopped at the door and flashed a grin before saying, "Y'all have a good night."

"You didn't need to do that. I have the money to pay her in my purse." Sylvia reached for her purse.

"Keep it. You can buy me dinner," Randall said dismissively.

Sylvia was too tired to protest. "Thank God the baby is sleeping," she said as she plopped onto the family room sofa.

"I'm going to stay for a while," Randall announced.

"What? Why?"

"Because you are still pretty loaded. If that baby wakes up maybe the two of us can handle her. I'm sober and you're experienced."

"Thank you. You are a jewel. The woman who gets you will be one wealthy lady. Can I get you something?"

"Just point me to the bathroom."

While Randall was in the bathroom, Sylvia got him a pillow and a blanket. When he returned, he and Sylvia sat on the sofa, turned on the television, and she went straight to sleep. Soon Randall leaned back in the opposite corner and dozed off also.

At six o'clock sharp, baby Cecily woke them both crying. Sylvia changed her, gave her a bottle, then sat and rocked her back to sleep. Randall relaxed on the sofa, watching Sylvia and the baby. "Like I said, you're a natural, Sylvia," he told her.

Sylvia beamed down at little Cecily. "I've got lots of experience."

Once the baby started back off to sleep, Sylvia placed her in the portable crib and asked Randall to stay while she took a shower.

"Sure, I don't have anything planned but sleep today."

After her shower, Sylvia found Randall asleep on the sofa. She covered him and climbed in her bed, quickly falling asleep. She awoke two hours later to the ringing of the doorbell by Sean and Camille. Randall was no longer on the sofa. Sylvia looked outside as she opened the door for her co-parents and noticed that Randall's car was gone.

"Looks like you had an overnight guest," Sean said as he eyed the folded blanket and pillow on the sofa.

"That's her business," Camille snapped at Sean and smiled at Sylvia.

The three parents gathered up the half awoke children and herded them out to the car with promises of more sleep when they arrived at their other home. Sylvia received many thanks from

Camille and accusatory glances from Sean as they left the house. After a call to Jim advising him that she would not be in until after noon and that he should call if he needed her, Sylvia climbed back into her bed and went fast asleep.

Chapter 13: Male Tail

"This cat's been brought up on charges for domestic abuse more than once – a different woman almost every time. He's got four incidents, one involving his mother, two with his wife and one with a lady friend. That's all we've got on him other than a few traffic violation and one resisting arrest tied to the domestic abuse incident involving his mother." Randall's old friend Lamont, who was a detective with the Houston Police Department, reported on Terence Solomon.

"Thanks for checking this guy out for me. Anyway to get more info on the severity of the domestic abuse," Randall asked.

"Nah, these reports don't give much detail. With the charges dropped the way they were, I'd bet the incidents were minor."

"Hey, thanks a lot Monty. I owe you lunch."

"No problem. I'm going to hold you to that the next time you're out this way. Take it easy."

Randall ended the call and placed one to Jerome to pass on the information he had just received from Lamont.

"So maybe we should pay this dude a visit in Houston and let him know we're on to him," Jerome suggested.

"His brother, Nathaniel, is staying in close contact so he'll know what or if Terence is planning anything. I think we need to let Sylvia and her family handle this unless it starts getting out of hand," Randall said.

"I don't want to wait for something to happen to my girl before we act. I believe in being proactive when it comes to dealing with fools like Terence. I don't know him well. Only saw him at Sugar's a time or two. I do know Nate and he's no punk. He's show nuff Sugar's boy. If he's got Sylvia's back, she should be okay but I'm thinking we need to get her a weapon and a concealed carry permit, if she doesn't already have one," Jerome advised his cousin.

Randall ignored the suggestion. He was certain Sylvia did not carry a weapon but would if necessary to protect someone other than herself. Randall felt it would take a threat more serious than the current one posed by Terence to get Sylvia to carry a gun.

"Sylvia and her partners are having a meeting next weekend. The niece that married the ball player is coming in from out of state and Terence and his sister Cheryl will be in from Houston. I think Sylvia wants me there to present the report from my audit. I want you there also. I want them to see you, not in the meeting but just outside."

"No problem, brah. I want to look that fool in his face so he understands not to mess with Sylvia and I mean that shit." Jerome sounded angry.

"Do me a favor and invite her to Aunt Zoe's for Thanksgiving dinner. The kids will be with the ex," Randall said.

"I think she usually goes to Jessie's for Thanksgiving," Jerome told him.

"They're all going to Tampa. That same niece – what's her name?" Randall asked.

"Retha. Retha Daniels. You know who she's married to?" Jerome asked.

"Some minor league player named Lindo, I guess. I've never heard of a MLB player with that name and I follow baseball."

"Nah, man. Lindo was her first husband. She's just using that name because she wasn't married when Sugar died and left her part of his restaurant. Her name is Retha Daniels, man. She's married to Daniels."

"Jaren Daniels?"

"Yes sir."

"Damn! She's the one they say turned Sugar's around. Jaren Daniels, he's the man. I never would have guessed it. I knew he got married a few years back but I didn't know his wife was from SA. Well this should be a really interesting meeting." Randall sounded excited.

"Wait till you see her," Jerome told him.

"If she looks anything like her sister," Randall began.

"That's right, you met Jessie. They're good people, man. Retha and Jessie look a lot alike except Retha is slimmer but just as fine. That Jessie's a fine old lady ain't she. She's about fifty."

"You lyin'," Randall said.

"No I'm not. Ask Sylvia," Jerome urged.

"Jaren Daniels, wow," Randall said before suppressing the child in him and moving on. "Don't forget to ask Sylvia about coming to dinner. I think she'll be more receptive to you than me."

"You like old Syl, don't you?" Jerome asked, not needing an answer.

"I like her company. She's good people. I spent the night on Saturday."

"What!" Jerome exclaimed.

"I slept on the sofa. She was lit up like the Fourth of July, man. I mean toasted."

"Not Sylvia."

"Yep. Your girl was blasted."

Jerome laughed at the thought of an intoxicated Sylvia and wished he could have seen her. "Man, you should have shot some video. We could have put her on blast all over the place." He and Randall shared a good laugh. "I'll get her to come over but you know she'll be working for a while on Thanksgiving. I'm betting they get real busy."

--

Sylvia was pleased to receive the invitation from Jerome to Thanksgiving dinner at his mother's house. Since she had never received an invitation to Thanksgiving dinner or any other dinner from Jerome, Sylvia assumed Randall was behind the invite. As her Thanksgiving Day wore on, she was having a complete change of heart. She had been on her feet since five o'clock Wednesday morning. She took a three hour break at midnight, went home showered, napped and returned at three thirty in the morning.

Sugar's was open for preorder pick up only on Thanksgiving Day. This was the second year the restaurant had offered full takeout meals for Thanksgiving. The great majority of the meals were picked up on Wednesday between five and ten pm. Rudy, her front of the house manager had suggested they offer a price reduction for orders picked up on Wednesday. The incentive for early pickup worked beautifully but Sugar's staff still had a large volume of food to put out before closing their doors on Thursday.

Two o'clock on Thanksgiving Day was the latest for patrons to pick up their orders. Once Sylvia closed her doors, they would not reopen for business until eleven o'clock Sunday morning. The staff needed the extra days to recuperate and gear up for the prolonged Christmas and New Year's rush.

Jim and Rudy would close up and get out of Sugar's between three thirty and four o'clock Thanksgiving Day. Sylvia should have left as soon as the doors closed at two but didn't leave until three. She got home, showered and washed her hair, and lay down to take a short nap.

Izola and Viola had been cooking since Wednesday morning also and had declared that Thanksgiving Day dinner would start at one o'clock "sharp", "no bullshit." The sisters agreed that they needed to sit down and enjoy the day along with everyone else. Viola had sent word to Sylvia via Jerome that she wanted one of those marble swirl cheesecakes that Sugar's was known for, without a doubt the most time-consuming and costly dessert in the house.

It was nearly seven o'clock when Sylvia jumped out of her bed, threw on some clothes, and barely any makeup. She considered backing out of the dinner invitation all together but did not want to spend the remainder of the holiday alone. She was also a little excited about spending time with Randall and his people.

--

Randall had to restrain his agitation at the day's events. He had been at his Aunt's house since eleven o'clock in the morning and was ready to leave. There was no sign of Sylvia who should have arrived two to three hours earlier. Both Jerome and Randall had called her but got no answer on her house or cell phone. To top it off, Debra, her mother; Denise, and sister; Janice, stopped by Aunt Zoe's for an uninvited visit, which had lasted more than two hours.

It had been a good day for Randall, spending his first Thanksgiving back in San Antonio with his family in more than fifteen years. Everyone was eating, laughing, and talking, and the kids were running in and out of the house. Jerome brought a date to dinner, a pleasant young woman named Jennifer who fit in well with the family. Martha, her husband Trace, and their four children were all present. Aunt Viola's son Mark had called from South Korea where he was serving in the Army. No less than twelve friends and relatives had stopped by to say hello and sample Izola and Viola's food. Yes, it had been a good day and only got stressful when Debra and her family showed up.

Martha had spotted Debra's family coming up the walkway to the porch. "Oh Lord, I wonder what brought them out this way.

When was the last time they visited?" She had nudged Randall with her elbow and grunted.

Aunt Vi had stood up from her seat to see who was arriving. "Have mercy! These folks ain't got no pride. Izola, you ain't gonna believe who is about to grace your humble abode. No pride."

Just then the doorbell rang and Martha let the new arrivals in. Everyone said their hellos. Martha introduced her husband to Debra and her family. Folks hugged like long lost relatives. Debra's mother, Denise, complimented Izola and Viola on how well they both looked. "Haven't aged a day" and "Look just the same" were bounced around by both families. The home renovations were lauded as lovely and making the rooms appear larger. Eventually the new comers had settled in for a good long stay.

A short time later, two of Jerome's friends and one of their wives stopped by and joined in the festivities. Martha who had been trying to get her husband, Jerome, and Randall to play a board game all day finally succeeded in gaining their participation. She and Debra chose their teams, with Randall being Debra's first choice. Izola, Viola, and Denise sat by and watched and yelled out answers in an unruly fashion. As the game drew to a close it was clear that the older women were enjoying the play more than the participants who were all having a good time. Sylvia walked in just in time to see Debra jump and throw her arms around Randall's neck and give him a kiss. This was Randall's reward for guessing each clue Debra had given during her turn and winning the game. Randall, caught up in the moment, accepted the embrace and the kiss with a warm smile and even returned the hug, holding on to Debra tightly.

Sylvia's Aunt Denise was happy to see her. "Sylvia, baby, I didn't know I was gonna see you over here. I haven't seen you in so long. How the babies? They must be with Sean. I talked to your mother just before we left the house. She say they all doin fine."

"Hi, Aunt Neida. Happy Thanksgiving, everybody." Sylvia greeted her aunt with a hug. She then spoke to her cousin Janice, followed by Debra, who gave her a huge grin before taking her up in an embrace and whispering in her ear. "I hope you can forgive me for being so silly, Cuz. You know I love you."

"I love you too," Sylvia replied.

When Debra finally released her, Sylvia moved around the house, greeted everyone, and thanked Izola for the invitation. Izola took her into the kitchen to put the cheesecake away. "I'm so glad you could make it, Sylvia. I can tell you're tired aren't you, baby? Were y'all very busy at Sugar's today?"

"All week, Miss Izola. It's been a mad house. I really appreciate you inviting me. I started to call you and tell you I couldn't make it but I wanted to be here more than anything." Sylvia graced her host with a pleasant smile and a hug she needed to extend.

"Don't you thank me. Those boys of mine are both in love with you. You know you are always welcome. You don't never need no invitation to Aunt Zoe's, okay." Izola patted Sylvia on her shoulder as a sign of confirmation.

"Bout time you made it, Slick. We been waiting on you all day. Where's that cheesecake?" Jerome entered the kitchen, gave Sylvia a kiss on the cheek, and started looking around for the cheesecake.

Randall came in right behind Jerome. "Glad you could finally make it."

Izola retaliated on Sylvia's behalf. "Lord, this child's got a job and a big one. Y'all leave her alone."

"They bothering you, Syl?" Debra asked as she entered the kitchen.

"No more than usual," Sylvia answered and thumped an unsuspecting Randall upside his head, causing him to duck and wince in pain.

"Want me to kiss it and make it better?" Debra volunteered.

Randall smiled, not wanting to be rude and protested, "One cousin wants to beat me while the other wants to kiss me. What is a man to do?"

"Sylvia will you cut me a piece of the cheesecake?" Jerome asked.

"No. I'm hungry. I'm going to eat. Cut it yourself."

"Okay but don't nobody say anything about how big of a piece I take or how jacked up the cheesecake looks when I finish butchering it."

Aunt Viola, who entered the kitchen to protect that very cheesecake from happenings such as those Jerome described, took charge. "Give me that knife boy. I'll cut it."

"Miss Izola," Debra spoke loud enough to capture everyone in the kitchen's attention. "Mama and Janice are getting ready to leave but I'm not ready to go yet," she announced. Debra then turned to her old high school boyfriend and asked, "Will you give me a ride home later on, Randall?"

Randall looked stunned and was at a loss as to how he could tactfully refuse the assistance requested. "I'm not staying much longer myself. It's been a long day," he said half-heartedly.

"That's okay with me." Debra looked at him in an attempt at conveying what she wanted.

"Yeah, sure." Randall turned and exited the kitchen.

The room was dead silent. Izola and Viola left the kitchen and returned to the living room to tell Debra's family and Jerome's friends goodbye. Sylvia finished preparing her plate of food and went into the dining room which adjoined the living room and sat down to eat. She had been starving when she arrived but found she had no appetite left. She wanted to go home, climb in her bed, and cry.

Randall had slipped into his old bedroom where he sat on the bed contemplating how best to handle Debra. She had met him for dinner two weeks earlier and Randall had told her he just wanted to be friends for now. He realized that the "for now" part had been a mistake. He had explained he was getting settled in to his new life. "I don't want to involve you in all my life changes. I've got a lot to accomplish over the next few years." Randall had been business like during their dinner. When Debra asked if he was involved with anyone, he had told her he was not. No, he did not tell her he wanted nothing to do with her romantically because he knew Debra would not accept the truth graciously. She might have slapped him, cursed him out loudly in public, threw a dish or maybe even jumped him. The restaurant was not the place to tell Debra the absolute truth. Then again, having Debra jump him when he drove her home might not be good either. Debra was the type that would jump a man and then call the police because he didn't let her kick his ass.

Randall was not afraid of Debra's wrath but he did worry how this situation would affect Sylvia. He knew hiding in the bedroom would not resolve his problem, so he headed out to face the music. "I hope Sylvia understands this shit because I sure don't," he complained to himself.

Debra and Izola were in the kitchen putting away food when Randall left his old bedroom  but no one else was in sight. He walked into the front room and found only Viola. "Where is everybody?" he asked.

"Martha, Trace and the kids left a few minutes ago. I think Sylvia is leaving right now. Jerome and Jennifer walked her out," Viola told him.

"She just got here. Did she finish eating?"

"She wrapped her plate and took it with her. She said she was tired and will stop by and visit with me and Izola tomorrow before I go back home. She's exhausted, poor baby. That sure is a good cheesecake. She says she baked it herself."

Randall stood in the middle of the living room floor with his hands braced on his hips as he looked around in frustration.

Jerome stuck his head inside the doorway. "You got a minute, brah?"

"What do you need?" Randall asked.

"Just need to talk to you a minute out here." Jerome was clearly upset because he looked unusually calm.

Randall followed Jerome out onto the porch where Jennifer sat lounging. "You want some privacy?" she asked as she pulled her ear buds from her purse.

"Nah, baby. You're fine where you are," Jerome told her, motioning for her to stay seated.

Jennifer proceeded to place the buds in her ears and turned up the music on her phone.

"Nigga, did you or did you not ask me to invite Sylvia over here today?" Jerome asked Randall with a calm lethal voice.

Randall was caught off guard by Jerome's hostility. He walked closer to his cousin. "Who you calling 'nigga'?"

"You, nigga!" Jerome answered with a now raised voice.

Randall stepped even closer to his younger yet much larger cousin. Jerome had two inches and twenty five pounds on Randall.

"What's going on out here?" Aunt Viola asked as she burst out the storm door with Izola right behind her. "I don't believe y'all out here acting like eighteen-year-old hood rats. Even if this is the hood, me and Zoe ain't raised no hood rats. I don't care what this mess is about, it ain't important. Randy, you supposed to be the older wiser cousin. Act like you got some goddamn sense."

"Excuse me ladies." Randall left the porch and entered the house more upset with his behavior than Jerome. No sooner than he sat down on a sofa, Debra exited the bathroom. "You ready?" he asked her.

"If you ready for me," was Debra's seductive answer.

--

Sylvia got home, plopped down on her family room sofa, and immediately began nibbling on her dinner without washing her hands or using any utensils. After picking at the turkey and the collard greens for a minute she wrapped the plate back up and placed it in the refrigerator before heading to her room and dressing for bed.

"I wonder if there are any episodes of *Scandal* I haven't seen," she spoke out loud as she donned a large shapeless faded pair of raggedy pajamas before dragging back into the kitchen and slicing a heart-mending sized chunk of a chocolate cake a customer failed to pick up. Sylvia poured out a pint sized glass of milk to wash down the cake and tuned in to her Netflix queue. It didn't take her long to finish off the cake and milk and direct her attention to the television set as she tried hard not to think about her evening. Within a matter of minutes her stomach started to feel uneasy so she grabbed an antacid and a bottle of water and headed to the shower, searching for something to sooth her body and ease the pain of her bruised heart.

The shower did help a little. Next came a huge goblet of wine and surrender to her misery. *What kind of game is Randall playing? I know he told Jerome to invite me to dinner today. Then I show up and he's all hugged up with Debra, grinning like the Cheshire Cat. Then I have to act like I don't care. I should have just gone slam off on his ass. If it wasn't for Aunt Denise and his aunts, I would have. Stop kidding yourself, Sylvia. You have never gone off on anyone in your life. God I wish I could be the diva just once and make people tip toe around me to make me happy 'cause they know I'll have a conniption if they cross me. How does that feel? Then I could get all sweet and smile real pretty and give men looks like, "I could fuck you real good just as long as I get my way". I bet he's over there doing her right now. He better not ever get in my face again, sorry piece of crap.*

--

Randall tuned his radio to FM 91.7 as soon as he and Debra got in the car. He had been listening to some hip hop and R&B but thought it best he play something calming on the ride. Hip Hop could incite and R&B has a tendency to excite, neither of which emotion he wanted from Debra. Trinity was the best Jazz station anywhere and they were rolling just the right mix.

Randall was quiet for most of the drive and thankfully Debra was also. *She thinks she has won; otherwise she'd be working on me. I better let her know before I get her home that I am not staying with her tonight.* "Debra when we talked the other night at dinner, did you understand I'm not interested in a relationship?"

"Sure baby. I understood. I'm not long out of a marriage myself. I don't want to be tied down either. But we can still enjoy each other can't we?"

"You mean me and you just screw and that's it. No strings attached." Randall glanced at her.

"Sounds good to me. How about you?" Debra looked at him and very subtly and seductively moistened her full beautiful mouth with her tongue.

There were times when Randall had a love hate relationship with his penis. It had a mind of its own. No matter what he told that hard-headed bastard, it did what it wanted and at that moment it wanted to be aroused. Randall breathed in deeply and released the air slowly. "Debra, if you and I had a sexual relationship, how would you react if I stopped having sex with you when I started dating someone else but"

Debra did not allow Randall to finish the question before she started her answer. "I would"

"but you were still alone?" Randall finished speaking over the top of Debra's voice.

"Honestly, I think once I do you, baby, you won't want to go nowhere else."

*Can she really have this much confidence in her sexual ability or is she just saying this?* "Debra, you and I have had two bites at each other's apple, baby. We choked both times."

Randall's passenger sat quietly for a few moments and Randall knew she was building up steam for a full frontal attack. He was glad they were only a few minutes from her home. Hopefully he could get her out of the car before she went off.

"So there is someone else? I thought you told me you didn't have anyone," Debra said.

Randall started to answer when his phone began to ring. *Thank you Jesus It's Aunt Zoe.* "What's up Aunt Zoe?" he answered his phone, grateful for the reprieve.

"Randall, baby, Vi went off and left her medicine at home. Can you pick it up and bring it here before you head home?"

"What meds did she leave? How do I get in her house?"

"Call me when you on yo way to Vi's and I'll tell you how to get in. Don't take too long because she needs those meds tonight before she goes to bed. She should have had them with her dinner this evening."

"Okay, Aunt Zoe. I'll make it quick."

"What's wrong?" Debra asked irritably as he ended the call.

"Aunt Vi forget her meds. I need to get them to her." Randall pulled in front of Debra's house with no further explanation. "This is the one, right?"

"This is it." Debra was deflated. She couldn't act the fool with Randall and push to get her way like she did when they were in their teens. Randall was not leaving her to take a gallon of milk home. He was taking his aunt her medication. Debra doubted that Viola would die without her meds but knew she could not ask Randall to disregard the request and stay with her. If she thought he'd stay, she would ask. She sat in the car for a moment and considered asking to ride with him to pick up the medication but that reeked of desperation on her part. When Randall got out and began walking around the car, she thought about offering to follow him to his place but before she knew it he was helping her from the car and nearly running her to her front door. He waited for her to unlock her door before turning on his heels to leave.

When Debra turned around to say goodnight she was surprised to see Randall halfway down the walkway. "No goodnight kiss?"

Randall kept walking, not bothering to look back.

"I know he heard me," Debra grumbled under her breath, mildly embarrassed.

No sooner than Randall pulled away from the curb, Izola called again. "Okay, Aunt Zoe, how am I supposed to get into Vi's house?"

"You already drop Debra off? You by yoself?"

"Yeah, why?"

"Well, that's okay about the medicine, baby. Vi found her take-along pill bottle in her purse. Hope we didn't ruin your evening."

"No problem, Aunt Zoe."

"Thanks, Randall. Me and Vi sure do appreciate you."

"Not as much as I appreciate the two of you. I'll see you tomorrow." Randall sighed deeply and then laughed out loud.

"That boy is gonna have to learn to be a little more mean, especially with women like Debra who don't believe in taking no for an answer," Viola complained.

"I believe he would have figured out a way to get away from her without taking any tail with him but a little tail won't kill him."

"Yeah, I wouldn't mind a little male tail myself about now." Viola responded, causing both sisters to laugh in agreement.

Chapter 14: You Got To Change Things Up

After relaxing on her sofa for a while, Sylvia found herself out for a walk. It was a nice cool night, though dark, grey, and misty. She walked longer and farther than she had planned and found herself in another neighborhood. She turned to head back home but noticed a group of people coming from that direction slowly moving toward her. As a matter of fact they were just limping along but getting closer to her very quickly. She realized that some in the group were crawling, some were in wheelchairs, and others were on stretchers. They were grotesque. She turned to run away from this mass of the undead but the only house on the block was Miss Izola's. She hesitated and looked around. Did she want to lead these beaten, battered, and even disabled zombies to poor Miss Izola's house? No, but that was the only visible place of refuge. The creatures were hobbling closer. Sylvia approached the home, ran onto the porch, and began banging at the front door but no one answered. *Oh my God! They're reaching for me.* She banged harder and harder.

Then the lead zombie called her name, "Sylvia."

She yelled, "Open the door!"

Sylvia jerked up from her sleep on the sofa with tears in her eyes. Thank goodness; it was just a dream. She almost jumped off her sofa when she heard banging at her door and realized someone was actually outside. "Who the hell is it? I got a gun," she declared as she tipped toward her front door.

"It's me Sylvia, Randall."

*Randall? What the hell does he want?* "What is it, Randall?"

"Open the door, Sylvia."

Sylvia opened the door and stood to the side so Randall could enter. When she turned around she found him right in front of her, so close she needed to tilt her head back to look him in the face. She quickly lowered her head and looked straight ahead into his chest.

"You mad at me?" he asked with the hint of a smile at the corners of his full mouth as he stepped back, allowing her a bit more room and giving himself a better vantage point of her face.

"Why would I be mad at you?" The corners of Sylvia's mouth were turned down in a scowl and she refused to look at him.

Randall took her chin in his hand and turned her face to his. He saw defiance and anger in her eyes. "You are mad."

"Where's Debra?" she asked. "Did you get her home okay?"

"I don't want to waste time talking about Debra." Randall leaned forward and gave Sylvia a gentle kiss on her mouth, causing her eyes to soften. Randall drew her close and kissed her again, deeply. Tears began to well in Sylvia's eyes and before long they were running down her cheeks. She pulled away from Randall, not wanting him to see how much her heart ached or how relieved she was that he was with her.

Randall held on to her and stopped her from walking away. "Where are you going?"

"I need to go to the bathroom," she told him as she tried to divert her face.

"Why are you crying, Sylvia? Come on baby, don't cry."

"I'm not crying. I've got to go to the bathroom." She jerked away and went to the bathroom to blow her nose and wipe her face. She was embarrassed. She was certain Debra never cried over a man. "I hate being so weak. Why of all the men in this world did I have to fall for Randall Craig?" Sylvia looked in the mirror, put in some eye drops and went back out to her guest.

"You okay?" Randall asked.

"I'm fine."

"Come here." Sylvia didn't resist as she sat next to him on the sofa and he wrapped her in his arms and kissed her again. When they pulled apart Randall looked at her for a moment contemplating what he wanted to say but nothing formulating in his head sounded right. He just went for it. "I need you, Sylvia."

"You want to spend the night?" she asked.

"That too."

Sylvia rose from the sofa, took Randall by the hand and lead him to her bedroom. He was surprised and pleased she was granting his request with no resistance. Once they were in the room standing next to her bed, she seemed at a loss as to what came next. Randall did not want to scare her but his cravings for her had been building for weeks and were strong and constant. He knew it was important that he please her, so he took a deep breath and told himself to wait his turn. As they stood next to the bed kissing, Sylvia did get a sense of the depth of his need.

Randall guided her onto the bed and sat next to her for a moment before asking, "Are you okay with this?"

Sylvia didn't answer but pulled him to her. Randall kissed her gently, pulled back, and looked at her for a moment before rising from the bed. She lay and watched as he began taking off his clothes, loving the sight of each newly revealed inch of his body and wishing she could see him better in the dark room. She wondered if she should start taking off her own pajamas or let him remove them. Randall quickly had her sitting on the edge of the bed and began pulling her top over her head. He pushed her back onto the bed then lay down next to her. Sylvia felt lost. In her mind, she had never made love and hoped that was what was about to happen between her and Randall – lovemaking. She felt hands and then his mouth on her breast and closed her eyes so she could relax and enjoy his touch. His fingers on her skin were like delicious raindrops trickling down her body. Randall moved his hands slowly, relishing her, everything about her, even as his body ached to be inside hers.

Soon he stood to pull off her pajama bottoms, lay back down next to her, and covered her mouth with his. His touch on her full thighs caused her to tense slightly. He pulled back and looked at her for a moment before reaching across her to turn on the bedside lamp.

"No. Leave the light off," Sylvia protested.

"Why? I'll turn it off in a minute."

They lay there side by side facing each other as Randall ran his fingers along the curves of Sylvia's body. He leaned forward, urging her onto her back as he kissed her breasts in turn and ran his hand up her inner thigh. Sylvia gasped when he touched her. "You're wet," he said as he fought to control his breathing. Sylvia parted her legs wider and gave him free access to her wet open crevice. Randall kneeled in front of her parted legs and planted a kiss on her inner knee before lowering his mouth to that most delicious valley between her thighs. Sylvia closed her eyes when she felt his tongue running very softly up inside her. She could not hold back her loud moan. He seemed to move even slower so he could capture every drop that fell from her body. "Goodness, by baby is sweet," he groaned and continued barely touching the tip of his tongue inside her.

After only a few minutes, Sylvia pushed his head away, stopping his conquest of her body.

"Why did you stop me?" Randall asked.

She lay back, throbbing and wanting more of him. "You know why." She took him into her hand but he only allowed her to touch him for a moment before he left the bed.

Randall pulled a condom from his wallet. He stood there and faced her while he eased the condom into place. Sylvia stared as his body rose in response to her gaze. He climbed back onto the bed not taking his eyes off her. Sylvia pushed him onto his back. He hadn't expected her to take any control and was pleasantly surprised at this turn of events. She straddled Randall and eased him inside her. His breathing became shallow. She didn't move her outer body but tightened herself around him while sitting very still. "Damn, Sylvia. Damn!" Randall grabbed her and slowly started moving. Sylvia leaned forward allowing him to make longer strokes inside her. It was not long before Randall began lifting her almost completely off him. Sylvia smiled as his eyes walled back and his head tilted back. His mouth opened and he started to groan uncontrollably. Sylvia wanted him to wait for her but knew all hope was gone. Randall couldn't hold on any longer. When she thought he was completely spent, she started to move off him but he said anxiously, "Don't move." Sylvia realized he was still coming inside her. "Damn," he sighed in completion but continued to hold her in place. Sylvia lay on top of him until she felt his arms relax from around her body. "Want me to bring you a towel?" She asked as she moved off him.

"Yeah," Randall could only whisper.

Sylvia stood in her bathroom and mumbled to herself. "What have I gotten myself into? Damn! He was so good." Sadly, the few times she and Sugar had tried to make love left much to be desired. Sugar was so ashamed of his lack of stamina, he had no heart to try and please Sylvia in any way. Eventually they didn't even bother trying though Sugar had people believing he was rocking Sylvia's world.

Randall was snoring hard when she left the bath. "Oh no, I'm not waiting for you to finish sleeping." Sylvia placed the hot towel over his wilted body, causing him to jump. "What, what?" Randall woke and looked around confused until he saw Sylvia. Smiling drowsily, he reached for her and said, "Sylvia, come here."

Sylvia crawled onto the bed, lay next to him, and squeezing her naked body close into his. Randall wrapped his arm around her and pulled her head closer, kissing her forehead. They laid there nestled together for a few moments until Randall got up and went to the bathroom. Sylvia was ready for him when he returned. He grinned big when he spotted the hunger in her eyes and headed straight to his wallet. He felt his body rise as he pulled the condom from its wrapper. When he turned around Sylvia lay back on the bed and gave him an open invitation. He climbed in with no hesitation. Sylvia's body was hot, wet, and jumping for him. Randall moved inside her and pulled almost completely out repeatedly with slow deliberate circular strokes. Soon their bodies began making wet clapping noises as they connected. Randall closed his eyes and listened. Sylvia clamped her legs around his hips and raised herself higher to meet his body with each stroke. She watched him and tried not to give in to the divine ache growing deeper and deeper in her body. She couldn't wait a moment longer. She grabbed his shoulders and groaned so loud she didn't realize the sound came from her. Randall held her tighter and squeezed her to him as he pushed harder and deeper into her. He continued for longer than he thought possible. The intensity caused his body to convulse just before his release. He collapsed onto Sylvia's body, breathing hard.

Now it was Sylvia's turn to ask, "You okay?" Randall did not respond. He lay on top of her, taking shallow breaths. Finally he said "Sylvia" and went quiet again. He lay so still that Sylvia began to wonder if he needed oxygen. She was elated, never imagining people made love with so much intensity. It was all new to her and she liked it.

--

"What's up?" Jerome asked Randall.

"What time you going to your mom's today?"

"I got a couple of clients, so I'll probably get over there after four, close to five. Why?"

"I'll meet you over there. You think you can get your young lady to join us?" Randall asked.

"Jennifer? She might be available. You gonna have somebody with you? Which one Debra or Sylvia?" Jerome wanted to know.

"Man you know I'm not interested in Debra," Randall said.

"I know Debra has always been good at getting you to do what she wants. She got you to take her home last night at Sylvia's expense didn't she?" Jerome felt angry at the thought of the previous day's events.

"Yeah, I know. That mother of yours saved me from a lot of drama last night," Randall said.

"How she do that?"

"She called just as I got to Debra's and told me Aunt Vi needed her meds ASAP. Said Vi had left the meds at home and I needed to pick them up and bring them right over. Debra couldn't start a fight when I left her because Aunt Zoe had declared a medical emergency." The retelling of the story caused Randall to laugh.

"So you went all the way back to Mom's and got Aunt Vi's keys and went and got her meds?"

"Hell no, man, that's the kicker. Aunt Vi didn't need her meds. Aunt Zoe was just getting me away from Debra. No sooner than I left Debra at her front door and pulled away from her house, Aunt Zoe called me again and asked me if I was on my way back. When I told her I was, she said Vi didn't need her meds. She'd found them in her purse. Man, I tell you she timed both calls just right. If I didn't know better, I'd think she had a GPS tracker on my ride. She's something that mother of yours, that Viola too."

"I know they keep me straight." Jerome hesitated for a moment before continuing. "Listen."

"Yeah," Randall said.

"We straight?" Jerome asked by way of apology.

"Always. See you at home," Randall said, pleased that he and his cousin had cleared the air.

"Right," Jerome replied.

Randall got home and took a shower before diving into his work for the weekend. He figured he could put in two to three hours each day over the next three days and be well ahead of his work load come Monday. He just needed to focus and not think about the woman who had captured his thoughts.

--

Sylvia lay in her bed until well after noon enjoying images of Randall floating inside her head. She tried to move her thoughts to places less pleasurable but her mind wanted to remain on Randall and last night. She blushed when she thought about the delicious things he did to her, the sweet things they did to each other. Sylvia had no idea love making could be so intense. Here she was a thirty-four-year-old woman whose only experience with sex had been the wham bam kind. She had not even received many "thank you ma'ams" for the time she spent in bed with men.

Sylvia and Sean were so young when they started making babies that before long they were gun shy about sexing each other. Only a few years into their marriage Sylvia became certain he had another lover. Once he became so mean and abusive she had often prayed for him to leave her for someone else. Eventually they had no sex life other than when he was drunk and forced himself on her just to show he had control over their lives. Sugar had wanted to love Sylvia and show her how to make love but physically he could not. He lost all his stamina the night he hit Sean upside his head with that pistol. Sugar just seemed to enjoy looking at Sylvia, sleeping with her, calling her his baby, and taking care of her. He liked spending his money most of all. She had known all his pampering was to make up for the physical love he could not give her. Sylvia had been with one man during the period between her marriages to Sean and Sugar. He was not worth remembering and she was certain the man felt the same about her.

Sylvia lay in her bed thinking about what she had missed all those years and wishing she had someone to tell about her new found sexual awakening. It would be nice to have a girlfriend she could giggle with and talk to. Right on cue her home phone rang. She answered and heard two voices greeting her with "Happy Belated Thanksgiving, Sylvia". Retha and Jessie laughed into the phone. "Girl we called you yesterday. We even tried Sugar's after you didn't answer your cell or home phone," Jessie told her.

Retha wanted to know, "How was your Turkey Day? We missed you."

Sylvia liked hearing she was missed by two of her favorite people. "My day was okay. You know we worked so hard all week and yesterday was crazy until the last order went out. Once we got out of there, the day got better. We're not opening back up until Sunday. The kitchen staff will work and prep some food items tomorrow. Hopefully they won't be there too long. We all need this break. Did Nate fly out?"

"Yes, he did. It's good having him here with us. Gerald didn't come but he called Nate yesterday and then talked to just about everyone in the house. He and Robert talked a long time. I think he might be having a bit of a change of heart. I hope he is. Nate and the fellas are out running around. You know how they do us women after the holidays. Nate's young lady, Jessica, is here too. Elizabeth and Rachelle took her and Nicola shopping. I think they talked my husband into a spree. He is such a soft touch when it comes to that sister and niece of his." Retha sounded breathless with all the guests and holiday making.

"Ida, Maddie, and Phyllis are here too," Jessie chimed in. Ida and Maddie, short for Madelyn, were Jessie and Retha's sisters and Phyllis was their brother Jermaine's wife.

"God, you have a house full. I really missed a good time," Sylvia complained.

"Wait a minute. I'm going into my bedroom. Just a minute. It's a little quieter in there. I have to sit across the room from Jessie so we don't get too much feedback." Retha said.

Once the sisters got situated in Retha's bedroom, Jessie asked, "Why couldn't we get you on the phone yesterday? Where were you? We called three times. I was worried about you being alone since the babies were with Sean."

"I was fine. Jerome invited me to his mother's for dinner. I didn't stay long because I was so tired, but the day ended good," Sylvia told her friends.

"How is Izola?" Jessie asked.

"She's good. I meant to call you guys but with the store being so busy, I didn't get around to it. I want to tell you something because I need to talk to someone and y'all are my closest family. I hope I don't offend you, Jessie."

"What is it?" Jessie asked.

Sylvia could hear the concern in Jessie's voice. "It's nothing to worry about. It's girl talk." She hesitated for a moment, then continued. "You know I loved Sugar but our relationship was really more like a father daughter thing than a husband wife relationship."

"Oh really," Retha said but Jessie remained quiet.

"I mean we loved each other but we weren't really intimate." Sylvia dragged that last piece of information out slowly and then paused. She couldn't hear any breathing on the other line. "Maybe I should just forget about this," she said.

"No, you can't start and stop like that. I won't get any sleep. You got to tell us now," Jessie pleaded.

"Keep talking and we won't say a word." Retha pushed Sylvia on.

"Well me and Sean were so young and inexperienced that we just had a horrible sex life. So I just had no idea what good sex is like until last night."

"WHAT!" Retha yelled with glee.

"OH MY GOD, who with?" Jessie yelled as she leapt from her seat. "Please tell me it was the CPA. I been dreaming about that boy myself."

"The CPA! Jessie says he is better than butta. Is it the CPA?" Retha shouted and jumped up and down excitedly.

"How did you know, Jessie?" Sylvia asked, surprised.

"Please girl. Stevie Jenkins Wonder could see that boy's got a thang for you," Jessie said.

Ida and Madelyn rushed into Retha's bedroom when they heard the commotion. "What's going on in here? What's all this noise about?" Sylvia heard Ida ask.

"Can we tell Maddie and Ida, Syl? They won't tell nobody," Jessie pleaded.

"Hi Syl," Maddie yelled. "Tell us what?"

"Can I tell 'em, Syl? They old ladies and they don't know people in San Antonio to tell," Retha begged.

"Retha!" Sylvia whined all the while wanting to tell the whole wide world about her new discovery, SEX IS DAMN GOOD!!!!!!

"Okay, if you want to get all closed-mouthed now," Retha pouted.

"You might as well let us tell 'em while you're on the phone because they are going to get it out of one of us before the weekend is over," Jessie honestly advised.

"Okay, Jessie, you tell 'em," Sylvia conceded.

"Why Jessie get to tell 'em and not me?" Retha complained.

"Shut up Retha and let me talk. I'm the oldest and can tell it where it doesn't sound low and dirty." Jessie then addressed her other two sisters. "Y'all remember that CPA I was telling you had the hots for Sylvia, the fine one?"

"Yeah, what about him?" Madelyn answered.

"He gave Sylvia some last night and it was so good she couldn't wait for us to get back to San Antonio to talk about it."

Sylvia was laughing so hard she was crying at this point. All four sisters were posing questions and it sounded like they might have been fighting over the phones. Finally Jessie said, "Sylvia you did the right thing in telling me this juicy morsel. You know I'm always available but answer this question for me."

"Yes," Sylvia responded.

"Put her on speaker. Put her on speaker," Sylvia heard one of the sisters yelling.

"This wasn't your first orgasm was it?" Jessie asked.

"Jessie!" Sylvia complained, enjoying her own embarrassment before sharing more. "No, it was not my first but it was the first time I experienced really good sex. I had never made love before."

"Lord have mercy!" Madelyn proclaimed in the background.

"Oh my God!" Ida declared.

"Don't y'all think bad of me. I just needed someone to share this with. What friends I had were so hard on me after I married Sugar and when I was married to Sean he ran off all my school friends. I've never had anyone to talk girl talk with. I don't know what I should tell or what I should keep to myself."

"Never tell another woman exactly what you and your man do in bed. You can tell them the sex was good but don't brag too much about how good your man is or the next thing you know he might be her man." Jessie schooled Sylvia.

"Tell her those other women will be looking at her man remembering everything she told them." Sylvia could hear Madelyn in the background.

"Tell her to never, never, never discuss the size of her man's penis unless she's trying to get rid of him. That's disrespectful and she don't want other women thinking about his penis every time they see him," Ida advised.

"No, I don't want y'all thinking about his penis. Hold on my doorbell is ringing," Sylvia said.

All four sisters anticipated imparting more advice to Sylvia about her new sexual exploits but they would have to wait for another day. "I'm back; it's him," Sylvia whispered. "He wasn't supposed to be back for another three hours. I gotta get cleaned up. I'm still in my PJs."

"Did you eat?" The sisters heard Randall asking in the background.

"I gotta go guys. I love y'all and thanks for being there. Talk to you later."

Wait a minute, wait a minute," Retha pleaded. "I didn't get to give my advice, Syl. Remember, you got to change things up sometimes and keep things fresh."

"Okay, we'll talk about that later. Love you guys." Sylvia rushed off the phone.

"Bye baby," Jessie replied.

"Bye, Sylvia," the other three sisters yelled in unisons.

Once they were off the call, Jessie looked at Retha and asked, "Change thangs up, what does that mean?"

Retha looked embarrassed and said, "I don't know. That's what Ida told me when I got married the first time. She didn't give me no specifics and I did not ask."

All eyes turned on Ida who pointed a finger at Jessie. "That's what you told me or have you forgotten. Poor Robert, that's why he looks so bored."

Chapter 15: Chick Magnet

Randall busied himself in Sylvia's kitchen preparing a light brunch of eggs, fruit, and toast while she showered and dressed.

"Am I interfering with your plans for the day? I couldn't concentrate on my work. After about ninety minutes I knew I was wasting my time," he admitted as he served up her meal.

Sylvia watched him and smiled to herself. ***Randall is adept in the kitchen like Sugar. What a pleasant surprise.*** She took her place at the table and watched him pour her coffee. "Are you joining me?" she asked and was disappointed when he declined.

"I picked up a couple of breakfast tacos on the way home. I will sit and have a cup of coffee and keep you company though." He took a seat and then got back on track. "You didn't answer my question."

Sylvia wasted no time starting on her specially prepared brunch. "I was going to do a little housework and try to catch up with my kids for a short visit before meeting you back here." For some reason she did not understand, she felt a little shy about their plans for later in the day. It was a date, she realized. They'd already done quite a bit more than date, so why feel shy?

Randall watched her as if he sensed she was thinking about him. "I can take off and meet you back here later or I can go with you to see your kids," he offered.

"You want to wait here until I come back?" Sylvia countered without looking at him.

"You mind if I do some work while you're gone?"

"No, not at all."

"What have you got – cable or DIRECTV?"

Sylvia smiled and said, "DIRECTV."

"Cool. I'll finish these dishes. Then I can work, watch television, or sleep on your sofa. Sounds like a plan. Take your time. Don't rush on my account." Randall left her at the table finishing her breakfast and went into the family room, grabbed the remote, sat down and stretched his long legs as he got comfortable. Sylvia was being sent away from her own home.

--

There was no sign of Sylvia's children or Sean when a feverishly ill Camille holding a hysterically crying Cecily opened the door for Sylvia. "Where are Sean and the kids?" Sylvia asked, unable to hide her dismay at Camille's appearance.

"Sean took the boys to some football day camp in Live Oak. Tani's in the room playing videos. She didn't want to go with them," Camille yelled over the top of Cecily who seemed to get louder with each passing moment.

"Camille you look terrible. What's going on?"

"It's just my allergies but I get these painful throat infections this time of year. I was pretty good yesterday and not horrible this morning but it has gotten worse as the day has gone on." Camille was trying to sound calm but her eyes pleaded for help.

"What's wrong with the baby? Is she sick too?" Sylvia asked.

"I don't think so. It's as if she knows I'm sick so she's irritated."

Sylvia reached for the child who was crying so hard she could barely catch her breath. Cecily who was usually clingy with her mother, went straight into Sylvia's arms and started to calm down though only slightly. "I'm going to check on Tani." Sylvia walked slowly and cooed, patted, and bounced the baby as she walked. Cecily stopped crying, taking rapid short breaths in that jerky way babies do when they are all cried out.

Sylvia found Bertani lying across the bed playing a video game in the room she shared with her baby sister. "Hi Mommy," she yelled excitedly and wrapped her arms around her mother.

"Hey baby. What are you doing? I missed you and your brothers so I thought I'd come see you."

"They're gone with Dad. I didn't wanna go. Can I go home with you? Camy is sick and I don't have nothing to do. I'm bored," Bertani pleaded.

"We'll see."

Sylvia, accompanied by Bertani, found Camille trying to prepare some lunch for Cecily in a kitchen that looked like it could have been on an episode of *Hoarders: Buried Alive*.

"Oh, is she hungry, Camille?"

"She probably is. My schedule is off today. We all got up late so she had a late breakfast." Camille cleared a spot at the table so she could sit and help the baby eat. Sylvia placed Cecily in her chair. The child looked at Sylvia like she didn't want her to leave. Camille and Sylvia both laughed. "She's not used to seeing me in such a state," Camille confided.

Sylvia started picking up the kitchen.

"You don't need to do that, Sylvia. I'm leaving it for Sean and the boys. They make all this mess and leave it like they've got maids. I don't know why I have to continually tell them the same thing."

"Good for you. Stay on them, girl, but I'm going to load these dishes and clean the kitchen so you'll feel better. There is no telling when they'll get back and you should not have to look at this and then argue with them when they get here. Bertani wants to go with me so I'm going to call Sean and see if he's okay with me taking her."

"I know he's got plans for later with the kids but she doesn't need to be cooped up in the house today. I feel bad that I couldn't keep her busy but I can hardly keep Cecily calm."

Sylvia felt bad for Camille and she was disgusted with Sean for leaving his wife in her condition. *Sean has made some great strides in his life but he can still be a selfish bastard. He wants more time with the boys. Not in this lifetime, self-centered toad.* She would not mention her feelings about him leaving a sick Camille at home with two children while he was off having a fun day with the boys. It was not her place to discuss his behavior toward his current wife. Sylvia remembered that some of her worst ass-whippings were after some family member or friend criticized Sean's behavior toward her. She had no reason to believe Sean was physically abusive toward Camille, but she remained cautious in her dealings with him.

She felt a little kinder toward her ex husband after speaking with him. He did inquire about Camille and the girls. She told him she wanted to take Bertani with her and he agreed to pick the child up later that evening before a planned visit to his aunt's home.

Camille sat resting on the living room sofa with a magazine and a box of tissue while Sylvia finished up in the kitchen. Afterwards, Sylvia found the two sisters dozing on the bed in their room. She laid the baby in her crib, covered her, and she and Bertani left.

--

"That's Uncle Romey's friend." Bertani told her mother as they stood and observed the nice hunk of manhood stretched out on their sofa.

"Uncle Romey's cousin. I told you his name is Randall. You can call him Mr. Randall." Sylvia whispered back at her daughter.

"Why does Jerome get to be uncle and all I am is a mister?" Randall mumbled in question as he emerged from the serene haven he had enjoyed for nearly two hours.

"We didn't mean to wake you," Sylvia apologized.

"Yes you did or you two would not have stood there discussing me in my presence. Hello Tani."

"Hello, Mr. Randall."

Randall gave Sylvia a loaded look, not caring to be called "Mr. Randall." "How was your Thanksgiving? Did you eat much?" he asked Bertani as he sat up on the sofa.

"Not so much. I didn't like the food at my dad's house. He always makes me eat stuff I don't like. My grandma had some better stuff but I couldn't eat there." Then turning to her mother, Bertani said, "Mommy, I hope you cook next year."

"I will, baby. Are you hungry now?"

"Not too much, just a little bit." At this, the child left the family room and went to her bedroom.

"I hope you don't mind if Tani comes with us to your aunt's house," Sylvia said.

"What if I do?" Randall responded and looked serious.

Sylvia's face turned into a scowl as she started to attack but Randall stopped her. "You'd dump me and tell me to go to hell. Why would you ask me something like that? I know if I'm going to spend time with you I'm going to spend time with your three beautiful and well-behaved children."

Randall pulled her down on the sofa next to him, but Sylvia backed away, giving him an assessing gaze. Up to this moment Sylvia had not given much thought to Randall's or any man's relationship with her children other than their father's.

"You guys ready to head over to Aunt Zoe's. I think I've worked up an appetite sleeping on this sofa," Randall joked.

--

"You are just a chick magnet ain't you, Cuz? I had forgotten that about you." Martha harassed Randall as he entered the kitchen where she, Izola, Viola, Sylvia, and their old family friend Miss Laverne were congregated.

Giving Martha a wink and a thumbs-up, Randall grabbed several bottles of water from the refrigerator to place in a cooler on the back patio.

"Don't pay no attention to her, baby. You know she loves to pick at you and Jerome," Viola told her nephew.

Randall did not comment but patted his aunt on the shoulder before heading back outside where he, Jerome, Jennifer, Martha's husband; Trace, and Patricia were having a heated political debate.

"I'm not picking, I'm just stating a fact. I have had more women up in my face asking me about Randall in the past two months. I'm about ready to start selling his cell phone number. I haven't seen Debra in this house since Randall's graduation party when she and her mother declared he jilted her. Yesterday was the first time I ever saw Sylvia in one of our houses. Today Patricia shows up with Miss Laverne in tow." Martha pursed her lips and looked at the ladies.

Sylvia jumped to her own defense. "Jerome and Miss Izola invited me to dinner yesterday and back today."

"Okay, you got a good excuse. I wonder what Patricia's excuse is. Whose idea was it for y'all to stop by, Miss Laverne, yours or Pat's?" Martha asked the long lost family friend.

Laverne got tickled as she dropped her head over the table with laughter. "God knows it was not mine. I was so tired after that dinner yesterday I just wanted to stay at home and scratch. I never guessed she was trying to get over here because of Randall. I didn't even know he was back in town." Suddenly Laverne's face turned into a scowl as she switched subjects. "So Debra was over here yesterday. Was that mother of hers with her?"

Sylvia had enough of folks disparaging her relatives in her presence. "Yes, my Aunt Denise was with her." Sylvia gave Laverne a challenging look when she made the statement. She knew there had been bad feelings between Denise and Laverne for years over some sorry man neither of them won and both were better off without. Sylvia knew the tale and was aware of Laverne's propensity to bad-mouth her aunt. She refused to sit with a table full of women and listen to one talk about her aunt, even if her Aunt Denise could be a diva of a bitch at times.

The ladies had moved on to safer topics of gossip, of which there were many, when Bertani busted in the door with Martha's nine-year-old daughter, Tristin, and Randall not far behind them.

Randall pointed to the hallway leading to the bathroom but Tristin took Bertani's hand and told Randall, "I'll show her, Cousin Randall."

Sylvia watched her daughter and shook her head, knowing Bertani had once again waited too long to go to the bathroom. That was a sure sign she was having fun outside playing with Martha's four children and Laverne's two grandchildren.

Randall immediately returned to the back yard where Jerome, Jennifer and the others were keeping up a ruckus and watching the kids play. Sylvia tried not to acknowledge the jealousy she had felt for the past hour or more because Randall had barely glanced at her since Patricia arrived and started swinging her hair and prancing around in her 5" heals and skinny jeans. *Am I supposed to compete with this? No way.* Patricia had walked past Sylvia trailing a scent so alluring Sylvia wanted to do her.

Bertani came out of the bathroom declaring she was ready to eat and not shy about specifying what she wanted. Her plate had to have, "some dressing with gravy, some cranberry sauce – not the jelly kind but the one with the berries in it, some greens, some potato salad and just a little piece of turkey, please."

Martha gathered up the rest of the children to eat and she, Jennifer, Jerome, and Sylvia got them all served.

Randall, Patricia, and Trace remained out on the patio, causing Sylvia's temperature to rise. She told herself, as she wiped down a counter, that she didn't care what Randall did or who he did it with. No sooner than this thought cleared her head, she felt him standing very close behind her. "You gonna eat something now, baby, so we can make a move?" Sylvia glanced back at him without answering. Randall continued, "I know we need to get Bertani home so Sean can pick her up." This was as much a question as a statement. Randall was so close that he had Sylvia pinned against the counter she was attempting to clear. She edged her way around him and noticed every adult in the room, including Patricia, watching them. Jerome and Jennifer smiled with pleasure, noting that Randall was declaring to the world that he was with Sylvia who was not sure she appreciated the declaration.

--

As soon as Sylvia, Bertani, and Randall arrived at Sylvia's home, Bertani exhibited the reason her parents seldom fed their children collard greens. "I got to go to the bathroom," the child announced before Randall had the car in park. Sylvia wasted no time following her daughter and unlocking the door to let the child inside. Randall followed at his usually easy pace.

Sean, Camille, and the children pulled up as Randall entered Sylvia's home. Normally, Sean would dispatch Justin or Billy to collect Bertani, but not today. The entire clan came inside for a visit. Sylvia was dismayed to see even Baby Cecily coming in the house, held by her father. The boys said hello and immediately ran to their rooms, happy for the opportunity to snatch up items they may have forgotten. Camille was slightly embarrassed but not deterred from her goal of checking out the man entering Sylvia's home. "I wanted to thank you again for helping me today, Sylvia. I felt so much better after you left, and the baby slept until Sean got home." Camille's gratitude was sincere but she couldn't keep her eyes from repeatedly straying to Randall who was casually lounging on the family room sofa.

"You don't need to thank me, but you are welcome. Let me introduce you to my friend, Randall. Randall Craig this is Camille Gaston, Sean's better half. Camille, Randall has recently taken over our accounting needs at Sugar's."

Randall stood, gave Camille a friendly smile, and accepted her hand.

"It's nice to meet you, Randall. Are you new to the area?" Camille asked.

"Well in a way. I was raised here but I've lived out of state for a number of years. I'm just moving back and getting settled in. My family is here," Randall explained.

Camille couldn't help but grin at Randall. He had that effect on women but seemed completely clueless. "Well, welcome home." She wanted to say more but was at a loss.

Sean watched the introduction and took in his wife's behavior. He glanced at Sylvia with an "I told you so" look and slightly shook his head in disgust. *You too Camille, you too?* Sean had managed to speak a few civil words to Randall without displaying any obvious disdain for "the ladies' man" as he called him, but his wife's reaction to the man had him ready to get as far from Randall as possible.

"Come on kids; let's go." Sean turned and walked out of the house, carrying Cecily with him. "You guys have a good evening," he said as he left.

"I guess we had better go." Camille actually giggled as she gathered up the children.

Sylvia stopped her sons. "Billy, Justin, do you guys think I can at least get a hug before you leave? I came to see you guys today but you were out at a football camp."

The boys hugged their mother in turn. "It was boring but I had fun with Dad," Billy told her.

Justin didn't agree. "It was cool. They wanted us to work though. But I learned some stuff. We got some awesome Cowboy's stuff too."

"Okay, you guys better go. I'll see you on Sunday. Call me tomorrow, okay."

"Yes ma'am," Billy answered.

"Don't forget."

"We won't," Justin promised.

Sylvia stood in the door and watched Camille and the kids out to the car and waved.

When she joined Randall on the sofa he asked, "Do you miss your kids much when they are with their dad."

"Not like I did at first. Most of the time now, I'm happy for the break." She smiled. "That sounds terrible doesn't it?"

"Not to me. You work hard and it's only natural that you would need time to yourself."

"I feel a little guilty about that though." She looked in his face, trying to get a sense of what he was thinking.

Randall just shrugged and sat quietly for a moment before speaking. "So, I'm your friend and your accountant?"

Sylvia wondered what was wrong with the way she introduced him to Camille. "How would you have me introduce you? Should I have not given you a status – just Randall?"

"That's a good question. I'll give the answer some thought over the next few months."

"What were you calling me at your aunt's today or did anyone ask you about me?" Sylvia asked.

Randall frowned. "What do you mean?"

"I mean Miss Patricia."

"That girl is looking for a husband," Randall said, curling his lip even more.

"Is that why you got so lovey dovey with me before we left?" Sylvia got up and walked into her kitchen with Randall following her to make sure she was not upset.

"I got 'lovey dovey' as you call it because I wanted to touch you. I hadn't touched you for hours," Randall responded in his defense.

"Humph. Why did you play it so cool with me almost the entire time we were there? I bet you were trying to decide if Patricia is someone you want to hit on." Sylvia looked at him quizzically.

"You know what? You don't sound the least bit jealous," he observed.

She let out a sarcastic chuckle. "You want me to be jealous?"

Randall shrugged. "You're jealous of Debra."

Sylvia gnawed on her inside lower lip. She wished she wasn't jealous of her cousin. She loved Debra and had always longed to be closer to her but Debra had not been available to Sylvia since their teenage years. There was a time when Sylvia thought Debra was her nearest and dearest relative and friend but that time had long since passed and it saddened her. "I wish I wasn't."

"So why no jealousy for Patricia?"

"I don't know Randall, should I be jealous of Patricia?"

"There is no reason for you to be jealous of either of them. Like I said, Patricia is looking for a husband and I'm not looking for a wife."

"What makes you think I'm not looking for a husband?"

"I think after Sean and Sugar you are finished with marriage and husbands."

"Sugar was a good husband." Sylvia would defend Sugar and her marriage to him to her grave though she still questioned the wisdom of the union.

"I know Sylvia, but he was twice your age and started dying no sooner than you got married. I bet you spent a lot of time caring for him." Randall realized he had spoken too freely and upset Sylvia. Sugar was definitely a sore spot for her. "I'm sure you loved Sugar. I don't get the impression you were in love with him. Tell me if I'm wrong?"

Sylvia looked sadder than Randall thought possible. She shook her head and sat down on a bar stool. "No, no you're right. I feel guilty about that. My life changed 180 degrees once I married Sugar. I was a scared poverty-stricken single parent depending on the government for handouts. Sugar made my life today possible. Sometimes I feel like he died saving me and my children."

"Come on Sylvia; stop being so hard on yourself. I bet Sugar was one happy man to have you with him. I know you make me happy."

Sylvia didn't know if Randall was trying to placate her or serious but she liked his words and she had to smile.

"And I really like the fact that you're not husband hunting like Debra and Patricia. I feel safe with you."

Now she was insulted. "You need to learn to quit while you're ahead. It sounds like the only reason you want to spend time with me is because I don't want anything from you."

Randall pulled her up from the stool but stepped back from her. "Do you? Do you want something from me?" He questioned her seriously. Sylvia noticed him swallow and knew he was excited because she was. She stepped closer to him and put her forehead on his chest. "How about coming home with me and spending the night? I'll treat you to a special brunch tomorrow and you can sleep in; I promise," he said.

"Okay." Sylvia hated to admit it but she no longer had the will to resist Randall Craig.

--

"You will never guess who Martha told me Randall is dating." Debra's quasi friend Charise Jemison told her. Debra was surprised when she saw Charise's name on her caller ID. Charise seldom called though she did text Debra on occasion to keep in touch. Charise was a fair weather friend and sought Debra out when there was something she wanted or when she needed to share some titillating gossip. She was the proverbial dog bringing a bone. If you wanted something known, she would carry that bone to anyone who would listen. Debra figured Martha wanted her to know about Randall and Sylvia. Why else would she tell a gossip like Charise?

The thought of Sylvia with Randall made Debra sick to her stomach. She never questioned the validity of the report. Charise may have not been the most reliable source for information but she was not a liar. If she said Martha told her about the relationship, Martha had, and Martha was the proverbial "horse's mouth."

*I could kill that sneaky bitch. She must not know who she's messing with.* Debra wondered who she should confront first, sneaky Sylvia or two-timing Randall. She was certain their involvement would be short-lived and that Randall was only toying with Sylvia, but she couldn't understand why he or any man would waste time with Sylvia when she had made herself so available. Debra remembered Sylvia advising her to stop pursuing Randall. *That is one bold slimy cow. Acting like she was concerned about me when she was screwing him all along. That's why she got so mad. I don't believe this shit.* Debra felt hot angry tears stinging her face as she thought about this betrayal. *I can't believe Sylvia would do this to me, not Sylvia.*

--

"Okay sleepy head. It's almost noon." Randall yelled at his house guest.

"I thought you promised I could sleep as long as I wanted." Sylvia raised her head from the pillow and grumbled over her shoulder.

"Yeah, but I also promised to take you to lunch and we need to talk business before tomorrow's meeting."

Sylvia sat up in Randall's king sized bed drawing the covering up around her naked breast. "Oh God, I hate to think about that meeting. Do we have to talk about that today?"

"Yes ma'am we do. I've been meaning to talk to you about it for days now. I want you to know about the status of Sugar's so you can absorb the info and ask me the questions before hand. You should not go into the meeting just as ignorant as your partners. This way you'll be prepared and ahead of the game. It's all good. You've got a damn good business, Sylvia. I'm not sure Sugar did but I know you've done a good job keeping food and employee costs down. So come on, you're going to be looking as good to your partners tomorrow as you look to me every time I see you, and from what I've heard, a couple of them will hate you even more because of that." Randall grinned.

"Oh God!" Sylvia fell back onto the pillow and pulled the covers over her head.

"Come on Sylvia; get up. I'm hungry."

Chapter 16: Assault Before Meeting

Sugar's Place had gone from busy to buzzing to humming since the doors opened four and a half hours earlier. It was as if all the customers from Friday and Saturday piled in with the Sunday crowd. People were clearly tired of Thanksgiving Day leftovers and pizza.

As Sylvia glanced out in the still full dining room she was traumatized when she saw Debra walk in and take a seat. "This cannot be good," Sylvia mumbled under her breath. "I cannot afford this distraction, not today. Why did I schedule this meeting for a Sunday? Sundays are never good days for meetings. What does she want? It sure in the hell ain't food."

"Did you say something, Syl? Joe, get those gumbos plated up," Jim asked over the roar of the kitchen without skipping a beat in the running of his domain.

"Nothing," Sylvia answered as she peeped back out front and saw Debra giving Marilyn, her wait person, a harder time than usual and ordering a full meal. Debra clearly had an agenda other than dining.

Sylvia watched as Marilyn turned to leave Debra's table and headed straight to the kitchen. Marilyn pushed her way in through the doors, looked around in a near rage, and spotted Sylvia. "Sylvia, could you please come and get yo' cousin? She's actin' like she wants to murder somebody out here and I cain't please her."

Normally, Sylvia jumped to the rescue when one of her staff complained about a guest but she was not ready for Debra yet and was well aware that things may only escalate if she confronted her cousin. She needed more guests to clear the dining area before she took Debra on. Sylvia raised her hand and really needed to say nothing after that because anyone who had worked for her knew what the raised hand meant, but she did tell Marilyn, "Handle it."

Sylvia remained at the back of the house until all the guests left except one. Debra was talking on her cell phone and barely eating her food. Fortunately, Sylvia's meeting was scheduled for five o'clock. She figured two hours was plenty of time to get Debra out of Sugar's. Of course Randall could have walked in the building at any moment and if he entered through the front, Sylvia expected an even bigger confrontation with Debra than the inevitable one about to take place. Running and hiding was not an option. The queasiness in her stomach was the result of guilt. Sylvia couldn't completely deny any accusation Debra threw at her. When she finally approached Debra, no one observing the two could guess the dread she felt. "What's going on Debra?" Sylvia asked.

"So you decided to come out and talk to me. I was wondering how long I'd have to wait."

"Did you come to talk to me or to eat?" Sylvia said, not bothering to pretend all was well between her and her cousin.

"Both actually, but as usual the food here is too salty, full of fat, and over seasoned. It's just plain nasty." Debra pushed her plate away and directed her gaze on Sylvia, raring for a fight.

"Do you want me to have that food taken away?" Sylvia asked.

"No," Debra said coldly as she stared at Sylvia.

"I'll be in my office if you want to talk." Sylvia turned to leave the dining room.

"I don't need to go into your office," Debra yelled at her back. "I just need you to answer one question. Are you screwing Randall?"

Debra spewed such venom with the question that Sylvia's body convulsed before she turned back to face her cousin. She looked at Debra with disbelief on her face before she turned and headed to her office. "Like I said, I'll be in my office if you want to talk."

"We can talk right here or are you ashamed for your employees to hear what a sneaking, conniving whore you are, screwing your cousin's boyfriend behind her back?"

Sylvia stopped, turned, and walked back to Debra. She wanted to beat her down but refrained from physical assault. She was trembling and wished she was in the midst of another nightmare. Sylvia got so close that Debra felt the need to take a half step back. Jim came from the kitchen and stood watching his employer and her cousin. "Debra, you can either come to my office or leave right now."

Debra placed both hands on her hips. "I'm not going anywhere."

"Jim would you call the police and tell them we have a customer who is causing a disturbance and refuses to leave." Sylvia turned and headed back in the direction of her office without a backwards glance at Debra who followed her.

"You still want me to call the police, Syl?" Jim asked as Sylvia passed him.

"We'll see." Sylvia entered her office and held the door for Debra. She then told Jim who had followed Debra to the office, "I need you and Rudy right outside my office door."

"You scared of me, Sylvia? You must not be too afraid or you wouldn't have slept with my man." Debra's voice was lower now.

Before Sylvia could close the door, Jim called her out into the hallway. "Sylvia, you don't need to be closed up in that office with that crazy woman."

"I'll be alright."

"No! You leave the door open or I'm coming in too," Jim insisted.

"I don't want her to have an audience. I know Debra. She loves an audience. I just need you by the door."

"I sure hope you know what you're doing." Jim submitted.

Sylvia did not answer but went back into her office, leaving the door slightly ajar. "What do you want from me, Debra?" She faced her cousin and asked.

"I want you to leave Randall alone and I want to know what you told him about me that made him leave me for you?"

The guilt that Sylvia had felt from the moment she first pushed any romantic thought of Randall from her being was shrouded with anger, disgust, and even pity. She said nothing but stood by her desk with her arms folded across her chest and breathed deeply.

Debra, not getting an answer, continued her tongue lashing. "You know how long I waited for Randall to come back to me? How could you do such a low backstabbing thing to your own cousin? I loved you and you stole my man and I want him back."

This speech touched Sylvia. She wished she could make amends but did not know how. "Debra, I hate that you feel this way but it's been almost twenty years since you and Randall were together. We were all still just kids. I didn't go after Randall. He and I have known each other for years and started spending time together because of business. We just grew to like each other."

"And screw each other," Debra yelled.

"Stop yelling, Debra. This is my place of business. I want to respect you as my cousin and my guest but if you yell one more time you will have to leave. I need to finish closing up for the day and then I have a meeting. I haven't spent time with my kids in days, so I can't meet with you today. Maybe we can meet tomorrow and have coffee."

"Oh, Miss Important can make time to talk to me tomorrow." Debra spoke calmly as she removed her car keys from her purse. "You'll make time for me on your busy schedule." Debra spoke the words so harshly that Sylvia became alarmed, but it was too late. Debra swung at Sylvia's face with all her strength. Sylvia reacted but not fast enough to evade the blow. Things went dark for a moment after the fist landed. Sylvia reached out for something to hold onto but missed and fell to the floor as her surroundings went from blue to orange before the room came back into focus. Sylvia could hear Jim and Rudy entering the room and had a blurred view of Rudy grabbing Debra. She was aware of Jim at her side reaching for her.

"You alright, Syl?" Jim asked with concern changing his voice pitch.

Sylvia wasn't sure but believed she was okay. She nodded slowly.

"I'm calling the police on yo' ass," Jim yelled at Debra who squirmed and yelled for Rudy to let her go.

"No!" Sylvia's vision cleared and Debra's struggling form came into view. Her beautiful cousin looked small and pathetic. "Get her out of here," Sylvia told Rudy and then said to her cousin, "Don't ever come back here, Debra. I mean it."

Debra shot fire from her eyes in defiance but left without further assistance.

"I'll get you an ice pack." Jim considered his boss and friend as he collected the items needed to attend to her bruised face. Jim had not thought much of that young woman who married the elderly Sugar over five years ago. He never thought she was conniving like some said, nor had he thought her bright enough to take over from Retha, then Sugar, and manage Sugar's Place. He was amazed and pleased that Sylvia had turned into such a wise and benevolent business owner but she had obviously made a misstep with this situation.

"Sylvia, you need to report this. That lady is dangerous," Rudy insisted after he returned from escorting Debra to her car and ensuring she left the premises.

"I just need the two of you and Marilyn to write statements about what happened here today. Don't leave anything out."

--

The partners started arriving less than an hour after Rudy escorted Debra to her car and watched her drive away, showing him her middle finger. Before long each of the co-owners and Jerome were present in a small party room off the main dining area.

Nothing seemed out of place except no one had seen Sylvia and all were denied access to her office. Also, the three remaining employees were quieter than usual. Jim did not come out of the kitchen to greet everyone and talk smack to Sugar's boys or Jerome, one of his favorite smack talking partners, nor did he come out to bestow hugs and kisses on Jessie and Retha. Something foul was in the air and everyone knew it.

Jim had directed Marilyn to set up a sideboard with coffee, tea, ice tea, and water. There were also a variety of the pastry chef's homemade cookies, a nice selection of cheese with crackers and some fruit. A lovely arrangement of flowers set the buffet off nicely.

Retha admired the refreshments and commented to Jessie, "I feel so proud every time I come in here and see how nicely Sylvia sets things up. I like to believe she learned a lot from me."

Jessie looked at her younger sister skeptically and smirked, "And who did you learn from?"

Retha laughed and grabbed Jessie by the shoulders. "You, of course."

"Well don't forget I was still here working with Sylvia when you were gone off to be Mrs. Big Baller."

"Okay, okay," Retha relented.

Jessie nudged Retha sharply, calling her attention to Randall as he entered the restaurant.

"Ooh, is that him. Oh my God. He's better looking than Jerome, dresses nice too."

"Stop staring," Jessie said to Retha.

"Stop grinning," Retha told Jessie.

Randall worked his way around the room, speaking and introducing himself to the restaurant owners. When he approached Jessie, Retha became embarrassed by her older sister's reaction. She realized that Jessie was telling the truth when she said being in Randall's presence caused her to blush. "Hello Jessie. Good to see you again," Randall said.

"You too, Randall. This is my sister Retha Daniels. She's one of the owners."

Randall waited for Retha to extend her hand before he reached to shake it. "Yes I know. Sylvia has told me good things about you, Retha." Then looking at Jessie he added, "She gives you two much praise for the success of Sugar's Place. I have to commend you because it is seldom you find such a well run mom and pop eatery."

Jessie's grin grew. She simply could not help it. The blush came along with the grin. "Thank you Randall, but Sylvia, my uncle, and sister here, along with Jim did most of the real work. I'm just glad to have a part in this. Sylvia says you have some valuable information for us."

"I sure hope you'll find it valuable. Actually, I know you will. Where is Sylvia? Why is the hallway to the office blocked?"

"They say she'll be out in a minute. I think she's changing," Retha told him.

"Excuse me." Randall headed to the kitchen, suspecting a problem. Just at that moment he saw Sylvia and Rudy clearing the chairs that blocked the hallway to Sylvia's office.

Retha and Sylvia met in a warm embrace. "What happened to your face?" Retha pulled back from their hug and whispered.

"It's nothing." Sylvia touched her face gingerly. "We had an unruly customer and I tried to hold her but she got me right in the face," Retha's young aunt lied.

All eyes were on Sylvia's swollen and bruised left cheekbone. It looked painful.

Jessie's eyes immediately found Randall. She hoped he didn't have a Jekyll and Hyde thing going on. She could see both anger and concern coming from him and knew he did not cause Sylvia's injury. One thing was certain, Sylvia was lying. She smiled but failed to meet anyone's gaze. It was clear she was hiding something.

"Did you call the police?" Retha asked.

"No. She lives in the area. She's got problems but her family picked her up." Sylvia quickly changed the subject. "Listen, Romey if you'd wait in my office, we can get started. You want to get something to munch on while you're in isolation?" She gave a little flat chuckle.

"Nah, baby. You still got a television back there?" Jerome asked.

"Sure do, with DIRECTV?" Sylvia answered without looking at her friend. Jerome gave her a hard mean stare as he passed close by. Sylvia kept her eyes averted as she shuffled through what now seemed like mounds of unfamiliar papers.

"That's some bad looking shit. You not lying about what happened are you, Syl?" Jerome asked in a low voice as he stopped directly in front of her.

Sylvia acted disgusted and swung some of her papers at him. "Get out of here, Romey," she said and gave another flat chuckle, trying to appear relaxed.

Jerome threw a hard look at Randall who looked just as menacing. He held his cousin's gaze for a moment then immediately turned his stare on Terence who tried but failed at returning Jerome's gaze. Sylvia's friend, who seemed in no hurry to leave the room so the partners could start their meeting, looked back at her. "Me and you gonna talk later. I'll have Marilyn get me something from kitchen."

Sylvia unnecessarily shuffled papers for a full minute longer and took a deep breath. Her unease was painful to watch for those who cared about her. Finally, she began. "I hope everyone has met Randall here." Sylvia laid her hand out toward Randall and then asked him, "Randall did you meet everyone?" She turned her head toward Randall but refused to look at him.

"Yes, I have." Randall glanced around the room and nodded.

Sylvia swallowed hard, took a drink of water, and continued. "As you may or may not know Randall is our new accountant. He has worked hand and hand with Jackson and Bruitt, the company that performed the business valuation report and he has audited our accounts. Randall will give us a thorough report and then we will have an open discussion. Randall." Sylvia's sigh of relief was audible as she turned the floor over to Randall.

"Thanks Sylvia. First I'd like to commend each of you for your part in maintaining and managing such a lucrative and well run establishment. I have given you each a report of the recent audit I conducted." Randall went through his report page by page. He told the partners there were only minor discrepancies found in the sampling documents reviewed. Much of what he explained was tedious but the partners were receptive. Upon finishing the audit review, Randall suggested a short break before he began the business valuation report. He hoped for an opportunity to speak with Sylvia but she remained engaged in conversation with Jessie and Retha, so he went to find Jerome.

Randall had barely stepped inside Sylvia's office when Jerome said, "I asked Jim what happened to Sylvia. He lied too. He knows what happened but ain't telling."

"You think it was her ex?" Randall asked.

"I thought about Sean until I talked to Jim. I don't think Jim would protect Sean, even if Sylvia asked him to. Also, Sean never bothered Sylvia when others were around. Jim saw this. He just ain't telling."

"Maybe it was a customer." Randall considered the possibility that Sylvia's story was true.

"Yeah, but probably someone we know," Jerome said.

Nathaniel entered the office and joined in the speculation. "What do you think happened to Sylvia? I don't believe a customer clocked her like that. That bruise looks like "ready, aim, fire to me." Jerome and Randall agreed.

Jessie had the group engaged in a conversation on the Dallas Cowboys star quarterback's worthiness when Randall returned and asked if everyone was ready to start back up.

Randall went through the business valuation quickly. He explained that placing a value on a business is a subjective process and could result in wildly diverging outcomes. He recommended that each of the partners take time over the next week to read the report thoroughly, write down their questions and concerns and submit them to him via email. He would, in turn, compile the questions and submit them to the valuation company, unless he was certain of an answer.

"As you can see the building has an appraised value of $725,000. That does not include any equipment, furniture, inventory, or supplies. Mr. Bruitt gives the total value of these items $213,000. By far the most subjective part of the valuation is the projected income. Mr. Bruitt places that at an average of $89,000 over the next five years."

Each of the partners looked around the room at their fellow partners. Randall cleared his portfolio and tablet from the table and Sylvia took over. "Does anyone have anything else for Mr. Craig?" she asked.

"Just thanks, man," Nathaniel said.

"Yes, thank you very much Mr. Craig," Cheryl added with a flirty smile.

Randall gathered his things and joined Jerome in the office.

Sylvia now had her composure. "Well, anyone have comments about Randall's reports?"

"I'm curious about what happened with the other accountant. Does this guy work for Frisk or is this a different agency?" Terence asked as if he had no idea of the answer.

"Frisk was frequently late with reports or documents I needed. I became dissatisfied with his work," Sylvia responded dismissively.

Retha held back a grin and nudged her sister's foot under the table. Jessie's face became even straighter as she looked around at the others in the room.

"Where did you find Mr. Craig?" Cheryl asked.

"We went to school together. His cousin Jerome and I are good friends. Randall has both excellent references and credentials. He has been very thorough and I'm pleased with his work. Plus, he's reasonable." Sylvia paused, waiting for more comments about Randall but none came.

"Well, moving on, we have this business valuation which puts Sugar's Place at a value far beyond anything I expected." There were nods and agreement around the table.

"The last time we all spoke there was a discussion of selling the business. Cheryl, Terence, Nathaniel, Gerald are the four of you still interested in selling your interest in Sugar's Place?"

"I'm no longer interested in selling," Nathaniel answered with no hesitation. Terence stared at his younger brother but was not surprised by his decision. Cheryl and Gerald didn't even bother to look up.

"What about the rest of you?"

"I'd like some time to think about it," Gerald told his partners, still not raising his eyes from the table.

"Based on the appraisal I'd say my share should be worth a little more than $160,000. I'll walk away for that amount," Terence declared.

Sylvia was expecting Terence to propose the maximum price for his share based on all the figures bounced around. Randall had prepared her well. "Remember, the valuation report is subjective. I think it is high on the projected income as far as profit. Also you have to realize, those of you who want out, the rest of us are left with all the risk. No way am I willing to pay anywhere near a straight percentage amount based on that valuation report. A straight percentage on real estate value seems fair but on the equipment and inventory, no and definitely not on the income projections. When you walk away you are guaranteed the money in your pocket. Those of us who stay have no such guarantee. We may make money or we could lose. Randall has advised me on this. He is willing to meet with each of you privately and advise you based on his knowledge of these types of situations. You may want to consult an attorney, if you are not comfortable with Randall." The room was quiet but everyone could feel the storm clouds forming inside Terence.

"Cheryl, what about you?" Sylvia asked.

"I want out but I don't want to lose money on the deal. This place is worth a lot of money."

"Yes it is," Retha chimed in with a smile.

Sylvia continued. "Gerald, you think about what you want to do. If you decide you want out, you, Terence, and Cheryl need to decide what you are willing to accept as a buyout amount. Those of us who want to keep Sugar's will make you an official offer no later than mid January."

"What if I find someone who wants to buy my interest in the business? Can I sell it to them?" Cheryl asked.

"No, you must sell it to the remaining partners. That was Sugar's stipulation in his will and we carried that over to our partnership agreement, if you recall," Sylvia explained.

"That doesn't seem fair," Cheryl protested.

Jessie decided to put her seal on this meeting. "Listen, we all understand that Uncle Sugar had his reasons for setting this partnership the way he did. He wanted Sylvia and the rest of his family to maintain control of this restaurant. That was his bottom line, his legacy. I am not willing to ignore his wishes and have a stranger making decisions about what happens to Sugar's based strictly on profit margin."

Terence shook his head in disgust. All possibility of him making a large amount of money on Sugar's was flying out the window. He was certain his best financial option was to remain a partner and push for expansion but Cheryl really wanted out. She wanted a new home in Sugar Land and a Louie Vuitton handbag, several of them. Terence planted the seed and now he needed to kill it and save face, but how? Sylvia had won again. He felt bile in his throat as he watched Sylvia. He absolutely hated her, yet she became more self-assured each time he saw her. Except for a moment or two of discomposure at the start, she had conducted the meeting like some high powered executive. Terence wondered how she stumbled onto the accountant. ***The guy is smart.*** Terrence thought. ***He explained the items in that forty page audit report without glancing at the pages once. One thing is certain, with him on board Sugar's won't lose money.***

Chapter 17: That's Just Taboo

Sylvia plopped onto her sofa, completely drained. After the meeting, Randall had tried to follow her home but she told him she needed to spend some time alone with her babies. "Will you call me once the kids are in bed?" he had asked as he tried to catch her averted eyes.

"Randall I'm exhausted. Can we talk tomorrow?" He had looked like an orphan, which he was, but that was the first time Sylvia had seen him look so dejected. She wanted him to meet her at the house and fit right in with her and the kids while she yelled at them and laughed with them, fed them, talked with them, listened to them, and finally settled them in for the night. She wanted to have him washing her dishes and waiting for her on the sofa to baby her and ask about her bruised spirit and face. She wished he was with her so she could tell him what an exceptional job he had done on the audit and presenting the audit and the valuation information to the group. She had not recognized Randall as the whiz kid he was until he stood before her partners earlier in the evening. Concluding he was the most remarkable being on the face of the earth, after her three children, she also determined to stay away from him except for business.

Her decision regarding Randall was shredded when the doorbell rang. Sylvia leaped from the sofa with a smile taking over her entire face, certain he was at her door. "He is so hard headed. I told him I'd talk to him tomorrow," she complained happily. "Who is it?" She yelled at the door with her heart fluttering.

"It's Jessie."

"And Retha."

Disappointment and pleasure all rolled up together at her front door. Sylvia was happy for the company but really would have preferred Randall. She opened the door for her nieces.

"We're not interrupting anything are we?" Jessie asked as both ladies stepped inside the house and looked around in quest of Randall.

"No, come on in. What would you be interrupting?"

Jessie walked further into the house, grinning as she looked around. Once she made it to the family room her look of glee turned into disappointment. "No Randall?"

"No Randall," Sylvia confirmed with disgust on her face."

"We bought wine." Retha pushed a bag with five bottles of wine into Sylvia's arms. "2009 Beaujolais, It's dangerous."

"We heard Jim tell you that you had better not come in tomorrow. Where the brats? They sleep already?" Jessie looked around, again. Since there were no fine men to ogle, she'd settle for Sylvia's children.

"I'm sure Tani and Billy are asleep, but Justin is still awake."

"I'm going to say hi." Jessie led the way upstairs with Retha in tow.

"The house looks good, Sylvia. I like these colors. What beautiful memories I made here," Retha whined.

Understanding that you never burst into a teenage boys room without knocking, Jessie knocked on Justin's door and waited for him to tell her to come in before attempting entry. She and Retha visited with Justin for only a few minutes. Retha gave him a new New York Liberty Jersey with Jaren's number 24 on the back. Justin's old lady cousins made him laugh whenever he saw them. They asked the usual school questions and Jessie made him blush by asking if he had a girlfriend. He answered in the negative. "Both Mom and Dad tell me there is plenty of time for girls." He grinned and added, "That might be the only thing they agree on." Retha gave him memorabilia for Billy, Bertani, and Baby Cecily before she and Jessie left the room.

The sisters found Sylvia opening a bottle of wine. She glanced at them skeptically as she poured out goblets of wine because they both seemed a bit tipsy. "Did y'all drive over here?"

"Nope, we have a chauffeur. James is picking us up later," Retha told her with a smug arrogant look and upturned nose.

"James?" Sylvia asked looking from Retha to Jessie with a questioning smile on her face.

Jessie explained. "Jaren brought us over. He got so pissed at Retha calling him 'James' he said we might have to spend the night. He was already mad because Robert wouldn't drive us. They're watching some football game Robert recorded earlier."

The friends settled in around Sylvia's family room sofa and Retha asked, "Okay, so, what's the deal? Who knocked the hell out of yo' ass today?"

Surprised by the question, Sylvia hesitated for a moment and thought about whether or not she wanted to answer truthfully. These were the people she confided in. She had declared Jessie and Retha as those closest to her. She knew they trusted her and she loved and trusted them and wanted them to love her also. Sylvia so needed competent adults to love her. "Debra," she confided without looking at either of her nieces before taking a long drink from her goblet. She had little experience with French wine. This was light with a hint of fruit, not sweet at all. Caught off guard by the intoxicating effect, she liked it. She stared at her wine goblet for a moment.

"Who is Debra?" Retha asked.

"My cousin." Sylvia scrunched up her face, rolled her eyes, and looked a little embarrassed. "She is mad about Randall. They used to date," she admitted.

"Oh hell, I knew there had to be something wrong with that man. He just seemed too perfect. Did you know he was seeing her too? Damn, what is wrong with men?" Jessie fussed, allowing no consideration for the possibility that Sylvia may have been partly responsible for any relationship violation.

"Jessie," Sylvia began to explain but was cut off by Retha. "Debra, she's Miss All That and a Coca Cola, the prima donna diva, right, the beauty?"

"That's my cousin – long legs, long hair, cafe au lait, and lots of style."

"Humph." Both Jessie and Retha grunted. The ladies sat around the coffee table and started their second $70 bottle of wine.

"Sylvia, baby, ain't nobody ever told you that it's against societal norms for you to mess with your cousin's man. That's just taboo. Cousins, sisters, any family member, best and good friends, actually friends period; the men who mess with those folks are all off limits. It's pretty sad really because that limits most of us to only about ten percent of the male populace," Retha philosophized.

Jessie was heartbroken and tipsy. "I would not have believed Randall is such a slime bucket." She looked downright distraught.

Sylvia relieved her misery. "Jessie they dated eighteen or nineteen years ago in high school and only a little in college when she wasn't screwing around with someone else."

"Are you telling me they haven't been together since he returned to San Antonio?" Jessie asked hopefully.

"He says he has had nothing to do with Debra since college and only a quick minute then. Debra has been trying though, and she is nothing if not determined. I tried not to like him but we were together so much it just happened. I knew Debra wanted to get with him. She made no secret of her feelings. I even tried to tell her that Randall wasn't interested in her, but she wouldn't listen. I have no idea how she learned about us but she came to the restaurant raising hell today, told me to stop screwing Randall. Tried to lay a serious guilt trip on me. Hell we just got together three days ago. If I didn't know better I'd think she hired a private detective."

"You sure he hasn't been with your cousin since he moved back to SA. I mean, should she have good reason to be upset with you or expect him to be faithful to her? Nineteen years is a long time ago," Retha protested.

"Maybe I'm in denial but I don't believe he has been with her or wants to be with her. I was invited to Randall's aunt's house for Thanksgiving Dinner. Debra, her mother, and sister showed up uninvited. She was all over Randall."

"Who invited you?" Jessie asked.

"Jerome invited me. He said Miss Izola wanted me to come but I figured Randall put him up to it. Anyway, I was late and hadn't been there fifteen minutes when Debra announced that my Aunt Denise and Cousin Janice were ready to leave but she wasn't, so she asked Randall to give her a ride home. He tried to give her an excuse but Debra doesn't take no for an answer. I left before they did. I was disgusted and too tired for games. She lives way out in Cibolo but Randall was at my house within an hour, asking if I was mad. I know it sounds childish, but we all know how she is. She will fight and throw a fit until she gets her way. That's how I got this." Sylvia pointed to her swollen purplish cheek bone. "I love my cousin but we have not been close since high school. Still I can't alienate myself from her and the rest of my family for Randall."

When neither sister commented, Sylvia pleaded her case. "Debra wants Randall because he refused to keep seeing her after college. She is obsessed with him because he rejected her. I should have known better, but getting involved with Randall is the easiest thing I've ever done. With him things simply fall into place." Sylvia breathed in deeply just thinking about the man.

"I don't know, Syl. Randall is quite a catch. Maybe your cousin really likes him for who he is. If I was single and a bit younger I'd make a play for him. I like that boy," Jessie laid it out there.

Sylvia sighed and poured out some more wine. "I don't want to talk about Randall or Debra anymore. How is Sugar Babe? You should have brought her with you. Is she talking much?"

Retha, like most parents, just needed a nudge to talk about her child. "Too much," she told Sylvia. "Jaren has noise-blocking headphones everywhere. I tell him that's not good parenting but he swears he only puts them on when we are both at home. She has already started the 'why' stage. We would not have been able to talk to each other if she was here. She repeats just about everything she hears. We have to be very careful what we say around her. She told Jaren to stop saying 'because.'" Retha started laughing. "Babe has been asking 'why' so much that Jaren has just started answering 'because'. Well she has figured out that 'because' is not a good answer, so she tells him 'Daddy, stop saying because!' He looked at her and cracked up. Babe gets this really serious look on her face and says 'I mean it Daddy.' So he tells her to stop asking 'why' all the time and he'll stop answering 'because.' Those two argue like they're both three-year-olds."

The ladies sat and enjoyed each other's company until Sylvia's phone interrupted their tete a tete. She had ignored two earlier calls from Randall but this time hurried to the phone, hoping he was on the line.

"Hey, baby. How you doing?" Jerome asked his friend.

Sylvia hid her disappointment as she responded. "I'm fine, Romey. Thanks for coming over today."

"Yeah, Randall thought I would be a good intimidator. Did I look menacing enough?"

Sylvia laughed. Over the years she had heard a number of people say Jerome went for bad, but he was one of the gentlest people she had ever known.

"Hey, don't hurt my feelings now. I thought I was so terrifying I damn near scared myself."

Sylvia was still laughing. "I'm sorry but I could never see that in you, Romey."

"I love you too, baby. Glad to hear you laughing."

"Jessie and Retha are here keeping me company."

"Wow! They got them old men with 'em?"

"No, their husbands are not here."

"I'll be right over."

"Stop it."

"Okay, but you know me and you gonna have to talk."

"We will," Sylvia agreed.

"Speak later," Jerome said in his ultra cool voice.

"Bye, Romey." Sylvia put down her phone and returned to her visitors.

"Jessie, I think Romey has a crush on you," Sylvia said with a wink and a smile.

"Girl, he flirts with me something terrible whenever he sees me; he's never disrespectful. Robert just ignores him. Of course, Jerome is awfully big for Robert to jump. Somebody needs to catch him."

"Jerome is much deeper than anyone realizes except maybe his family and me. He doesn't hang out much anymore, makes lots of money, takes good care of his money and doesn't spend it on foolishness," Sylvia told her friends.

"What does he do?" Retha asked.

"He is the Director of VIA's Health and Wellness program. He also owns a gym with several employees and does some personal training."

Retha thought for a moment before commenting. "He sure is a looker to be out there on his own. That boy's got testosterone dripping all off of him, goodness! Does he like women?"

"You mean is he gay? No, I'm pretty sure Romey is straight but he's so deep that he's a bit of a mystery to me. He reads everything. He likes big girls, fit but big. I think the woman he finally snags will have to be as intelligent and kind as him. He does not do shallow."

"Izola did a good job with those boys. Viola's kids are pretty nice too. That Martha is a talker but I like her," Jessie said.

"I know. She embarrassed me on Friday. She called Randall a "chick magnet." Said women were coming over to Miss Izola's just because he was back in town."

"She said that with you sitting there?" Jessie asked.

"Yes she did, called me out specifically."

Retha and Jessie laughed and Retha asked, "What did you do, Syl?"

"Looked stupid and said Jerome and Izola invited me over."

A knock at the door announced Retha's husband had come to pick up Sylvia's guests. As Retha went to the door, Jessie told Sylvia, "We're making pizzas tomorrow night. You and the kids come for dinner. Everybody will build their own."

"What should I bring?"

"Just come."

Jaren entered and looked around his old home for a moment. "Looks good in here, Syl. I missed you on Thanksgiving." He gave her a huge hug, lifting her from the ground. "How you been, girl? You look good except for that shiner you got there."

"It's a beaut, isn't it?" Sylvia beamed at Jaren who always made her feel more than special.

"Kids sleep?" Jaren asked as his eyes continued taking in the house.

"Yeah, I'm pretty sure Justin is out now. Thanks for the gifts you sent them."

"You're welcome, but your niece makes sure she collects every treasure she can get her hands on for your kids and Jevon. When are you guys coming out to visit? You need to come before the season starts so I can spend some time with the kids."

"Maybe next year if I can get away from Sugar's long enough for a decent visit."

"Old Jim will do fine without you for a few weeks." Jaren grinned as he thought about Jim. "I hear you guys are thinking about expanding your operations to other cities. That's going to be a lot of work."

Sylvia glanced at Jessie and Retha who both looked excited at the prospect of expansion. Jessie shared her thoughts. "I'm thinking Houston and Austin. You know those fru fru people in Austin like to pretend they are liberal. As long as you have lots of clean options on the menu, they'll support you. Houston has plenty of room for a good comfort food restaurant. Sugar's offers some of the best food I've eaten anywhere in the country and I'm not just saying that because I'm an owner." She looked around and received agreement from even Jaren.

"We better get going before Robert starts calling for his brah-in-law," Retha advised. They all laughed, knowing it was likely the case.

--

Debra, there's a gentleman here to see you. He says he doesn't have an appointment. His name is Craig, Randall Craig." The receptionist at Coldwell Banker Realty gave Randall a pleasant smile as she spoke into the phone.

"Did you say Randall Craig?" Debra was stunned. *Why would Randall be here? Is he here to confront me about Sylvia or maybe he wants to make up? That fool has come to his senses. I knew he couldn't stay away.*

"Debra." The receptionist jerked Debra back to reality.

"I'll be out in a moment. Do I have anything scheduled over the next two hours?"

"Not until three," the receptionist answered with disgust just before ending the call. Debra maintained her own calendar and could have just as easily checked it herself. Debra was one of the two out of eight agents who acted as if the receptionist was her personal assistant.

"She'll be out in a moment, Mr. Craig. Would you like to help yourself to some coffee? It's freshly brewed."

"Thank you. I'm fine," Randall responded with a lackluster smile.

Randall thought a lot about the attack on Sylvia the day before. When he first learned about the incident, he knew Sylvia was lying and covering for someone. His first thought was her ex husband but Jerome had assured him that Jim would have called the police on Sean. Jerome was sure Jim was covering also. The sick feeling in the pit of Randall's stomach told him it was Debra but before the certainty settled in his head, Jerome spoke what Randall hoped was not true. "Man, I bet it was that crazy-assed Debra. You remember how she was with you in school. How many girls did she jump just because she thought they liked you?"

Two too many. Randall got embarrassed remembering how crazy Debra acted and the worst part was he had been flattered at her aggressive behavior. She had went at him a couple of times when he tried to break up with her. If Martha and Debra's mother, Denise, hadn't stopped her, she would have jumped him when she learned he was moving away from San Antonio all those years ago.

Work and thoughts of Sylvia and how to deal with Debra had kept him awake until four in the morning. He had made two calls to Sylvia after they left the restaurant but she hadn't answered. That rejection added to his sleepless night. He had managed to finish a good portion of his work and was completely caught up by the time he lay in his bed. Visions of Sylvia's bruised face and averted eyes met his consciousness as soon as he awakened. He wondered what he could do to protect Sylvia from her own cousin. Debra did not understand hints or subtleties and she obviously believed she could force her desires into reality, no matter what Sylvia or he wanted.

--

"Nice digs." Randall eyed Debra's beautifully decorated office. He couldn't help but observe that her office was like her home and both were a reflection of her, extravagant; well-thought out; and beautifully put together but lacking in character or warmth.

Debra watched Randall with a smug proud expression on her face. It was as if she read his mind and responded with why do I need personality and warmth when I can shop and coordinate? "This is a very pleasant surprise. I wondered when you would find the time for me. What can I do for you?" she asked with expectancy.

Randall took a seat without being offered one. "I wanted to stop in and talk to you about Sylvia. I probably should have done this before now but I didn't think it was necessary until your altercation with her."

Debra went into high alert. She got up and walked from behind her desk and started toward her office door. "I'm not sure what you're talking about," she lied and reached to close the door.

"Would you mind leaving that door open?" Randall asked.

Debra looked insulted but was so surprised by the request that she honored it and moved back behind her desk, feeling nervous. She had not thought Sylvia would tell Randall about the incident. *I can't believe she told him, anything to make me look bad.*

With a remarkable calm, Randall picked a piece of lint off his pants and waited for another denial. When one did not come, he continued. "I'm certain you know exactly what I'm talking about. Debra, you know I'm very capable of making my own decisions.

You and I are no longer children in high school. You can't throw tantrums and get me to do what you want."

"I haven't thrown a tantrum. What did Sylvia tell you happened yesterday?"

Randall got his confirmation much quicker than he had expected and his temperature rose. He had held out a morsel of hope that his relationship with Sylvia had not been the cause of her injury. He questioned how he had ever been attracted to a woman as self-absorbed as Debra.

"Sylvia didn't tell me anything. She would never betray you like that."

"Oh damn she wouldn't. She is sleeping with you isn't she? If that's not betrayal I'd better go look the word up on Wikipedia, sneaky fat cow."

Randall got up from his seat and stepped toward the office door. "Sylvia and I like each other and if she lets me, I'll be spending some time with her and her kids. I want you to leave her alone."

Debra was speechless. Randall was in her magnificent office telling her he wanted to be with Sylvia. What did he expect her to do? She had to lash out in some way. "I hope you don't think I'm going to wait for Sylvia's leftovers. I thought Jerome was the one into the big girls. I didn't know you liked lard too."

Randall would not allow Debra to provoke him. "I understand that you and Sylvia are cousins. I know you used to be close. We are all different people now. You and I were finished back in high school. Yeah, we tried again but we are not good together, never have been. I know what I want in a woman when I see it. Give yourself some time. A beautiful woman like you will see what you want also. You don't have to settle for Sylvia's leftovers or your own because I am just that, your leftovers." Randall smiled and prayed his message got through. "You deserve better, something new and fresh."

"Don't patronize me, Randall. I know Syl must have told you something about me."

"You won't believe me about Sylvia, so let's not talk about her. You and I are too different, Debra. Let's just leave it at that."
Randall turned and left Debra's office.

Chapter 18: Out of the Woodwork

The week following Thanksgiving found Sugar's nearly as busy as the week leading up to the holiday. Jim and Sylvia accepted the idea of bringing on extra help for both the front and back of the house. "Well it's a little late but we could use that catering department you been talking about right now," Jim told her as they left late one evening. Christmas party orders had been increasing daily and Sylvia had Marilyn on the phones taking orders just about full time. She would need to sit down with Jim and Miss Mildred, her pastry chef, and establish some cut-off dates before they became overwhelmed and failed to meet orders they had already accepted.

In a matter of days, Sylvia had two new temporary kitchen staff and three more wait staff on the books. Letty, who ordered supplies and maintained inventory, managed to get exceptional pricing on much of the products they would need throughout the remainder of the holiday season. Jessie and Retha had both volunteered to come in and help with catering orders in the evenings. They loved the work, shared great talent when it came to food preparation, and were real sticklers about quality. Jim enjoyed having them in the kitchen but Miss Mildred was somewhat territorial and had to warm up to the nieces all over again each time they offered their services.

Sylvia should have been overjoyed about all the extra business but had grown sadder with each passing day. Whenever she stopped moving her eyes welled up with tears. She blinked them dry, went in the restroom to blow her nose, and tried to stay as busy as possible to keep ahead of her ever pursuing blues. Randall had contacted her one time in the past eight days via email to inform her that he had documents he needed her to review and sign and that he would have them to her by week's end.

Sylvia had felt a bit better after receiving the email because she assumed Randall would deliver the documents in person. On Sunday, she stayed around a little longer than necessary hoping he would show but after an hour she surrendered to her exhaustion and went home to rest, knowing she'd need all her energy in the weeks to come. She found the documents waiting on her desk the next morning. Jerome had dropped them off. The packet contained a short formal handwritten note from Randall and a self addressed return envelope for his Post Office box.

Either Randall was avoiding her or had no desire to see her but she fiercely wanted to see him. She wondered if she had turned him off when she ignored his calls after the partnership meeting. She remembered how sad he looked when she refused to let him follow her home. A week ago she was determined to stop seeing Randall. Now she prayed he hadn't given up on her or gotten involved with someone else.

--

The man on Sylvia's mind and slowly taking over her heart was not involved with anyone but his status was not due to a lack of effort. He was totally baffled as to why women were throwing themselves at him. Martha had called him a chick magnet and he was beginning to wonder if there might be some credence to her designation. Women were coming out of the woodwork at him.

His ex-wife, Jillian, had tracked him down the night before and called under the guise of needing some help with a tax problem. ***Hell, this is December. Who worries about a tax problem in December?*** She had asked if she could come out to Texas and bring her paperwork. He told Jillian he could not work on or advise her on her tax issues. Then she had the nerve to try and sound sad and told him she just needed to see him. Randall and Jillian had been divorced more than five years but, like Debra, when there was no man in her life Jillian tried to get back to Randall. Also, like with Debra, he had let her back in his life more than once; the need for sex had been mutual. Randall stopped playing that game years ago, but Jillian continued to call, sometimes just to talk and sometimes for sex. Last night's call had definitely been for sex.

Debra called before he was out of bed, apologizing to him for hitting Sylvia. When he asked her if she had apologized to Sylvia she whined, "Don't ask me to do that, baby. You know I'll do anything for you but please don't ask me to do that."

By the time Randall ended the call with Debra, he wanted to throw his phone but before he could sling it across the room, Maris called with one of her inane conversations. He tried his hardest to be polite and not rush the woman off the phone. He liked her in a way and wished Maris didn't try so hard at getting him in her bed. She didn't offend him but he imagined that if she were the man and he the woman, her behavior would be threatening. Her persistence was pushing him toward the decision to drop her as a client. Once again, he dismissed the idea of resigning from her service because he dreaded explaining such a decision to his old friend Ray Rutledge.

Randall listened and chatted as long as he could tolerate the conversation. Maris never ended a call with Randall. If he left it up to her, this tiresome chat would last an hour or more. "Listen, Maris I've got to get back to work. Have you got anything I need to take care of for you? Is everything going okay?"

"Oh the main reason for my call. I'm sorry, Randall, sweetie. I've got a friend who needs an accountant. She and her husband are recently divorced and she asked about you. I've bragged so much on how you've gotten me on track. Do you think you can make it out to the house for lunch to meet her one day soon?"

"Maris, I will not be taking on any more clients until after tax season. If your friend is still looking for help in May of next year, I might be able to help."

"Oh, Randall," Maris complained.

"Sorry Maris, but I've got all the work I can handle. I do appreciate the referral. I mean it, but I would be cheating you, her, and the rest of my clients if I took anyone else on right now. Thanks though."

"Well, we can still get together for lunch. Call me."

"Take care, Maris."

Randall was only able to concentrate on his work a few hours before the calls started up again. First there were three client calls he was compelled to take and then the most important call of the day came from Izola. "Randall, baby I'm sorry to bother you. I know you workin' but I need to know if you busy this comin' Saturday."

"Aunt Zoe, I told you not to worry about calling me during the day. I work at home on my own schedule and I can always take a break to talk to you and Aunt Vi."

"Well, I just don't like interrupting you. I know you have a lot of work."

"If I can't answer, just leave me a message and I'll get right back to you. It's not a problem." Randall had given both Izola and Viola the calling guidelines but the aunts did not operate under the current day premise that a person is always available. To them, one should only call a working person before or after working hours unless there was an emergency.

"I remember what you told me Randall. I know when to call but what about Saturday?"

"What about Saturday?" Randall asked, not remembering Zoe's reason for calling.

"Are you available to go with me and Vi to Laverne's? She's having her annual Christmas party and me and Vi thank we'd like to go. Martha wanted to go too but Trace is having some function at his job on Saturday so she has to go with him and Jerome says he don't want to go and for me to see if you'll go with us. I know she probably only invited us this year because Pat put her up to it but that Laverne puts out a nice spread and I sure would like to go."

"Man, Aunt Zoe, I don't know. Can I think about it?"

"Well sure, baby, but don't thank too long because if you not gonna take us, me and Vi will probably go up to Austin and spend the weekend with our cousin, Vernia. Let me know pretty quick."

"I'll give you a call tomorrow. Is that soon enough?"

"That's fine. When are you gonna stop by?" This was a not so subtle request to see her nephew.

"I'll stop by tomorrow. How about that?"

"It'll be good to see you. Bye, baby."

The idea of dealing with Pat made Randall hesitant about escorting his aunts to Laverne's party. He was pretty sure Pat understood he was interested in Sylvia, but didn't think that fact would deter her behavior. Pat did not come on to him in a direct way. She was a seductress. She batted her lashes and looked at him with lowered eyes and an alluring smile, wore clothing that displayed her assets to their best advantage, and fragranced body lotion that would make any man turn his head to follow the scent. She asked lots of questions, listened to her prey's every word, and laughed sexily all while running her fingers through her hair nonstop. She was the type of woman who did not say she was interested but displayed her interest by turning her back to her partner on the dance floor and rubbing her ass as close to him as possible. Her technique was very effective but pretty boring once you had succumbed to it enough times, unless easy sex was the ultimate goal. Still, Randall wanted to avoid the enticement if at all possible.

He was uncertain about his involvement with Sylvia. He liked her but she cut him off immediately after the incident with Debra. Knowing Debra was her assailant, he wasn't sure how to proceed. Debra had not given up on her pursuit of him; this was clear, and she probably wouldn't anytime soon. Like Jillian, Debra liked to win. It didn't matter the price, winning was all that really mattered. He couldn't ask Sylvia to deal with Debra's craziness and the risk of another attack, possibly one more serious than the first. Randall realized that he should have considered the relationship between the cousins before he got involved with Sylvia. The thought that he might need to give her up in order to protect her sickened him. It would have been selfish for him to ignore the quandary he had caused for Sylvia and he understood why she might want to end their involvement.

Randall was leery about that word "involvement." He continuously reminded himself to slow down and let things happen at an easy pace, not only with Sylvia but with other women he had dated since his divorce. It seemed like once he and Sylvia put their arms around each other they were swallowed up by a sinkhole. Two days with Sylvia had turned into a full-fledged relationship. Maybe, he thought, Debra's attack on Sylvia was a warning for him to slow things down. After all, he was just getting settled in San Antonio and needed to get his footing before diving in too deeply.

The party at Miss Laverne's might be a good change of pace and get his mind off Sylvia. His aunts would climb into their cars and drive all over the state of Texas during the daylight hours but both had given up driving at night. His decision to return to San Antonio was so he could help with the ladies' quality of life and relieve Jerome and Martha of some of the responsibilities of elderly parents. Well his aunts needed an escort to a party and Jerome did not want to escort them and Martha was unavailable. Randall had nothing planned, so it looked like he'd be going to Laverne's. The only dilemma was how to avoid dancing with the lovely Patricia.

Once Randall's mind started bouncing all over the place, he knew it was time to quit work for the day or at least take a good long break. He began organizing his work area and contemplated heading to Jerome's gym for a good workout. He cursed under his breath when he heard the chime of his doorbell and hoped it was Jerome. Shock and awe ran through his body when a glance through the peep hole revealed the identity of his visitors. "So, what, did we put a man on Mars or something? To what do I owe the pleasure of this visit?" he asked as he opened the door to not only Sylvia but her three children also.

Before Sylvia could answer, Bertani started walking into Randall's home. "Hi Mr. Randall. We just come to bring you some papers." Sylvia grabbed her daughter by the hood of her hoodie before declaring, "You just wait a minute, miss. We haven't been invited in." She stood outside the door holding Bertani's hoodie and watched Randall with a look that read, "Well, are you going to invite us in or what?"

Randall stepped aside as he opened the door wide. "Please come in; forgive me for being rude. I'm just surprised to see you guys."

Once inside, Billy took off running and exclaimed "Whoa, look at the view in this place. Justin and Bertani quickly joined him.

Sylvia stood just inside the doorway and handed a packet of documents to Randall. "I thought I'd drop these off personally since the kids and I were going to the Purple Garlic for pizza. Thought you might need them quicker than snail mail would get them to you." She casually perused his home as if she'd never seen it before.

"This place is awesome. I thought it was just a regular old apartment building but this place is huge and really cool. I'm going to have a place like this when I get old," Billy announced.

Randall grinned at the "get old" reference and then told Sylvia. "There was no rush on these, but I'm glad you stopped by. Sit down."

"We can't stay. I've got to get the kids fed and home to bed. School tomorrow, you know. Did you eat yet?"

"No, not yet. I hadn't really given dinner any thought. I had kind of a late lunch today."

Sylvia stood there and tried to think of what else to say to prolong her visit now that she had turned down a seat and Randall hadn't accepted her hint for him to join them for dinner. She decided being direct is always the best approach, so asked, "Why don't you join us. I owe you dinner."

"You do? For what?"

"You said I could buy you dinner when you paid the sitter for me, remember, after Luis and Olga's wedding."

"Hey, Mr. Randall, is that an XBOX IV?" Billy shouted, he was so excited."

"Yeah, I play a little when Jerome or someone else with serious skills stops by."

"Billy, what did I tell you my Nana used to tell me about hey?" Sylvia asked her middle child.

Billy looked downright disgusted and answered with a smirk. "Hay is for horses."

"You need to try and remember that sir and please don't use that word when talking to an adult. It's disrespectful."

"Yes ma'am." Billy went back and sat near the windows with his brother and sister.

Sylvia looked at Randall who was watching her. "So, do you want to join us?"

"I could eat, but I need to get cleaned up. It'll take me a few minutes. How about letting the kids play a game while I get ready."

"I don't care if you don't."

Sylvia sat and flipped through a magazine while her children played on the XBOX and Randall got ready. When they left his home Billy beat his older brother to the punch and asked if he could ride shotgun with Randall. Sylvia hoped Randall wouldn't abandon his own car in the middle of some San Antonio roadway because Billy could talk. There were times when she'd tell her middle son to stop talking and take a breath.

After they arrived at the restaurant and seated themselves, Randall directed all his attention to the kids. Not much time passed before Sylvia began to wish she had saved the "I owe you dinner" excuse for a time when she could have had Randall to herself. He gave her some rather peculiar looks but no words that encouraged her in her feelings toward him. Soon Randall and Justin were deep into a discussion about football with Billy throwing in his opinion periodically. Bertani, who was in tune with her feelings and saw no reason to deny them, other than the wrath of her eldest brother, did her best to change the conversation and claim some of Randall's attention. She wanted to know when she could return to Miss "Zola's" house to play with Randall's young cousins, where Uncle Romey was tonight, how many more days 'til Christmas, she gave the complete unabridged version of her Christmas list, and told Randall all about the pizza party at their Aunt Jessie's house who is not really their aunt but Sylvia made them call her that because Aunt Jessie is so old. Randall directed his attention to Tani when she demanded it but got right back to talking with Justin and Billy about football after she completed each speech or he answered her question.

Sylvia was happy to be in Randall's presence but she had no idea her children would consume him. The most she was getting was a little eye contact, an occasional smile, and every now and then a reference to her. She ate her food, drank her ice tea, and acted as if she was interested in the conversation her sons and Randall seemed to be enjoying so much but she wanted to tell the boys to shut up and eat so she could talk to Randall. Normally she might do that but she did not know what to say to him. They hadn't spoken in days and though he seemed pleased to see her and the children, Sylvia wondered if he was still interested in her as more than an acquaintance and a client. She sat there barely finishing her food and wanting to scream.

There was one lady present who decided to handle the situation. Bertani slouched her chest forward, let her head drop back onto her shoulders as far as it would go, half closed her eyes, and let her exasperation out. "Grrrr, football, football, football, I get so tired of football."

"Tani!" Sylvia exclaimed. "Don't be rude."

"Well that's all they talk about Mommy. They talk about it at Dad's all the time and now they want to talk about here."

"Nobody said you have to listen, girl." Billy, who was barely participating in the conversation took up the mantle of protection of the never ending football discussion.

"And nobody said you have to talk, knotty head," Bertani screamed back at her brother.

Now Sylvia had to pretend serious indignation at the name calling though she was in complete agreement with her daughter about the football talk. "What did I tell you about that name calling Miss Bertani Inez Gaston?"

"Dad calls him that all the time. He calls both of them that," Bertani protested in her defense.

"No he doesn't. Dad never calls us knotty head." Justin, who had been above the ruckus until now, jumped in.

"Yes he does too." Bertani stuck to her guns.

"Dad doesn't call us knotty head, stupid. He calls us knuckle head." At that point, Randall turned his head and clamped his teeth together to keep from falling out of his chair with laughter.

"Okay, that's enough," Sylvia said sternly as she cut her eyes at Randall, well aware of his amusement.

"But, Mom," Billy tried to get in a word.

"I said that is enough! Not one more word from any of you."

The table went stone silent. Thankfully, Sylvia had paid at the register when they ordered so she could quickly free herself from the misery of dinner out with Randall and her children.

Randall walked them to their car, gave the boys daps, accepted a hug from Bertani, thanked Sylvia for dinner while giving her a light hug, and headed to his car without a backwards glance. During the ride home, Justin, Billy, and Bertani, started a discussion about their dinner which quickly progressed into an argument, but Sylvia didn't hear them until she was nearly home. She was so busy trying not to think about Randall that only a full blown fist fight would have captured her attention at that moment.

--

The very next day, a call from Ray Rutledge inviting him to lunch pulled Randall's attention away from the accounts he had been working on since six in the morning. He was thankful for the break. He was pleased Ray was downtown so he could take him to Sugar's and show the place off. He praised the food at Sugar's Place so often and with so much fervor that Ray had expressed a desire to visit the eatery.

The restaurant was packed as usual for lunch but it didn't take Randall long to spot the back of Ray's balding head along with the distinctive golden mane that identified Maris Kleinholz. Randall wasn't totally disappointed that Maris was joining them for lunch. With the restaurant owners' hopes for expansion, every additional customer was beneficial and Randall was well aware of Maris's ability to influence those of her circle.

Randall received friendly greetings from the wait staff as he approached the table occupied by his friends. Ray stood and gave him a hearty handshake and a huge grin. "This is a pretty nice place here. Food must be pretty damn good with all these hungry faces.

We haven't ordered yet, waiting for you," he told Randall as they took their seats.

"Maris." Randall nodded a greeting. "I wasn't expecting to see you today. How's everything going?"

"Good. I couldn't resist inviting myself along when Ray told me he was meeting you for lunch. We were attending a business meeting together at the Westin Building. Glad to see me?" she asked.

"Always," Randall answered and started advising Maris and Ray of the items he had eaten on the menu and which were his favorites. The two men decided to try the special of the day, Creole beef steak with rice and beans, fried plantains and a side salad. Maris wanted something lighter, so she went with the salad medley of chicken salad, mango walnut, and bacon spinach and tomato.

Ray flirted shamelessly with Marilyn who waited their table. Maris was doing a fair bit of flirting with Randall, causing Marilyn to throw questioning looks at him. Marilyn was tempted to tell Sylvia that Randall was in the dining room with a date but knew better; she could have misread the situation. She did pull Rudy to the side and ask him to check out the woman at the table with Randall. Rudy wasted no time working his way around to the table in question as he asked guests, "Everything okay?" and "How's your lunch?" In order to make it appear as if he was simply checking on his guests and not being nosy, Rudy asked two more tables about their dining experience after speaking to Randall and before reporting back to Marilyn. "Who is that woman?" he asked Marilyn with his eyes stretched wide.

Marilyn hunched her shoulders in the universal sign for "I don't know."

Sylvia had no idea Randall was in the dining area until she spotted Elder and Sister Ware and went out to greet them. No sooner than she exited the kitchen, Randall spotted her and went on alert. She remained at the Ware's table a little longer than usual discussing Sister Ware's arthritis and the recent death of a longtime church member. She visited with guests at two other tables and was contemplating approaching Randall and his friends when he caught her eye and called her over.

Randall's demeanor changed once Sylvia approached their table. Everything about him said he liked the owner manager of Sugar's Place. "Hey, Syl," Randall addressed Sylvia, sounding so much like Jerome that she had to do a double take to make sure Jerome wasn't hidden behind him. Maris immediately sensed the degree of familiarity between Randall and Sylvia. Randall barely took his eyes off the restaurant owner during her visit to their table, yet Sylvia was cool with him.

"Ma'am, are you the chef?" Ray asked with a big smile.

"No, I am not. That would be Jim but he does allow me to assist him. I've learned a lot over the years," Sylvia admitted.

"Well, listen," Ray took on a serious tone, "I'm just a little upset that I had to wait for Randall to move back to San Antonio before I got here. This is some of the best eatin' I've had in a long time. My compliments and I mean that from the bottom of my heart."

"Well thank you, Ray. I hope you will come back and visit with us and please let me know if you need anything else." Sylvia bestowed her best smile on all three and no one observing this interaction would have guessed that she sensed she and Maris shared the same interest, Randall Craig. She hoped Maris was not the reason he was keeping his distance.

Chapter 19: Biscuits Versus Pancakes

Sylvia's Saturday evening was her most productive at home in some time. After a six to two shift at Sugar's, she went grocery shopping for her home. Her neighbor Lola met her at the house at four o'clock and helped her clean until a little after eight. Having such a busy schedule kept Sylvia from longing for what could be in her life. She had become quite adept at not worrying when her days were full and they usually were filled to the brim.

Even an unexpected call from her mother had failed to throw her off track except for the ten minutes or so they were on the phone. As unexpected as the call may have been, Sylvia had been waiting for it to come. Dianne may not have had a close relationship with her oldest daughter but she and her sister Denise and nieces, Janice and Debra were tight as a brand new pair of jeans on a sixteen-year-old girl's butt. When Sylvia crossed Debra, she crossed her own mother and her aunt also. Janice would stay out of the fray, though following the drama closely.

The task at hand had not required much attention when the call came through. Sylvia had been so absorbed in sorting dirty laundry that she had not bothered to look at the caller ID or she might have at least considered letting the call go to voice mail.

"Sylvia, what in God's name is going on down there between you and Debra?" Dianne had asked without bothering with the pleasantries of greeting her daughter or inquiring after her grandchildren.

There was a complete void of emotion in Sylvia's voice when she responded to her mother's question. "What did Debra tell you?"

"Debra didn't tell me anything. My sister called and told me that you and Debra got into it over Randall. Denise says Debra is through with you because she can't believe you'd do anything so low as mess with her boyfriend. I told Neida there has to be a mistake."

Sylvia was stone quiet on the phone, barely breathing. She was afraid that she would say something mean or disrespectful to her mother so she held her tongue until she could speak civilly.

"Don't you go quiet on me, Sylvia. I know you hear me. What the hell were you thinking letting that boy fool with you? You know he will just use you, throw you out and try to go back to Debra Jean and you know how much she loves that boy. Why would you be so evil and try to mess things up for your cousin like that? She can't very well take him back after he's been with you but it serves you right if she does. Debra has always been good to you and you go and backstab her like this."

"Mama, I don't want to talk to you about this. I'm sorry but I can't. How are Marie and Jason doing?" Sylvia asked about her brother and sister who were always on her mind and in her heart.

Dianne had been nice to her daughter up to that point. She was accustomed to Sylvia going quiet on her because that had always been Sylvia's strategy for dealing with her mother. Dianne talked and Sylvia listened. It was a strange phenomenon for her daughter to respond disdainfully. "I can't get down there anytime soon so you might need to come up here so we can talk. This is some bullshit you trying to pull and it's going to backfire on you and hurt the entire family. Cousins don't fuck their cousin's man, Sylvia. You leave Randall alone. Don't make me have to come down there."

*Hurt the entire family. What a joke. Like I should care.* "Mama, I've got to go. I'll talk to later. Have a Merry Christmas and tell my sister and brother hello for me and I'll kiss my kids for you. Bye."

--

It was nearly nine o'clock when Sylvia finally settled into a warm soothing bath and it took her all of five minutes to fall asleep. The ringing of her cell phone woke her, but she refused to leave the tub to answer. A few moments after the cell phone stopped ringing the house phone began to ring, but Sylvia let it go to voice mail also and remained in her tub. She was dozing again when she was startled awake by her doorbell and banging at the door.

"Damn it. One of my kids had better be injured. This had better be Sean or Camille." When Sylvia realized what she was saying she changed her grumbling to, "Please don't let this be about my kids." She grabbed a heavy terry cloth robe and stomped to the door, leaving puddles of water in her wake. "Who the hell is it?" she yelled at the door.

Hearing the venom in her voice, Randall stepped back from the door and yelled with merriment in his voice, "Open the door, Sylvia."

"Randall, damn you!" she cursed as she granted his request. "Why didn't you call?"

"I did; twice." He stepped inside, looked her up and down, and spotted the water on the floor before starting to laugh out loud. "You were in the tub. I'm sorry, baby. Go ahead and finish. I can wait. I brought you a plate."

Sylvia looked at Randall with disgust and disbelief before she turned and left him standing in the middle of her foyer holding a plate full of food out to her.

"You want me to warm it for you?" Randall yelled at her departing figure.

Once back inside her bathroom with both her bedroom and bathroom doors closed, Sylvia climbed back into the tub. She decided she would continue to soak just as long as she would have if Randall had not shown up at her door. *I hope this is not a booty call. I'm not going to be his afterthought.* She continued to lie in the tub fighting the urge to get to the man who was most likely parked on her family room sofa watching television. As she washed her body, she wondered where he'd been and with whom. She told herself she didn't really care because she had no time for a relationship with Randall Craig. Justin, Billy, and Bertani were the only people she was willing to have a love affair with at this stage of her life. Between them and Sugar's Place there was no room for anything or anyone else. *I wonder where he's been.*

Finally giving in and getting out of the tub, she took her sweet time patting herself dry, moisturizing her body from head to sole and putting on her oldest and most comfortable PJs and a robe.

Sylvia tried not to appear upset or pleased when she entered her family room. Randall was leaning on the kitchen island aiming the television remote and flipping channels. "Man they said the Horns would be on tonight. Damn, I can't find 'em."

"Maybe they're off already. It is nearly ten o'clock you know." Sylvia gave her guest an accusatory glance which he seemed to miss completely.

Randall turned the television off and placed the remote on the counter before asking, "You want me to warm this food up for you. It's damn good."

"Who cooked it?" Sylvia tried to sound disinterested.

Randall gave her a smirk of a smile. "I got it from Laverne's house. She had a Christmas party this evening."

Displeasure and jealousy took over Sylvia's face. Her lips pressed together and poked out slightly as her mouth twisted up to one side and nostrils flared. If there were a picture of disgust in the dictionary, it would be an image of Sylvia's face at this moment.

Randall watched her expression and called her to task. "You are one jealous woman, Sylvia, considering I can never get you on the phone unless you're at Sugar's."

"I'm not jealous. Why would I be jealous of Laverne? I just don't understand why black folks always feel the need to haul off plates of food when they leave dinner parties. It's ridiculous and really bad etiquette. It's like they're afraid they won't get their full share or something – tacky, just tacky." Sylvia plopped into a kitchen chair and turned the television back on.

"Wow, that's exactly what Aunt Viola said when you left Aunt Zoe's on Thanksgiving," Randall said.

Shock was the new expression on the face that turned toward Randall with a gaping mouth. "Your aunt said that about me?"

"Tacky, I know." Randall barely looked at her and kept a straight face.

"You're lying on Miss Viola. You should be ashamed of yourself."

Randall laughed sarcastically. "So, why was your face all turned up like that?"

"Not because I'm jealous of no Miss Laverne, that's for sure."

"Okay, play crazy. You got to try these crab cakes. They're the best I've ever had and I'm a connoisseur."

"I don't want no crab cakes."

"Okay, but it's your loss."

Sylvia sat and watched Randall, giving him the evil eye as he started heating the crab cakes on the stovetop. "Why not use the microwave? It'll be faster," she suggested

"Microwave might mess 'em up – dry 'em out." He gave Sylvia a wink and a wicked smile. He knew she was jealous and it made him happy.

Sylvia turned her head away and started biting on her thumb nail.

"Hey, hey, look at me, Sylvia."

When she turned her head back toward Randall with a wide-eyed gaze, he told her, "I tried to get Aunt Vi and Aunt Zoe to leave earlier so I could see you at a respectable hour but they were having a good time. I didn't want to spoil it for them. I was their chauffeur, their date, their waiter, and babysitter. I had to help Zoe get her shoes off when I got them home. Her feet had swollen. Why do women insist on wearing shoes that are too small and too high? I had to walk them to the car one at a time because their feet were hurting so bad they both needed all my support."

He got a laugh out of Sylvia with this description but she got back to what was foremost on her mind at the moment. "Did Pat behave?"

"Just like always," Randall answered, sounding full of himself. "I'm beginning to believe Martha knows what she's talking about with the chick magnet thing."

"Have you been drinking?" Sylvia asked with disgust.

"I told you I was the DD. No booze for me. I had precious cargo. Got any beer?"

Sylvia got up and pulled one of the Heinekens he and Jerome had left weeks before from the refrigerator. Randall placed the now crispy and thoroughly warmed crab cakes on a plate with a small container of Miss Laverne's homemade remoulade sauce and placed the treat on the table. Sylvia didn't hesitate to pick up a fork and dig in. After she completed one and noticed Randall starting on a second, she protested. "I thought you brought these for me."

"Told you they were good. Want me to get you the recipe for Sugar's."

Sylvia looked hopeful. "You think she'd give it to you."

"I might have to sacrifice my body and sleep with Pat but anything for you, baby." Randall had gone too far and knew it when he saw sparks flying from Sylvia's eyes. "I'm just messing with you, Syl. I have no need or desire to get with Pat."

Sylvia's face softened. "So how are you going to get me the recipe – by making a play for Laverne? She wouldn't have you," Sylvia chuckled.

He smiled at her, turned his chair, and scooted close, pulling her chair between his legs as he leaned forward and nibbled on her neck. Sylvia pulled away and wiped her neck, complaining that his stubble tickled. Randall ignored the complaint, pulled her head to him, and kissed her deeply. He smiled and said, "You taste like crab cakes," when he pulled away from the caress.

"So do you," Sylvia whispered and picked up her fork to finish the now unwanted delicacy before her.

Randall turned her face back to face his and made her look at him. She held his gaze and felt warm relaxing in his eyes. There was something special in the way he looked at her that relayed the depth of his feelings. Every reservation Sylvia had about her involvement with Randall dissolved when she was in his presence. She kissed him as he sat still, not wanting her to stop. She pulled away slowly keeping her eyes on him. She surprised herself with that kiss and wanted to see Randall's reaction. He didn't bother to speak but took her hand in his and gently kissed the palm. The caress caused a shiver to run through Sylvia. The couple sat quietly looking at each other for a moment before Randall spoke. "When are you going to feed me?" he asked.

Sylvia looked at him with surprise. "I bought you dinner a few nights ago."

"I want your food."

"Every time you eat at Sugar's you eat my food, Mr. Craig."

Randall pushed his chair back from Sylvia's so he could get a better look in her face and asked, "How did you feel the morning I came over and fixed you breakfast?"

"What do you mean?" she asked.

"How did it make you feel when I fixed breakfast for you?"

She looked thoughtful for a moment before answering. "Special, I felt special." Sylvia smiled, remembering that morning.

"I'll share something with you," Randall thought for a moment and began. "I grew up loving my mother's biscuits. To this day I believe she made the best biscuits ever tasted by man. Both my parents cooked, sometimes together, sometimes separately. My father liked biscuits but he preferred pancakes, those were his specialty, all kinds of pancakes. It does my heart good to think about my dad making biscuits, which were not very good, for me. When he cooked those biscuits it was because I was special to him. When my mother made biscuits instead of pancakes it was her telling me I was just as special as my dad to her.

"When I came to live with my Aunt Zoe and her family, she made a point of baking biscuits for me. She and Uncle Jake could have cared less if they ate biscuits, pancakes, or toast but Jerome cared. Jerome decided he preferred pancakes. Now I know the brother really prefers biscuits because he and I have eaten many a late night breakfast out together and he always orders biscuits. But Aunt Zoe, Uncle Jake when he was alive, and even me often cook pancakes for Jerome because pancakes make him feel special. They are for him, no one else. Everyone needs to feel special, Sylvia, even me." Randall's voice was low and emotional and he had to look away when he finished his biscuits versus pancakes discourse.

"Are you telling me I don't make you feel special, Randall?" Sylvia asked quietly, saddened and feeling emotionally connected to the strong man who had shared his tenderness with her.

"Whenever I'm with you I feel special, but I guess I want you to go out of your way for me. I have been with some fairly assertive women – my wife, your cousin. Guys would look at me and say stuff like 'you lucky dog' but I would not have been with either of them if they hadn't chose me. It feels good to choose someone I want to spend time with but I need to know that you're okay with me – that you want to spend time with me also. I don't want to be in this all by myself. Sometimes I get the impression you're just going along with me like I used to go along with Debra and Jillian. I don't want to be involved in that type of relationship."

Sylvia's head hung down and she sat very still. She wanted Randall so badly it scared her and she did not want to be overly anxious. *How do I respond to this? What is the right thing to say?* She wondered

Randall continued, "I want to thank you for coming by the other day. We hadn't talked in days and I was beginning to wonder if you wanted to keep seeing me. When you showed up with the kids you gave me hope. I must admit that I did feel special having you bring the kids by my place. That was a real treat. They're good kids, Sylvia."

Sylvia smiled a thank you. "So when are you available for me to cook for you?"

"I control my own schedule so I can work around yours. Just let me know and I'll be here."

"Well, Sean usually has the kids on Wednesdays, so how about this Wednesday?"

"Your kids are a part of you, Syl. Any night is fine. I know you've got a lot going at Sugar's right now with the holidays, so I'm willing to wait."

"You won't have to wait long but to be honest I'd like to cook dinner for you without the kids first. My kids demand lots of attention and I'd have a hard time showing you how special you are to me."

When Randall didn't respond she continued with a change of subject. "It's funny or I should say odd, not funny at all."

"What's that?" Randall asked.

"When I listen to you talk about living with your aunt, uncle, and Romey you don't sound like an orphan. You lost both your parents who you loved a lot and I can tell loved you more. You are blessed to have such a good family with your aunts and cousins and to have had your uncle. I, on the other hand, never knew my father but still have my mother right there in Houston – so close but very distant. I have a brother and a sister. I married out of my mother and stepfather's home though I only lived with them off and on over the years. As much as my grandmother tried to make up for my father and mother, I still felt like an orphan my entire childhood. I never knew for certain where I'd sleep from one night to the next." Sylvia paused and thought about how much of her past she wanted to share.

Randall leaned back and put more distance between Sylvia and him. He wanted to see her as she spoke so that he would have a clearer understanding of her words.

She continued, "When I was very young I was seldom with my mother but I would spend time with her family, my Grandma Dora and Aunt Denise. They weren't mean to me but I never belonged there. I was always the afterthought, never very important. My father's mother, Raelene always wanted me with her and I realized at a very early age that was the very reason my mother kept me away from Nana. But once my mother met my stepfather the two or three days a week she could pawn me off on her family was not enough. She needed more time alone with him and free of me. That's when I started living with Nana most of the time. She tried so hard to make up for the fact that I had a sorry mother. She felt sorry for me; I could see it in her eyes. I felt sorry for her too because she was powerless to protect me against my mother's stupidity. Sometimes my mother would call out of the blue and announce that I needed to 'come home.' I didn't even have a room at mother's house. I was enrolled in school based on Nana's address. Nana went to the parent teacher conferences and all the school programs. My mother never once asked about my grades."

Sylvia wanted to stop sharing her sad history but Randall was listening intently. She told herself to change the subject. "Where did you live before you came to live with Miss Izola?"

"I lived in San Diego with my parents. I still have family on my dad's side there. They've been asking me to visit for a long time now but I've been putting it off. My dad's family is huge. I'll probably head out that way next year." Randall wanted to know more about Sylvia's childhood. He probed further. "Do you remember your father?"

"Way back here." Sylvia rubbed the back of her head. "Nana had pictures of him around the house. I have them now. I can remember him swinging me by my arms one time and spinning around. I think we were laughing. I know I wasn't afraid. I also know he was just visiting. I don't think I ever lived in the house with my father. My grandmother loved him very much. He was the only family she had. Damn, I am making myself so sad telling you all this stuff. I wish I could stop. I've never told anyone all this before, not even Sugar. He'd say don't worry about all that nonsense because we all have mess in our backgrounds. He didn't like for me to talk about my background. I think it made him sad."

"Maybe you should get it out. I don't mind listening if you don't mind sharing." Randall gave her such an earnest look that she could tell he meant his words.

"This will teach you to show up at my house unannounced late at night." Sylvia laughed lightly, trying to clear the somber mood that had taken over the room.

Randall said nothing. He knew there was more Sylvia needed to say and did not want to hinder her in any way. "You want another beer?" she offered."

"I guess."

Sylvia got their beers and they moved into the family room to sit on the sofa. She turned off the television and they relaxed in the soothing sounds of Cassandra Wilson.

"You've got good taste in music, Sylvia."

"Why thank you."

She took a drink of her beer and laid her head back on the sofa. It wasn't long before she found herself talking about her past again. "My mother used to buy me clothes, lots of pretty clothes. All my friends envied me for my clothes, even Debra. She and Janice always borrowed my things. They'd keep stuff forever. I didn't really care because I didn't go to all the special outings and parties they went to. Yeah she'd spend money on clothes for me but never once took me shopping. How she always knew what size to buy, I don't know but she did. The stuff always fit perfectly. Expensive clothing but I don't think she ever gave my grandmother any money for keeping me all those years. The clothes pretty much stopped after Nana died and I went back to live with my mother. I guess she figured she had to feed me so why buy me clothes. Do you know I had no idea that my mother was receiving a social security check and another check because of my father's military service to care for me until the checks stopped when I turned eighteen. That's when she announced I needed to find a full time job because she wasn't receiving money from my dad's social security for me any longer.

"When my mother's husband got out of the air force and got a job in Houston, I was not included in their relocation plans. I was a grown woman, if you can call nineteen grown, but I didn't have anywhere to go. I was not ready to be on my own. Sean wanted to get married and I needed a place to live.

"I have only seen my brother and sister twice since they moved to Houston. I never get invitations to dinner, or graduations, birthday parties, nothing. My mother calls me four to six times a year. Matter of fact she called me tonight. I don't think she remembers my children's names. No gifts, never had a baby shower. I know I sound wretched and I was at one time but not anymore."

"And what changed for you, Sylvia, because the person I see shows no sign of the neglect you say you experienced from your mother. How do you manage to be so content? It's not a facade is it?"

"Marrying Sugar changed my life. I was so scared and insecure when I walked into his place and asked for a job. Since the day I got hired on, my life has gotten better. You know how we always say other people can't make you happy? I mean another person might be able to provide momentary joy but you have to find happiness for yourself. At least that is what my grandmother always told me. But

Sugar and his family made me happy. They included me and my children in everything. Those nieces would tell me off like I was family and get in my business. I thought they would forget about me once Sugar died but they drew me closer. They are like the sisters I never had. I have to admit that I'm still a little hesitant about joining in their family activities because I don't want to impose but I'm getting better."

Randall had his head back on the sofa alongside Sylvia's, watching her as she spoke, emptying the garbage of her past. "Sounds like you, Miss Sylvia, are a shining example of 'if it doesn't kill you, it will make you stronger.' You seem comfortable in your own skin."

"I'm much more comfortable than I ever imagined I'd be."

"And you know that stuff your Nana told you about another person not having the ability to make you happy? Well, I hate to disagree with sage wisdom but I will. I think we have to do all we can to get ourselves straight so we can be happy. If we're jacked up then no; there is nothing anyone can do to make us happy for any length of time. But I know that when we are straight and have things in order inside, the right person can make us happy. I'm happy whenever I'm with you, Sylvia. I enjoy you. I hope you don't mind me saying that."

Sylvia's saddened expression caused Randall to worry that he had come on too strong. "Did I say too much? I'm just being honest. I want to spend time with you, Sylvia but I don't want to be in this alone. I know things are never equal. I've been with enough women to know that but I need some balance. I want you to be happy with me also. I'm doing my best not to move to fast here. We both have a lot going on in our lives and need to take things slow." Randall watched her in anticipation of some declaration.

The bad thing about any amount of alcohol is the effect it has on honest speaking. Sylvia had just knocked off a Heineken, a brew that would give a regular beer drinker a buzz. Sylvia was not a regular beer drinker. She sat up and leaned forward as she began to confess all. "I don't know if being happy with you is enough for me. I'm afraid of my feelings for you, Randall. It feels too good. I ache for you when I don't see you. I think about you when I go to sleep and when I wake up. I know you don't want me to feel this way. I know you just want us to take it easy and enjoy whatever happens but I don't know if I can. I don't want to be clingy and pitiful so I try and not be jealous. I don't want to run you away but I'm so afraid of the time when you will leave that I can't enjoy the present. God I'm a mess."

Randall reached for her, pulling her back onto the sofa. "You're not a mess. You're just a little bit lit up. Let's talk about this later."

Sylvia had shared so much with Randall that she felt foolish and was more fearful than ever that she may have turned him off with all her honesty. She wished she could take her words back. Rising from the sofa, she carried her empty beer container into the kitchen. "Well, I've got an early start tomorrow so I've got to get some rest."

Randall did not move from the sofa. He had not expected Sylvia to send him away, at least not so early. He wanted to stay with her but knew she had reservations about sleeping with him after the long break they had from each other. "So, I guess you're sending me home? What if I want to stay here with you tonight?" he asked.

"I can't just let you show up at my home all hours of the night and sleep with me. You said you want to take things slow but I guess that means you want to sleep with me when you get the urge? I'm not that sophisticated, Randall. I don't really know how to separate sex from a committed relationship. I don't know how to make love with you and not get jealous when you talk about other women, or ignore me, or show up at my restaurant with a beautiful blond. That's not who I am."

"I'm not interested in any other women, Sylvia. I told you I want to spend time with you."

"What does that mean? Does it mean we get together and have sex on occasion? Does it mean we go out socially and cook meals for each other sometimes or are we just testing each other for size and fit, what?"

"Come on, Sylvia; why are you acting like this?"

Sylvia sat back down on the sofa next to Randall. "See what I mean. You think I'm being difficult or that I'm upset. I don't know much about relationships, Randall. I've had two serious relationships in my life and as bad as my first marriage was and as strange as my second marriage was, I understood the rules. I don't understand what you want from me or what you are willing to give me. I agree we should take it slow, but in my mind taking it slow does not include sex. We don't know each other well enough to make a serious commitment." She stopped and looked away in frustration. "Am I just supposed to play this by ear or what, Randall?"

"Damn, Sylvia, no more Heineken for you." Randall was attempting to make light of all she had said but Sylvia could hear the agitation he was trying to hide. He wanted her and it was clear he did not want to abandon his quest. Sylvia questioned if sex was all he wanted from her. She felt he wanted more but she didn't want to fool herself into believing that there was a future for them. They sat on the sofa listening to the mellow music drifting through the air and waited. Sylvia would not act because she wanted Randall to stay with her as much as he wanted to stay but she did not want to be easy for him. She never considered herself a woman that a man had to wine and dine before she would have sex with him but she felt slighted that Randall had never taken her out except to a wedding that they were both invited to attend. Sure he took her to his aunt's house once and fed her brunch one day but that was after she spent the night with him. Sean was too young, crude, and self-absorbed to make love to her in a nonsexual way and Sugar too ill and crotchety. Sylvia wanted to date and be courted but more than that -- much much more than that, she wanted to have sex with Randall tonight.

Sylvia stood in front of him and asked "Do you want to stay the night?"

"Yes, yes I do."

"Then tomorrow we start taking it slow."

Chapter 20: Christmas Cheer – New Year's Trouble

Just before Christmas Randall persuaded Sylvia to accompany him to a small intimate dinner party given by Ray and his fiancé, Karen, at a local steak house. JT, Rhonda, and their children; Maris and her date, Jeff; and several other distant Rutledge family members were also present for the holiday dinner.

Randall was relieved that Maris had a date for the occasion but before long found he remained Maris's quarry of choice, dates or no dates. Jeff, the rugged looking man Maris had with her, did not appear to mind his date's obvious interest in Randall. As a matter of fact, he engaged two of Ray's young female cousins and Sylvia throughout dinner. Randall would have chalked the man's overtures up to the norms of Texas society, but since Jeff could not keep his eyes off Sylvia's breasts, that hardly seemed the case.

Maris was only a degree less discreet in her attempts to engage Randall's time and attention throughout the evening. When she had little success with her usual tactics of captivating the male species she tried to belittle her competition by asking Sylvia a barrage of personal questions including what university Sylvia attended, how she became owner of Sugar's Place, how many children she and Sugar had and their ages. These questions would not be offensive to many but based on the circumstances of Sylvia's life, Maris's questions seem targeted to embarrass. Sylvia answered the queries with a cool smile and the indulgent demeanor of an adult responding to someone else's rude overbearing child. Maris's attempt at putting Sylvia in a bad light backfired and she could not hide her frustration. To make matters worse, Randall openly displayed his affection for Sylvia, who was reserved in her regard for him.

Ray eventually took on the task of entertaining Maris and lifting her out of the funk that enveloped her. Indeed her mood seemed to improve somewhat as she dined, though she shot daggers at Randall the remainder of the evening, causing him to question his past behavior toward her.

Once Sylvia and Randall were safely inside his car and headed toward Sylvia's home, Randall apologized for Maris's behavior. "I hope Maris didn't make you uncomfortable with all those questions.

I wouldn't have brought you here if I had any idea she would act so crazy."

Sylvia gave him a look that, thankfully, he didn't see out of the corner of his eye and due to the poor lighting inside the car. "She's got a thang for you. I guess I should be getting used to that by now."

"What do you mean? I can't help the way that woman acts."

"Yeah, Randall. It's not your fault that women can't control their behavior where you're concerned. Patricia snubbed me in the supermarket the other day. The lioness back there verbally assaults me. Debra physically assaults." Sylvia caught herself but it was too late. She had no intentions of telling Randall that Debra had been her attacker weeks ago, but knew she had already said too much.

Randall waited for her to continue, but when she didn't he asked, "Did you think I didn't know Debra was the person who attacked you Sylvia? What I don't understand is why you would keep that secret."

Sylvia was ashamed. Had she let that slip purposely? She wished she could forget that she was now sleeping with the man her cousin had been wishing, hoping and, praying for the past fifteen years.

"Why the secret, Sylvia? Why do you feel the need to protect Debra?"

"I'm not trying to protect Debra. I think I've done enough to Debra when you consider what's going on between us. I'm not going to try and make her look bad."

"Hell, are you really feeling guilty about Debra. I dated Debra twenty years ago. I used to consider her an old friend but not anymore, not after she attacked you like she did. You should have pressed charges on her ass."

"Do you remember telling me on Thanksgiving night that you didn't want to talk about Debra?"

Randall glanced over at Sylvia. "Yeah, I remember; so what?"

"Well it's my turn now. I don't want to talk about Debra."

Randall took a deep breath and let it out slowly. He knew, no nookie tonight.

--

Terence Solomon sat across the table from his wife of thirteen years, Lynette, and watched her consume an order of tiramisu and wondered how she maintained her figure. Lynette wasn't a slender woman but she was fit, fine, and exquisite and Terence had grown to love her with a passion over their years of marriage. When they first started dating it was more about status for Terence. Lynette was from a wealthy family and had recently joined a large Houston law firm. Now she was a full partner and made boat loads of money as a litigator. She was tough as hell and took crap from no one except Terence which she repaid tenfold.

Terence was no slouch in the money making business himself but he did not clear half the income his super performing high speed wife pulled in on a yearly basis. He had enjoyed the wealth and fine living when they first married but now he hated the subtle innuendo hanging in the air that he was riding on his wife's coat tails. Lynette was the head of the Solomon household and everyone familiar with the couple was aware of that fact. His desire to increase his standing in the world on his own was one of the reasons Terence wanted control of Sugar's Place. He saw ownership and control of a chain of restaurants as a way for him to gain in stature and income. There was no doubt that Sugar's business model would do exceedingly well in Houston and Atlanta for starters. He had envisioned fancying up the newer locations and marketing them to the hilt, maybe even bringing in some live entertainment on the weekends. Americans love the "new place to be seen." Good food would help but location, ambiance, and marketing were the real keys.

He and Lynette sat quietly and drank their coffee, each in their own world of thought when Terence received a text message that read "n town. need to c u #11001."

"Something important?" Lynette asked as her eyes attempted to pierce his skull. She had become adept at reading Terence over the years and expected him to lie when he answered.

But their years together had taught Terence some things also. He knew that telling as much of the truth as possible fooled Lynette's radar. "An old friend from San Antonio is in town and wants me to stop by the Hilton to see him. I'll catch him tomorrow if I have time."

"I've got a few hours of work ahead of me tonight when we get home. I'll be okay if you want to go by and see your friend before you come home."

"What time do you think you'll be finished or should I ask?" Terrance said.

"Don't ask, but tomorrow night I have nothing planned so we can spend some time together if you're available."

He became aroused at the way Lynette said, "we can spend some time together." He would wait for tomorrow, make sure he was available, and be happy about it. His wife had taught him years ago that she could be very giving in the bedroom when she was well-rested. Lynette was well worth the wait. "I'm always available for you, baby," he told his wife with a wink and a smile.

Terence made no attempt to leave his wife until she left the restaurant. It was important that he not show Lynette how anxious he was to follow up on the text. Once he saw her off, he thought about the message. During the drive he questioned why, after all these years of no personal contact, his old friend was asking for a meeting in a private hotel room? He pulled up to the Hilton and left his car with the valet before heading up to room #11001 with his curiosity rising along with the ascent of the elevator.

--

Christmas and New Year's came and went with only a modicum of drama for Sylvia. The restaurant functioned like a well run machine requiring constant tweaking to keep it running smoothly. Jessie and Retha worked at the restaurant and were invaluable in getting out holiday catering orders. The increase in staff allowed a much larger volume of sales, resulting in the greatest holiday season sales ever and a profit increase of more than thirty percent over the previous year.

Sylvia and her kids spent much of their time during the holidays with Jessie and Retha's families. Retha hosted Christmas dinner at her greatly underutilized San Antonio home with the desserts catered by Sugar's. Each of the twelve adults present for Christmas dinner prepared a dish. Jessie was responsible for all the condiments and drinks. Sylvia's children, Jessie's grandson, Jevon, and Retha's three-year-old, Morning (no longer known as Sugar Babe or Babe), all pitched in and made a salad under Justin's strict supervision.

Sylvia was pleased to find both Nathaniel and Gerald and their lady loves at Retha's home when she and the kids arrived. Billy and Justin attacked there stepbrothers like they were super heroes.

Sylvia's boys had grown close to Sugar's sons during their years together. Justin and Billy frequently questioned their mother about their much older stepbrothers.

"Man you cats have grown." Gerald beamed at the boys. "What are you feeding 'em, Syl? He then spotted Bertani. "Come on over here, Little Bit. You standing over there acting like you don't remember me."

Billy declared, "She probably don't. You guys don't come see us and we don't know how to find you." Everyone who heard this declaration was moved -- out of the mouths of babes.

"I do to remember him and I remember Nathaniel too." Bertani approached Gerald and gave him a hug. He picked her up as if she was still the two-year-old he had fallen in love with five years earlier.

This reunion was a little heart-wrenching for all who observed. Sugar and his two youngest sons along with Sylvia and her children had established a frail but love-filled family when a strong storm of death pushed through, causing severe damage. Those left standing did not have the wisdom or the stamina to repair the severed unit. Sylvia had hoped she could maintain the remnants in some healthy form but the destruction had proven too great for her. Maybe she should have let her stepsons know she needed and wanted them to remain a part of her family. Sylvia was so distressed after Sugar's death that she had never considered the effort needed to maintain a close relationship with her two youngest stepchildren, never given thought to developing a relationship with Cheryl, and although she forgot the particulars, heeded Sugar's warning to stay away from Terence. So Sylvia never reached out to her stepchildren or them to her. Everyone present hoped that the holiday gathering at Retha and Jaren's home would help restore Sylvia and her children's relationships with Nathaniel and Gerald.

Retha and her family departed San Antonio two days after Christmas so they could spend New Year's with Jaren's family in Tampa. Their absence put a damper on the party for New Year's but those remaining in San Antonio managed to enjoy the fireworks, champagne, and tamales while sitting in lawn chairs in Jessie's front yard. The children ran around playing and begged to shoot off fireworks but the closest any of them got was Justin passing the next explosive to Robert or his son, Mykol, to shoot off.

--

That modicum of drama just before Christmas came in the form of Sylvia's mother who, for the first time in nearly ten years, visited her oldest daughter's home. Dianne arrived uninvited and unannounced on a Saturday evening. She kissed her grandchildren and had a hard time focusing on her mission to set Sylvia straight in regards to her treatment of Debra because she was too busy looking around her daughter's home. She had no idea that Sylvia lived so well and had not expected such a nicely kept home. The last time Dianne had been in her daughter's home she was living in a small dingy two bedroom apartment with Sean and two young children. That had been a depressing little place. Now Dianne took in her surroundings and realized that there was much about her daughter she did not know and it crossed her mind that she should spend more time with Sylvia and maybe even her grandchildren.

Dianne did eventually broach the subject of Sylvia's violation of Debra's claim to Randall but it was useless. She was the worst possible emissary, holding no sway whatsoever with her daughter. In exasperation she asked "What has Debra ever done that would make you care so little for her feelings?"

"The only problem I have with Debra is this." Sylvia pointed to a darkened spot on her cheekbone that remained discolored from Debra's blow.

"What do you mean?" Dianne asked.

"Debra came into Sugar's, cursed at me, refused to leave or calm down and when I wouldn't give her what she wanted she closed her fist around something – I don't know what – and knocked the crap out of me. I will forgive her but I don't want her around me because I can't trust her. She literally knocked me to the ground. The only reason I didn't try to take her out was because I was hurt too bad; she got me good. Every time I think about it I get so mad at myself for not beating the hell out of her. If I had got just one good lick in, I probably wouldn't be so mad about this, but I didn't even get to hit her back. She's banned from Sugar's. I told her if she ever comes back, I'm calling the police."

Sylvia's mother had to take a better look at her daughter to make sure she had the right person. Her oldest daughter had always been so passive and such a lady. That was the one thing she felt her daughter had over her sister Denise's girls, she was so well behaved. On this occasion, Sylvia was sounding just as tactless as her cousins. "Well, I'm not going to have no fighting between you two. You were raised better than that. I want you to sit down and talk this out. Old as y'all are, fighting over a man is just pathetic. He probably ain't worth a damn. I hope you're not trying to still see him?"

This sneaky tactic didn't work any better than the direct approach had earlier. Sylvia drank her tea and did not comment. She wondered that her mother expected to have influence on her behavior. Sylvia wanted to ask Dianne if motherhood, void of love or sacrifice, still warranted some form of deference but she held her snide comment and kept her silence. She felt no victory when her mother got up to leave. Sylvia understood that her mother was much like Debra; they didn't release their prey without a long hard fight.

Toward the close of business the next day, Dianne; her sister, Denise; and nieces, Debra and Janice all showed up at Sugar's for dinner. "You want me to tell them to leave, Sylvia?" Rudy had asked with concern on his face.

Sylvia shook her head no and remained in the kitchen. She had other guests out front she wanted to greet but could not bring herself to go out and speak with those guests while ignoring her family. Turmoil tore through her. She felt disrespected and small and thought she was being disrespectful toward her Aunt Denise and Cousin Janice by not going out, but she refused to approach their table. She considered that her mother may have thought she was making the rift between the cousins better or was she purposely trying to offend Sylvia. Thankfully, it was Rudy's day to close so as soon as he locked the front doors, Sylvia walked out the back door, got in her car, and drove home.

Later, when her mother called trying to raise hell about her lack of respect, Sylvia fired back. "I told you Debra is banned from Sugar's but you come stepping up in there with her anyway. She would not have come if you had not brought her. I didn't have Rudy ask her to leave or call the police out of respect for my aunt. Debra does not need you to fix our relationship and I sure don't need your help with this. Please stay out of it. We have to figure this out for ourselves."

Dianne was floored. The person on the phone could not possibly have been her easy-going daughter who never gave her an ounce of trouble. Dianne had been accustomed to speaking to Sylvia in whatever tone suited her and using any and all forms of disparagement and not receiving a word of backtalk. She had strong suspicions as to why her meek child had turned into this strong woman. "So you got a little money now and got yourself a nice house and figure you don't need your family anymore. You think you can just do us any kind of way and it don't matter. Well you might want to get down off that high horse of yours and remember what goes around comes around. You spending time with those people who have a little bit of money and you think you're better than the rest of us. Well let me tell you something, Daughter. When they get tired of you, they're going to leave you flapping in the wind and you gonna wish for your family then. Mark my words."

Sylvia felt ashamed of her attitude toward her mother and knew that, although her grandmother, Raelene, cared little for Dianne, she would have cared less for Sylvia's attitude toward the woman at that moment. So our girl held her head back, took a deep breath, and pulled up some humility. "Look, Mama, I'm not trying to change the relationship I have with you and the family and forgive me if I seem disrespectful toward you; I don't mean to be. I would never disregard my family. I need family but Debra and I have to figure this one out ourselves. I feel she owes me an apology but at this point I feel it is better if she just stays away from me because I'm mad at her and I know she's still angry with me. There is no sense in either of us pretending like we can just kiss and make up."

--

"Mr. Solomon my name is Jason Reardon and I am an investigator with the Enforcement Division of the Texas State Board of Public Accountancy. I have received a letter of complaint concerning Mr. Randall Craig and his services for a restaurant in San Antonio called Sugar's Place. A Mr. Terence Solomon alleges a possible conflict of interest by Mr. Craig. Are you and Mr. Terence Solomon related?"

"Terence is my older brother," Nathaniel answered in shock. He continued listening to the caller but not really hearing the words spoken. He knew this was another attempt by Terence to make trouble for Sylvia and possibly strong arm the sale of Sugar's Place. *Talking about grasping at straws. Does this fool really think that getting rid of Randall will get the other owners to sell Sugar's – not if I can help it?* Nathaniel wondered what Terence thought this agency could do to advance his cause.

The caller proceeded to tell Nathaniel that Terence alleged an inappropriate relationship of a sexual nature between Sylvia Solomon, a co-owner/manager of Sugar's and Randall Craig and that Mr. Craig had made adjustments to the financial records to benefit Mrs. Solomon's interest in the business. "I take it you are also related to Mrs. Sylvia Solomon?" Mr. Reardon asked.

Nathaniel explained that Sylvia was his deceased father's widow. After a moment, Reardon cleared his throat and scheduled Nathaniel for a recorded interview the following week.

"Will that be the end of this or is this just the beginning?" Nathaniel asked, knowing the answer.

"We are just getting started with our preliminary investigation. Our findings in the prelim will determine if we need to have an official hearing or take any further action. We act quickly, so we will be ready to move on to the next phase of our investigation in just a few weeks, if there is a next phase. It helps a great deal when we have cooperation from individuals who are close to the situation and may have knowledge of any violations. I appreciate your availability Mr. Solomon. We will not take up much of your time. Thanks again and you have a good rest of the day."

--

The peacefulness of the New Year was coming to a sudden end for Randall as he stood just outside the United States Post Office opening a certified letter from the Texas Board of Public Accountancy. Upon reading the document, Randall was floored. It was no secret that he and Sylvia were dating and of course that could constitute a conflict of interest but he had done nothing that violated any ethical behavior. He had saved each of the owner's of Sugar's a great deal of money. Why would Terrance want to cause him trouble? There were plenty of good accountants that could easily step into his shoes, especially since he had gotten the restaurant's financials laid out in such an orderly fashion.

Randall stared at the document for some time and thought about the trouble it foreshadowed. He figured the best course of action was to let Sugar's go and help Sylvia find a replacement for him. The thought of Terrance pushing him out angered Randall and made him want to fight to stay on with the business, but he doubted the resulting trouble would make a fight worthwhile. In his years of experience he had seen any number of situations similar to this and knew that as long as he had committed no crime the pending investigation would be squelched once he dropped Sugar's as a client. Though Sugar's paid him well for the service he provided, he could easily manage without that income or pick up a new more lucrative client.

The real problem this troubling allegation could cause was the effect it might have on his relationship with the skittish Sylvia. When she told him they would start taking it slow, she was serious. Randall had never done so much wining, dining, cooking and courting to spend time in a woman's presence. Sylvia had shut him down cold. She accepted nearly all of his invites and extended her own to him but she was not giving him access to her bed or her body. They had a date for the coming Saturday, St Valentine's Day, and Randall had been certain she would allow him the pleasure of her sweetness. Now he feared that once she heard this news, she would keep him away. He knew sex should have been the least of his concerns based on the seriousness of the allegations in the correspondence before him, but he had his priorities and at the present time getting into bed with Sylvia was pretty much number one.

Randall considered not mentioning the investigation to Sylvia until after the holiday but thought better of it. There was a good possibility the agency had already contacted her and if they hadn't they would soon. He called Jerome, told him about the investigation, and invited him to a late lunch at Sugar's Place.

When he called Sylvia to set up a meeting for the close of business, she told him she was aware of the allegations and wanted Jessie to join them.

Chapter 21: I Saw Stars

Relaxing in the dining room at Sugar's, Randall and Jerome took in their surroundings and watched the staff close down the business for a Tuesday afternoon. The cousins had been waiting for a while but neither had much on their schedule for the next few hours so there was no rush. Jerome flirted shamelessly with Marilyn and the other female wait staff, causing the ladies to fall behind in their usually efficient shutdown process. Rudy and the two male employees were slightly annoyed but smiled and graciously tolerated the unwanted guests in the dining area.

Jerome was always overbearing when he dined at Sugar's but he was well-liked by all the staff and loved by their boss so he was definitely hands off. Randall was polite and friendly but commanded a great deal of respect by his demeanor. The two cousins flustered the staff when they came in together because they found it hard to make jokes and harass Jerome the way he liked when Randall seldom engaged in the banter.

"What did she do, call you and tell you she was ready to meet?" Randall asked Jessie when she showed up right on cue as Sylvia exited the kitchen and invited them into her office.

"No. I just know how things run around here. I've put in my share of hours in this place, young man," Jessie quipped then asked Jerome, "You joining us too, Romey?"

Jerome looked around somewhat doubtful. "I think that's why my cousin treated me to lunch today. Is it okay with you if I sit in?" He gave Jessie his sexiest smile.

Before Jessie could respond, Randall explained that he invited Jerome to sit in on the meeting because he might be able to help them out.

"That's fine with me as long as he can keep a secret," Jessie continued with the light kidding.

When they entered Sylvia's office and closed the door she informed them that Nathaniel would be joining them soon. At that moment Nathaniel knocked on the door and entered the office. "You're right on time," Sylvia told her stepson as he gave Jessie and her hugs and kisses.

Everyone except Randall grabbed a chair and after only a few moments of small talk they got to the reason for their impromptu meeting. "Well, this is a bit embarrassing and I thought about talking to each of you separately but decided we might as well be open about this whole thing. Both Jessie and Nathaniel have been called by a Mr. Reardon with the Texas Board of Accountancy," Sylvia began.

"Public Accountancy," Randall corrected her.

"What?" Sylvia asked with a frown.

"The Texas Board of Public Accountancy, that's the name of the agency conducting the investigation," Randall said.

"Whatever," Sylvia responded with irreverence, causing Jessie, Jerome, and Nathaniel to shoot questioning looks at each other as she continued. "Anyway, I have not been contacted, but Randall has received a letter from that agency. I guess the letter is the most reliable piece of information we have. Randall, would you mind telling us what this is all about. I'm sure we all know by now but just to make sure we have everything out in the open." Sylvia's voice trailed off as she ended this little speech with her face turned down toward her desk.

Randall gave the group the specifics of the allegations and told them the complaint was filed by Terence Solomon.

"That boy never ceases to amaze me," Jessie mumbled.

No one else commented, so Sylvia spoke, "So I guess we need to discuss what we should expect and how we can help Randall. Well first, Jessie, Nathaniel, I should have asked you guys this before I brought you all in here together but do either of you have concerns about the service Randall is providing our business and would you tell me if you did? I guess it is stupid for me to ask you this in front of Randall." Sylvia looked disgusted and shook her head at her blunder.

Nathaniel responded first. "Hey, I have no problem with Randall. He has saved us a boat load of money. I may not look at all the paperwork as thoroughly as I should but I went over everything pretty good yesterday and I don't know why Terence is wasting all of our time with this. The only thing I can figure is he wants to embarrass you, Sylvia. I thought he might be trying to get rid of Randall but what would be the sense in that? We'd just find another competent accountant."

Jessie just smiled at her young cousin, pointed to him, and said, "What he said."

Jerome tackled the elephant in the room. "How did Terence find out that you two are involved?"

Jerome's direct approach caught Randall off guard but that was the reason he brought Jerome along, to play devil's advocate. No one seemed to have an answer to his question. "Somebody had to tell him or he had to see you two together or something," Jerome concluded.

Nathaniel was a little put off at this point. He moved his gaze from Sylvia to Randall and asked, "So are you telling me there is something going on between you two? I mean, are y'all dating?"

"What rock have you been under?" Jessie asked.

"Does that make a difference to you, Nate?" Sylvia asked, looking directly at her stepson.

"Hell, nah. I don't care about that. I just didn't know. I thought Terence was pulling this stuff from his ass." Nathaniel checked himself, not meaning to show his much older female cousin any disrespect. "Excuse me, Jessie."

Jessie simply nodded in response, not willing to give him too much leeway.

Nathaniel's face turned into a huge grin as he looked from Sylvia to Randall. Jerome and Jessie were grinning also but Jerome got back to his question. "Is there any chance Gerald told him?"

"Believe me if I didn't know, Gerald didn't and he would tell me something like that." Nate got quiet for a moment and then said to Jessie, "You know Gerald is like Jermaine and Dad when it comes to gossip." Sugar and Jessie's youngest brother, Jermaine, loved to indulge in juicy gossip.

Nathaniel directed his next comments to Randall. "He would have told me if he had known you was hit" Nathaniel caught himself and cleared his throat, deciding that "hittin' it" might not be the best phraseology. "He would have told me. He doesn't know and he hasn't been contacted by the accounting people."

Now everyone in the room was curious as to how Terence became aware of the relationship between Sylvia and Randall. It wasn't unfathomable that someone saw the couple out together and mentioned it to Terence or an acquaintance of his, but it seemed unlikely. Nathaniel was only aware of a few people, outside of family, that Terence knew in the city. Terence was not a man that formed lasting friendly relationships.

Jessie asked, "Who besides the people in this room know you two have been spending time together."

"It's not a secret Jessie. We're not trying to be on the down low or anything like that. We just date sometimes," Sylvia answered defensively.

"What about people here at the restaurant? Is there anyone who would tell him? He seems kind of a ladies' man," Randall said.

"I'm pretty sure Marilyn and Miss Mildred are the only ladies working here who know Terence and Jim and Rudy are the only guys; none of them care for Terence. Marilyn says he gives her the creeps," Sylvia said.

"What difference does it make who told him? Sylvia just said it's not a secret." Nathaniel looked perplexed.

Jerome had his reasons and he knew he spoke for Randall. "Listen, man, I know we talkin' about your brother but we can't figure out how he knows something so personal about my cousin and Sylvia. That's a problem for me. Terence didn't accuse them of spending time together. His complaint is they are having an inappropriate relationship of a sexual nature." Jerome turned to Sylvia. "Not saying the relationship is inappropriate, Syl." He then addressed Nathaniel again. "You didn't know that and you live in San Antonio. Now how the hell would he know the nature of their involvement just by someone telling him Randall and Sylvia were out together?"

Randall was quiet. He did not want to scare Sylvia again but worried that Terence may have someone watching them.

"I go back to my original question. Who else knows the personal details of your relationship?" Jessie asked again.

Sylvia and Randall finally made eye contact. They had both been looking at each other and glancing away, afraid of what they may or may not have seen in the other's eyes but now they held the gaze. "My family knows," Sylvia admitted. "Debra, my mother, aunt, and Janice, they all talk a lot."

Jessie shifted in her seat as a way of conveying the message that she had a revelation. "Does Debra know Terence?" Jessie wanted to know.

"I don't think so," Sylvia answered hesitantly.

Nathaniel did remember a history between his older brother and Sylvia's cousin. "They know each other. Debra worked at the beauty supply store around the corner one summer when Terence was down here. She came in here pretty often. They talked a little bit. I remember that now."

Sylvia looked at Nathaniel and frowned as if she recalled events from the past also. She remembered that as the summer just before Randall went away to college, the same summer Debra decided Randall was too young for her and ended their relationship because she had fallen for an older guy who lived out of town. She started going to visit with some distant cousins in Houston every chance she got because that was where her new man lived. She called him "T". Sylvia had never met the mysterious "T" but she and Debra had started weaning off each other after Debra got so caught up in Randall. By the time her cousin started dating "T", Sylvia hardly saw her except during large family gatherings. It was not long before Sylvia was married and no longer invited to those gatherings so she never learned what happened to end the relationship between Debra and the older man from Houston. "Debra used to date an older guy in Houston she called "T". Sylvia finally admitted.

Randall remembered Debra's affair with the older man. "That's right, she did. Every time they broke up she would get in touch with me, but they must have had a big blow up right before I graduated because she came up and tried to start back up with me. That's right. You think that could have been Terence? Why doesn't anybody know about them?"

Nathaniel chuckled. "My brother is nothing if not ambitious. Sylvia, you met Lynette, his wife, at Dad's funeral didn't you?"

"I think so; I don't remember that day so well, there were so many people."

"I remember her, Miss Designer Everything, a big beautiful woman, lots of confidence and very friendly. I remember thinking 'friendly but deadly.' I'd almost forgotten Terence is married. That girl keeps a low profile. The funeral was the first and last time I met her because I wasn't invited to the wedding, you know." Jessie recalled her resentment at the slight she had been given by her cousin.

Nathaniel smiled as he recalled Jessie and Retha fussing to his father because they were excluded from the wedding and Sugar's complaints after they'd left his cousins that day. "Hell, I wish I could send them in my place. I sho hate to have to put on a suit and act like I give a damn about them people and act all happy. I hope this here girl is worth more than Terence and she can straighten him out 'cause she gonna be in a heap of trouble if she's a weak one," Sugar had said.

"Nah Jess, you got her with the "friendly but deadly." Lynette is a litigator and she is high speed. Terence tries not to cross her. The thing is, he tried to get her for a long time before she agreed to marry him, I mean years. If he is the man Debra was seeing in Houston, he was keeping Debra on the down low because if Lynette had gotten a whiff of her on his clothes, she would have dumped him. He had a couple of women down this way he would slip off and see. I think he still does, but Terence was determined to get Lynette. Not only is she high speed she comes from money. I think after she put him off so long, he fell in love with her. Once Lynn agreed to the marriage, he knew he had to get rid of those other babes or at least see them less often."

"Sounds like Debra and Terence might be back in contact, if they ever stopped having contact," Randall surmised.

Sylvia wondered if this was the case. Could Debra have been involved with Sylvia's nemesis all those years ago and kept it a secret for so long? Could they still have contact with each other and how did all this matter? "Who cares if Debra told Terence about us? It's neither of their concern."

"Sylvia, baby, we just need to be sure we don't have spies around here talking about stuff they have no business talking about. But since you are certain none of our people here at Sugar's would have done that, we have another concern." Jessie looked around at the three men in the room, none of whom wanted to say what that concern might be so she continued. "We don't trust Terence and we wonder if he's got someone watching you and maybe Randall. It doesn't sound to me like that's the case. Now it could just be somebody gossiping that meant no harm, but that also seems unlikely. If it is Debra, we can all breathe a little easier because she is a known entity. We just need to decide what if anything we want to do about her."

"Why would we need to do anything? So what if she told Terence you two are seeing each other? The damage is done, right?" Nathaniel didn't understand the concerns over Debra.

"Debra was the person who attacked Sylvia and gave her that shiner last Thanksgiving."

"Thanks Jessie," Sylvia said with sarcasm dripping from her words.

"Why'd she do that? What happened?" Nate asked even more perplexed.

"Over Randall. Debra dated him in high school and wants to get back with him." Jessie did not miss a beat in sharing Sylvia and Randall's private affairs.

"Oh, shit!" Nathaniel said, not even bothering to apologize for his language this time. "This is like bleeping reality TV or something. She just walked in here and clocked you Sylvia? You didn't even try to fight her back?"

Sylvia had her face down with her eyes closed and was using eight fingers to rub her forehead as her thumbs massaged her temples. There were four pairs of eyes on her and the heads encasing three pairs of those eyes wanted an answer to a question they had wrestled with for awhile now, "Why the hell didn't Sylvia beat that bitch down?"

Sylvia's shoulders began to move up and down and it looked like she was crying uncontrollably though no sound escaped her. Randall wanted to comfort her, they all did. As he started to move toward her, she looked up and surprised them with her laughter. She tried to speak but couldn't because she was out of breath. The others looked around at each other and wondered what Sylvia found so hilarious. They couldn't help but grin at her glee. Finally, with her eyes watering and between gasps for air, Sylvia squeezed out the words, "I saw stars." She then leaned back in her seat and covered her face with both hands and continued to laugh uncontrollably.

Jerome and Jessie joined her in laughter and Nathaniel grinned. Randall was the only person who found little humor in her words but even he had to smile.

"That heifa took something in those boney fingers of hers, made a fist, and hit me so hard, I hit the ground. Everything went black, blue, then orange. I actually saw stars. I think I was just glad to be alive when I could finally see clearly. Rudy had her out of here before I was off the floor. Then I was mad and ashamed that I hadn't got her back because if she had left me standing, I would have got her ass."

Sylvia shook her head thinking about what could have been if she just could have gotten up off that floor fast enough. "Ooh I wanted to get her for weeks after that but how would it have looked for me and Debra to be in here fighting over Randall? Couldn't you just see a KSAT reporter standing outside of Sugar's in front of a couple of squad cars reporting a domestic disturbance. Then me and Debra being escorted out in hand cuffs with our hair all over the place and me trying to hide my face and her cursing and screaming at me and the cops."

Sylvia put her hand up to her mouth and pretended she was holding a microphone "We are here on the Northeast Side of San Antonio just outside a well known local eatery where a serious altercation has just taken place. Employees of Sugar's Place tell us that the problem was between two female cousins, one of which is a co-owner and manager of the restaurant. That's the big one with the nappy hair on the left. It seems one cousin accused the other of sleeping with her man and then all hell broke out. Fortunately, no one was seriously injured. From the looks of them, I'd say the only thing wounded is their pride and that a trip to a hair salon is needed much more than a trip to the hospital. This is Marilyn Moritz reporting for KSAT News. Back to you, Mike."

Sylvia had everyone except Randall in tears at this point. Randall could only stare in amazement. This was a side of Sylvia he had no idea existed.

"Yep, me and Debra rolling around on the ground over Randall." Sylvia looked at the man in question and gave him a sly smile. "Not to say he ain't worth it."

Randall who was standing with both his arms and legs crossed and leaning with his back against the wall finally moved from that spot. "Stop it," he told Sylvia and left the office.

Sylvia wiped her face and nose and tried to contain her laughter but found it hard because the others kept cracking up.

Randall returned to the office with a pitcher of ice water and some cups. He poured out two glasses and handed them to the ladies before he poured a glass for himself.

"What about us, man? You not gonna serve us any water?" Jerome grinned and teased his cousin who perched casually on the edge of Sylvia's desk.

"I got you, man," Nathaniel helped himself and poured out a glass for Jerome also.

Randall tried to get back to the business at hand. "If Debra is the one who told Terence about us, that's two things she's done to get at you, Sylvia. I'm afraid she may try another tactic if she doesn't get any satisfaction from this investigation. We need to stop her now. As far as the investigation goes, if we stop doing business together that will most likely squelch any further inquiry."

"What if we don't want you to quit? You've done a good job for us and we'd like to keep you on." Jessie spoke for the others.

"Believe me, I prefer to keep you as a client but if for some reason they decide to conduct a thorough investigation, you will all want to discontinue my services. This type of investigation can cause a lot of trouble. The agency has very little to go on and may decide they want to dig really deep. I can't deny my relationship with Sylvia, so half the allegation is true. If the investigator decides to do everything possible to prove the other half, we are looking at a really invasive process. There is nothing for them to find, but they can still make a big mess digging."

"How long does an investigation like this last?" Sylvia asked seriously, with no sign of the laughter she displayed just minutes earlier.

"I really don't have any firsthand knowledge of Texas investigations. I know the ones in Maryland and DC could go on for months. There are a lot of variables. If the investigators have a lot of work or other cases they deem more important, a case like this one could go by pretty quick but first they have to get to it. If they are backlogged we could be waiting some time for them to even start an extensive investigation, if that's what they decide to do. I'm sure there are timelines they must follow. I'm the one that will be in limbo during the process waiting for their findings and decisions."

"What can we do to help in the mean time?" Nathaniel asked.

"Get your brother to withdraw his complaint," Randall laughed and stood up from the desk. "No, I guess the most any of you can do is be honest when questioned and provide the investigator any requested information as quickly as possible. We don't want to upset the investigator."

"So, if Terence were to withdraw his complaint, you think it would go away?" Sylvia asked.

Randall appeared thoughtful for a moment before he answered. "I don't see why it wouldn't. I doubt he has provided any documentation to back up his allegations that our relationship has caused a conflict of interest that has benefited you to the detriment of the other owners. Our relationship is not a problem as long as the co-owners, your partners, do not believe it benefits you unfairly. If Terence withdraws his complaint stating that he is now satisfied there was no unfair benefit to you, I'm fairly certain the agency would end the investigation with a somewhat terse letter to him. I doubt we can expect him to drop the complaint though."

There seemed to be little else to discuss in regards to the pending investigation but Jerome had a question. "Didn't you offer to buy Terence out of this business? I thought he wanted to sell and move on. What happened with that?"

Nate took Jerome's question. "Yeah, well that seems to have died down considerably. We made them an offer and have not received a counter. I know Gerald has changed his mind. I think he felt that once he told me, I'd pass it on to the rest of you, which I did. Terence nor Cheryl have mentioned selling their interest in the business. Maybe they've come to their senses."

"Well, frankly I would much rather buy them out than to have to continue with the turmoil they've been causing this past year. It's hard for us to proceed with any plans toward expansion with Terence constantly creating trouble. I wish he would bow out so we can move on," Jessie complained as she stood up to leave. "You got anything else for us, Sylvia?"

Sylvia was caught off guard by the question. She had been thinking about Randall declaring he would resign as Sugar's accountant. "No. I'm good. You guys think we should meet again or what?" She directed the question to Randall.

"Let's see what comes up and go from there," he said.

As they started to leave Sylvia's office, Jessie stopped and spoke to Randall. "I hope you plan to wait awhile before quitting on us. I meant what I said about not wanting you to leave. I think we are in good hands and I know my sister and Nathaniel feel the same." She winked and patted him on the shoulder with a smile.

"Thanks, Jessie. I appreciate the vote of confidence," Randall responded with no commitment to stay on as their accountant or to leave.

Sylvia's cell phone began beeping. Before she answered she asked, "Randall, can you stay a few minutes? Did you and Jerome ride together?"

"No, he drove. What's up?"

Sylvia spoke to her caller. "Hey, this is a surprise. Hold on just a minute."

"Will you lock the front while I take this call?" she asked Randall.

Randall looked slightly put out but did as Sylvia asked. When he returned he found her talking in a near whisper with a smile on her face. Upon seeing Randall reenter her office, she changed her tone to a normal level and made plans to meet with her caller the following day.

"Who was that?" Randall asked.

"Just an old friend," Sylvia said evasively.

"Male or female?"

"You're not jealous are you, Randall? I thought I was the jealous one."

Randall sat down in front of her desk and watched her for a moment before answering. "No, I'm not jealous. Just curious with all the whispering and shit going on."

"If you're not jealous, why did you ask me if I was talking to a male or female?" Sylvia asked with a smile.

"Forget it, Sylvia. What did you want to talk to me about?" Randall said irritably.

Sylvia came around and leaned back against her desk, right next to Randall's seat. Her expression changed from playful to one of concern. "Are you seriously thinking about resigning as our accountant?"

Randall had little patience for Sylvia's concern that he might quit as their accountant. "Syl, I can get you hooked up with another CPA, a good one. That won't be a problem. I can keep an eye on things for you and review reports with you. You won't even know I'm not doing the work. Let's not make a big deal out of something so unimportant. This investigation is a big deal for me and it could cause some problems for the business. If my resigning as your accountant will squelch this thing then that's a small price to pay."

This was the first time Sylvia had seen Randall appear upset. Usually he was laid back and seemed to not have a care in the world. "Could this investigation hurt your business much?" she asked.

"No. There is nothing to this crap and they'll see that once they get started. I'm damn good at what I do and I'm not sloppy. They might learn a few things but, honestly, I'd prefer not to go through a full-fledged investigation for them to learn there's no substance to this bullshit." Randall got up from his seat and walked to the door and stood there facing it. He got angrier every time he thought about the hoops he'd have to jump through to accommodate the investigation because of personal vendettas against Sylvia and him. He should have known better than to get involved with Sylvia as her accountant, especially since there was already so much turmoil between the co-owners of Sugar's. He stepped into a quagmire with his eyes wide open.

Randall stood there with his hands on his hips and head held down for a moment hoping the tension in the back part of his neck would ease. The touch of hands gently gliding through his arms and around his waist moved his spirit ever so slightly. He couldn't help but be thankful when he felt Sylvia's head rest on his back. They stood there, silently feeling each other for a few quiet moments in time. When Sylvia started to remove her arms from around his waist, Randall grabbed them and held them in place, so she settled back in against him and began kissing him gently on his back. These unexpected caresses were like golden coins to a peasant and Randall did not want them to end. When he loosened his hold on her arms, Sylvia ran the tips of her fingers up and down his outer thighs as she kissed and gently bit his back through the thin cotton shirt he wore. As Randall faced her, she stood on her tip toes and kissed his neck, running her tongue to his Adam's apple, sucking and nibbling on it gently before kissing her way to his chin. Randall stood there with his head held back and relished those sweet intimacies. He didn't know what had brought this on but wanted to do nothing to stop it.

When Sylvia started pulling his shirt tail from his jeans, Randall considered stopping her but couldn't. He was caught up. "What are you doing, Sylvia?" he asked helplessly.

"Nothing," was her only reply as she smiled at him and started unzipping his fly.

Randall watched in blissful confusion as Sylvia dropped to her knees and took him in her mouth. "Wait, no wait! Damn, baby! What are you doing?"

Chapter 22: Revelations

Blackmail was an ugly word. Could it be considered coercion or something less sinister, Sylvia wondered. Whatever it was, it was ugly and hateful and she wanted no part of it. She contemplated her weakness and wished she was willing to ruthlessly go for the kill. That's what winners do. They use whatever tools available to strike down their opponents no matter how frail or weak. Sylvia's opponents displayed no sign of frailty or weakness and she feared the continued exertion of their ruthlessness, because she believed both possessed a limitless store of that particular trait.

There had been this tickling in Sylvia's brain that represented something she knew but only in pieces. The pieces had been trying to come together for awhile now but the edges remained blurred and did not fit well. Now that the fuzziness had cleared and the edges were well-defined those pieces of memory all fell into place and Sylvia wished for the bliss of ignorance.

When Randall's cousin Martha had asked Sylvia to meet that afternoon, Sylvia had suspected the meeting concerned Randall. Why else would Martha want to meet with Sylvia in such a clandestine manner? "Don't tell Randall you're coming by, Jerome either," Martha had told her. Sylvia had been certain she recognized the Chevy SUV parked in front of Martha's house but had still been caught off guard to find her cousin Janice visiting with Martha.

The ladies had greeted each other cordially and after Sylvia had taken a seat and was offered and received something to drink, Martha got to the point of the meeting. "Sylvia I want to tell you something but I don't want Randall or Jerome to know I told you. They both say I talk too much and Randall always tells me I have no filter – whatever the hell that's supposed to mean. You have no idea how much trouble I stay in with those two." Martha picked up the remote to turn off the television and then yelled at her two youngest children who were giggling and playing with each other to, "Stop running in and out of that kitchen and get that damn homework done," before she continued speaking to Sylvia. "They'd both be really mad at me about this, but when I heard them talking about all the mess that's been going on, I knew I had messed up again with my mouth."

"I don't understand. What mess are you talking about?" Sylvia asked, looking over at Janice for answers.

"I was really happy to see you with Randall that day after Thanksgiving. I think I would have shot him myself if he had started back up with Debra." Martha stopped, looked at Janice, and simply shrugged as a way of apology before continuing. "After I saw you guys together and could see how much he likes you -- and just let me tell you, I have known Randall my entire life and I have never seen him like anybody like he likes you -- well, I had to gloat it over Debra, so I called and told Charise. I knew that big mouthed cow would tell Debra. I knew she would."

"Oh. I wondered how Debra knew so quickly that I was seeing Randall," Sylvia said.

"It was me, but I couldn't tell Randall. He would have been so disgusted with me and I just don't know if I could have dealt with him like that, you know. But Sylvia, baby, I felt so bad when I heard him and Romey talking about Debra jumping on you the very next day after I opened my mouth. I'm so sorry that happened. My mother and auntie keep telling me not to be such a gossip and I know they're right. If I had any idea that cousin of yours would have done something so stupid I would have kept my mouth shut; I swear. I hope you can forgive me."

Relieved that Martha didn't have some heartbreaking revelation about Randall and amazed at the lady's sweet sincerity, Sylvia accepted the apology.

Having forgotten that Martha and Janice were friends from way back, Sylvia waited to hear why her cousin was present. Janice had sat through Martha's confession slightly teary-eyed but had not said a word.

Sensing Sylvia's curiosity about her cousin, Martha explained, "I called Janice and asked what I should do because I remembered how vicious Debra could be when it comes to men, Randall in particular. I wish I had remembered that before I started talking to Charise."

"Sylvia," Janice addressed her cousin in an eerily quiet voice, causing Sylvia to jerk her head around. "I want to stop Debra from bothering you. I'm sorry this happened to you, baby. You know Debra didn't tell us she jumped on you. Never said a word about that all while talking about you like you were the trashiest whore on earth for messing with Randall. She said she and Randall were back together until you stepped in. I just found out last night from Martha that Randall refuses to have anything to do with her. Aunt Dianne told us you claimed Debra jumped you but she also said you were lying. I know you've never been a liar and Debra lies about the time of day, but I just went along to keep the peace like always. I should have stood up to Debra, my mother, and yours a long time ago. Sylvia, I should have stayed closer when you needed me but I was so afraid of being left out in the cold myself that I tried not to worry about you. I didn't fit their mold either, but I clung to them. I thought they were all I had. I would have been better off if I had let go like you and went my own way." Tears were trickled down Janice's face and she stopped to wipe them away before continuing.

"That's enough of that," Janice declared as she straightened her posture and moved on. "I wanted to talk to you because I need you to know some things. This is harsh and cruel but sometimes the only way to stop mean, self-centered people is with their own style of warfare and Debra and Terence are waging war against you and we have to stop them."

--

The inclination to spend time with Ray Rutledge in order to glean some sage advice had steadily increased for Randall. He and Ray spent time together with little expectation of each other. Ray liked to talk and Randall was a listener, seldom forgetting anything he'd heard. This dynamic was likely another reason Ray often preferred Randall's company over that of his son, JT. JT talked just as much as his father and the two often spoke at the same time. Ray also had a soft spot for Randall because he was present in the young man's life back during high school when Randall lost his Uncle Jake. Understanding that Randall had lost his father as an adolescent and then his beloved uncle who had taken on the role of father, Ray grabbed hold of Randall, hugged him hard, and never let go. Randall held on tight. The embrace had worked to the benefit of both men.

The friends were sitting in the library of the Rutledge home when Ray, looking deeply concerned, said to Randall, "You know, I may have misjudged Maris. I think she really has a serious interest in you. You got any designs in that direction? I hate for her to just be wasting her time and get her feelings hurt again."

"To be honest, Ray, I'm pretty involved with someone else right now."

"With Sylvia, I know. She seems like a sweet girl and is real nice on the eyes too. That doggone Maris just don't have no real interest in white fellas. Mostly I've seen her with the Mexican guys. Her husband was one of them real fair Mexicans. I thank she only married him because he would pass Old Kleinholz's color test. That didn't last long and after the split she gave into her inclinations, the darker the better. She only dated one other black fella that I know of. JT is the only white boy I've known her to date."

Randall found Ray's gossiping humorous and was pleased to get some insight into Maris. She seemed to have taken on a nearly obsessive interest in him though they had spent little time together. "What about the guy she had at your Christmas dinner party? Anything happening there?"

"Nah, I'm pretty sure she brought him along because Karen told her you were bringing a date. I think she was fit to be tied when she saw it was Sylvia. I was downright ashamed of how Maris tried to embarrass the girl. That Sylvia holds her own pretty damn good, I'd say. She don't need no rescuin', that's for sure."

This observation made Randall laugh. He'd love to be Sylvia's hero and have her indebted to him. That was a most unlikely scenario.

Randall's thoughts turned back to Maris. "Hopefully Maris finds someone she likes to settle in with. She's a beautiful woman."

"You are right about that," Ray agreed. "You know, JT used to have quite the crush on her when they were kids. She wasn't so skinny then and had the most beautiful head of hair. Of course she straightens it now but back then it was a curly mass all over the place; just about the most beautiful thing you've ever seen. She and JT made quite a pair." Ray got up and headed over to his book shelves and reached for a picture album. "I believe this is the one."

He sat and flipped through the album for a bit and when he spotted the photos he was looking for, passed the album to Randall. On the page was an old photo of JT with Maris, looking like they might make a happy couple one day. Randall noticed that there were younger pictures of Maris on the previous page, so he flipped forward until there were no more shots of her and then turned back to the original page and back through the album. There were several more pages with photos of Maris with JT, Ray, other members of the Rutledge family, and some with people Randall did not recognize. On the last page of the album Randall saw several photos of Maris Kleinholz with the "other black fella" There was one with the couple posing on horseback and several shots around the pool. Randall sat and looked at the photos closely. He definitely had a better understanding of Maris by the time he left his old friend's home.

--

"Debra, I need you to come to the restaurant next Saturday to meet with me and Randall," Sylvia told her cousin.

"And why would I want to do that?" Debra responded angrily to the strange request.

"I want to get this mess straightened out. You and I are not talking. I don't know if you and Randall are talking or not but this is not working for me. Also, Debra, it would be best for everyone if you didn't tell Terence about this meeting. He and I are not on the best of terms and I guarantee you, he will screw things up. After we meet, dinner is on me. Eight o'clock at Sugar's, okay?"

Debra was at a loss for words. She wanted to curse Sylvia out like she had never cursed before. She wondered how Sylvia knew about Terence and what exactly she knew. One thing Sylvia was right about; Terence would screw things up given the chance. The invitation sounded more like a warning than a threat and Debra had to admit, if only to herself, she trusted her cousin Sylvia more than any one.

"Debra, will you be there?" Sylvia pressed.

"I'll think about it."

"I hope you come, Debra. I can't guarantee all this shit will blow up if you don't show but I am certain things will get better if you do."

--

"Terence, this is Randall Craig."

There was silence on the line for a moment as Terence got over the surprise of a call from this man he had only met once and despised. "What can I do for you?" he finally responded.

"I think you and I need to talk," Randall said.

Terence figured Randall must be desperate to call him with an active inquiry into his accounting practices taking place. Terence liked the rush of power this gave him. "I don't have anything to say to you, man. You shouldn't be calling me."

"Yeah, well I need to talk to you. I don't want any more trouble for me and especially not for Sylvia. She's been through enough. I believe we can get all these issues resolved."

"What can you do for me?" Terence asked, sensing victory near his grasp. He just needed to reach out and take it. He no longer cared about the business of selling the restaurant. Why cut off your nose to spite your face? That was a poorly planned scheme to get back at Sylvia. He'd rather ride in on her coat tails as they expand and make a mint. He would insist on overseeing a Houston location, maybe two or three, using his investors. He smiled to himself, certain Sylvia was crying "uncle." Having Randall walk away and leave Miss High and Mighty Sylvia flapping in the wind would be the icing on the cake. He knew she could easily get another accountant but doubted she would find one she enjoyed sleeping with as much as Randall. This could be quite a coup and Terence would be the one to close the deal that brought Sylvia down a notch or two.

"Sylvia will have to tell you what she is proposing but I think in the end you'll be relieved. You need to meet with me and Sylvia next Saturday at Sugar's at eight thirty. It will definitely be to your benefit. I think it best if you don't discuss this with the other owners until you and Sylvia come to an agreement."

"I'll see what I can do." Terence ended the call. Randall was certain he would show.

Chapter 23: A Valentine's Day Without Pressure

Taking a much needed five minute break to choke down half a sandwich, a banana, and glass of water, Sylvia sat at her desk near tears. She had deluded herself into believing she could get away from Sugar's before closing on Valentine's Day. She nearly gagged on a piece of sandwich upon hearing the unease in Randall's voice when he answered the phone. "I can't make it tonight, Randall. There is no way I can get out of here before closing. We are swamped."

"I thought you had a couple of extra people coming in to help out." Randall sounded upset.

"I did but we are busier than I thought possible. It's a mad house. We might run out of food. I'm sorry, Randall. Can we make it another time?"

"What time do you think you'll get out of there?"

"I would guess about nine thirty, as soon as we get the last guests out the door. I'll be so tired by then and it'll be too late for me to get changed and out someplace decent to eat."

"You're right about that." Randall hesitated and breathed deeply before he went on. "I hate to ask you for a favor but can you pass by here when you get off and take me to pick up my ride. I had some work done on it today and it took much longer than it should have. I could call a taxi I guess, if I have to."

Sylvia wanted to tell him "no" but felt she had already ruined his evening, so agreed to give him a lift. She was more than a little pissed when she hung up the phone. After all, she would have been working for over fifteen hours by the time she left Sugar's, yet Randall wanted her to play limo driver for him. "Damn there is no telling what time I'll get in my bed tonight," Sylvia complained out loud, then set aside her concern over Randall's inconsiderate request and headed back into Sugar's kitchen.

--

No sooner than Rudy unlocked the door of Sugar's to let out a young newlywed couple, Sylvia and Jazzy, the cashier, cleared the till for the day and Sylvia left. She grumpily started her car and instead of heading toward home went in the opposite direction toward downtown San Antonio. She attempted to lighten her disposition because she didn't want to appear upset with Randall although he was the main cause of her irritation. As she neared his home, she called him on his cell phone but got no answer. After trying his cell a second time she called his home phone but the call went straight to his voice mail.

Sylvia lost her resolve to hide her irritation with him as she rode the elevator up to his floor. Randall answered the door to a tired pissed-off Sylvia who didn't bother to step inside his home and barely looked at him. "I'm downstairs. Why didn't you answer your phone?" she barked before turning and heading back toward the elevators.

"Hey, wait a minute." Randall grabbed her arm. "Come in for a minute. I've got a couple of things I need to finish before we head out. I don't want you waiting downstairs for me," he said.

Incredulity pretty much summed up Sylvia's feelings at that point. Randall had been at home nearly all day while she slaved away at Sugar's and now he needed her to give him a ride to God knows where but wait for him to finish work he had had all day to complete before she could give him said ride. Sylvia never wanted to tell anyone off more than she did at that moment, but instead of going off she allowed Randall to pull her back into his condo.

"Did you eat?" he asked as he walked toward his office. "Have a seat. It won't take me long. You look really tired."

Sylvia didn't answer but sat on the sofa and grabbed a coffee table book of Ghanan photography to flip through as she waited.

"Do you want to get something to eat on our way?" Randall asked again.

"I'll just grab something out of the fridge at home when I get there. I'm too tired to stop." Sylvia didn't even bother to look up until she felt Randall's hand on her arm reaching for her.

"Come here; I need to show you something," he said.

"What?" she asked, not hiding her perturb.

Now Randall went mute and maintained a tight hold on her hand as he walked her into his bedroom and then into his bath, flipping a switch which did little to illuminate the room.

Sylvia had followed him with a big question on her face. When she entered the bathroom she noticed lit candles on the window sill and around the tub, fresh towels on the edge of the tub, a vase of red roses, and a bottle California Syrah with two wine glasses on a serving tray. Her eyes opened wide and mouth dropped open but not a sound escaped. A lovely string rendition of Erik Satie's Gymnopedie 1 flowed quietly over Randall's sound system.

Sylvia swallowed hard to keep from crying, turned toward Randall, and asked in a near whisper, "Is this for me?"

"It is. I thought since we couldn't go out we could just have a nice night here, if it's okay. I was worried you might have called and cancelled your sitter so I called her and asked if she'd stay. She said it's not a problem and for you to enjoy yourself and not worry about the kids."

Sylvia swallowed again as her eyes began to water. "This has to be the nicest thing anyone has ever done for me, Randall."

That beautiful man's heart began to ache hard as he watched tears stream down Sylvia's cheeks. He wrapped Sylvia up in his arms and said, "Hey, no crying. This is supposed to make you happy. I want you to climb in that tub. There's plenty of hot water so you stay in as long as you want. I picked up dinner from Central Market. Nothing fancy but I've been promised that my selections 'are exquisite.' That's a quote."

"I don't have any clean clothes. Do you have PJs I can borrow?" Sylvia mumbled in his shoulder.

Randall went to the bathroom counter and picked up two elegantly wrapped boxes and handed them to her. "Your Valentine's Day gift. I think you'll find all you need in these. This was a first for me. I mean I've bought lingerie before but – well open them and you'll see."

Sylvia sat down on the edge of the tub while Randall poured two glasses of wine. She started to open one of the gifts but he stopped her and asked her to open the larger box first. Inside Sylvia found a full outfit of clothing to include bra, panties, and sandals, all in the right sizes. She held up the mid length mitered skirt and delicate short sleeved cropped lace top. "Is this the type of thing you'd like to see me wear?" she asked.

"You don't like it?" he asked with disappointment on his face.

"It's all beautiful but how did you know my sizes? Did you call my mama?" Sylvia joked.

Randall smiled and answered proudly. "I guessed."

In the smaller box, there was a short sexy night shirt, house slippers, and body lotion.

"I hope those are okay. I thought about doing something a little more revealing but I want you to be comfortable and relax tonight. No pressure here, okay, baby."

The tears started to flow again. "Randall, I haven't even bought you a card, yet. I thought I'd have time. I'm so ashamed."

"Shut up and get in the tub. I'll come back and finish my wine with you, if that's okay. Then I want you to relax. Sleep if you want."

Sylvia was obedient and emerged from Randall's bathroom fresh and energized nearly two hours later. She found him stretched out on his sofa sound asleep. Before waking him, she looked around and saw a beautifully set table, a bottle of Champagne in a chiller, and even more roses. *Goodness, he went all out for me. How do I keep this man?*

She woke Randall and hoped he felt as rested as she. Sylvia had to insist Randall allow her to help get dinner on the table. They sat and lingered over a luscious meal of stuffed cilantro lime chicken breast, roasted red pepper pasta and a spinach and sweet hot house tomato salad. They drank Champagne and laughed nonstop, giving no thought to circumstances that caused them anguish just a few days before.

"Tell me, Mr. Craig, do you treat all your women so well?"

"What all my women are you talking about? I hate to disappoint, but you are my only woman, Sylvia."

"I meant women you dated before me. Am I really your only woman?"

Randall reached across the table and took Sylvia's hand. "Look at me, Sylvia." When he had her full attention, he said, "I have never gone to this extent to please any woman, not even my Aunts Zoe and Vi, and yes, you are my only woman."

Sylvia swallowed hard and fought back tears. She hated that she felt so emotional when it came to Randall but couldn't help herself. Randall was one exquisite man and he treated her well. He was the absolute best of Sean five times over and Sugar all rolled up in one man. Sylvia knew he had his faults but she hadn't seen them yet. She sat there and watched him watch her, feeling her heart ache as he held her hand across the table. Then Maxwell's "This Woman's Work" flowed out of Randall's system.

"Let's dance. We haven't danced since Luis and Olga's wedding." He pulled Sylvia to the floor and held her close as the music played. "You like me Sylvia?"

She nodded a yes into his shoulder.

"Good. I'd hate to think I did all this for you and you don't even like me, because I like you a lot, but I'm sure you know that."

"Randall?"

"Yes?"

"Please don't break my heart."

"I promise I won't break yours if you don't break mine first."

Randall stopped dancing and tilted her head back placing his mouth to hers. They stood in the middle of the floor kissing until he pulled away and began unbuttoning her shirt. Once the shirt was hanging open he reached inside, cupped one of her breasts, and gently ran his thumb across the nipple.

"You plan on taking advantage of me now. I can hardly tell you no after you've spent so much time and money on me today," Sylvia whispered, enjoying his touch. She then reached out and started removing his tee. No sooner than she had that shirt off, Randall pulled hers from her shoulders. He took two full steps back and looked at her as if he had never seen her before. Sylvia smiled at him, tilted her head to the side and asked "You like what you see, baby?"

Randall moved toward her but she backed away with her eyes glowing and a smile on her face as she looked him up and down. "Take your pants off first. I want to see you, all of you."

"You take them off for me," he said.

"Come on, baby. Take them off so I can see you," Sylvia pleaded seductively.

Randall loosened the drawstring on the pajama pants, lowered and stepped out of them before starting to move toward Sylvia again. She backed away again. "No, Randall. I want to see you," Sylvia told him as her smile grew with her approval.

"Show me yours and I'll show you mine," Randall bargained.

"I've been standing here with mine showing."

"Yeah but I want to see more."

"Ooh Randall, you're nasty."

Randall stepped toward her and caught her up in his arms and kissed her deeply as they pulled each other onto his large area rug.

He continued kissing Sylvia until he had her flat on her back. Then he sat up and said, "Let me see you Sylvia as he pulled on her bent knees.

"What will you give me," she asked playfully.

"Me, I'll give you me."

Randall positioned himself in front of Sylvia as she gave him a full view of all he desired at that moment. He put his middle finger in his mouth and wet it before using it to touch Sylvia in her most titillating spot, causing her to arch her back for more. "Oh, you like that don't you." he told her with a smile.

Randall got up after a moment and left Sylvia lying there with her body fully exposed. "I'll be right back," he said as went to his bedroom.

Sylvia lay there for a moment before getting up to refill their Champagne flutes. She entered the guest bath, relieved herself and sat there for a moment, thinking about how much she loved being with Randall and wishing she could spend time like this with him whenever she wanted. She found him waiting for her when she returned.

Randall eyed Sylvia as she moved from the bathroom, through his living room, on to the kitchen where she retrieved their Champagne flutes, walked over to Randall and kneeled on the floor beside him. He accepted the flute of Champagne she offered, then leaned forward, taking one of her breasts in his mouth and gliding his tongue across the nipple.

"You want to get in the bed," he asked when he pulled back.

"Maybe later. I like it here. It's different for me." She smiled at him as she sat back, crossed her ankles, and hugged her knees up to her chest, all her inhibitions hidden.

Sylvia was experiencing something new and Randall wanted to savor each moment. He kept his eyes on her with his excitement rising and his body growing hard. Sylvia took a drink from her glass, got on her knees, leaned across his chest and kissed him deeply. She pulled back slightly and ran her tongue across his lips before moving her mouth to his neck.

Randall loved the play but simply could not participate any longer. He produced a condom from Sylvia knew not where. Once his protection was in place he laid back, grabbed Sylvia by her arm, pulling her on top of him and entering her at the same time. She sat there straddling Randall and taking deep breaths. He held onto her butt as he tried to control himself but couldn't. Randall started to move inside Sylvia but she barely moved with him. After a few minutes, he stopped and rolled over on top of her. They laid there for a moment and then Randall began to kiss her, moving his mouth from her face to her breast then her stomach. He ran his tongue around her belly button before having her turn over onto her stomach as he knelt next to her. His eyes moved along the curvatures of Sylvia's back and butt to her shapely thighs, all the way down her calves. He followed the trail blazed by his eyes with his fingertips and then his lips and tongue softly caressing each sweet spot.

Sylvia turned her body and pulled on his arm. Randall quickly heeded her request and within a matter of seconds was sliding his body inside hers. Neither could hold back any longer and both fully yielded to their desire for the others body. Sylvia fought to hang on with Randall, determined not to reach her goal before her lover. This was an endurance race not a sprint and Randall was winning. He watched her, knowing she couldn't outlast him and smiled as he remembered her gift to him just a few days before. The thought brought him closer to the end. He slowed down and began to withdraw but Sylvia locked her thighs on his hips and yelled "Don't stop now," causing him to move inside her more forcefully than before. Sylvia closed her eyes and began moaning loudly. Her heated noises excited Randall and he felt his own release approaching much sooner than he wanted. There was no stopping it so he gave in and went for it with every ounce of energy he had left, holding on to Sylvia's thighs as if he needed to carry her across the line with him. The lovers collapsed with their bodies melded together as they laid there breathing hard and sweating on each other.

"My backside hurts," Sylvia complained.

Chapter 24: They Know

The Spurs game was set to record but Robert Polanco was not sure when or if he'd get to watch the game. His wife, Jessie, was dragging him off to meet up with the other owners of Sugar's Place. Since Retha and Jaren had invited him and Jessie to visit with them in Tampa for a week, this game may be lost to him forever. If he learned the score before he had a chance to watch the game, he wouldn't even bother putting it on. Such was the life of a sports junkie.

As much as he hated missing one Spurs matchup during the eighty two game season, his pleasure at attending the New York Liberty preseason games for the next week far out-weighed his disappointment. Of course his "brah-in-law" would be on the field or in the dugout but Jaren's father, Charles, would keep Robert company in the stands. Jessie had declared she might attend a game and he graciously feigned excitement at the prospect of her company.

Robert just wished he didn't have to forego tonight's Spurs versus Oklahoma City Thunder game to accompany Jessie to some fru fru event at Sugar's.

--

Jaren Daniels had, just days before, listened to his overly cranky, newly pregnant wife tell him, "I need your clout by way of your presence. I just need you to be there, do what I say, and don't look too friendly."

Jaren had laughed at Retha's demands. This was their second child and he had always regretted that he and Retha were not together during the first two trimesters of their first pregnancy. Jaren now considered that separation may have been a blessing in disguise. For all his wife's moodiness and foodiness due to her inability to keep most foods down, he was as happy as ever. The preseason was just kicking off, his appetite was just fine, and there was a baby on the way; life could not be better.

Retha and Jaren Daniels, accompanied by Jaren's sister, Rachelle, climbed aboard their chartered flight for San Antonio at five thirty eastern standard time and touched down at their destination at five minutes after seven central time. They stepped from their flight dressed for the evening and headed straight to the home of Jessie and Robert Polanco.

--

A dinner invitation from Ray Rutledge caught Maris slightly by surprise. He had called a day before and questioned her about her plans for that Saturday. When he learned she had none, he asked her to leave the evening open and said he'd get back to her. He was pretty jovial when he called back and asked her to join Karen, Randall, and him for dinner, explaining that Karen had been pestering him about dining at Sugar's and he had just confirmed that Randall would be available to join them. "You know it won't be a party without you, sweet pea. How bout it?"

Having kept her night free as requested, Maris accepted his invitation. Ray had offered to pick her up but she chose to drive herself. She might get lucky and get an invite to drop in at Randall's home afterwards; a girl needed some flexibility. Obviously, he and Sylvia had cooled down some; otherwise, she doubted Randall would want to dine with her at Sylvia's place of business.

--

When Terence Solomon pulled up to Sugar's Place, he found the parking lot nearly full of cars. It was surprising to see so many cars when the place closed at nine o'clock. As he walked up to the restaurant entrance, Terence was stopped by a young man in a San Antonio Police Officer uniform. "Excuse me sir, are you attending the private party," the officer asked.

"I'm one of the owners of this place. I'm here on business."

"Your name, sir?" the policeman said.

Terence did not like this one bit. If the guy were a regular rent-a-cop, he'd probably refuse to give his name but the real cop uniform and real cop gun made him more cooperative. "Solomon, Terence Solomon. What's going on?"

"There's no problem, Mr. Solomon. I can only allow the invited guests of the private party through the front. I was instructed to ask you to enter through the back. Ms. Solomon is expecting you," the officer explained.

"Thanks." Terence headed to the back of the business and nearly fainted when he walked upon Jerome standing outside the kitchen door apparently waiting for someone. Terence looked around anxiously, wondering if he was being set up and felt nothing but relief when he saw Robert Polanco and Jaren Daniels exit the kitchen door.

"Terry, hey dude. What's going on? I ain't seen you in ages," Robert declared with real pleasure.

Terence was not only relieved but genuinely happy to see Robert who was the only person that could get away with calling him "Terry." Terence shook the older man's hand and accepted a light bro hug.

"You two know each other?" Robert looked from Jerome to Terence and the two men nodded without comment.

"Have you ever met my brother-in-law, Jaren? Jaren this is Uncle Sugar's oldest boy, Terence."

Jaren extended his hand and looked Terence straight in the eye. There was no smile on his lips and his eyes were not friendly. "What's going on man? I knew your father well, a good man," Jaren said.

Terence remembered seeing Jaren at his father's funeral and wanting to meet the superstar baseball player but the man had been so distant looking he didn't try to approach him. "Yeah, I remember seeing you at the funeral," he said coolly. He then turned his attention to Robert. "I'd like to stay and catch up but I've got to get inside and meet with Sylvia. We'll talk later."

After Terence went inside the building, Robert looked at Jerome and asked, "What's that cat doing here? What's Sylvia up to?"

Jerome rendered only a shrug in response.

Upon hearing Sylvia's "come in," Terence entered her office to the surprise of his life in the form of a very timid looking Debra. "What the hell are you doing here?" he asked Debra and then threw an accusing look at Sylvia. "What kind of bullshit are you trying to pull, Sylvia?"

At that moment Randall walked in and closed the door behind him. "Glad you could make it, Terence. Pull up a seat," Randall said.

"Kiss my black ass. I'm leaving," Terence barked at Randall and turned toward the door.

"No, don't go, Terence, please!" Debra pleaded.

Terence glared at her with disbelief before turning to look at Sylvia who was seated at her desk. "What the fuck is going on here? I thought we were here to talk about the business."

"We are, Terence. Why don't you sit down and we can get this over with in a few minutes," Sylvia told him.

Terence took the seat between Debra and Randall and leaned back with his ankles crossed and finger's intertwined on his chest. "Okay, Sylvia. Your boy here tells me you want to get things resolved; let's start resolving shit."

Sylvia looked at Debra but remained quiet.

"They know, Terence," Debra spoke in a low voice.

"Know what?" Terence asked, not even bothering to look at his old girlfriend.

Now it was Debra's turn to look at Terence in disbelief. "You know what. Don't try to act like you don't know what I'm talking about."

Terence jumped up as if he would snatch Debra out of her seat as he yelled at her. "What did you tell them?"

"Sit yo ass down man." Randall placed a strong hand on Terence's shoulder. Terence jerked away and wanted to swing on Randall but the look in the eyes that met his dared him to take that swing.

"Debra hasn't told us anything. Actually, I've been doing most of the talking and I'm tired of talking, but I will tell you that I know you and Debra dated and there are reasons, one very serious reason in particular, you two have kept that relationship quiet all these years." Sylvia looked at Debra who looked awful. She had cried earlier and the tears were flowing again.

"So what is this, some type of blackmail or what?" Terence looked directly at Sylvia.

"No, I wouldn't do that to Debra or her son. They are my family but you have put me and Randall in an uncomfortable position. Now we have information that will allow us to repay the favor in spades, as Sugar used to say, but we won't. We do, however, want to lay everything out on the table in the hopes that you will reconsider your complaint against Randall."

Sylvia now directed her attention to Randall. "Debra says she had nothing to do with the complaint filed against you."

Debra quickly spoke up. "I swear I didn't, Randall. I'd never do that to you. I decided weeks ago to let it go." She dropped her head feeling ashamed of her thoughts but decided to share them. "I figured I would wait it out and that you'd get tired of Sylvia soon enough."

Not bothering to respond to Debra, Randall asked Terence, "Who told you about me and Sylvia."

"Is that supposed to be some big secret or something? Don't nobody give a damn about you and Sylvia. I got better shit to do than worry about you two."

"So why the complaint to the board, if you care so little about me and Sylvia," Randall asked.

"I was just trying to get even." Terence looked at Sylvia. "You turn my stomach, Sylvia. Marrying an old man and talking him into leaving everything to you that should have been left for his children. You're a disgrace."

Terence's words were harsh but Sylvia had always known his feelings. Randall on the other hand was ready to take Terence to task until Sylvia stopped him with her hand in the halt position.

"I'm a disgrace. You have got a lot of nerve calling me a disgrace. I may be a lot of things but disgraceful is not one of them," was Sylvia's cool retort.

"Oh, maybe I used the wrong term. What you are is a," Terrance began.

"Man if you are not careful you're not going to have a tooth left in your fucking head when we leave this office," Randall told Terence who tried to blow off the threat but visibly squirmed in his seat.

Sylvia gave Randall a "are you finished" look then lit into her stepson. "Terence. I have no idea why you hate me so much but it really doesn't matter. I know now that I deserve all the good things that have come into my life and that includes your father. I would never try to deny that my life is much better since I met and married Sugar."

"Yeah and you made a lot of damn money once you whored yourself out to him," Terrence spat out the words.

At this point, Sylvia had to run around the desk to make Randall let go of Terence's shirt collar. Debra jumped in front of Terence and backed him into her seat.

"I ain't afraid of you mothafucka. We can take this outside right now," Terence barked with the two women separating him and Randall.

Randall realized the meeting was getting out of hand and there was only so much he could do in Sylvia's tiny office without endangering Sylvia and Debra, so he stepped back and took a seat before speaking very calmly. "Terence, I don't need you to be afraid of me. I'm going to say this just one time. If you call Sylvia out of her name again I'm going to let you. I won't stop you from saying anything you want. We not gonna fight or even sell wolf tickets over these ladies. So if you want to get shit off your chest at Sylvia's expense, you go for it. I just need you to know, you've used your last pass on that. We'll deal with it when we leave this office."

The men were making the task at hand difficult. Sylvia knew she couldn't keep them closed up in her office much longer but she had to get some things off her chest. "Terence you can call my relationship with Sugar whatever you like because you can't change what it was. I loved your father and he loved me and yes my life changed for the better once we married. But what I know now is my life would have gotten better with or without Sugar because I was determined to make it better.

"When your father got deathly ill, I had just started classes to finish my degree, but my husband needed me with him. Where were you, Terence? I saw you twice during the five months Sugar suffered and died. He was so mistrustful of you that he insisted me, Retha, Jessie, or Robert be in the room when you came to visit. He didn't trust you."

These words took the fight out of Terence who had never dealt with the state of his relationship with Sugar before his death. He sat staring at Sylvia and clinched his teeth. He had no defense.

Sylvia was determined to speak her mind to the stepson who was the least helpful during Sugar's illness and had caused her the most trouble since his death. This would likely be her last opportunity to express these feelings. "For months, until Jaren hired nurses, I sat up every night with my husband and nursed him. I bathed him, changed his diapers, fed him, did my best to make him comfortable, and loved him. He was safe with me. Where were you?"

Terence could no longer look at the others in the room.

"When he groaned in pain, I was there searching, always searching for something to make him feel better. I dealt with his crankiness just glad he could speak that day. Where were you, Terence?"

Sylvia moved back behind her desk and stood there for a moment, thinking there was no point in saying all the things she wanted to convey to this selfish man, but the words would not cease. "Just before he died, he asked for you. 'Think he'll come see me?' He could barely speak above a whisper. Imagine how amazed I was when he said 'Terence.' I asked if he wanted me to call you and all he could do was nod a yes. I called but couldn't get you on the phone. I left you a message that your father was asking for you. I also told you in that message that I didn't think he had another full day. He was better that next evening after I told him I'd called you. I thought he might make it a while longer. The next morning he was gone."

Sylvia stared at her stepson, wanting him to say something that might make this situation better. "Thank God I had plenty of help taking care of Sugar while he was ill, your brothers; Jessie; Retha; Robert; Jaren; even Lizzie would make a point of coming and sitting with Sugar when she was home from school. But you and Cheryl never offered any help in any way. I almost understand Cheryl because she never spent a night in her father's home. They had no relationship but he still thought enough of her to leave her in his will. I believe you both owed him so much more than you gave."

Feeling exhausted, Sylvia sat down at her desk. "I gave your father everything I had to give and I'd do it again. He wanted me to be safe and happy and I work real hard to make good things happen in my life. Sugar told me life requires a lot of work, you can't just sit and let it pass you by. You should be thankful your father saved me, because he could have saved a sorry woman and things could have turned out much worse or he could have been alone. I am a good woman and Sugar was a damn good man. You should try to be half the man he was."

The room was quiet until Randall got up to leave telling the others, "We need to finish this."

--

By the revelry of the partiers out in the front of Sugar's Place, no one would have believed the war going on in the tiny office at the back of the building. Sylvia's guests were having a ball at the expense of Randall and five of the restaurant owners. There was plenty of food, wine and beer and all for free. The amazing thing was that most of the people had no idea of the occasion. Sylvia explained to the owners that the party would help bring some resolution to the recent complaint filed at the Texas Board of Public Accountancy and help resolve the concerns over the ownership of the eatery. Most of the other guests were there because Sylvia or Randall had invited them to a party at Sugar's Place with the only stipulations being to dress to impress, be nice, and party hard. The hint that the Major League Baseball player Jaren Daniels would be in attendance assured a full house.

By the time Randall walked out of Sylvia's office, Ray, Karen, and Maris had been waiting for him nearly forty minutes, but he had not been missed. Jaren had pulled a chair up to their table and done a fine job of entertaining them. Robert and Jessie also joined them at the table for a while. Retha stayed away because she didn't want to distract her husband from the task at hand. She sat a few tables away and watched him work his magic. At some point she thought he might be enjoying the flirting with Maris and Karen a bit much but she just sucked it up and drank some more lemon flavored water.

Ray Rutledge had left his table a couple of times and chatted up other guests. He spent a good amount of time with his old friends, Izola and Viola and made a date to go to Izola's for dinner. He took particular note of Jessie who flashed him a smile and introduced herself as one of the owners of Sugar's Place. Ray spent ten minutes complimenting her on his new favorite place to eat. He was a little disappointed later when Jessie showed up at his table holding Robert's hand but kept flirting with her anyway.

So no one felt Randall had been remiss when he returned to the table because they were all having a very good time. "You think I can steal Maris for a moment," he asked Karen and Ray as he touched Maris on her shoulders to get her attention. She was quite flattered and failed to notice the look of concern that crossed Ray's face when Randall asked to steal her.

"I've got some people I want you to meet with," Randall told Maris.

Ray understood that Randall was certain Maris was behind the complaint against him at the state. When Randall had told Ray his suspicions, Ray had hoped rather than believed Maris would not pull such a dimwitted vindictive act but he had known her since her birth and was well aware of her capacity to be malicious.

The blood left Maris's face when she entered Sylvia's office and saw Terence Solomon sitting there with no fight left in him. She looked around and did not recognize Debra who she had only seen once before "What's going on?" she asked.

"Sit down Maris; we won't keep you long." Randall told her in a soft kind voice.

Maris considered turning and leaving the room but her feet felt too heavy. She looked toward Sylvia but did not see her. Her eyes glassed over.

Randall explained, "Maris we are putting everything out on the table tonight. What we want is for no one in this room to remain under the thumb of anyone else. A week or so ago I learned that you and Terence dated some years back. We have been trying to figure out why Terence would file a complaint against me with the board of public accountancy. Did you have anything to do with that complaint?"

"Why would I do that? I never told Terence to do any such thing," Maris protested.

"No, she didn't," Terence confirmed. "She made a special trip up to Houston to ask me if I could get Sylvia to stop seeing you. She thought I had sway. When I told her that me and Sylvia don't care for each other she got pissed and told me that I had better think of a way to separate you and Sylvia or she would make sure Lynette found out that Trevon is my child. Told me how one night when me and her were together she saw me looking at the ultra sound and smiling before I folded it up and put it in my wallet. Said she heard me later on that night on the phone with Debra asking her to get rid of the baby. I guess while I was sleeping that night, she went in my wallet, found the picture of the ultra sound with the little arrow pointing to Trevon's penis," Terence chuckled sarcastically at this point, then continued, "and made a copy. Waived it in front of me like it was a piece of candy in that hotel room. Up until then I didn't know she knew about Trevon. When I told Debra, she freaked. Said Trevon would be devastated if he learned we had been lying all these years and that her ex is not his real father." He looked at Debra then at Randall. "She begged me to do something. I didn't think the complaint would work but at least it kept Maris quiet for a while."

Terence leaned back in his chair, closed his eyes, placed both hands on his head, and began massaging his forehead and temples. The room was quiet as everyone watched his actions. "I'll withdraw the damn complaint first thing Monday." Without another word to anyone, Terence got up to leave the office. No one tried to stop him.

Everyone's eyes were on Maris during Terence's confession. She had her head bent forward so her face was completely shrouded by her hair. Sylvia knew she was crying.

"Randall, would you excuse us ladies?" Sylvia said.

Randall sent her a questioning look but respected her request. He found Terence standing outside the door leaning on the wall with his head back. Randall joined him but they didn't speak. They stood in silence. Randall was relieved. He could see the light now and knew he and Sylvia were emerging from the muck that had encapsulated their relationship from the beginning.

Terence looked over at Randall and wanted to ask his advice. He wanted to ask, "Man, how to you stay so clean and keep your head above water?" but he would not dare ask something he considered so juvenile. He and Randall were different people and came from different backgrounds. Terence couldn't help but stand there and reflect on his life. He had no children that he could openly claim. He loved his wife and they had a great sex life but that's about where it ended. He worked hard at making a living in his financial services business but didn't know how to live well and was too proud to ask for help. His mother begged nonstop and their relationship was difficult during the best of times. He let his father die without ever telling him he loved him. He had lost the respect of his most beloved brother. He looked at Randall and declared, "I could use a drink."

"Come on; I'll buy you one," Randall offered.

--

Once Randall left the office, Sylvia held out a box of tissue to Maris. "So Maris, how can we get you to keep my cousin's secret?"

The lady slowly raised her head and took the tissue. She looked from Sylvia to Debra as she blew her nose. "You two are cousins? Y'all sure don't look alike."

Both cousins smiled at this observation. "Well, we are cousins and we like the same man." Debra attempted to make light of the situation.

Maris looked at Debra and asked, "You like Randall too?"

Debra answered, "We dated in high school. He don't want me anymore."

"Don't feel bad, honey. He never wanted me," Maris told Debra.

Maris was quiet for a minute until the tears stopped streaming down her face. She asked Debra, "I bet you never knew anything about me before all this, did you?"

"No, no I didn't." Debra shook her head.

"I knew about you and I sure knew about the lovely wife, Lynette. I was the least important of all. He would call you both and didn't care if I knew. I just accepted it to keep him coming around but once he and Lynette got engaged I hardly saw him for a while. Then he started back calling and I just couldn't resist that charm. I wanted to throw him out of my house when I realized he was seeing you again too. I was so jealous about your baby. That is the one time I seriously considered confronting him. But I knew I'd get my chance to hurt him. We stopped having sex after I found out about your baby. I only called him about business after that but he always stayed in contact. I guess you could say we became allies. Last year he called and wanted me to invest in this place; I agreed. Then I met Randall and I wanted him. I tried to hold back and not be so aggressive but Randall knows what he wants and it sure ain't me." Maris looked at Sylvia as if she was conceding victory.

What she said next freed Debra from weeks of worry "I would have never told that. I just get so desperate when it comes to men. I pick the wrong ones and I'm so bull headed I always try to make things be the way I want them. I shouldn't have threatened Terence the way I did. I think I wanted a fling in bed with him more than anything when I made that trip to Houston. He wasn't interested and I was angry. I'm lucky I didn't end up dead, threatening him that way." She looked at Debra and said, "You don't have to worry about me and I know I'm not the one to give advice but I can't see how you can live under the weight of this lie for the remainder of your life. You even have to worry your boy might find out after you're dead and gone."

Debra began crying for the third time since she'd entered Sylvia's office.

There had been enough soul-wrenching speeches to last a good month or two and Sylvia wanted to end the group meet session. She encouraged both women to fix their makeup and after fifteen minutes of primping all three ladies exited Sylvia's office with no sign of the marathon struggle they had just endured.

Debra was pleased to see her mother and sister present and shocked at the scope of the party taking place at Sugar's. Sylvia's aunt gave her a big hug and said, "I told your mother you'd get this straightened out. I knew you wouldn't stay mad at Debra long. You have always been the peacemaker." Sylvia held on to her aunt, happy for the affection, and looked over at her cousin Janice. They passed winks and smiles.

When Sylvia left her aunt and cousins, she was grabbed from behind by Retha. "Can I go home now, Syl. I'm so tired."

"Oh, I'm sorry, baby. How early are y'all leaving tomorrow?"

"Jaren and Robert are taking the charter back but I'm sleeping in. I'll fly out late tomorrow afternoon with Jessie and Rachelle. Jaren's mother has Morning and I already told her I won't be in until late tomorrow. Maybe I'll get to see you before I leave."

"Yeah, we have to talk. You guys flew all the way here to help and I think everything is working out fine but we'll talk about it tomorrow. Call me when you get up and I'll come over.

Sylvia watched as Retha and Jaren told everyone goodnight. Their departure was the catalyst for the other guests to start winding down and clearing out. Nathaniel came up, gave her a hug, and told her Terence was spending the night with him. He was so pleased you'd have thought he had just won season tickets to the Spurs games.

Chapter 25: That Special Dinner

It was well into summer before Sylvia had Randall at her home for the special meal she had promised him months earlier. She had invited him on two previous occasions but Randall refused to let her cook for him until her children would be present for the meal. "How am I supposed to cook something special for you and satisfy my kids? They complain at every meal because one, the other, or all three don't want to eat something on the table. Now I have to try and please them and you too. It will never happen."

Randall looked at her and smiled with that laid back manner of his and told her to "Just cook something they'll like. I'm easy to please. You should know that by now with the little attention you give me. I'm happy with whatever I can get from you."

"I thought this was supposed to be special for you."

"And if you cook it, it will be. I just want the kids there too."

So, although Sylvia, Randall, and her children spent a good deal of time together; dinner at her home, prepared by her, was as evasive as a cool summer night in San Antonio.

Pondering the question of what to prepare for this monumental meal, Sylvia asked the children what they would like. They were each a bit put off by the question. I mean their mother actually cooked dinner for them once or twice a week. Their sitter, their father, and their stepmother also cooked meals for them and when no one cooked they went out or ate take out. What made this question odd was that Sylvia had learned ages ago not to ask her children what they would like to eat; there was no consensus. Now if she asked them separately she might have a slim chance of agreement, but asking the three of them at the same time was sheer foolishness and resulted in quite the argument. If you did not know better, you might think Sylvia was intentionally trying to start trouble between her children.

So, dinner for Randall and the children proved to be quite the challenge. Sylvia was thoroughly stressed by the time her guest of honor arrived at her home with roses and wine for her and Ben and Jerry's and a new video game for the children.

The menu consisted of a roasted tomato salad, vegetable fried rice and Tandoorie chicken which she had made for her children before and knew they all liked. Justin loved the roasted tomato salad but Billy and Bertani only tolerated it; two out of three wasn't bad when it came to Sylvia's children. Homemade brownies and ice cream were dessert.

As a special treat, Sylvia served dinner on the patio. Bertani was so excited about the dinner party that she had remained in the kitchen with her mother all afternoon and had been more help than Sylvia would have guessed. The brothers had been well-behaved and helped when called upon. Justin, very much aware of his mother's jitters, remained at the ready with any assistance he could provide.

Once they settled in at the table everyone was eerily quiet and concentrated on their food. Billy was the first to break the silence by declaring "This is really good, Mom." Bertani nodded her head and gave Sylvia a greasy thumbs up. Justin agreed, "It sure is." Randall just smiled. Sylvia beamed and told her children thank you.

The table got progressively noisier as stomachs filled and mouths became less so. The children were ecstatic and talking nonstop by the time they finished eating.

Randall leaned back in his seat and asked, "How did you know Tandoorie chicken is my favorite?"

"I didn't." Sylvia grinned. "Did you like it?"

"I think it was the best I've ever eaten. That was a delicious meal, really special." Randall smiled at her with that special look Sylvia had begun to recognize as hers alone.

"Wow! Thank you. That's some compliment," she said.

Sylvia and Randall sat there and gazed at each other across the table, forgetting about the children for a moment.

"Can we have dessert now, Mom?" Billy asked.

"Help me clear the table and get these dishes in the dishwasher. Then we'll have dessert."

The children dove into their brownies and ice cream as if they hadn't eaten all day. The adults passed on the dessert but sat at the table with the kids while they indulged. After they inhaled their dessert, the children went inside and got ready for bed before coming back down to play with their new video game.

Sylvia gave Randall permission to play with the children while she put the finishing touches on the kitchen. He joined her back on the patio after about thirty minutes of play, declaring he lost on purpose so he could keep her company. "You're going to have to cook some of that chicken for Romey. You know he loves that stuff as much as me."

Sylvia smiled in response.

"You work hard Sylvia. I remember Romey saying that the first time I came here with him. You remember that?"

"I remember. He made me cry. Debra called looking for you. That seems like years ago."

Randall looked around appearing a bit nervous and spoke quietly. "I was wondering if you want some help."

"What? What kind of help?" Sylvia asked.

"Mommy, it's my turn and Billy won't let me play," Bertani whined, pulling back the screen on the opened patio door.

Sylvia became alarmed because Randall appeared overly concerned and fidgety "What's the matter?" she asked him.

"Nothing, nothing. I'm cool."

"Excuse me. I've got to get them off to bed," Sylvia said as she rose to leave the patio.

"Mommy, no. I'm supposed to get another turn." Bertani tried to conjure up tears that would not come and would do no good at this time and place. She sometimes forgot that the tactics that worked on her father and stepmother bounced off of Sylvia like golf balls on pavement.

"Let's go missy. You're tired; I can tell," Sylvia told her child.

"Goodnight Uncle Randall," Bertani whispered in a whiny voice as she ran out onto the patio to bestow a hug and kiss on Randall. Thank you for coming to dinner and for the game and the ice cream.

"You're welcome, baby. I'll see you tomorrow, okay," Randall said, returning the embrace.

"Okay," Bertani replied pitifully.

The boys came out to the patio and thanked Randall before saying goodnight. Sylvia went upstairs with the children so she could casually supervise the end of their night. She had learned that if she was nearby, teeth got brushed, dirty clothes went into the hampers, toilets got flushed, and life was all together easier. Billy and Bertani would be asleep in less than fifteen minutes but Justin would listen to music or watch some television before passing out.

She found Randall pouring out glasses of wine when she returned. "This is a nice wine," he said to her as he took a second sip of the now beautifully aged Beaujolais Retha had left with Sylvia during the holidays.

Sylvia sat and took a drink from her goblet before asking, "Now what was that you were saying about help."

"That was stupid and not at all the tone I was trying to set." Randall laughed nervously. "We can talk about it later."

They sat and listening to music as they drank their wine. Randall pulled his chair close to Sylvia's, leaned over, and placed a delicate kiss on her lips for the first time all evening. She returned the caress, looked at him and wondered what was bothering him. "What is it Randall?" she asked.

Again, that nervous laugh. "I just realized I've never done this before."

"Done what?"

"I've never been in love before. I love you, Sylvia." Randall's voice cracked and Sylvia fought to remain calm.

"I love you too, Randall. Thank you for telling me that. I needed to hear it. I was scared to tell you before you told me."

Randall stood and pulled her out of her seat, wrapped her in his arms and kissed her long and deep. When he pulled away he said, "That's not all I need to tell you."

"What is it?" Sylvia's eyes searched his face. The anxiety she saw scared her.

"Give me a minute." Randall guided her back to her seat and then sat back down. "I work pretty hard myself, Sylvia. I make a good living." Now he smiled at her as he thought of the laundry list of things he had rehearsed to tell her. "I'm patient. I'd like to have another child but if that doesn't work for you, I can live with that."

Sylvia's mouth opened slightly as she guessed at, hoped, prayed, feared, and thanked God for what she thought Randall was trying to say. She felt herself slipping into a dazed state and told herself to pay attention. Could she have been imagining or misreading his intentions. *Pay attention, Sylvia! Damn you!*

"I know you love Sugar's Place and want to expand. That will take a lot of work and you'll probably put in a lot of time getting things in place for that. I can help you with that."

*Oh God. Is that what he is talking about, but he said something about another child. What happened to that? I want another child too. What the hell is he talking about? Please let him get back to another child.*

Sylvia's look of calm had turned into one of despair as Randall talked on. "I'll love your children, Sylvia, but I won't step on Sean's toes unless they need stepping on. I can take good care of you and the kids and I know you will take good care of me." Randall reached in his pocket, pulled out a box, and opened it. "Sylvia, you're the first woman I've ever loved. I want us to live together and make a home together. Will you marry me?"

"Yes, yes, yes, yes!" Sylvia shouted. Randall held onto the ring as she jumped out of her chair and flung her arms around his neck, nearly knocking him to the ground as she showered his face with kisses.

Sylvia surprised Randall on a regular basis but he had no idea she could get this excited over anything. She finally released him, stepped back, snatched the ring out of his hand, and began jumping up and down. Randall watched her and had to laugh. "I should be filming this you know, so years from now when you get mad at me, I can show it to you and remind you how happy you were to get me."

Finally, Sylvia sat down and looked at her ring. It was an exquisite conflict free three carat radiant cut diamond solitaire. "It's a beautiful ring, Randall."

As Randall removed the ring from the box and placed it on Sylvia's trembling hand, she asked, "When?"

"When do you want?" Randall laughed at her excitement.

"Tomorrow!"

"Come on Sylvia be serious. That's a little soon, don't you think?"

"You don't think we can get a license that quick?" she asked seriously.

"Don't you think we should talk about our lives together? Do some planning. Where are we going to live -- sell, buy, move, stay. I'd like to tell my family here in San Antonio. Give my family in California a chance to come to the wedding; put an announcement in the papers."

"Wedding?" Sylvia sounded shocked.

Randall now looked at Sylvia as if he was seeing her for the first time – surprise, surprise, surprise. "Don't you want a wedding, Sylvia?"

Sylvia pressed her lips together and shrugged her shoulders. "I never thought about a wedding."

"Did you have a wedding before?" Randall asked.

"No," was her plain and simple answer.

"You never wanted one?"

"I guess when I married Sean I wanted my mother to give me a wedding. I didn't want her to spend a whole lot of money but, you know, make a big ta do over my marriage and have a small but nice reception after. Shoot, old girl married me off like I was eight months pregnant and Sean was off to the war. When me and Sugar got married, we just decided to tie the knot. We didn't discuss it with anyone, just went away for a few days and came back married. Did you have a wedding with your first wife?"

"Jillian wouldn't have it any other way. I hardly remember it. Both my aunts and Jerome came up. It was okay," Randall shrugged.

"So why would you want to have another wedding?" Sylvia whined.

"This won't be another wedding. This will be our wedding. You said you never thought about a wedding. Did you think about marriage, to me?"

"Yes, a lot," Sylvia responded softly.

"So where do you see us living?" He asked her.

"Honestly?"

"Honestly."

"Here, right here in this house," Sylvia confessed.

"Okay. That works for me, for now," Randall agreed.

Sylvia smiled. ***That was easy.***

"I've given you something. Now it's your turn to reciprocate." Randall tried to negotiate.

"Wait a minute; you didn't tell me we were making deals," she complained.

"You didn't ask. Let me tell you what I want," he said.

"You already said you want another child, right?" Sylvia guessed with a huge grin.

"We are not talking about that yet. I want a wedding, a church wedding with all the frills. Then I want a reception just like the one Luis and Olga had but with some R&B, Neo Soul, Hip Hop and of course a little Jazz. I can do without the Mariachis unless you want them. We do need a little bit of country and some Rock. We'll do like our friends and stay the entire reception and turn that motha out. I want us to start off with a bang." Randall was quiet for a moment, and then with a look of genuine desire said, "Let me give you a beautiful wedding, Sylvia. I want to throw you a great party, nothing ridiculous. I love you. I love your people and mine. I really want to do this."

This required another kiss for Randall, a long, soft, deep caress. When Sylvia finally pulled back she asked, "Can I help?"

Chapter 26: There's No Backing Out Now, Dude

Sylvia and Randall had a four-month engagement. They set the wedding day for mid-November, allowing time for Retha to recuperate after the birth of her child and serve as Sylvia's matron of honor. Also baseball season would be over and Jaren would be able to accompany his wife and children to San Antonio and attend the wedding.

There had been little stress associated with the upcoming wedding for Sylvia or Randall. They only told their closest friends and family they were engaged until two months prior to the wedding date. Upon learning the news of the engagement, those closest friends and family took over the planning for the big event. Randall quickly found he just needed to show up and have his credit card out when requested. Jessie became chief wedding planner with her Mini Me, Retha, refusing to be left out. Izola and Viola asserted their will and let it be known that every major decision needed to be ran past them. Martha, sworn to secrecy, was pulled into the fold because she would have most likely broken down and cried if left out. So Sylvia had a wedding planning committee that frequently ran things past her for approval and she was fine with that.

Retha and Jaren offered to pay for the reception as their wedding gift but Randall flatly refused, though very graciously. Randall happily made a call to "the man," Jaren Daniels and thanked him for the offer. Jaren understood and countered with a request that he be allowed to provide additional limos and have them on standby for those late night partiers leaving the reception who may be in no condition to drive home. That offer Randall accepted.

Some discussion went into Sugar's Place catering the reception but Sylvia insists that her friends at Sugar's have the day off to attend the wedding as invited guests. Jessie lined up reception venues for Sylvia and Randall to select from. Sylvia did take serious interest in selecting her own gown and reluctantly selected colors for the wedding. Jessie and Retha picked the dresses for the bridesmaids, flower girl, and Bertani. Although Retha, with her baby due any day, was not present, she insisted on paying for all the floral arrangements. Sylvia and Jessie found a small local florist and gave very detailed instructions about the beautiful simplicity they desired. Miss Mildred and her pastry staff would bake the wedding and the groom's cakes with the caterer providing cake cutting service. The wedding would be held at Sylvia's home church which she seldom attended. Pastor and Sister Ware were overjoyed to host the ceremony. Pastor Ware was to officiate and Sister Ware, an accomplished keyboardist, would arrange the music.

--

"Debra, there is a Sylvia Solomon here to see you."

"I'll be right out." Debra wondered what Sylvia might be coming to see her about. The cousins had forgiven each other but their relationship remained distant and strained.

They couldn't help but smile upon seeing each other as Debra entered the receptionist area of her real estate firm. Although there remained a strain in their relationship, there was also a growing connection, a respect that did not exist prior to their conflict over Randall. "What are you doing here?" Debra asked as she hugged Sylvia. "Come on back."

"I just stopped by for a minute. I guess I should have called but I needed to talk to you and decided to take a chance on catching you free," Sylvia said.

Once they entered Debra's office, she indicated for Sylvia to take a seat as she sat behind her desk. The ladies got loads of small talk out of the way, everything from children and parents, how they spent their summers, and things they did as children. Finally there was nothing small worth discussing and Sylvia broached the big deal.

"I wanted to tell you before you heard it from anyone else. Randall and I are getting married," Sylvia informed her cousin.

"Married, you and Randall? You guys were even more serious than I thought." Debra fell back in her seat. "This is a surprise. I don't know why, but it never crossed my mind that you two would tie the knot. Did he propose or what?"

Sylvia smiled before answering. "Yes, he proposed. Why is that so strange?"

"Don't get in a tiff, Sylvia. Back when we were kids and Randall and I dated, all those many moons ago," Debra had spread the fingers on both hands and raised them to the sky. "I took the lead on everything. I told him when to come and when to go. He had no interest in anything we did. He didn't even ask for sex, just accepted it when I gave it up. Of course that was a long time ago and he really didn't care much about me that way. God that's hard for me to admit." Debra looked at Sylvia and gave her a thoughtful smile. "When's the wedding?"

"In November, two months and eight days from today," Sylvia said. "The invitations go out in the mail next week. I wanted to tell you before yours arrived or someone else told you."

"I'm invited to the wedding?" Debra asked in shock.

"Of course you are; we're family."

Debra's eyes welled up and her voice cracked when she told her cousin, "Sylvia, you know there are some people that would say you were wrong for getting involved with Randall even if he was just my high school boyfriend and two decades have past?"

Sylvia had prayed they were past this because she wanted an amicable relationship with Debra and the rest of her mother's family. "I guess I'd better go." Sylvia stood to leave.

Debra stood and walked around her desk. "They'd be wrong, baby." Debra caught Sylvia up in another embrace and then pulled back from her. "You'd be a stupid woman to pass on that good man because he was somebody I used to know. Randall was never particularly interested in me. I think the only thing he was really interested in back then was football and sex, in that order. But as little as he cared about me he was good to me. He's just a good man, so good it's hard to believe he's real. I hope I can find one like him. He is the real deal and if he asked you to marry him, he is really in love."

It was Sylvia's turn to hug her cousin and hold on tight. "Thank you for that, Debra."

"You are a good friend, Sylvia. I hope you know I love you and that I can regain your trust after being so mean. I will be at the wedding."

"One more thing," Sylvia said before she exited Debra's office, "I'm going to ask Janice to be one of my bridesmaids."

Debra thought for a moment and responded with, "I guess it would be a little awkward for me to be in the wedding, huh?" She shook her head, feeling that Janice was usurping her spot. "Thanks for telling me that because I might have been a little upset behind that one. I'll be as supportive as I can."

"Bye, baby and thanks for being so understanding," Sylvia said.

"I'm a work in progress." Debra laughed.

--

"Justin, I need to ask you for a favor," Sylvia said to her oldest son as he sat down on the side of her bed. "This is just between you and me for now, because I don't want you to feel pressured in anyway."

"Okay," Justin responded hesitantly, wondering if he had done something wrong.

Sylvia looked at him and smiled because she could tell he expected something he did not want to hear. He seemed to have matured by five years since Sylvia and Randall became engaged. The moment Justin heard the news, he changed. The changes saddened his mother because it didn't seem right to baby him any longer. Of course, he had resisted the babying for some years but now coddling seemed downright ridiculous.

Billy and Bertani had reacted much like Sylvia when they heard Randall would become their stepfather. Bertani had asked, "You mean like Camy is my stepmom?" and glowed when the answer was "Yes, like Camy is your stepmom." Justin, however, had been far more reserved upon learning about his mother's engagement. She had worried he might be unhappy about the prospect of having Randall in the home with them but in a matter of two days he confirmed that was not the case when he asked her for Randall's cell phone number so he could program it into his phone. Over the months since the engagement, Sylvia's oldest child had grown closer to Randall and called him frequently to talk about Sylvia knew not what.

"What Mom?" Justin asked in anticipation of bad news.

"Well," Sylvia responded. "I think your brother feels a little sad that you will walk me down the aisle and present me to Randall. I was wondering if you would be okay with sharing that honor with Billy."

"Is that all?"

"That's it."

"That's cool; maybe I won't be so nervous," Justin chuckled.

"I didn't know you were worried about it. You don't need to be. Just don't let me fall down, okay?" Sylvia said with a smile.

"Me and Billy will hold you up, Mom. This is a big deal, isn't it?"

"The ceremony is not a big deal, baby, but the marriage is. Now give me a hug."

Justin hugged her and held on tighter and longer than he had in a long time. Sylvia was proud of her son. He was growing into a strong man. She thanked God that he had good strong men to influence his life.

--

After their engagement, Sylvia and Randall got into the habit of spending several nights a week together, but during the weeks leading up to the wedding each slept in their own bed. Sylvia and Randall were much alike in their decisiveness. Once either made a decision, it was a difficult task to change their mind. Sylvia decided the time apart would make the wedding night beyond special and no matter how hard Randall tried he could not change her mind.

"You know I have to be out of my condo at the end of October so the tenants can move in on the first. Where exactly am I supposed to sleep for that week?" Randall had asked as if he would be completely out of options once he moved out of his condo. Sylvia had only smiled and given him no response. He hated it when she did that because it was a sure sign he was fighting a losing battle. She was more aware of the options available to him than he was. He could have stayed at Jerome's, Aunt Zoe's, Aunt Vi's, and if he didn't have those family options, he could have gotten a hotel. Randall was far from destitute, so a place to sleep was really not the issue.

He had watched her, getting more irritated by the moment as she refused to answer his question. "Hey, don't start making these arbitrary decisions that affect me without talking to me first. Don't even start that shit," Randall warned.

"You said you wanted a traditional wedding with all the frills. Well, I've gotten into the whole idea of this wedding and I want it to be as special as we can make it. I feel like it will take something away from all this hoopla we're making if we climb out of bed together on our wedding day and just make a point of riding to the church in different cars. I thought you wanted to make this wedding special for me. I want to make it special too and I think we should spend some time away from each other for a few days before our big day," Sylvia pleaded.

Randall understood her point but still didn't care for the idea.

Sylvia could see the wheels turning and knew she had just about gotten him onboard. "The kids are excited. Jessie and Retha, your aunts, Martha, my mother and aunt, Janice, even Sean and Camille are all excited. This has turned into a big deal and I don't regret it. But I want it to be a really big deal for us too," she pressed her advantage.

"Well I'm sure not going to want to stay at the reception long. I can tell you that," Randall declared rebelliously.

"I'll tell you what. You do this for me. Allow us to take a break from each other for the weeks leading up to the wedding and I will leave the reception whenever you say, just so long as it's after we cut the cake and have our first dance together as husband and wife, okay?

He gave her a look of disgust. "I did want this didn't I?"

"Yes sir, you did."

"And you are happy about all the planning, and the growing guest list, and the changing venue, and your mother's wrath at not being asked to help plan the wedding and because your sister won't be in the wedding?"

"Well, I'm not happy about all that but I am happy about having such a big beautiful party to celebrate our marriage and I am happy my children are so happy and will be a part of something so special. I didn't realize how important a wedding would be to them. They are actually having fun."

"I was going to tell you that we could just cancel everything and go downtown and tie the knot if you want, but if the kids are that much into the whole wedding thing, I guess we're stuck," Randall conceded.

"I think we are," Retha said.

"So," Randall rose from his seat, stretched, and twisted his back. "emergency contact only for the three weeks before the wedding, right?"

"I didn't say that. We don't need to go to that extreme." Sylvia looked at him with shock on her face.

"Yes, I think we do. I've been thinking about this since you mentioned it to me the other day and as much as I don't like the idea, it might be good for us to spend some time apart. I feel it is best we see as little of each other and talk as seldom as possible before our big day. It will give us time to reflect on things."

Sylvia's face was full of doubt. She was not sure she liked not being able to call him several times a day and not seeing him every day. Randall walked over and gave her a kiss on the forehead before exiting the bedroom. "Be careful what you wish for," he told her as he walked out feeling like he had just struck a blow for all men.

--

Not fifteen hours into their pledged hiatus from each other, Sylvia punched Randall's number on her cell phone. She lay in her bed listening to the phone ring, fearful she might not reach him. The separation was proving harder for Sylvia than Randall. "Hey," he finally answered.

"I just wanted to say goodnight. What are you doing?" Sylvia asked.

"Right now, I'm lying here wondering why you're calling me. I thought we were taking a break from so much contact."

"I know. I just wanted to hear your voice. I haven't talked to you all day. You doing okay?"

Randall could barely hold back his laughter. Sylvia's misery was apparent and he considered letting her off the hook by hanging up the phone, driving to her place, and demanding she let him in her bed but he would follow her lead and accept whatever decision she made concerning the time they spent together before the wedding. "Oh, I'm good. I'd be a lot better if you were in the bed with me right now, but I'll be okay. You?"

"I'm fine." Sylvia was a little whiny now because Randall hadn't given any strong indication that he thought they should see each other.

"Kids okay?" Randall was grinning from ear to ear. The separation was Sylvia's idea and he knew she wanted to change her mind.

"They're good. Asking for you. I told them they can call you if they want to see you."

"That's cool."

"Well, I guess I'll let you get some rest. I love you, Randall."

All of the sudden, Randall no longer found humor in the call. Sylvia had never told him she loved him over the phone. He felt his heart beat and his maleness rise. He reconsidered making that drive to Sylvia's but decided to stick to their agreement. "I love you too, Sylvia," he told her.

"Goodnight," Sylvia said.

"Baby?"

"Yes, Randall?"

"I'll stop by for lunch in the next day or two, okay?"

"I'd like that."

The self-imposed separation that made Sylvia so sad was not nearly so bad for Randall. One week into the separation, his cousin Mark arrived in town from Seoul, South Korea on permanent change of station leave from the Navy. Mark was overjoyed to be home with his family, excited about serving as one of the groomsmen in his cousin's wedding, rolling in cash, single, and ready to party for the next forty five days. Jerome and Randall wasted no time getting on board with their young cousin and making plans to enjoy themselves. The three took road trips to Houston, the Dallas Metro area, and several trips to Austin over the two weeks leading up to the wedding.

Randall stopped in at Sugar's one time during that period – that's it, once. He was having a blast with his boys. He did manage to remain faithful but between the temptations presented to him while hanging out with his cousins and no Sylvia, that was not an easy task.

--

Although Sylvia felt she had far too much to do the day before her wedding, she reluctantly spent the better part of the day at a spa with her mother, sister, aunt and cousins. The spa day was a wedding gift from her mother and aunt that she could not bring herself to refuse. The gift proved to be far more pleasurable that Sylvia could have guessed and relieved much of her anxiety. She got everything waxed, her nails done, a facial, a full body scrub and wrap, and a massage.

The rehearsal dinner at Sugar's Place started off somewhat strained because Sylvia invited her mother, sister, and brother to meet the group at Sugar's for the dinner but excluded them from the actual rehearsal. Dianne, who had complained nonstop since she learned of Sylvia and Randall's engagement, was offended to tears by what she considered yet another slight. Thankfully, the tears had no effect on Sylvia, who did not see them. Sylvia's Aunt Denise, who had not been included in either invitation, told her sister to just be happy for Sylvia and stop all her "belly-aching."

The atmosphere at the dinner warmed up quickly and soon there was more laughter and joking than eating taking place. Randall and Sylvia even warmed up to each other after spending so little time together over the past few weeks. Jerome who was best man and JT, one of the groomsmen, had been teasing Randall for weeks about Sylvia's decision to stay away from him. They continued the ribbing, though discreetly, throughout the rehearsal and the dinner.

The only real damper was the always reliable Dianne's observation to her nervous daughter, "I hope you plan on doing something with that hair. I thought you would have had it straightened already."

Accustomed to her mother's criticism, Sylvia just shrugged and told her, "Not yet, Mama. I've got my hair appointment tomorrow morning. It'll be fine." She moved away from her mother's bad Karma as quickly as possible and on to Izola and Viola to bask in those ladies' refreshingly adoring eyes.

Jessie and Retha had planned on spending the night before the wedding with Sylvia but once Dianne and Sylvia's sister, Marie, announced their plans to stay, the nieces graciously conceded that right. They did pile their wedding garb in Sylvia's closets in wait for their early arrival the next morning.

Jessie and Retha had Sylvia's wedding day scheduled down to the minute. This schedule allowed Sylvia to sleep in relatively late and some free time so that she was well-rested for the day. The only thing Sylvia would have to do for herself was bathe. Sylvia's first appointment on her wedding day was at nine o'clock with her natural hair stylist who had agreed to come to Sylvia's home. Ma Harper's would deliver lunch at noon. Makeup was scheduled for two o'clock. The ladies would help Sylvia dress at two thirty and then be off to the church.

Sylvia's home was crammed full of ladies slinking into their wedding garb on the day of her wedding. Her mother, daughter, aunt, sister, nieces and cousin, all dressed at Sylvia's.

In a break with tradition, Bertani would carry the bridal bouquet for her mother and walk behind little Morning Daniels, the flower girl, and just ahead of Sylvia, Justin and Billy.

Justin and Billy spent the wedding eve at their father and stepmother's home. Sean and Camille would assist the boys getting dressed and get them to the church to meet the wedding party no later than three thirty for the four o'clock ceremony.

--

The hodgepodge of planning that created Sylvia and Randall's wedding and reception did not disappoint. The little church on San Antonio's East Side had not seen so many attendees in a great while. The florist had tastefully transformed the rundown temple into a floral wonderland while maintaining the sanctimony of the place of worship.

Sister Ware was in high form and she had a guitarist, a flutist, and her daughter who was a gifted singer accompanying her. The music was so engaging that Robert told Jaren they should have used Sister Ware's trio for the reception.

When Randall, accompanied by Pastor Ware, Jerome, JT, and Mark entered the sanctuary the humming of conversation lessened, though only slightly. Randall was obviously nervous but more handsome than ever in his custom tuxedo. Aunt Zoe and Aunt Vi started sniffling as soon as they set eyes upon him. No sooner than the groom and his entourage got situated the wedding march began and the guests all rose.

Randall heard JT whisper loudly, "There's no backing out now, dude," causing all five men to grin. Randall barely noticed the bridesmaids and ushers leading the processional. He was aware of the guests' chuckles, oohs, and ahs as Martha's youngest boy, Reginald, concentrated hard on staying in step with the music and holding on to that ring cushion, followed by young Morning Daniels who was putting all her effort into distributing rose petals evenly across the aisle. Randall's vision cleared a bit as Bertani approached carrying the bridal bouquet for her mother and looking straight at him. He smiled his approval at the child and then immediately focused on Sylvia, his soon to be bride, who was focused on Justin and Billy, her two young escorts. Before Randall was prepared to greet her, she was before him accepting kisses from her children and her bouquet from Bertani. Suddenly Randall felt dizzy. He had seen videos of grooms passing out during their wedding ceremonies and hoped he wasn't the future star of a YouTube video with thousands of views. Once he stopped taking in Sylvia's splendor and looked into her eyes, his head began to clear and he heard Pastor Ware ask, "Who presents this woman and this man to each other to be married?"

Izola, Viola, Justin, Billy, and Bertani all answered in unisons, "We do." The guests laughed.

The ceremony went on without a hitch. Randall managed to remain conscious and he and Sylvia delivered their short well-rehearsed vows with the only problem being Sylvia's slightly tearful delivery which caused tears to flow freely throughout the sanctuary. There was so much sniffling that Pastor Ware eventually said, "I sure hope these are tears of joy being shed with all this nose blowing going on." Again the church went up in laugher. Before you noticed, the ceremony was over and Pastor Ware was presenting Randall and Sylvia as Mr. Randall and Mrs. Sylvia Craig. The pastor turned to Randall and said, "Randall, you may kiss your bride!" Randall placed a nice warm kiss on Sylvia's lips but nothing to breathtaking, causing a nice round of applause. The couple held hands and jumped the broom with laughter and still more applause accompanied by cheers.

By the time the bride and groom arrived, the reception was in full force. This was the best party most of the wedding guests had attended in a long time, if ever. The band and DJ, both chosen and hired by Jerome, proved well worth their fees. Sylvia was one happy hungry bride when they sat down to consume their dinner but before they ate, Randall took a moment to focus on his wife. He kissed her hard on the mouth with complete abandon. It was the kiss he wished he had given her earlier, at the altar. Sylvia wrapped her arms around his neck and kissed him back. The entire room went up in a loud cheer.

The Craigs spent the remainder of the evening greeting their guests and partying like they might never have another chance at such revelry. They wanted to make the best of the event that would only happen once for them.

After all the speeches were made, cakes cut, and traditional dances completed, Jessie and Retha dragged Sylvia off to a room in the hotel and presented her with one of several gifts. Retha had gotten Sylvia's measurements from the bridal gown company and had a Dolce & Gabbana cocktail dress made for her to wear the remainder of the evening. The sisters helped Sylvia freshened up, change, and get back down to her husband and guests in less than half an hour.

Sylvia captured every eye when she reenters the ballroom in that exquisite designer dress made just for her. Randall actually did a double take when he saw his wife. Mark cupped his hand over his mouth, leaned back and said, "Damn!" Jerome grabbed Sylvia and moved her onto the dance floor before Randall could get to her. As Randall approached, Jerome told him, "You gonna have to wait your turn man, you gonna have to wait your turn." Randall didn't miss a step. He didn't even look at his cousin as he moved him to the side and took Sylvia in his arms. This brought on another tremendous cheer from the crowd.

Finally, Sylvia and Randall decided to make their departure. Jessie's daughter Elizabeth caught the bridal bouquet and her cousin Nathaniel caught the garter. The cousins sneered at each other and declared they didn't want to dance together before choosing more appealing partners to bump and grind around the floor with.

The celebration wound down and the newlyweds climbed into a limo and headed off to the honeymoon suite at the JW Marriot where they would remain for two days before flying off to Hawaii for a two-week honeymoon.

--

"Do you want me to carry you across this threshold?" Randall asked with a slightly worried expression.

"No!" Sylvia answered and then just to scare him, with glimmers of hope radiating from her eyes, she said, "Not unless you want to."

"Oh God, Sylvia!" Randall groaned, sounding exhausted.

"I'm just kidding, Randall." Sylvia slapped lightly at his chest and started to walk into the suite. Suddenly she felt Randall's hand on her arm holding her back and just as quickly, he scooped her up into his arms as if she were a feather. Sylvia threw her head back with laughter and shouted. "I can't believe this. Randall, you're going to hurt your back."

Randall looked in her eyes and told her, "Don't worry baby. I've been working out at Jerome's gym preparing for this very moment. I'll carry you whenever you want or need me to; I've got you."

Sylvia stared back at him as he carried her across the room and responded with, "I've got you too, baby, I've got you too."

~~~

Thank you so much for reading *Sylvia's Solace*. I hope you enjoyed the novel as much as I enjoyed writing it and that you will take a moment and visit your favorite retailer's site and leave a review for fellow readers. You may also share your thoughts and comments on the *Cinda's Books facebook page*.

Thanks again!

## About the Author

Cinda Brea is a native of the city of Carthage, Texas, located in the East Texas Piney Woods and grew up in the city of Seaside on the beautiful Central California coast where she attended Monterey Peninsula College. Cinda is retired from the United States Army after 22 years of service. She has degrees in culinary arts and restaurant management. She is the wife of one, mother of four, grandmother of four, great grandmother of two pooches, a family member and friend to many. She and her family make their home in San Antonio, Texas. *Sylvia Solace* is her second novel.

## **Novels by Cinda Brea**

*An Industrious Woman*
*Friends No Longer*
*Romancing Retha*
*Sylvia's Solace*

Contact Me
www.cindabrea.com
follow on Facebook at
https://www.facebook.com/pages/Cinda's Books
contact via mailto:cindabrea@gmail.com

www.ingramcontent.com/pod-product-compliance
Lightning Source LLC
Chambersburg PA
CBHW031958190626
46808CB00018B/1779